STRIVERS
ROW

During the 1920s and 1930s, around the time of the Harlem Renaissance, more than a quarter of a million African-Americans settled in Harlem, creating what was described at the time as "a cosmopolitan Negro capital which exert[ed] an influence over Negroes everywhere."

Nowhere was this more evident than on West 138th and 139th Streets between what are now Adam Clayton Powell, Jr., and Frederick Douglass Boulevards, two blocks that came to be known as Strivers Row. These blocks attracted many of Harlem's African-American doctors, lawyers, and entertainers, among them Eubie Blake, Nobel Sissle, and W. C. Handy, who were themselves striving to achieve America's middle-class dream.

With its mission of publishing quality African-American literature, Strivers Row emulates those "strivers," capturing that same spirit of hope, creativity, and promise.

DREAM IN COLOR

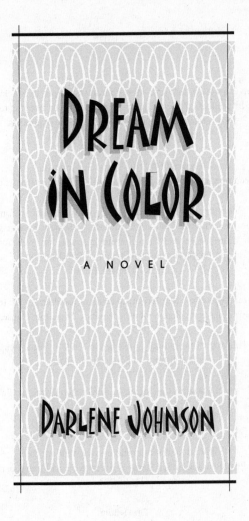

DREAM IN COLOR

A NOVEL

DARLENE JOHNSON

STRIVERS ROW

VILLARD / NEW YORK

VILLARD BOOKS is a registered trademark of Random House, Inc.
STRIVERS ROW and colophon are trademarks of Random House, Inc.

This work was originally published in 1999 by Brandywine
Publishing, Indianapolis, Indiana

Library of Congress Cataloging-in-Publication Data is available.

ISBN 0-375-75841-0

Villard Books website address: www.villard.com
Printed in the United States of America on acid-free paper.
24689753

First Edition

For my sons, Malcolm and Douglas.

My life would be empty without you guys.

And to Marcus—your memory

and your light will always shine within us.

You all are my pride and joy.

ACKNOWLEDGMENTS

So many wonderful things have happened in my life since the self-published edition of *Dream in Color* was released. First, I must give testament to God. There have been so many times when I didn't know how I would be able to see the light at the end of the tunnel, but without fail, a way was made. I am nothing without Him.

I am surrounded by family and friends who have always believed in me, especially my parents, George L. Johnson and Deloris Johnson. We all inherited your strength. Hugs to my crazy sisters, Annette, Elondra, Carolyn, and Felicia, for teaching me how to stand up tall and be a lady at all times, and to my brother, Morris, for just sitting back, watching and shaking your head at us. To my cousin Vincent Lewis and all my relatives in Cincinnati, Ohio, and the Hartsfields, Johnsons, and Shacks in Bessemer and Brighton, Alabama.

Special thanks go to David, for putting your faith in me and believing in my work (kiss), and my first cover artist and dear friend, Carolyn Carey-Jones, for becoming another sister. Thank you, thank you, to my first agent, Delin Cormeny, for working her butt off. Girl, what can I say other than you were the best. And thanks also to my editor, Melody Guy, for reading this story, feeling it, and believing in it.

Bear hugs go to my sister-friends Sheila Allen, Tracy Harris, and Angie Niebling. I can depend on you ladies to keep the little girl in me alive. And Diann, I know my tab is running pretty high, but you give it to me straight, girl, and there is nothing I can do but love you for it. Michael Jackson, you know you've come through for me many times. I have nothing but love for you and all those folks at Conseco. Thanks, Fadi and Ron, for not walking me out the door when we both know you should have.

This is a special shout-out to ALL my nieces and nephews. There is simply not enough room to name all of you but you guys know who you are and you know I'm talking about you. FIND YOUR LIGHT. All of you are talented and beautiful and there isn't anything in this world you cannot do if you put your heart and soul into it and make it happen.

I want to thank the bookstores and book clubs that read and sold the self-published edition of *Dream in Color*. Lloyd Hart, Tariq Jones, Angela Holmes—you are more than booksellers to me now; you are my friends and I love you guys. If I failed to mention someone here, please forgive me!

Malcolm, I know you don't understand why I sit in front of the computer so much instead of playing Dreamcast with you, but thanks for playing on without me. I promise to get a game I can play too.

I want to thank everyone, old friends and new, for all of the support you've given me. Thank you and God bless you all.

DREAM IN COLOR

1

VICTORIA

I couldn't remember the last time I'd actually enjoyed sex with Gerald. Things had gotten so bad that I hated seeing nighttime because it usually meant that I would have to lie beside him, with my hands clenched against my body and my legs tightly closed. I always made a point of sleeping as close to the edge of the bed as possible. The last thing I wanted was for him to accidentally touch me.

There were times when his hand would slap on my back or stomach as he slept, and the moment he realized that a warm female lay beside him, he was ready to have sex. It never mattered if I wanted it. It didn't even matter if I enjoyed it. My sole purpose was to provide the necessary body.

But this day my thoughts of sex were different. I'd had a dream the night before that I couldn't shake. It had been a long time since I'd felt that special tickle between my legs when I thought about making love, and it was something about that dream that forced me to sit at my desk while I worked and squeeze my legs together.

Neither the face nor the voice of the man in my dream resembled Gerald's, and I was inclined to believe that that added to the excitement. The infidelity of the mind was just as real to me as if I had actually lain down with another man.

I shivered again, perhaps for the hundredth time that day. I wasn't sure what it was that aroused me and kept me at that incredible height, but one thing I did know: for the first time in a long time, I *wanted* to be touched.

There were two things on my mind as I drove the familiar roads home that evening. The strongest thought was of being touched and trying to control the hormones that were creating a river between my legs. The second thought was of how I was going to seduce my husband. Over the past few years, I hadn't shown any initiative in seducing Gerald, and I had my reasons. The passion and joy of lovemaking left our marriage many years ago, and it was due in part to the fact that I felt more like a sexual object than a sexual partner. I know that many people would contest that there is a difference, but there was for me, and feeling like a sexual object took the pleasure out of making love and turned it into just another household chore.

Tonight I was willing to forget all that and become a partner. Perhaps afterward Gerald would notice the difference as well and respond to me as a partner rather than just an object for getting off.

When I walked into the house, I followed the sound of voices into the family room. Gerald and our daughter, Reese, were sitting on the sofa watching television and joining the laughter from the picture box. They looked comfortable, Gerald with his legs stretched out, Reese curled up at his feet.

It was always a pleasure to see those two together, no matter how hellish our marriage was. I smiled at them and walked to the window and pulled the curtains back, letting the remaining rays of sunlight strike me and add more heat to a kettle that was about to boil over.

"Gerald," I said, bouncing on the sofa beside him and taking his hand. I followed his eyes as he looked first at my hand touching him and then at me. "I asked Stephanie to watch Reese for a few hours for us tonight."

Gerald squinted.

"So that you and I can enjoy a nice, relaxing evening alone." I leaned forward and gently kissed his cheek.

Gerald pulled back from me. "What's up?" he asked in his usual suspicious tone.

"Nothing. I just want to spend some time with you. Some real time. We haven't done that in a while."

He continued to look at me suspiciously.

"Nothing is up. I promise. I just want to spend some time together. Cook a nice dinner, listen to some good music, and have some fun." My faint grin hinted of enticement.

Gerald picked up on the tone and nodded. "Sounds good to me," he replied.

I was surprised that he didn't turn me down cold and cite my disinterest in sex and anything associated with it as the reason. Perhaps he was missing that integral part of our relationship as well. I knew that one night wasn't going to send the five-year downward spiral of our marriage into an upturn, but it was a start, and we needed that more than anything else.

"Wonderful!" I exclaimed. "You go ahead and drop Reese off while I get things started here." I jumped off the sofa and practically ran into the kitchen to start our meal. A few minutes later I heard the door close, but not before Gerald yelled into the kitchen that he'd be right back. With that, I began preparing for a date with my husband.

The entrée of choice was his favorite, salmon steak. I covered two large, pink steaks in a special lemon marinade that was a recipe from Gerald's mother and set them in the refrigerator. I started cooking some wild rice and prepared the asparagus to steam later while the salmon cooked.

I ran to the cellar to select a bottle from our collection of prized wines and champagne. I chose a sparkling white that best resembled what I hoped would be the mood of the evening, energetic and definitely bubbly. I ran back upstairs and placed the bottle and two of our best goblets into the freezer for a quick chill. With a push of the remote control, I started the CD player.

I stood in the middle of the living room with my hands folded in front of me. I closed my eyes and listened to the smooth melody. Pleased, I nodded, then returned to the kitchen to finish dinner.

With the meal prepared and the music going, it was time to work on me. I danced into our bedroom and selected my best nightgown.

Tonight was not an occasion for the usual sleep shirt. I reached into my closet and took a long, black silk gown from a satin-covered hanger. I held it against my body and examined myself in the mirror. After five years and several ill-fated attempts with fad diets, I was still unable to shed fifteen of the pounds I had picked up during my pregnancy. Every exercise program I went on kept my interest for about a month. I spent hundreds of dollars joining an exercise club in the neighborhood, and during the first month I could be found there almost every day working feverishly on every machine. But after that, as with all the regimes I tried, the motivation subsided and my visits became more sporadic until they stopped completely.

By most standards I was not fat, but I wasn't pleased about the extra weight. There were times when I looked in the mirror and hated the image that stared back at me, when the added fifteen pounds seemed like a few hundred and the depression would set in. I'd convince myself that I would never be thin enough, never glamorous enough, and never sophisticated enough. Nothing I ever did to my hair, my face, or my body seemed to get the results necessary to override the despair.

But this night was different. The gloom that usually shadowed me wasn't there. I toyed with my hair and modeled in front of the floor-length mirror before walking confidently into the bathroom for a quick shower.

After I showered, I splashed myself with Gerald's favorite body scent, then tiptoed barefoot into the living room hoping to find Gerald waiting for me. I glanced around and was slightly disappointed that he hadn't returned yet.

"Ump," I mumbled. He should have been back by now. I looked toward the open window. It was dark outside, and the streetlights that lined the narrow street had come on, spilling light through the pulled-back curtains. I walked to the window and drew the curtains.

I walked around the living room and counted ten candles scattered about. The wicks had never been lit, and all of them were covered with dust. I blew the dust off and lit each candle. With the small flames softening the room, I inched myself down on the sofa and looked at the clock. It was eight o'clock. Gerald had been gone almost two hours, even though Stephanie lived only twenty minutes away.

Perhaps he stopped at the store on his way back. Maybe he decided to buy flowers. I smiled. That would be nice.

I tucked my legs underneath me and relaxed on the sofa. I listened to the clicks of the CD player switching to the next disc.

The sound of another click woke me up, and once again the music of Sade filled the room.

Slightly confused, I sat motionless on the sofa. We had a five-disc CD changer. Why was Sade playing again?

"Damn." I jumped from the sofa and quickly turned to look at the clock on the wall. It was eleven o'clock!

"Gerald!" I screamed out his name and waited for a response. I heard nothing but Sade.

"Gerald!" I called out again. I walked to the stairs and called for him again, but still no answer. I walked back into the living room and peered out the window. His car wasn't in the driveway. I opened the side door and peeked into the garage. It wasn't there either.

"What the hell." Now I was really confused. I walked into the kitchen to see if anything had been disturbed. Everything was exactly as I had left it. I took the food from the oven where it was keeping warm and placed it on top of the stove. I put my hands on my hips as I stared at the food and shook my head. The once perfect dinner was now dried-up ruins.

Reese. I panicked and ran to the telephone to call Stephanie.

"Stephanie, is Reese there?" I asked hurriedly into the receiver as soon as Stephanie had answered.

"Yeah, she's asleep. What's wrong?" she asked, sounding confused, perhaps picking up on the urgency in my voice.

"Gerald's not here. How long ago did he leave your place?"

"He dropped Reese off about six-thirty."

I didn't say anything for a moment.

"Did he say anything to you about going anyplace else?" I felt ridiculous asking Stephanie such questions.

"No, he just dropped her off and left."

I took a deep breath and let it out slowly.

"Okay," I said, trying to hide the hurt in my voice. "I'll pick Reese up in the morning." I hung up before Stephanie could ask me questions I couldn't answer.

If there had been an accident, I was sure I would have heard by now, so this could mean only one thing. Gerald had stood me up.

I plopped down on the sofa, numb. "He stood me up," I said softly beneath my breath. I was in such shock that I couldn't even close my mouth after I had said it.

Tears began to fill my eyes, and I reached up and quickly wiped away one that threatened to fall. "Nope, nope, nope," I repeated. I stood up and paced the floor. "You are not going to cry," I told myself. I fanned my hands furiously and blinked until my eyes were dry.

After regaining my composure, I walked into the kitchen and slammed the food into the garbage, splattering some, but at that moment I wouldn't have cared if the food was smeared all over the kitchen wall. I never wanted to see salmon steak again.

"Oh, shit," I murmured, and rushed to the freezer. I cringed as I pulled open the door and peered inside. As I suspected, the goblets were now chunks of glass, and the semifrozen contents of the wine bottle had forced the cork from the neck and now made a neat pile of alcohol slush. I slammed the door shut. I wasn't going to deal with the mess tonight.

Listlessly, I walked upstairs into our bedroom and replaced the sexy black silk nightgown with a cartoon-character sleep shirt. The charmed evening had turned into a total mockery that reminded me of the sham my marriage was and had been from the start. Tears burned in my eyes as my determination not to cry grew stronger. I lay flat on the bed and stared up at the ceiling.

Why did he ask me to marry him? I thought as I blinked at the white space above me. Not even from the first day of marriage had he made an attempt to treat me as anything other than Reese's mother. A friend, a confidante, a partner . . . I was none of those. What I was, was the woman who bore his child. If Gerald felt anything more for me than that, I didn't know it.

Disgruntled, I did manage to fall asleep again sometime during the night, but I couldn't sleep deeply because my mind was a boggled mess. At one o'clock the muffled sound of Gerald's car pulling into the garage awakened me.

I listened to the squeaks of the door opening from the garage into the family room. Then I heard his softened footsteps creep across the hardwood floor making only an occasional resonance in the floorboard. Gerald was a big man, and there was no way he could walk across hardwood floors that quietly unless it was intentionally and scrupulously.

I remained motionless on the bed, staring into the darkness. The house fell silent. I listened intently for any indication that Gerald had tiptoed into the carpeted bedroom, but there wasn't any.

Immediately, I knew that he had no intention of facing me and offering an explanation for what he had done. I sprang from the bed and stormed downstairs. When I stepped into the family room I saw him stretched out on the sofa. With the exception of his shoes, which were strewn alongside the sofa, he was fully dressed. I reached for the light switch on the wall, which turned on both table lamps.

Gerald reached to cover his eyes from the sudden brightness.

"Turn the light off," he mumbled, and tossed about on the sofa.

I walked farther into the room, then stopped when I got a whiff of the strong stench of stale cigarettes and beer in the air around him.

"Where the hell have you been?" I shouted.

"I stopped by Anthony's to give you time to get everything ready, and we ended up going to get a few beers. I just lost track of the time."

"You have been gone since six o'clock this evening. How could you lose track of the time for seven hours?" He didn't answer, so I continued. "You had no intentions of coming back, did you?"

"We'll do it again some other time."

"What?"

"It's no big deal, we'll do it again some other time," he repeated.

"No we won't!" I yelled. "Do you even care how you've made me feel tonight?"

Apparently annoyed, he turned his back to me.

"You haven't even apologized."

Gerald said nothing as he buried his face in the cushion.

"Why do you even bother coming home?" I asked, my eyes never leaving him.

"Because I live here," he answered.

"And that's all you do. You've never made an attempt to include me in your life, and I am not happy about it."

"Your happiness is not my responsibility," he said bluntly, then turned to face me. "Reese is my responsibility."

"Reese is a part of me. How can you care about her happiness and not mine?"

"I am not going to have this conversation with you tonight, Victoria." There were times when I loved to listen to the sound of my name roll from his lips. This was not one of those times. He was patronizing me. He made me feel as if I were a child who needed to be scolded and corrected.

"I have spent the last five years trying to be your wife, and you go out of your way to destroy anything I try to build. Why have you convinced yourself that I am not worth your love?"

Gerald said nothing.

"Why are you so determined to make me hate you? Is it because if you actually gave us a chance, you just might like me?"

He shifted on the couch, seemingly more from agitation than from the thought of having to answer me. "Turn the light off, please," he said, offering not even so much as a bandage to cover the wounds he had inflicted on my spirit.

"I didn't have Reese to trap you. She was not a punishment."

He snorted but said nothing, and I was not going to keep speaking to his back. For some reason Gerald had decided that he was not going to let me into his heart. The harder I worked to get in, the harder he worked to keep me out.

I looked at him while my resentment grew more intense. It wouldn't have taken much more for me to pick up an object, any object, and swing it at him. Maybe then our pain would be equal. But I didn't. I turned and walked back upstairs and into the bedroom. As I lay in bed, the tears I had fought so hard to control streamed down my cheeks.

I found comfort as I thought of my parents' marriage. My parents had been married for almost forty years when my father died. My father did everything for my mother and made sure she had whatever she needed. As far back as I could remember, my mother never worked, and she never questioned my father about money or whether or not the bills were paid. They trusted each other and respected each other. I wanted that kind of marriage. Gerald tended to most of the household expenses and I didn't have to worry, but when it came to my personal needs, he simply didn't care.

My mother was one of those immaculate women who made sure her family ate dinner at the same time every night at the dining room table. My sisters and I laid our clothes out every evening before bed, and they were neatly pressed. Our hair was carefully combed in either pigtails or braids every other day, and we slept in scarves. She had her rules but she was fair. There was one thing that puzzled me about my mother. Although I thought she lived a charmed life with a man who loved her and catered to her every need, I rarely saw her smile, and I never understood why.

I tried many of the same tactics with my house that I remembered my mother using. I did the laundry the same, I cooked the same, and I cleaned the same. I did everything I could think of that would make me as good a wife as my mother was to my father.

I had hoped that Gerald would become a husband like my father. I wanted a marriage like my parents'. Reese was my angel, and she deserved to have a family like the one I was raised in. I had a joyous childhood, and some of my best times were spent vacationing and hanging out with my father. I wanted the same for Reese.

But as my thoughts returned to the spoiled dinner and Gerald's heedless attitude about the failed evening, I found it hard to imagine that the tears drenching my pillow were worth the prize.

2

The music is playing. I hear music. Fun music. Fingers snapping, feet tapping. Listen to the music.

Smile, Victoria. Remember how young this used to make you feel? Remember that song?

That's your favorite song. You haven't heard that song since . . . since college. You used to smile when you heard that song.

I haven't seen you smile in a long time. Wipe these tears from your eyes.

I opened my eyes slowly and stared into silent darkness. I was dreaming. I knew I was dreaming because I heard music. I closed my eyes again and fell asleep.

Come on, Victoria, let's go dancing.

3

JAMES

They rode around town after leaving the restaurant. Reese was with her father, so there was no point in rushing back. The radio was on full blast as Victoria began to drum the beat of the music on the steering wheel of her truck.

"Come on, Victoria. Let's go dancing," Monica said for the second time.

Victoria looked down at her clothes and frowned. "I'm not dressed to go out." She wore a colorful wool Eddie Bauer sweater, black jeans, and ankle boots. She looked presentable but much too casual to go dancing.

On the dance floor the music always took control of her body. She would dance, flinging her arms through the air, snapping her fingers to whatever beat was playing while her legs moved as fast as the music allowed. Even as the perspiration trickled down her cheeks, Victoria would not sit down.

"You look fine," Monica said. "Look at *me.*"

Victoria looked at Monica dressed in a pair of Lycra khaki pants, a green pullover shirt, and brown loafers.

"Should we go home and change?" Victoria asked. The thought of the wool sweater sticking to her body didn't appeal to her.

"Nah, that will take all night. We'll only stay for a minute," Monica reassured her, then they headed for the Wilderness.

During their college days, the Wilderness was the happening place and they hung out there two or three days a week. The music was good, the company was great, and the cover charge and liquor were cheap.

Despite the brisk, cool autumn wind, a small crowd stood patiently in line in front of the club. Women wearing miniskirts or sheer garments stood bunched together trying to shield their exposed bodies from the night air.

"Too cold out here to be cute," Victoria said, snickering.

The Wilderness hadn't lost its momentum for attracting large young crowds. Tony, the doorman, saw Victoria and Monica as they walked toward the entrance and waved them up front.

Victoria stood back while Monica had a quick but obviously very sensual exchange with Tony.

"What was that?" Victoria asked as they walked inside and immediately felt the comfort of the heated nightclub.

"It was nothing," Monica said, and quickly walked ahead to avoid any more questions.

Victoria immediately noticed the youthfulness of the crowd. Memories of her college days rushed to her mind as she glanced over the new patrons of the Wilderness. Just as it was when she was a regular, everyone seemed barely over the required age of twenty-one.

"We're getting too old for this!" Victoria screamed to Monica over the music.

"You're never too old to dance, my dear." And with that, Monica headed straight for the dance floor.

Victoria smiled and joined her. They never bothered to wait for anyone to ask them to dance, and Victoria doubted that anyone would ask tonight. She and Monica were simply not dressed to steal the attention from the scantily clad women bouncing beside them.

After college, Victoria and Monica became removed from the nightclub scene. Three-day-a-week aerobic classes at the gym replaced the all-night dancing. On the few occasions when they braved the hip-hop crowd, they loved it when the DJ played old school jams, music that was popular when they were in high school and college. With their fingers snapping and hands swinging through the air, that was their time to shine and do the dances from those days.

They danced until the DJ decided to put on a slow jam. It was their cue to walk off the floor. Victoria pulled her sweater away from her body while she and Monica searched for a corner to stand in to cool off.

They found a perfect spot near the bar where they had a clear view of the happenings inside the club and could also get some relief from the heat whenever the bouncers opened the door to admit a new patron.

Monica walked to the bar to get drinks while Victoria looked at the couples on the dance floor. She could always distinguish the lovers from those dancing together for the first time. The lovers always danced raucously, making their intimacy obvious. They'd grind into each other, and the woman would arch her back as her partner pulled her closer to the bulk that was developing in his pants. It was always an interesting sight to behold.

Victoria sighed, feeling a pinch of envy. It had been a long time since she'd been one of those lovers, and she missed the feel of a man holding her and squeezing her breasts against his chest. She sighed again to relieve the weight that bore down on her.

The door opened and the brisk breeze offered a welcome relief from the heat. She leaned her head back and gladly accepted it. As the cool air seemed to linger at her face, she took in an incredible scent. She inhaled deeply, then slowly exhaled as she opened her eyes to see where it had come from.

Her eyes caught a group of men standing inches away. The one directly in front of her held her stare.

Victoria gasped. He was without a doubt the most beautiful man she had ever seen. His flawless skin was rich milk chocolate. His hair was cut clean and even. Because of the way he stood Victoria only saw three-fourths of his face, but it was enough to notice the thick curves of his eyebrows and the radiance of his wide brown eyes. A perfectly trimmed shadow beard rounded his face and gently touched the top of his lips.

As he laughed with his friends, Victoria listened to the sound of his virile voice. She froze when his eyes turned to meet her stare with a smile still stretched wide across his face. He didn't acknowledge her presence. It was as if his eyes had simply gone straight through her and he was staring at a wall.

Monica nudged her, and Victoria broke the gaze long enough to take the tall glass of Long Island Iced Tea. Monica started talking, but Victoria had become completely oblivious to everything else that was going on that didn't include the sight in front of her. She watched as a trio of ladies approached the men. A young lady took *her* guy by the hand and escorted him onto the dance floor. She wore a thin, two-piece skirt ensemble that exposed a perfect midriff. The humidity inside the club moistened her smooth brown skin and provided a nice glow against tiny specks of glitter sprinkled on her body. The coifed hair shaped a youthful, radiant face. Makeup added just a hint of color to an otherwise perfect face. The only jewelry she wore was a pair of delicate diamond studs. She slid comfortably against him and wrapped her arms around his waist. Their bodies began to sway with the music as their feet stepped to the rhythm. Victoria followed their moves. He placed his arm around his partner and pulled her into him. Nimbly, he slid his hand along the small of her back and gently maneuvered her body to move with his.

They're lovers, Victoria decided. She exhaled deeply and looked away from the dance floor as she sipped from her glass. She eyed the wall of mirrors behind the bar and took in a view of herself as he would have seen her. The crumbled napkin she used to wipe the sweat from her face after dancing had more makeup on it than her face. The heat had diminished all the curls and bounce in her hair, and the bulky sweater seemed to add ten pounds to her frame.

The music became lively again, and the stunning couple promenaded off the dance floor and retreated to the other side of the club. Victoria quickly pulled herself from the bar and headed in his direction.

Seeing her approaching, he stepped aside for her to pass, but she purposefully widened her stride and bumped his arm.

"Excuse me," she apologized. His hand was at her waist to keep them both balanced.

"No problem," he said.

Victoria grinned wickedly as she walked past. She headed for the dance floor snapping her fingers. Expecting to see him staring back at her, instead she turned and caught sight of his posse heading for the exit. Her fingers stopped and the music faded behind her. She gazed after him until she saw the tan metal door close behind him.

Shaking her head, she mumbled, "Good-bye, beautiful," and danced on.

4

Victoria tried to make it to her truck without dropping the packages. The wrapped presents were too large to fit into shopping bags, and she struggled with them as she hurried down the busy mall corridors.

When she got to the mall exit, she juggled the packages in her arms and reached for the blue button that activated the automatic door opener installed for the handicapped. But the packages moved off balance and tumbled to the floor despite her effort to catch them.

"Damn this mall," she muttered. "You'd think they'd just install automatic doors for everyone." She knelt and began picking up the packages. She didn't notice the young man who had walked up behind her.

"Let me help you."

Startled, Victoria glanced up and felt her heart thump hard against the wall of her chest. "Oh, hi," she said, remembering his face from the Wilderness. She could never forget his face.

"Hi," he drawled, catching the hint of the familiarity in her voice.

"You don't remember me, do you?" *Of course he wouldn't*, Victoria thought.

He shrugged.

"Well, actually we've never formally met. I bumped into you at the Wilderness last weekend." Most of the packages were still on the floor, but she couldn't bring herself to stop gawking at him.

He smiled and handed her a few of her things. "I bump into a lot of people at the Wilderness, but I never remember them."

"You stood out," she said, and immediately she wished she could take it back.

"Oh, really!" He laughed, revealing perfect white teeth.

For the first time Victoria felt he finally looked at her, and once again she wished she had taken more care in her appearance. She wore just foundation, mascara, and eyeliner. She had brushed her hair away from her face and held it back with a white headband that matched the white button-down shirt she wore under a blue blazer.

"And why didn't you ask me to dance?" he said.

"For one, you were never alone, and second, you left too early."

He laughed. "Is there anything else you noticed about me that night I should be aware of?"

Embarrassed, Victoria covered her eyes with her hand.

"I think you're blushing," he said, and took her hand away from her face. "Yup, you're blushing."

"Okay, you can stop now." Victoria tried to laugh off her embarrassment, but she felt the heat on her cheeks.

"Would you like some help to your car?" he asked, reaching to push the automatic door opener.

"Only if you promise not to make fun of me anymore," she said and chuckled.

"Promise." He waited until she had walked out the doorway before he stepped beside her. "But you should have asked me to dance," he continued.

Victoria shook her head. "I wasn't dressed."

"Then you really should have asked me to dance."

They laughed. His humor dispelled any notion that he would be a conceited, self-absorbed bastard. He seemed very likeable.

Victoria kept up with his strides while taking a good look at the way he was dressed. He wore loose black jeans with a fashionable cream pullover knit sweater. Even his choice of shoes delighted her. Contrary to the men she had met lately who preferred the latest overpriced athletic shoe, he wore brown leather loafers.

"What's the occasion?" he asked.

" 'Scuse me?" she asked. She was busy noticing everything about him.

"What's the occasion?" He nodded toward the packages in his arms.

"Oh. Birthdays."

"I celebrated a birthday myself a few months ago," he said. "If I'd met you earlier, one of these packages could have been for me."

"That's very possible, but I hope I would have gotten it sooner." Victoria laughed. She breathed in the air filled with his cologne. She considered herself a connoisseur of men's cologne, but she could not place this scent.

"I don't recognize your cologne," she said. "I don't think I've smelled it before."

"Is that good or bad?"

"Very good," she said, nodding.

"Good," he said. "But you're right, you probably haven't smelled it before. My parents brought it back from Italy when they celebrated their twentieth wedding anniversary."

"Oh." That was not what she would have guessed. She would have thought it was simply a popular brand she hadn't encountered yet.

Relax, relax, Victoria repeated to herself, but her heart pounded so hard that she wondered if he could hear it.

Using her remote, she unlocked the door of her green Ford Explorer when they were just a few feet from it. He opened the back door and moved papers scattered about the seat and the floor and carefully placed the presents in the car.

Victoria groaned when she peeped inside and saw what a mess it was. She had been meaning to clean it up but kept running out of time.

"By the way, I'm James," he said, taking the packages from her and placing them neatly beside the others. When he turned around, he stuck his hand out toward her.

Victoria momentarily stared at his extended hand before she gathered the courage to touch him. "Victoria Chandler," she said, and put her hand into his. A shiver went through her when their energies connected. Her hand lingered in the palm of his.

"Victoria," he repeated. "That's one of my favorite names."

Victoria half grinned. "Oh, that's weak."

James laughed. "Yes, it is, but it's the truth. Does anyone call you Vicki?"

"Only my father, but so can you."

"Then I'm in good company."

Victoria was mesmerized by the glint in his eyes. They stood awkwardly facing each other as the moment approached for them to go their separate ways.

"I was thinking of grabbing a bite to eat," he said. "Would you like to join me?"

Victoria's eyes widened and she hesitated.

"I know a wonderful Italian restaurant not far from here if you're interested."

"Really?" she said giddily. Instantly she felt foolish. She had a bachelor's degree in education, and that was the best she could do. This was the time for brilliance.

James continued. "I'm parked just a few aisles down." He pointed in the opposite direction.

"Okay, sure." Words still failed her. Victoria climbed into her truck and James closed the door behind her. She started the engine and followed close behind him as he hurried across the parking lot.

"This is incredible," Victoria muttered as she watched him. She waved at him when he turned to make sure she was still there. A nervous smile tightened her face as she watched him unlock the door of a late-model black Ford F-150 truck and get in.

"Okay, he has a job," she said aloud. "That's a good start, and hopefully it isn't his girlfriend's or parents' car." She chuckled softly.

She glanced at her watch while waiting for him to back out of his parking space. It was six-thirty. *Good*, she thought. That gave her a few hours to spare. She'd told Monica that she would be back by eight o'clock, but she had finished shopping early because she knew exactly what she wanted and where to find it. Reese's fifth birthday was the next day, and Monica's twenty-seventh was the day after.

Less than ten minutes later they pulled into the parking lot of Luciano's, an Italian restaurant. James parked his truck and Victoria parked alongside him. She watched as he quickly jumped out and began walking toward her. She noticed the disappointment on his face when she opened her own door. She couldn't remember her husband ever making such a gesture. She made a mental note to allow James the honor the next time.

"You have a nice truck," she said. "How long have you had it?"

"A year," he answered.

Check one, Victoria thought. At least now she knew he wasn't driving someone else's car. Now she had only a few more questions to confirm that he was worth the pursuit.

They walked toward the restaurant, and James placed his hand gently at her back. She exhaled and closed her eyes for a quick moment, feeling surprisingly at ease with his touch. They reached the entrance too soon for Victoria as he removed his hand to open the door.

"Thank you," she said and stepped inside.

The fragrance of Italian spices surrounded them. A plump, middle-aged woman met them at the door with a wonderful, friendly smile. Her gray hair was pulled up into a bun on top of her head, and she wore a spotless white apron over a black floral dress. She spoke with a strong Italian accent and ushered them to their seats.

Immediately, Victoria noticed the immaculate table settings. The fresh, white cloth napkins were edged with gold embroidery and delicately placed on top of cheerful red tablecloths spread across each table. Glowing candles sparkled in crystal holders. Victoria took a whiff of the enticing aromas coming from the kitchen. She noticed the waitresses and waiters making a point of stopping to chat with the patrons before returning to the kitchen for more food.

Victoria and James were seated at a small table near the rear of the restaurant. A couple looking intensely into each other's eyes sat three tables from them. James pulled the chair away from the table for Victoria before seating himself in the soft leather chair opposite her.

"This is a wonderful place," Victoria said as the hostess handed her a menu.

"Just wait until you try the food."

"What do you recommend?" she asked after scanning the menu. Everything looked delicious.

"Do you like spaghetti?"

"Yes, very much."

"Wonderful." He took the menu from her and placed the menus on the table. "They have the best spaghetti and meat sauce, and trust me, one plate is more than enough for two people. I have never eaten a full plate by myself." When their waitress arrived, James ordered a plate of spaghetti. But to start, he ordered a plate of shrimp antipasto.

When the appetizer arrived, Victoria examined it closely before picking up her fork. Consisting of small shrimp, roasted artichokes, and garlic over baby spinach, it didn't look like anything she was interested in eating.

"Here, try this. It's good," he said, guiding a forkful toward her mouth.

Reluctant, Victoria opened her mouth to receive the delicate appetizer and slowly began to chew. "Umm," she said, surprised by the tastiness and the fact that he felt comfortable enough to share his fork with her, a virtual stranger. "That is good."

"Told you," he said, and put a helping on his plate. "Help yourself." He motioned for her to dig in, which she did.

Their waitress returned with fresh-baked bread and a pitcher of iced tea. A waiter followed and placed white china bread plates on the table in front of them. Victoria sat up straight and eyed the plate of steaming bread. Garlic butter melted along the crust, leaving the center soft and moist.

Victoria picked up a slice of the warm bread and gently bit into it. There was an unmistakable goodness about the taste of fresh bread that set it apart from anything purchased at the supermarket.

"This is good too," she said. "Everything here is good."

"You haven't had the spaghetti yet."

Victoria had started on her third slice of bread when the spaghetti arrived. The waitress placed the enormous platter between them, then refilled their water glasses. The steam from the plate curled up to her nose and made her mouth water.

Victoria followed James's lead and twirled the spaghetti on a wide-tined fork.

"Oh my God," she moaned. "I could gain twenty pounds in this place." She twirled her fork into the spaghetti again and made sure she picked up a chunk of the seasoned tomatoes. "You must bring a lot of dates here," she concluded. That would be the only way he would be so knowledgeable about this place and the menu.

James grinned. "I have brought a few dates here, yes."

Victoria blushed, but the answer didn't really satisfy her. She was hoping he would tell her if he had a girlfriend. She had to find another way to get him to reveal whether he was available.

They talked, ate, and toyed with their food by having a sucking contest to see who could slurp the fastest. James won. Victoria ended up with spaghetti sauce splattered across her white shirt, but it was so much fun, she didn't think twice about it.

"I like this song," James announced as he stopped and listened to the jazz melody playing softly.

"If you like this, you should go to the Wilderness on Sunday nights," she said. "It's their jazz night, and it's very nice."

"Can't," James said and reached for a slice of bread. "I have school on Monday morning."

"Oh. What school do you attend?" Victoria asked.

"Xavier."

Victoria nodded. "Good school. I know a lot of people who have graduated from there."

James shifted in his chair. "I have an interest in going into law when I graduate. Maybe even take some summer classes. Senator Parker is a good friend of my parents and I've volunteered in his office during the summer. He's convinced that I should pursue it." He kept his eyes on the piece of bread in his hand, as if the issue was still a debate in his mind.

"His opinion would be very credible." She nodded.

"He's a great mentor," James agreed. "He has also offered to write a letter of recommendation for me if I decide to go to law school."

"Very impressive."

James shrugged. "We'll see."

"Well," she said abandoning the conversation and placing her elbows on the table and leaning closer to him. "I want to thank you for inviting me to dinner."

James looked at her before returning his slice of bread to his plate. "I wish you would have asked me to dance."

Victoria was quiet as she took this in. Was he saying he was attracted to her? Her eyes stayed with him until she felt a sudden vibration against her side. It was her cellular phone. She quickly glanced at the Caller ID and then at her watch. It was Monica, and she was late.

" 'Scuse me," she said, and turned slightly away from him.

"Yeah," she said quickly into the phone. She turned and smiled apologetically at James as she spoke. "Okay, I'll be there in about fifteen minutes. Bye." She closed the phone and looked at James. "I have to leave," she said, gathering her purse and reaching for her wallet.

"Don't worry about it. I'll take care of it," James said, closing his hand over hers before extracting his wallet from his pants pocket and motioning for their waitress. When they rose to leave, he took Victoria's hand and entwined her fingers with his own.

"Thank you for a wonderful dinner," James said when they stopped at her truck. "Maybe we can do it again sometime." He dropped her hand and reached to open the door for her.

Victoria sat in the truck as James closed the door behind her. "I'm sorry to rush off, but I really have to go. Thank you for inviting me. I had a good time." She smiled as she started the engine. She sat for a few awkward minutes wondering if he was going to ask her for her phone number, but he didn't.

"Bye," she said, putting the truck into reverse and taking her foot off the brake. She peeked into her rearview mirror and smiled again as she watched him pull out and turn in the opposite direction. She wished he would have asked her for her phone number, but maybe the reason for that was the young woman she had seen him dancing with at the Wilderness. She was grateful for the time with him. She was able to listen to his incredible voice, take in his wonderful scent, and stare at his flawless smile. It had been a perfect evening, and she wasn't going to press it any farther than that.

5

Friday night was girls' night out again for Victoria and Monica, but Victoria had an ulterior motive. She wanted to see James again.

This time she was prepared. The red velvet spaghetti-strap dress showed off her strongest assets—her strong athletic legs and enticing shoulders. It slipped comfortably over her body and rounded her delicate curves.

Monica wore a beautiful above-the-knee black dress. The loose-fitting material flowed at the bottom to give her plenty of room for dancing.

After a drink, they left the house and drove in Victoria's truck with the music blaring, preparing them for a night of dancing. They laughed as they recapped the happenings of the week. The Wilderness was a few short blocks away, so it didn't take them long to get there.

As usual, a crowd waited in line outside the club while inside the music played at full blast. As they walked toward the door, Tony waved them up front and they walked on in.

"You're going to tell me about that one of these days," Victoria whispered to Monica as they walked past Tony. She knew she wasn't going to get that information out of Monica voluntarily. Blackmail seemed appropriate.

Walking in the door, Victoria took a quick look around. Monica tugged on her arm as she spotted an empty table near the back. Immediately they headed for it.

They sat down and took in their surroundings. They were about ten feet from the dance floor and approximately twenty feet from the nearest bar. The ladies' room was just behind them if they needed to make an emergency escape from a pestering man.

"Do you want anything to drink?" Monica asked once they were comfortable.

"The usual." Victoria never ventured too far from Long Island Iced Tea. Monica stepped away to get their drinks. When she returned, they talked about the other dancers and their moves.

Victoria kept her eyes glued to the entrance, carefully inspecting each person that walked through the door.

"Oh my God, he's here," Victoria said and hid her face.

"Who?"

"James. The guy I told you about."

"Then why are you hiding? Go say hi to him," Monica urged. "He's all you've talked about for a week."

"That would be too obvious. I can't do that." Several songs went by and Victoria continued to sit at the table. Her eyes followed James around the club until she lost sight of him in the crowd.

"I'm going to dance," she finally announced as she stood. "Are you coming?"

"No, go ahead," Monica replied. "I'm going to sit this one out."

Snapping her fingers as she walked out on the dance floor, Victoria squeezed through the crowd until she was among the other dancers twirling on the floor. As she turned from side to side, she finally saw him out of the corner of her eye. He was on the other side of the room, dancing.

She sighed.

She noticed every move he made as the sweat began to trickle down the side of his face. His steps were on beat with the reggae music. Victoria inched closer to him as the tempo sped up and the guitar was replaced by the sound of drums. She stopped when she saw he was not alone.

She looked from James to the young woman he was with. It was the same one as before. Victoria quickly turned away and attempted to walk in the opposite direction only to be blocked by a young man who had followed her. He was dancing in front of her, urging her to join him. Making it off the floor now was not possible. She smiled and began to dance.

"Hey."

She heard the voice and turned toward it. James was standing beside her. "Save one for me, okay?"

Victoria nodded and then turned away from him to find the gentleman still with her and grooving to the music. Suddenly she was grateful that he was there. She would have felt stupid if James had seen her dancing alone.

The song ended and Victoria touched her partner's arm to indicate that she'd had enough. Victoria smiled at him and began to walk off the floor when someone grabbed her arm. She turned, hoping it wasn't the same man.

It was James. "Dance with me," he said, pulling her back onto the dance floor.

He had her on the floor and was dancing in front of her before she had the chance to protest.

"I was hoping to see you tonight," he said as he twirled her around to him.

Victoria nodded as she began to dance. Her feet couldn't keep up with his as she struggled to control her excitement. Her ears were deaf to the music, and the only sounds she was aware of were the thumps of her heart. Her eyes fastened on him as she noticed every detail about him. He wore a Calvin Klein sports shirt tucked neatly inside a simple pair of Lee stonewashed black jeans. The top of his shirt was unbuttoned, and she clearly saw the sprinkle of hair on his chest. One wrist sported a leather-band watch, and the other a gold-faceted bracelet.

The next song began and the crowd burst into the electric slide. Victoria had wanted to learn the dance but had never mastered it. She moved slower than the other dancers while she watched them stepping and sliding left to right and dipping. She stumbled, trying to keep up with James and the other advanced sliders as they added fancier moves.

Three slides to the right, three slides to the left, three steps back, shuffle, and then turn.

Victoria stumbled.

James took her hand and slowed down as he guided her through the steps. He directed her when to slide right, when to slide left, when to dip, and when to turn.

She turned the wrong way, and they tried again with James

moving closer and placing his arm around her waist. The beat got faster, and everyone around her picked up the pace. She had to keep moving to avoid getting stepped on.

When the song finally ended, she was panting hard from the excitement. She touched James's arm to signal she was sitting down. He took her hand and led her off the floor. Victoria directed him to her table as they wove cautiously around small cliques standing about.

When they reached the table, Monica moved their purses from one of the unoccupied seats and placed them on the table.

"Can I buy you ladies a drink?" James asked, and gently touched Victoria's bare shoulder.

Victoria nodded. "Yes, I'll take a Long Island Iced Tea." She made a mental note that it would be her last drink of the evening.

"Gin and tonic," Monica followed.

James nodded, then walked away.

"I think you have a new friend," Monica said, smirking, as soon as James was out of earshot.

"I hope so."

"I have to admit," Monica said. "He can sure dance his ass off. He seems a little young though."

Victoria frowned. "I know. I've been trying to ignore that. How old do you think he is?"

"Well, at least twenty-one, maybe twenty-two."

Victoria rolled her eyes up, calculating. "That's what, three, four years younger? That's not too bad. I can deal with that."

"Yeah, a twenty-two-year-old man has the mentality of a seven-teen-year-old. You need a man in his forties to be a mental equal to us."

"True," Victoria said, laughing. Her eyes found James standing at the bar. His eyes turned to meet hers, and his smile went through her like a lightning bolt.

He carried three glasses back to the table, careful not to bump into anyone. Victoria noticed he only had a glass of ice water for himself.

A man who doesn't drink, she thought. *That's refreshing.*

When he sat down Victoria introduced Monica and he shook her hand.

"I'm glad you came out tonight," James said, returning his attention to Victoria. "It's good to see you again."

Victoria took a sip of her drink to calm the nerves jumping about in her stomach and between her legs. "Yes, it's good to see you too. We had a wonderful dinner. And just in case you're wondering, I did get the stain out."

"Good, now I don't have to buy you a new shirt."

"You wouldn't have had to buy me a shirt."

"The spaghetti was my idea."

"Well, next time, buy me a bib." They laughed.

Monica broke in. "How did you learn to dance like that?"

James laughed, and before he could answer, a group of young men approached them and tapped his shoulder. He excused himself and began talking to them.

"Victoria, I have to go hang with them for a minute. Please don't leave before dancing with me again, okay?"

"Okay."

He gently squeezed her shoulder as he walked away. Victoria shifted in her seat as soon as she felt the heat from his hand.

"Is it a sin for one man to be that sexy?" Victoria shivered.

"And I think he likes you too," Monica said as they watched James and his friends circle a group of women already on the floor.

Victoria didn't reply as she watched him dance. Soon a small crowd blocked her view of the dance floor and she lost sight of him. Monica began bouncing in her seat and soon trotted off to the dance floor. Victoria remained at the table in hopes of James returning.

With the sound of the banjos, it was time for the Showdown; a half hour of nonstop, fast-paced music. This was one of the live-liest times of the evening at the Wilderness because you never knew what the DJ was going to play next. The selection ranged from rock, reggae, hip-hop, and occasionally even a little country. Every-one gave all the energy they had to the music, determined not to drop.

"Are you going for it?" Victoria turned and saw James standing behind her.

"Yes!" she exclaimed, jumping from her chair and reaching for his extended hand.

James led them to the middle of the floor. She didn't know where the energy came from, but she kept up with him easily. They were jumping to reggae tunes by Bob Marley and Inner Circle, then rock songs by Limp Bizkit and Rage Against the Machine. Then the DJ threw in some George Clinton funk. The minutes flew as they jumped about on the floor, laughing and bumping into each other and at some points holding hands, feeding off of each other's energy. With the beat of the banjos again, the Showdown was over and Victoria collapsed in his arms.

"We did it!" she exclaimed, trying to catch her breath.

Quiet Moment followed the Showdown as the ballads began. Victoria recognized the first song as "All My Life," by K-Ci & JoJo. James continued to hold her as they began to sway with the music. The dance floor was empty, save for just a few who survived the Showdown with enough energy to remain upright.

Her mind emptied as she melted into his embrace. She felt his hands at her back, pressing her breasts against his chest. She took in his cologne as she closed her eyes and moved with him. After a few moments James stepped an arm's length from her, and holding her right hand, he spun her around quickly, then effortlessly dipped her.

The move caught Victoria so off guard that she was looking up into his face before she realized what had happened. They laughed as he straightened her to face him. A small trickle of sweat formed along her hairline. He wiped it away. They remained in the embrace for a minute after the song ended. As they stood on the floor swaying, dancers returning to the floor bumped them.

Victoria said softly into his ear, "I'm going to go sit down."

James slipped her fingers between his as they headed off the floor. Victoria sat down, James opposite her.

"I hope you're enjoying yourself this evening." He spoke softly as he held her hand.

Victoria leaned onto the table. "Yes, I am. Are you?"

James nodded and moved his chair closer.

Relax, Victoria thought as she felt his breath against her face. She picked up a paper napkin and wiped the sweat from his forehead as it trickled down his face.

James took her hand as he looked down at each finger.

"Victoria, I—" James began.

"Excuse me." A voice invaded their space. They turned to see a young woman standing with her arms folded in front of her. One leg was slightly in front of the other, her body weight resting on her back leg, causing her to tilt casually to the right.

James dropped Victoria's hand as he looked from the young woman to her.

"James, can I talk to you for a minute?" the young woman demanded, and didn't bother to wait for him to reply. She pivoted on her back heel and walked away.

"I'll be back," he said, excusing himself and hurrying off in the woman's direction.

Victoria threw her arms in the air, wondering what had just happened. *Well*, she thought. *That wasn't pretty.* She watched as James and the angry young woman became engaged in a shouting match.

"Hey, where's James?" Monica asked when she returned to the table. "I saw him sitting here with you." Victoria pointed to where James continued a heated discussion with the young woman.

"Whoa, looks like he's in trouble. Who is she?"

"I have no idea, but it looks to me like she might be his girlfriend." Victoria watched the angry exchange until she decided she had seen enough.

"Let's get out of here," she announced as she stood and prepared to leave.

"Wait," Monica objected. "Are you going to find out what this is all about?"

"No!" Victoria exclaimed.

"Victoria," Monica protested, "give him a chance to explain."

Victoria sat down, regaining her composure. "Monica, I've been through this before, remember?" She shook her head in disgust. "What was I thinking? When will I ever learn?"

"You should at least give him a chance to explain."

Victoria thought for a moment. "Monica, I know what I'm looking for." She took a deep breath and looked again at James. "I want something that I've never had before. I want the kind of relationship with a man that is real. I am his girl and he is my guy, and there is no doubt whatsoever about that." Victoria thought about her marriage to Reese's father. She remembered the pain of learning about his extramarital affairs. She remembered the loneliness and depression she felt after the divorce.

"Why would I think that James would be any different?" She continued to eye him across the room. "I don't want to play games anymore. I don't need another relationship that has no chance of growing." Victoria's disappointment was mounting.

"Are you okay?" Monica asked, placing a comforting hand over hers.

Victoria shook her head. "No, but let's get out of here," she muttered. They walked quietly out of the building and into the parking lot. The cool night air helped calm her disappointment and dried the tears that filled her eyes.

"Victoria." She turned, hearing her named called from behind her. James was eagerly walking toward her.

He reached her and then took a deep breath before he spoke. "I saw you walk out, and I just wanted to catch you before you left."

Victoria paused before she spoke, watching him pant from his brisk walk across the parking lot. "It was time for us to leave," she said.

James took her by the arm and led her away. "I know how that must have looked, but give me a chance to explain."

Victoria said coolly, "Listen, James, I am not trying to cause any problems, nor do I want to be a problem, if you know what I mean."

"Yes, I know what you mean, and I promise you there isn't a problem." James hesitated. "Can I see you again?"

Victoria shifted, shaking her head. *What is he pulling?* she wondered.

He touched her arm as he walked closer to her. "Trust me with this," he said. "There isn't a problem."

The look of conviction on his face told her that he meant what he said. This was not a man who was trying to squirm his way out of punishment after being caught with his hand up the wrong dress.

Victoria shivered. She was torn between her attraction to him and the idea that he already might be involved with someone else. There was no way she was going to get involved with someone who couldn't stay committed to the relationship he was already in. She didn't need or want that heartache.

But James wasn't relenting and his stare didn't falter. "Vicki, I really do want to see you again. At least to explain everything. Please don't say no."

"We'll talk," she said, succumbing to his pleas. Her decision made, she took out a pen and paper from her purse and quickly scribbled down her name and number.

"I'll call you." He glanced at the number quickly and tucked it safely into his pocket. "Are you free for dinner tomorrow night?"

Victoria drew back. "That's quick."

"I'm not going to give you time to change your mind," James said with a crooked smile.

Victoria couldn't help but soften under his charm. "Tomorrow night shouldn't be a problem."

"Good, I'll call you tomorrow." James kissed her on the cheek, then hurried back into the club.

Victoria stood in silence before getting into the truck. She wanted to see him again but was scared to death of setting herself up for another great heartbreak. She climbed into the truck, where Monica was waiting.

"Oh God, I hope I don't regret this," Victoria said, and she tapped her head lightly against the steering wheel before driving off.

6

"Yes!" Victoria yelled after she hung up the phone. James had called her to give details of their date that evening. Their conversation was brief, and she was still eager to know everything about him. They hadn't yet drifted into anything personal. She definitely wanted to know the extent of his relationship with the young woman from the Wilderness.

One thing was certain. She was completely intoxicated by him. She was like an addict; the more of him she took in, the hungrier she became.

She hurried about the house, scrambling through closets searching for something to wear. At moments like these, she never seemed to be able to find anything appropriate. She picked up a red dress and held it against her in front of the mirror. She frowned. She had worn the dress on her first date after her divorce. It had been a disaster because she spent the entire time talking about her failed marriage. She tossed the dress onto the bed.

She took out a long black dress and held it against her. Once again she frowned. She had worn it to Grandma Mae's funeral. She quickly tossed it aside. Each time she picked up a dress, she made a quick decision. The green dress was too short. The white dress was out of season. The brown dress was the wrong color.

She held the gold, knee-length dress against her and slowly examined herself. Perfect.

"That's a pretty dress, Mommy," Reese said, walking into her bedroom.

Victoria stopped and picked the little girl up, hugging her. She kissed Reese hard on the cheek, then placed her on the bed while she walked about the bedroom looking for accessories.

Reese began to bounce up and down on her knees, seeing how high she could spring into the air. "Where are you going?"

"Mommy has a date tonight," Victoria said, searching through her jewelry box. "Aunt Monica is coming to pick you up, and you're going to stay with her. Is that okay?"

"Yep." Reese jumped off the bed and walked to the dresser to help Victoria select jewelry. "Wear these." Reese held up a pair of faux pearl earrings.

Nodding, Victoria said, "Thank you. I think I will wear these." Victoria kissed her again on the cheek.

"Are you hungry?" It was lunchtime, and Monica wasn't due for another five hours. Pleased with her selection, Victoria set everything aside to be with her daughter.

She held on to Reese's small soft hands as they walked down the winding stairs. When they reached the kitchen, Reese jumped onto the white wooden stool and rested her arms on the island countertop in the center of the floor.

The kitchen was one of Victoria's favorite rooms in the house. She had won the old ten-room house in a housing lottery. When she and Gerald had separated, she and Reese had stayed with Monica while Victoria searched for an apartment to rent. Then she read about a housing lottery in the local newspapers and decided to apply. A few months later she was notified that she had been selected and was offered a contract to purchase an abandoned, semicondemned house for one dollar on the promise to rehabilitate it and live in it for at least two years. The house was located in an area called Over-the-Rhine, not far from downtown Cincinnati.

When Victoria first saw the house, it was horrendous. Like the houses around it, it had wooden planks covering all of the windows. There were missing floorboards, and the walls were scarred with large holes. The second floor was inaccessible.

When Victoria took her family to tour the house, they suggested she return to her husband and the beautiful suburban home she had left. Victoria refused and decided to accept the contract and restore the old home. She was able to obtain a fifty-thousand-dollar loan. She used the money to hire wonderful but inexpensive electricians, carpenters, plumbers, and painters.

After two years, Victoria had satisfied her lottery contract but decided to keep the house, which she could now sell on the market for one hundred and fifty thousand dollars. The area had become a haven for young professionals, who were moving back to the inner city and rebuilding older homes. The houses around hers, which had once been no more than piles of brick, dirt, and broken glass, were now reconstructed masterpieces.

Victoria's mind stayed on James and the impending date. The attraction between them was palpable. She melted whenever he took her hand. Her knees wobbled when he stared into her eyes. She had never before met anyone she was instantly titillated by. She'd been attracted to her ex-husband, Gerald, when they met, but never like this.

Since her divorce, Victoria had been with only one man. There was no romance involved. He was just someone from her past, and they spent one night together. Male companionship was something she longed for but hadn't been actively seeking.

There were times when loneliness surrounded her and, to beat it, she would lie in bed, wrap her arms tightly around herself, and squeeze. She couldn't give in to the despair and the heartache. Luckily, those times were few and far between.

<hr>

Victoria was upstairs putting the finishing touches on her makeup when she heard the doorbell. Nervously, she walked to the door, stopping to check herself in the hall mirror before she opened it.

"Hi," she said, swinging the door open and taking a full look at him. She took a deep breath. His hair and beard were neatly trimmed. He wore a black trench coat over an olive double-breasted suit. Victoria took two quick deep breaths before she let him in.

James returned the greeting. "Hello. You look beautiful."

"Thank you." *You do too*, she thought as she stepped aside to let him pass. James stepped forward and kissed her softly on the cheek. Victoria thought quickly of his kisses. Both had been on the cheek.

"Would you like to come in for a drink before we go?" Victoria asked.

"No, I think we should be leaving. The reservation is for seven o'clock."

"Okay, let me get my coat." Victoria walked to the closet, took out her black leather trench coat, and draped it over her arm. James took the coat from her arm and helped her put it on. Then he opened the door for her.

A gentleman, Victoria thought.

They walked to his truck quickly in silence. When they reached it, he opened the passenger door for her. Before she could sit down, she noticed a bouquet of assorted roses placed neatly on the seat.

Victoria gasped. "For me?" she asked, scooping the roses up. She immediately brought them to her nose and took in the sweet smell before sitting down.

"Of course." James closed the door, then walked to his side and got in.

"You better be careful," she said, looking over at him as he sat opposite her. "I could get used to this." She still held the bouquet to her nose.

"That is my intention."

He flashed a smile and Victoria twitched. A powerful jolt went through her and turned on every emotional switch in her body. She wanted to reach over and touch every inch of him. Instead, she dropped her eyes and took another long whiff of the roses.

The drive to the restaurant was short. They engaged in idle chitchat about the changes in downtown Cincinnati over the past few years.

The restaurant James had chosen was on Covington Landing, just across the bridge from Cincinnati. Victoria waited while James took care of the valet parking. She glanced over at the Cincinnati side of the Riverfront. Although most of the Riverfront area had been ripped up to make way for new stadiums for the Cincinnati Bengals and Reds, it was still one of the most beautiful and serene places she had ever seen.

She felt James's hand on her back, getting her attention as they began walking toward the restaurant. They waited just a few minutes before being escorted to their seats.

Their table offered a beautiful view of Cincinnati as a backdrop. The restaurant lights were dimmed, and she heard smooth jazz melodies softly playing overhead.

"Is this okay?" James asked.

Victoria nodded. "It's perfect."

The maître d' pulled the seat out for her and handed them both menus as he recited the daily specials. They listened attentively but chose to look through the menu instead.

Victoria looked out onto the river, captivated by the thousands of soft lights playing off the calm water. "This is just absolutely beautiful," she said. "Do you come here often?"

"No, I don't. It isn't exactly an everyday type of place. I'm your typical fast-food junkie." James laughed.

Victoria smiled at his honesty.

"I've been here a few times with my family," James continued. "My parents live for places like this. I'm more at home at Luciano's." They sat quietly for a few minutes looking over the menus. Finally, James opted for the filet mignon, while she chose the blackened salmon.

They talked, mostly about the view around them, until the food arrived. Over dinner they compared the beauties of Cincinnati to other cities they had seen. To her surprise, James had traveled abroad several times, something she had not had the opportunity to do yet. He and his family had vacationed in Spain, England, Paris, and parts of Africa. He talked incessantly about Africa, explaining that it was quite different from what was portrayed in the media, which was why his parents had taken him.

"I never expected Nigeria to be this totally beautiful, very modern country. I was expecting to find a ravaged, dirt-street countryside, but it was nothing like that." He stopped talking long enough to take a sip of his water. "Don't get me wrong," he continued. "There were parts that we were told not to go to, but there are parts of the United States where I wouldn't want to go either." James took another sip of his water and looked at her over the rim of his glass. "You're not talking. I hope I'm not boring you."

"You must be kidding. I think this is absolutely fascinating. I enjoy listening to you talk." Victoria leaned forward on the table. "You tell wonderful stories."

James nodded his thanks. "You have a beautiful smile, Victoria," he said.

She was surprised by the sudden compliment. "Thank you," she muttered. "James," she continued, suddenly uneasy, "about the woman at the Wilderness—"

"I was wondering when you were going to get around to that," James interrupted. "She's an on-again, off-again girlfriend."

"So what is the current status?" Victoria asked.

"Definitely off." James looked at her. "Tai and I have known each other since grade school, and I just don't think we've learned when it's time to stop. She will probably always be my friend, but not a girlfriend." He took Victoria's hand and squeezed it. "I know it was awkward for you because it was for me. I just didn't want to get into that conversation with her in front of you."

Victoria nodded, satisfied by his explanation. She felt no need to press for more information.

After they had eaten, they shared warm chocolate-chip cake that was absolute heaven and melted in their mouths. James commented on her figure, and Victoria admitted to being a calorie watcher. Thinness was not a genetic trait in her family. James placed the last bite of the cake into Victoria's mouth before they rose to leave.

They walked out of the restaurant and into the wonderful, cool night air. The light from the full moon and the surrounding buildings lit their way. James's truck was brought to them, and they drove off. He held her hand as he drove around to Cincinnati's side of the Riverfront.

He parked, and they began to walk toward the concrete walls to sit down. This side of the landing was always peaceful, save for a few lovers enjoying the view and each other. When they reached the concrete walls, they stood in the breeze and held each other. Victoria's arms were tucked warmly inside his coat as he pulled her closer to him.

She loved the feel of him. She felt his breath on her face as he began to shower small kisses on her cheek, inching closer to her lips. She closed her eyes and turned to meet his lips.

It was a simple kiss at first. Her lips remained open as he brought his to meet hers again. Then his tongue explored her mouth until he touched her tongue with his.

The sound of a boat horn broke the trance. Slowly Victoria opened her eyes as their lips parted. She rested comfortably in his arms and placed her head against his chest.

James squeezed her against him, then took her hand as they walked alongside the concrete walls. A comfortable familiarity had settled between them.

"This is one of my favorite places," Victoria said, pulling James closer to her. "It's a great place to come to sort things out and to think."

"Think about what?" James asked. He pressed her against him and kissed her temple as if to comfort her.

"At the time, my marriage and my daughter."

James stopped walking and looked at her, his eyes wide in surprise.

"You're married?" he asked.

"No." Victoria chuckled. "Divorced, and I have a five-year-old daughter."

"A five-year-old daughter?" James repeated.

"Yes, Reese Alexandria." Victoria smiled.

"You have a five-year-old daughter?" he asked again.

Puzzled by his reaction, she slowly responded, "Yes." Her eyes narrowed as she looked at the expression on his face.

"How old are you?" James asked.

Excited by his inquisition, she answered him. "Twenty-five. Why?"

"Twenty-five." He closed his eyes and shook his head.

"Why are we having the parrot effect?" Victoria watched his expression but didn't know what to make of it. "Is something wrong?" she asked.

James opened his eyes and looked at her. He wasn't smiling, and the look in his eyes was one of distress.

"Before we go any further, I need to tell you something," he said. Then he took her by the arm and led her to the concrete wall. "Have a seat."

Her stomach tightened at the seriousness that came over him. She took a deep breath and held it before letting it out again. "Is something wrong?" she asked. Curiosity was getting the best of her.

James bit his lip before he began. "Victoria, I'm sev . . ." He stopped, bit his upper lip, and closed his eyes. "Seventeen."

Victoria leaned forward. "You're *what?*"

James paused before he continued. "Victoria, I'm seventeen years old. I turned seventeen four months ago."

Victoria jumped from her seat on the wall. "What the hell do you mean, you're seventeen years old?" she yelled.

James stood with her.

She continued to scream. "Is this some kind of a joke?" She stared at him, waiting for him to burst into laughter.

James shook his head. "Damn, I wish I could say it was, but no. No joke."

Victoria slumped down and leaned her back against the hard concrete wall. Her chest was heavy with the weight of her heart pressing against it.

"You're lying. That is not possible." Victoria stood and stepped down from the wall and looked up at him. She stared into his face. She mentally removed the neatly trimmed beard. She looked into his glossy eyes searching for signs of maturity that came with age.

"But you said you attended Xavier," she said, trying to piece together a puzzle that didn't seem to fit.

"I do. Xavier High School."

"Oh my God." She retreated to the concrete wall once again. Her visual inspection of him confirmed it. "James, I teach at Roosevelt High School," she said, looking up at him.

Wide-eyed, James sat down beside her.

Furiously, Victoria jumped from the wall away from him. "Why in the hell didn't you say something?"

"Because I didn't know you were a teacher, and if you had known I was seventeen you wouldn't go out with me."

"You're damn right," she continued to yell. "How do you get into the Wilderness?"

"Fake ID," he said casually.

"Wonderful," she said sarcastically as she sat down again and shook her head in disbelief. "This can't be happening. You are the same age as some of the kids in my classroom. This is a nightmare." Victoria stood and began to pace the wall.

"I'm sorry. Maybe I should have told you sooner—"

Victoria snapped, "You're damn right you should have told me."

"Look, you can stop yelling at me. I think this was an honest mistake."

"This was not an honest mistake. You deliberately kept that from me." She sat on the wall again and leaned against the hard concrete. She couldn't look at James or anything else. Her mind was in a haze.

James watched her as she shook her head. He took her hand in his and squeezed. "You're right, and I'm sorry." They sat silently for several seconds before he continued. "So, where do we go from here?"

Victoria turned and looked at him. She couldn't believe the absurdity of the question. "What do you mean, where do we go from here? I feel like a complete idiot. You are a seventeen-year-old. I am twenty-five. I was married and I have a five-year-old daughter. You have not graduated high school."

"I understand that."

"Then why are you asking me such a ridiculous question?" She pulled her hand from his and began heading toward his truck.

Hurriedly, James ran to catch up with her.

"Wait a minute." He reached her and turned her around to face him. "Is that it? We just forget about the attraction we feel for each other? Do we forget that kiss?"

"Do we have a choice?"

"I would like to think so," he continued. "I know we've just met, but I am not too young to know that there is something between us. We haven't spoken many words to each other, but it seems like we've known each other for years."

His words touched her but she had no choice. "James, you do not seem to understand," she spoke softly to him. "You are still in high school, and I am a schoolteacher. I could lose my job, and if my ex-husband found out about it, I could lose my daughter." Her voice cracked with every word she spoke. "Take me home, please."

"So, you're just going to ignore everything? The dancing, the way we feel right now, the kiss? You are going to ignore it, like it never happened?"

"I don't have a choice," Victoria snapped again. "I can't be with you." The words burned as they rolled from her lips. She couldn't stand near him any longer.

"Take me home. Now." The tears began to roll down her cheeks.

"Victoria, there has to be something we can do," James pleaded, but she ignored him.

They rode back to her house in silence as James drove the truck slowly, purposely taking the long way, stretching a ten-minute drive to twenty minutes. When they reached her house, Victoria quickly stepped from the truck.

"Don't," she said, stopping him from getting out and following her. She jumped out of the truck, leaving the roses on the seat, and walked toward the house looking straight ahead, not daring to look back. She felt his eyes burning a hole through her heart. She quickly opened the door and closed it behind her. After she was safely inside and away from his glare, she threw herself on the sofa in the living room and cried.

7

VICTORIA

"Victoria." Gerald nudged at my arm. "What's wrong with you? You look like you're spaced out."

The dream of James was fresh in my mind. I reached up and wiped a tear from the corner of my eye. "What did you say?"

"I said I'm about to go play some ball," he said and walked away. "You've been off in your own world a lot lately."

I watched him as he took a pair of shorts and a T-shirt from the dresser.

He actually noticed? The idea that he noticed anything about me got my attention. I rose from the bed and pulled the curtains open. The heat from the morning sun caught my face and blinded me, but I stared straight into it and stretched high toward the ceiling.

"Let's take a walk on the Riverfront," I said. If he took the time to notice that I had not been myself lately, perhaps I could entice him to join me for a walk. I found the thought of walking alongside Gerald and talking quite pleasing. It would be wonderful to engage in conversation and laugh, which was something we hadn't done in a long time. Perhaps there was a chance that we could even hold hands.

"Maybe some other time," he said, quickly eradicating any hope I had. He walked into the bathroom, and I followed him. I watched as he began to undress. There were times when the sight of his body instantly caused a stir between my legs. His strong legs, his tight ass, muscular chest . . . all of it was enough to make most women want to drop to their knees and let their tongue explore every inch of his—

"Victoria," Gerald snapped.

I quickly looked up at him.

"Towel." He pointed to the towel behind me.

I reached for the small burgundy towel and handed it to him. "Can you skip the game this morning? Reese is at your mother's house, and it's beautiful out. Let's take a walk."

"No, I really feel like I need to exercise this morning." He started the shower and stepped in.

I never understood why he took a shower just to go get sweaty and then would have to take another one when he got home. It made no sense to me. "Well, I'll go with you and we can take a walk afterward."

Where there's a will, there's a way was the old saying. I wasn't ready to give up. The thought of making love to the Gerald I had first met was too enticing to dismiss. I couldn't forget how good it had been between us. I missed those times.

Even if we were to come back home and nothing about our relationship had changed, a walk in the park and a time to communicate would provide me with the ammunition I needed to prove that there was hope. If only I could just hold on for a little while longer. Things had to get better. They just had to.

". . . and besides." Gerald had been talking while I had drifted in my own world. "You'll be the only female there, and I'm not going to want to walk downtown all sweaty," he said. And just like that, any hope I had remaining of rekindling the intimacy between us was extinguished. Again.

I looked through the glass shower doors at his silhouette as he scrubbed the lathered washcloth across his body. It was obvious that it didn't matter what I proposed, he was going to turn me down. My presence was not invited.

"Do you think you will be able to find any time for me today?" I had raised my voice, annoyed by his rejection.

Gerald peered from behind the sliding glass door. The water continued to beat down on his body as steam rose to the ceiling. "Not today. I'm not in the mood."

His body didn't have the same appeal it had just a minute ago. The churn of desire became a whip of antipathy. Lowering my head, I walked out of the bathroom. I grabbed my purse and headed out the door to enjoy the burst of sunshine alone. As I drove through the streets heading for the one place that gave me solace, I was convinced that one day soon I was going to get tired of having my feelings hurt.

Gerald stayed away all day, came home, got dressed, and went out again. The argument we'd had the night before about his late hours didn't seem to matter. This was an ongoing battle for us. Week after week, I would tell him how it made me feel when he didn't come home from his night of partying, but he never seemed to care. His pace never slowed; his eyes never made contact with mine. My ears stayed attuned to every sound he made, longing to hear him utter the words "I'm sorry."

I remembered one of those nights when I decided I needed a break as well and fled to a dance club, the Wilderness. I ran into a friend from the old days, an older man with uncanny perception. He offered advice I'll never forget.

"Why aren't you home with that man of yours?" he asked with a knowing smile, slipping a comforting arm around my waist. His touches could never be mistaken for advances. He never offered a hint of taking our conversations farther than casual friendship.

"He went out with his friends, so I decided I'd do the same. I just want to know what keeps his attention for so long into the night," I told him, hoping I sounded more convincing than I felt.

"Let me tell you something, little lady," he offered, sending out a whiff of the sweet rum and Coke on his breath. "The only thing open after two-thirty is some woman's legs." Perhaps he knew more about the situation than even he was willing to confess. Tears filled my eyes. He did not have to go into detail for me to decipher the warning. His words stabbed me, and I drove home that night with tears streaming down my face.

There were times when being in the house alone made me feel so empty I was numb. I walked about, looking at each picture hanging neatly on the walls. Each one told a unique story, but most were simple snapshots of Reese. There was one family portrait that hung away from the others; it was the only one I failed to dust.

Taking the portrait off its hook, I traced the images with my fingertips. Dust separated from the glass and lingered in the air above the photo. It was a perfect picture taken at one of the most prestigious studios in town. They did an exceptional job capturing our likenesses. Not one strand of hair was out of place. Our clothes were neat and unruffled, our smiles wide. I returned the wooden frame to its position on the wall and felt the need for a stiff glass of cognac. I went to the wet bar along the far wall of the house and poured a full glass, then walked to the sofa and sat with my legs curled up beneath me. Slowly sipping from the glass, I wondered how long ago loneliness had come to sit beside me.

"Ah," I sighed as I felt the warmth of the liquid flow through me. The alcohol began to relax me, but unfortunately it did nothing for the despair.

Gerald had all the looks I dreamed of in a man: beautiful brown eyes, thick, full eyelashes, and a dashing smile. In the earlier stages of our relationship, Gerald was my reigning Prince Charming, and I wasn't the only one who found him so attractive.

Everywhere we went, I noticed heads turning, women's eyes following him, wishing, appreciating. They would start at his feet, checking out his shoes. Their eyes slowly ascended his legs and stopped for a pleasurable glimpse at his round firm butt as I watched the carnal thoughts show through their eyes. A glint of a smile revealed entertaining thoughts of standing close to him, touching the well-toned muscles in his chest and arms. The journey ended when their stares met mine.

I remembered the night Gerald and I met. He raised his eyebrows at me with an interested expression and pointed to the dance floor. And then we danced. Standing close to him, I took in his cologne. Every step I took seemed to lift me higher above the earth. I was under his spell, and nothing could have shaken me from it.

The remainder of the evening we clung to each other, and at the end we exchanged telephone numbers. I rushed to the phone whenever it rang in hopes of hearing his voice. Not long after that night, mornings for us began with breakfast in bed. Our evenings ended with passionate lovemaking, and I was reunited with school-girl laughter. At sunrise I would open the curtains and allow the rays of sunshine to brighten my room. When I walked about, there was a bounce in every step as if I was about to leap for the sky. I was on the threshold of heaven.

I knew Gerald received a lot of invitations from women. He was a good-looking man, so it was to be expected. But I didn't doubt it for a second when he told me how much I meant to him.

When I met him, I was in my second year of college at Ohio University, majoring in business administration. Although in high school I excelled in all my subjects, I only received mediocre marks in college and I wasn't sure exactly what I wanted to do with my degree. I never successfully answered the question of what I wanted to be when I grew up.

Most of my dates with Gerald consisted of dancing at night-clubs, then returning to my apartment, where we would make love all night. I lived off campus in an efficiency apartment that I could afford working part-time at an auto-parts distribution center. Every semester I registered for a full course load, but usually by midterm I would have dropped at least two or three classes. I never could maintain a focus on management or higher-level computer-related classes. I found it all very boring.

We seldom went to Gerald's apartment because although it was larger, it was a typical bachelor's place—always a mess—and the telephone rang incessantly. He wasn't much for going out other than to the club. I decided he was a recluse and the club was his way of breaking free.

Gerald had graduated from Xavier University a year before I met him, and he talked about going back to get his graduate degree in electrical engineering or an MBA. I loved lying beside him after we'd made love and listening to him talk about his plans for the future and having a family. There would always be a huge grin on my face the entire time he talked. I was so proud of him.

Then that day came. The first day I was late, I knew I was pregnant because I was never late. I made an appointment with my doctor to confirm it. Gerald talked about having a family so much, the image of his excitement played repeatedly in my mind as I rushed to his apartment. When I knocked on the door I heard his footsteps, and it took all the control I could muster not to blurt out my news in the hall.

"Victoria, what are you doing here?"

As I thought back to that day, I recalled the nervousness in his voice as he opened the door.

"I have some news," I said, bouncing into the apartment and tossing my purse on the sofa.

"What is it?" he asked hurriedly.

"Do I get a kiss or a hello at least?"

He kissed me quickly on the lips then stepped back. "I'm expecting someone from work to stop by, and I'm trying to get things straightened up. You should have called first."

I looked around the apartment and saw that he had been cleaning. I'd never seen Gerald's apartment clean. Because of the pile of laundry that had become commonplace in his living room, this was the first time I had actually fully seen his black leather sofa, and he'd even taken the time to shine it.

"Okay, I'll make this a little quick," I said, then handed him the vial with a blue plus sign in the middle.

"What's this?" He shrugged as he looked at it.

"I'm pregnant." I don't precisely remember, but I think I bounced and clapped when the words spilled from my mouth.

Gerald quickly looked up from the vial and stared at me. "You're what?"

"I'm pregnant."

"What the hell do you mean, you're pregnant?"

This wasn't the response I had envisioned. The look on his face was not of amazement but of immediate contempt. Before I could answer him the doorbell rang.

"Shit," he said beneath his breath, then turned to walk toward the door. When he opened it, an attractive young woman stood on the other side, stylishly dressed in a casual black pantsuit and carrying a large leather briefcase.

"Kelly, come in." Gerald stepped aside and let the young woman in. "Kelly, this is Victoria. Victoria, Kelly." He did not mention that I was his girlfriend or a friend.

"Hello." The woman smiled and stretched her hand out in greeting. "Pleased to meet you. Are you Mrs. Chandler?"

"Oh, no." I laughed it off even though I liked the sound of it. "I'm his girlfriend, and we just found out we're having a baby," I said excitedly, ready to share the news with anyone who happened my way.

Gerald tossed me a scornful look as if I had done a terrible evil.

"Wow," the young woman said, and turned to see the dismal expression on Gerald's face. "Congratulations to the both of you." She returned her attention to me and smiled warmly. "Is this your first child?"

"Yes, for both of us."

"You must be very excited. Congratulations." She nodded. "Gerald, if you would like to reschedule, we can do that. You can come by my office tomorrow if you'd like."

"Yes, that would be great. Thanks," he mumbled, and escorted her to the door.

Kelly stopped in the doorway and waved at me as she left. "It was nice meeting you, Victoria," she said before Gerald closed the door behind her.

"She was very nice," I said with an enthusiastic grin on my face.

"What the hell do you think you're doing?" Gerald yelled as soon as the door was closed. The rise of his voice startled me, and I jumped back. "What the hell made you think I want to have a baby?"

My mouth dropped open. What was he talking about? How many nights had he and I stayed up talking about what it would be like having kids running around the house and all of us taking family vacations? I was speechless.

"I think we should talk about an abortion," he said.

I choked. "An abortion?"

"Yes, an abortion."

"I'm not having an abortion." I was dumbfounded. "Why are you so surprised about this? We haven't used any protection, and we've talked about it. Why are you acting like I've sprung this on you? All you ever talked about is having a family."

"Yes, but I never said I wanted one now and I never said I wanted one with you. Damn." He walked away from me.

My heart felt like it had stopped. The air was completely taken from my lungs.

"I'm not ready for this, Victoria," he continued.

"If you weren't ready for this, then why have you led me to believe that we were working toward a family together?"

"Everything that we've talked about was after several drinks and in the middle of the night."

"So you're telling me that you were lying to me the entire time?"

"Nooo," he said. He picked up a crystal vase from the kitchen counter and slammed it back down. The noise of the shattering glass ricocheted throughout the apartment.

I jumped.

"I'm not ready for this," he repeated. He didn't seem to notice the tiny pieces of glass scattered across the counter.

"I'm not having an abortion. I can't abort a child I'm excited about. I didn't feel that this was a mistake."

"So what do you want from me?"

I was flabbergasted that he would ask me that. "What do you mean, what do I want from you?" I yelled. "I am having your child!"

Gerald just shook his head.

I had been prepared for an initial shock, but not for contempt. "I don't believe this. I thought we were working toward something here. Was I wrong?"

Gerald threw his hands up and walked into the kitchen. He leaned on the breakfast bar with his head buried in his hands. "I really think you should consider having an abortion. Victoria, I think you are a nice person and we have a nice time together, but I'm thinking about going back to school and I'm not ready for a baby or a family right now."

My heart dropped into my stomach. *A nice person?* What the hell was he saying?

I yelled, "I practically danced into the doctor's office to have a pregnancy test. I rejoiced with the receptionist when the results came back positive. What am I supposed to tell these ladies? Am I supposed to go back and tell them that my boyfriend thinks I'm a nice person but he doesn't want to have a baby with me?"

"I don't care what you tell them. I'm just not ready for this."

I shook my head again in defiance. "I'm not having an abortion."

"Then I think you should leave." He walked from behind the breakfast bar and headed straight to the door and opened it.

At first I just stood there with my heart pounding as if I had run a four-minute mile. Then I picked up my purse from the sofa and walked out. I stopped outside his door and leaned against the wall in the corridor of his apartment building to brace myself. My heart had not settled, and I kept forgetting to breathe. I was numb. Tears flowed from my eyes as I drove home. I couldn't believe what had just happened.

How could he do that to me? All the talk was just that: talk. He didn't give a damn about me or a future with me. But now there was a baby. It was too late for him to change his mind. He was going to be a father.

When I reached my apartment I threw myself on my bed and cried myself to sleep. Later that night I called my girlfriend Stephanie, and she came over to console me.

"But you guys really didn't have a relationship," Stephanie said as she held my hand. "You just slept together."

"Stephanie, I couldn't tell you how many times Gerald and I stayed up all night and talked about having a family. I really thought that he was referring to me. To us."

"But why are you in such a rush to have his baby? I thought you wanted to finish school?"

"I do want to finish school, and I am going to finish school. I can always go to school part-time."

"It's going to be a lot harder for you to finish school with a baby."

"So are you saying that I shouldn't have this baby?"

"No," Stephanie said, backing down. "I'm not going to be the one responsible for giving you that advice. But it's going to be a little difficult going back to school after the baby is born. Personally, I don't understand why you're in such a rush to have a baby. You're only nineteen years old. You haven't experienced enough of the world yet."

I shrugged. "Because I'm ready to settle down. I'm tired of going out to the clubs. I want to be a mother, and I would love to be Gerald's wife. I love the way he smiles, the way he walks, and the way he laughs. I love him."

Stephanie shook her head. "What are you going to do now?"

"I'm going to have this baby. Maybe after the baby is born his attitude will change. But I'm going to have this baby."

───── 〰〰〰〰〰 ─────

Reese was born eight months later at three o'clock in the afternoon. She weighed in at seven pounds, five ounces, and she came out screaming.

When the labor pains started, I'd given Stephanie a list of people to call. She called Gerald at his job and told him to meet us at the hospital. Surprisingly, he showed up. Ms. Chandler, Gerald's mother, was also on the list. It wasn't until I was six months pregnant and threatened to tell his mother myself that Gerald accepted that I was not having an abortion. After he finally told her, she called and invited me to her house for dinner. She greeted me at the door with open arms and a smile that stretched from ear to ear, and she made one of the most delicious meals I'd ever had.

"Welcome to the family," she said, and sat me down to fatten me up. She had to make sure she fed her grandchild. No grandchild of hers was going to be malnourished, and according to Ms. Chandler, I was just too skinny. I certainly didn't agree with her about my weight, but I loved her from the start.

Everyone Stephanie called came to the hospital, and we had quite an anxious crowd: Stephanie, my parents, my sisters, and Gerald's mother all waited until Reese was born, then they were escorted into the recovery room to see her for the first time. Gerald sat quietly in the delivery room with me. After Reese was born and the nurse cleaned her up, she handed her, wrapped in a blanket, to Gerald. He looked at her, and for the first time that day I saw him smile. She had his nose and the shape of his head. She looked just like him.

When Gerald's mother strolled into the recovery room, it was comical watching her and Gerald together. In his mother's presence, Gerald instantly reverted to being the child. He did exactly what she said, and the intimidation was evident by the stern look on his face whenever his mother was present.

"I told Gerald I didn't want my grandbaby to be no bastard for the rest of its life just because he's not finished chasing skirts," Ms. Chandler said as she sat on the chair in my room. Gerald rolled his eyes and walked to the window and looked away. "No offense to you, Victoria." She patted my hand and continued. "But there is no reason for someone else to raise his child. He needs to settle down and marry you. You're a fine young lady. As fine as they come. I don't know what his problem is." She shook her head.

I only smiled at her, but I never understood why Gerald let her banter on without interrupting. He always let her have her say and never acknowledged or commented on it.

"Oh my Lord, look at your twin," his mother said to Gerald, looking at the baby. "She looks just like you when you were a baby. You can't go denying this baby is yours. You're not going to be like your father." Gerald never talked about his father or why he left, but Ms. Chandler hinted that Gerald's father left after she became pregnant.

Still Gerald said nothing. He looked at everyone in the room, then turned and glanced out the window again.

"Isn't she precious?" she asked, and took Reese from me and cradled her against her bosom.

Reese was a month old when I got the call that my father had collapsed at work and died en route to the hospital of an apparent heart attack. My father and I were very close, and his death was devastating. I ended up dropping the two classes I had enrolled in that semester and started working full-time at the auto-parts distribution center.

I worked harder after Reese was born because I didn't want to bother Gerald about money. The last thing I wanted him to think was that I'd had Reese only to extort money from him. Even though Gerald worked full-time and my salary was only a dimple compared with his, I felt I had something to prove. For some reason it was important to me that he see I was a good person and a good mother. I knew I would be a great wife to him if he'd just give me the chance.

He visited Reese a few times a week, and she immediately bonded with her father. Whenever Gerald was around, her tiny face lit up and she squealed in delight and would not let him sit her down. She'd be in his arms the entire time until he rocked her to sleep. Every time I saw Reese and Gerald together, my heart melted and I wanted so desperately for us to be a complete family. I knew in my heart that we would be good for one another.

Gerald and I never stopped having sex even though there was no real relationship. My hope was that he would finally understand how I felt about him and the dream I had for us and our daughter. I even thought that maybe we would consider having another child one day. I didn't have the desire to pursue another relationship, and every time I saw Gerald and Reese together, I couldn't imagine bringing another man into her life.

But there were times when my patience wore thin and frustration set in as I struggled to handle the enormous cost of single motherhood. Going back to school was no longer an option because I made too much money at the auto-parts distribution center to qualify for child care assistance. All of the money I made went toward paying my bills and Reese's day care while I worked.

I remembered the day Gerald gave me twenty dollars. All I could do was look at the crisp new bill lying on the table. There was a time when twenty dollars meant dinner out and a movie, but since Reese was born, twenty dollars didn't amount to much.

"What's this for?" I asked, picking up the bill and looking at it.

"Whatever you need it for" was his simple response, as if he'd just given me an amount equivalent to the national debt.

I frowned. "Twenty dollars?" The look on his face proved that he was completely ignorant about the surging expenses I faced taking care of our daughter. It was either that or he just didn't give a damn. I would rather think the former was true.

"Reese's day care is one hundred and fifty dollars a week. Her diapers are twenty-five dollars a bundle, and she goes through at least a bundle a week. Baby food runs fifteen dollars more. I pay two hundred and fifty dollars a month for a two-room efficiency apartment; my car payment is one hundred and fifty dollars a month, and I am consistently late paying it. And I have deferred payments on my student loans for as long as I could. Why are you giving me twenty dollars?"

His face went blank and he said nothing while I stared at him. "I don't know what to tell you," he finally said, and sat Reese down in her playpen. As usual she didn't like it and began to whimper. "You were the one who insisted on having this baby."

I quickly turned toward Reese as she kicked her legs and held her arms out for him to pick her up again. Her screams became louder as soft tears rolled from the corners of her eyes down the sides of her face. My only hope was that she was too young to grasp the full meaning of the words her father so carelessly uttered.

Over the years when I thought back on that incident, I felt it was my responsibility to make sure Reese always knew that she was loved and wanted, and I never repeated those words to him or Reese. But after he said it, I simply snapped.

"And your ass was a willing participant in the events that led to 'this baby,'" I yelled. "You never tried to make sure it didn't happen. We have a daughter now, Gerald, and things cost money. If you don't want to start helping out, then I'm going to be forced to take this a step further."

His eyes cut sharply at me. "And by that you mean what?"

"What do you think I mean? You live in a secluded condo with a fireplace and a view of the Ohio River. You go out every weekend and have maid service once a week. I sleep on furniture my sister gave me because I can't afford anything new. Sometimes I don't eat because after I buy everything Reese needs I don't have enough money to buy groceries for myself. I've never complained to you about anything. And now you give me twenty dollars that I'm supposed to be grateful for because everything's my fault. What type of shit is that?"

"Well, you know my situation. I have bills too."

"What situation are you referring to? You're driving a new car, and you just bought a new leather sofa because you found a scratch on the old one. You sold the old one when you could have given it to me."

"It was an expensive sofa."

"And we're not worth it?" I asked with my hands firmly on my hips.

"I work hard," he said, dismissing my question, "and I should not have to compromise my standard of living just because you wanted to have a baby."

I threw my hands up in the air. "I'm finished talking to you. I know what I have to do."

"What are you going to do? You going to make a case out of this?"

"I'm going to do what I have to do."

Gerald shook his head. "Now I see what you're about. Why don't you take it upon yourself and get a better job? I finished school, and I shouldn't have to pay because you screwed up your life."

My mouth fell open and my eyes began to water. "It took the both of us to conceive her, just in case you didn't know."

"If you want me to buy her diapers, all you have to do is ask."

"What about providing a roof over her head, getting her back and forth to day care, and making sure the utilities are paid?"

"I'm not taking over your bills. Just because you have my daughter doesn't mean I am obligated to support you."

"You're not supporting me, and Reese needs more than diapers."

He shook his head. "No. I'm not going to do that."

"Then you leave me no choice."

"I advise you not to do anything stupid," he said.

Was he threatening me? That sounded like a threat. "Get out." I walked away from him quickly to keep from lunging at his throat.

"What?"

"Get. Out." I repeated it slowly so that there was no way for him to miss the anger in my voice.

"I came here to spend time with my daughter," he said, not budging from his seat.

I was flabbergasted. Nothing he said made sense. How could he confuse the notion of supporting Reese with providing support for me? "Sitting in my apartment costs money and you don't seem to want to give us any, so you have to leave."

Our eyes locked and neither of us blinked. Absolute silence fell between us before he finally relented and made his way out the door. He stopped in the hallway, but before he had the chance to utter another word, I slammed the door.

———⊗⊗⊗⊗⊗⊗⊗———

Gerald didn't bother calling or coming over for several weeks after that. After I told his mother what had happened, she advised me to take him to court for child support. She called regularly, checking to see if Gerald had come to his senses and left money for me. She had a subtle way of asking about my finances, and it always caught me off guard. Although I was mad as hell at Gerald, I didn't gain any pleasure out of rattling on about our problems to his mother.

There were many times when I went to the mailbox and found checks for several hundred dollars from her. As much as I wanted to give them back, I really needed the money. When I called to thank her, I held the sobs deep in my throat.

"You don't have to tell me that you need money," she explained one day. " I know you need money. My son is not going to do to you what his father did to me. I'll see to that." And she made good on her word. I never knew how Ms. Chandler got through to Gerald, but a week later he began coming over regularly again and he brought money with him each time. After two months he announced that we should get married. It wasn't a heartfelt proposal that brought tears to my eyes. He didn't drop to one knee, and he didn't look up at me adoringly with love in his eyes. But I accepted anyway because I still had something to prove.

———⊗⊗⊗⊗⊗⊗⊗———

Now I sat comfortably on the sofa, slowly sipping the cognac. I closed my eyes and imagined a comforting hand over mine and a gentle kiss on my cheek.

I couldn't make Gerald love me, but I could always return to my dreams.

8

I have two passions that I can think of besides my daughter: dancing and reading. I can sit for hours completely absorbed by the written word. If the book happens to be a romance where the heroine is swept away by her adoring handsome lover, then that is an added bonus. Unfortunately, I couldn't help but notice that just as I'm becoming engrossed in a delicious love scene, Gerald frequently decides to begin a conversation. It leaves me having to choose between meaningless talks with him or enjoying a nice escape into the lives of the characters in my book.

Tonight Gerald was preoccupied with a video game while I was transported to exotic Belize. I jumped suddenly when the table began to vibrate, then realized it was only Gerald's pager.

"You're being paged," I said, keeping my eyes glued to the book. I could see Gerald stretch from the floor and grab the pager to shut it off as he headed downstairs to phone in to his job. There was always some crisis or another at his job throughout the night. Most of the time he was able to talk himself out of going into work, but on a few occasions when there were power outages during severe storms, he had to go in.

I quickly forgot about Gerald and the pager as I returned to Belinda Miles and her handsome Caribbean lover, Martín, making love on the white sandy beaches. I fancied the way he held her and looked adoringly into her eyes and told her that he loved her. It didn't matter that it was only as far-fetched as the romance writer's imagination. I still wanted to be Belinda.

I paused long enough to notice Gerald had walked back through the bedroom and into the adjoining bathroom. I heard the soft sounds of the water hitting the shower floor as I continued to read. When I looked up again, Gerald was standing by the light switch ready to turn it off.

"I'm not finished yet, I only have a few more pages," I said, and returned my attention to the book and the scene where Belinda was about to climax.

"I would like to get some sleep," Gerald said. "Go downstairs."

"I'm almost done," I mumbled. My eyes scanned the pages and my breathing halted as I read of every touch and felt the eroticism as their breathing grew heavier and heavier.

It took a few seconds for my mind to register that the room had gone dark. For a moment I thought that I had joined Belinda in her height of ecstasy, but I hadn't. Gerald had simply turned off the lights.

"What the hell are you doing?" I howled as I stared into the darkness. The thought of reaching an erotic zone, then suddenly having your lover withdraw was enough to cause a murderous scream.

"I have to go to work early tomorrow," Gerald announced as he climbed into the bed and pulled the blanket to his chest.

My mouth dropped open. I stared at his silhouette in the darkness. "I wasn't done yet," I shouted.

He said nothing while he turned on his side with his back toward me.

I wanted to get up and flip the light back on again but decided against it. It wouldn't matter now anyway. I was out of the mood. There was no way I would be able to return to Belinda's peak. I slammed the book shut and tossed it on the nightstand beside the bed.

I lay in bed most of the night with my mind wandering to thoughts of Martín's hand between Belinda's legs and teasing her nipples until they pointed at him. The churning in my stomach immediately left when Gerald coughed and brought me back from the abyss. I looked over at him as he slept and silently cursed him.

Sometime during the night, the random thoughts that ricocheted in my mind finally stopped and I fell asleep. But it didn't last. I couldn't have been asleep long because my body had not moved but I was acutely aware that Gerald was tugging at my underwear.

I sighed and pushed his hand away. I maneuvered my body so close to the edge of the bed that if I had sneezed I would surely have greeted the floor with a thump.

But Gerald wasn't fazed. It seemed the more I resisted, the more excited he became. "I'm not in the mood," I said sharply. "Go to sleep." Agitated, I pushed his hand away from me, but he continued to tug at the thin strings that hugged my hips. I touched his wrist and felt the determined grip he held on the flimsy fabric until the next sound I heard was the rip of the strings.

Gerald chuckled.

It was all a joke for him, playful fun that I found no pleasure in being a part of. Gerald tossed the torn underwear across the room and took the feel of my bare ass as an invitation to enter me. He didn't bother climbing on top of me, that would have been too easy. Instead he lifted me into the air until I straddled him on the bed. I assumed this was another victory in his manly game.

I could have continued to fight him, but at that point I was uncertain if I was fighting him or feeding his ego. It was obvious that resisting him was like adding gasoline to an open fire, so what was the logic of fighting a losing battle?

Just do it and get it over with, I said to myself as I stared down at him. A small ray of light escaped into the room from the streetlamp outside our bedroom, and I was able to catch a glimpse of his face. His eyes remained closed and a faint smile appeared in the corner of his mouth. My mind returned to the words of the book that lay by the side of my bed.

And he looked adoringly at her . . .

Yeah, right, I said silently and stared into my husband's face. Gerald was definitely not Martín. I should consider lending him the book so he could learn a few things about the thoughts and desires of a woman. I considered reaching for the book and reading it to him. Perhaps that would get him thinking about how I wanted to be touched.

I shook my head. There was no way Gerald would ever humble himself to learn from a romance novel, and the insult of me telling him that his lovemaking was not pleasing would only unleash the fires of hell.

I looked over at the book and vividly imagined Martín and Belinda rolling together, Belinda's legs wrapped around his body, taking him deeper into her while they made love on the white sandy beach. I looked away from the table and returned my attention to Gerald. He didn't seem to notice that my mind was not on the lovemaking taking place in our bed.

His eyes never opened and his hands never caressed me.

How could he make love to me without looking at me or touching me? I thought, and it made me shiver. "I don't want to do this," I said, and tried to separate from him.

But Gerald was not ready to stop. He tightened his grip around my arm and pulled me toward him. His effort to kiss me left a drip of saliva on my lip.

I sneered and tensed with disgust as I tried to wiggle from him. The more I pushed away the tighter his grip became. He released one of my arms only to slide his finger inside me during his feeble attempt at foreplay. He was trying not to excite me but rather to determine if I was moist. I wasn't, but that didn't deter him.

Gerald was going to have me whether I wanted it or not, and I was not strong enough to resist. I couldn't scream, and if I could, what sound would come from my mouth? "Rape?" Gerald was my husband. Who would believe that my husband was raping me? I needed to distance myself. I needed an emotional out.

Think about something else, I thought. I looked away and stared at the handsome lovers embraced on the cover of my book. I closed my eyes and entered into the world of Martín and Belinda again.

Martín kissed her softly on the lips, pulling gently at them as he squeezed her breasts into his chest.

He took her supple nipples into his mouth and licked them as a moan escaped Belinda's lips.

"Belinda, my love," he whispered . . .

Ouch. I flinched as Gerald pulled on my nipples between his lips until they hurt. He hands were now at my waist. He pushed himself deep inside with one quick thrust. I felt his hardness rubbing against my dry walls. No moans of pleasure escaped my lips.

I opened my eyes when he gently pushed me aside, but my hope that the event was over was short-lived as I watched him change positions. He separated my legs with his body and resumed pounding inside me.

Again his eyes remained shut, and I wondered who he was fantasizing about. I was certain it wasn't me. I too closed my eyes and returned to the beach, but this time I was Belinda.

I listened for the usual sound that Gerald made whenever he had reached his crowning point. When it began, I didn't dare give him any reason to put it off a second longer. His paced slowed and he slumped exhausted on top of me as his warm fluids heated the inside of my body. The sweat dripped from him and soaked my sleep shirt. I remained motionless until I was sure it was safe to move. His heart pounded inside his chest and vibrated against my breasts.

Within seconds he was fast asleep, and I didn't hesitate to nudge him off me. He drew his legs toward his chest and snuggled under the blanket with his back to me. His usual sleep position.

I lay on my back with my legs pressed together trying to ease a nagging ache. The pain had become a familiar feeling over the last year, and enjoyment of sex a thing of the past. The sheets took on the scents of the room and Gerald's bath soap. I used to love those smells together, but now they sent me scurrying into the shower to remove all traces of Gerald from my body.

When I reached the bathroom, I quietly closed the door behind me and stood in front of the mirror. I looked at myself, tilting my head first to the right and then the left. I stepped out of the wet sleep shirt and stood naked in front of the mirror. I stared indifferently at my body.

There was a time when I felt sexy and alive and loved the sight of my nakedness and how it enticed the men in my life and how they made me feel whenever we made love. "When was the last time you had an orgasm?" I asked the reflection in the mirror.

I shook my head, certain that something was wrong with me. I had not felt sexual pleasure in a long time. My doctor told me that I was many years away from menopause, but I didn't believe him.

I couldn't feel anymore. I didn't get excited. Gerald's touches did nothing for me. The tingling feeling that makes your toes curl no longer happened.

I took a deep breath, licked the tip of my finger, and gently touched my right nipple. I felt a stirring between my legs. Taking another deep breath, I slid my finger from my breast to the itch between my legs and gently stroked my clitoris until the guilt of the sensation made me stop. I didn't want to sit in the bathroom and pleasure myself when I had a husband sleeping in the bed beside me. The thought of that made me feel freakish.

Maybe I just needed to try harder, but it seemed the harder I tried, the more Gerald pushed me away. Every effort I made to feel passion for him blew up in my face and left me wondering why I even bothered. I made the water as hot as I could stand it and jumped into the shower hoping that I could just wash it all away and make everything better.

When I could no longer sniff Gerald's scent, I stepped from the steamed shower and draped my bathrobe tightly around me. I returned to our bedroom and stared at his shadow and listened to him snore. Instead of sliding into bed beside him, I walked out of the bedroom and tiptoed down the hall. I peeked inside Reese's room and watched her breath brush the bright red ribbon wrapped around the neck of her favorite teddy bear. I walked in and looked down at her.

She was so innocent. I wondered if she knew that things were not normal between her father and me. She'd never seen me with another man, and as far as she was concerned, Gerald and I were happily married. I never argued with Gerald in front of her, and I certainly never criticized him in her presence. Reese had no idea that she did not have a perfect family.

Before I left her room, I kissed her gently on the cheek. I only wished that she knew the sacrifices I was willing to make for her. I headed back to our room but decided against it. Instead, I grabbed a blanket from the linen closet and inched down the stairs, careful not to make too much noise.

If I had a Martín, I wouldn't be sleeping on the sofa tonight, I thought as I made my way slowly down the carpeted stairs. If I had a Martín, I would cuddle under his arms, naked with my legs wrapped around his body, hoping he would wake up and make love to me again.

"I gotta find me a Martín," I whispered as my foot touched the bottom step.

Before I retired to the sofa, I picked up the remote control and began flipping through the channels looking for anything that could soothe me. I finally stopped at the music channel, then settled on the sofa and spread the blanket over me.

Music was always my best friend. I loved all music, with R & B and jazz being my favorites. Depending on the mood, I could jam to Aerosmith too. Before I got married, Stephanie and I would carouse the nightclub scene and dance all night. Those days were long gone, but my love of music continued. I fluffed a pillow under my head and rearranged the blanket over me. I stared narrowly at the screen until sleep began to catch me. My eyes could no longer stay open, but I continued to listen to the zigzag of music ranging from rock and rap to pop and even a little of the New Country, as they were calling the songs by Faith Hill and Shania Twain.

I positioned myself in such a way that it was easy to imagine Martín's muscular arms wrapped around me. His strong hold kept me from falling to the floor. I pushed my back against the sofa that I envisioned was his chest. The brush of air that blew from the air conditioner became his breath at the nape of my neck. My eyelids became heavier as I blinked through the commercials. Somewhere between the new 7UP commercial and a Kid Rock video, I fell asleep.

9

MICHAEL

Victoria and Sharon were picked up from the dormitory at precisely five o'clock by a long white stretch limousine. The evening's itinerary included dinner before the concert at one of Cincinnati's finest restaurants, the Montgomery Inn Boathouse, with a member of the band Kaleidoscope, although it was uncertain who it would be. Sharon hoped for the lead singer and guitarist, Michael Prince.

They walked into the restaurant and were greeted by the radio disc jockey and the band member known only by the name Bobby. If Sharon was disappointed, it didn't show when she leaped into his arms.

However, it was Victoria who was introduced as the contest winner, and she amicably shared the spotlight with Sharon, who knew everything about the British band. Victoria willfully faded into the background and was grateful to be there. She listened to the conversation going on around the table but offered little input. She did, however, find Bobby very nice, and he did not measure up to the bad-boy rock-and-roller media interpretation of Kaleidoscope. He was polite and courteous and tried several times to include her in the conversation. Unfortunately, she was not up to par concerning the happenings of the rock industry, and the conversation always ended up drifting into unfamiliar territory before she crawled back into her shell.

Victoria cringed. This was not the beginning of a good evening. She couldn't believe she allowed Sharon to talk her into this escapade. She would be a fish out of water at the concert.

"I'm going to be the only black person at this concert, you know," Victoria had said as they prepared for the night's activities. Each of them had bought a new outfit, Sharon's a little skimpier than hers. Victoria wore a long cream-colored floral silk skirt and matching spaghetti-strap cotton knit top. Even though her outfit showed little flesh, the contours of her body were easily noticed.

"No you're not. There are plenty of black people who like Kaleidoscope," Sharon replied, trying to convince her. Victoria looked at her for a brief moment. They both laughed.

Victoria was the grand prizewinner of an essay contest Sharon had told her about. A local radio station on the college campus had sponsored the contest. Knowing Victoria was an excellent writer, Sharon asked her to submit an essay and Victoria won.

The only problem with the original plan was Victoria never

entered the contest in hopes of attending the concert. Her intentions were to give the prizes to Sharon, but she was disappointed to learn that she must attend the concert in order for her guest to reap any of the contest's benefits. It included dinner before the concert and backstage passes afterward to mingle with the band and the entourage—prizes that Sharon would never have forgiven her for passing up.

And Victoria couldn't disappoint her. Sharon would have been absolutely devastated if she missed out on the chance to meet Michael Prince. Sharon's walls were draped with posters of him dressed in tight spandex or jeans screaming into a microphone. Some showed Michael Prince steaming hot, his face showered with sweat. Sharon's favorite poster was of Michael Prince dripping wet from head to toe in the shower, with a small towel draped around his lower body.

How bad could the concert be? Victoria had thought. But she hadn't intended on having a really bad day and a really bad headache. There was no way she could cancel.

Dinner was over and they were on their way to the concert. The radio DJ wouldn't be joining them there, and Victoria was grateful for that. She found him obnoxious. Bobby left the restaurant and was escorted to a private limousine waiting for him. Victoria and Sharon returned to their limousine and began the journey to the coliseum.

They were dropped off at the front entrance and had to push past a youthful crowd. Once inside, they were ushered to their reserved seats. To Victoria's dismay but Sharon's delight, they were seated in the third row, a few feet from where the musicians would be prancing about onstage. Victoria looked around to see if there were any other blacks in the audience. She didn't see any.

"Would you just relax," Sharon said. "We are going to have a great time. Consider this a cultural experience."

Victoria laughed, put her arms around Sharon's shoulders, and gave her a quick hug.

They had been best friends and roommates since freshman year. They arrived the same day on the campus of Ohio University and checked into their dorm in Franklin Hall, a newly constructed coed dormitory that resembled a large apartment building. At first Victoria worried that they wouldn't have much in common. Sharon was raised in an upper-middle-class all-white suburb in Boston and went to private schools. Victoria was raised in a blue-collar, middle-class black neighborhood in the city of Cincinnati and attended public schools. But after their first conversation, the apprehension quickly diminished and they were not just roommates, they were friends.

The opening act was a band Victoria had never heard of, and they were awful. The music was too loud and the words were screamed unintelligibly into the microphone. By the time the band exited the stage she had a roaring headache. Sharon appeared to be having the time of her life.

This is not my idea of music, Victoria thought. *This is noise.* Maybe Kaleidoscope would be better. Maybe someone would stop beating that hammer against her head.

Sharon went to get them sodas and talk with other friends who had attended the concert. Victoria was in no mood to socialize. Twenty minutes went by as the stage crew prepared for the featured act. Victoria searched her purse for an aspirin, to no avail. She would have to suffer through the experience.

With an enormous smoke screen, Kaleidoscope was onstage. The lights went out, the stage lit up, and the crowd went wild. Fans rushed the stage as the guards pushed them back to their seats. Victoria's nightmare continued as she fought nausea from the smoke. She closed her eyes, sank in her seat, and prayed for the end of the night.

When she opened her eyes she saw Sharon reach toward the stage along with at least a hundred other women who rushed the stage. Two band members had walked toward them and were only inches away. She looked into the face of one of them. It was Bobby, but he looked much different now as he stood on the stage performing. She looked at the other man and recognized him. It was Michael Prince. He screamed into the microphone, but she couldn't understand what he was saying. She followed his lips until their eyes met.

He fixed his gaze on her as she stared into his face. The whites of his large brown eyes were streaked with red. Sweat poured from him as it did in the posters. His wet stringy brown hair swung loosely from side to side as his head bobbed up and down with the beat of the drums. Victoria noticed he had full, wide lips. His nose seemed to point right at her. He opened his mouth and she saw his tongue. He licked his lips with his tongue, and the women around her went wild. He pointed the microphone toward her as he sang.

He's pointing at me, Victoria thought. He must be wondering what the hell I'm doing here. She closed her eyes and concentrated on getting rid of her headache.

<hr/>

She was almost home free. *How long could this take?* she thought. They were going backstage so that Sharon could meet her idol, then they could leave. Another hour; could she endure it for another hour? For Sharon's sake she would.

As everyone pushed their way out of the coliseum, Victoria and Sharon followed one of the ushers toward the back. He directed them to the party rooms, then left. The area they were in was jam-packed with concertgoers. A bodyguard stood between them and the corridor to the party rooms. He was enormous. His muscles bulged out of his shirt, which was two sizes too small. Victoria was sure that was an intimidation tactic. Surely he knew the shirt was too small before he put it on.

When he took the passes from them, he stared at Victoria. Victoria knew he was thinking the same thing she was: that she didn't belong there. He returned their passes and signaled for them to walk through.

At the end of the corridor was another guard in front of a closed door. They could hear the music and the laughter from the other side. Once again they had to show their passes before he let them continue. When they walked into the room, smoke rushed into their faces. They could tell immediately it was not just cigarette smoke. The room was filled with groupies, members of the entourage of both bands, and famous rockers. Sharon grabbed her arm and pointed to every rocker she recognized.

"Do you see him? I don't see him," Sharon said as she scanned the room.

"See who?"

"Michael Prince. I don't see him."

"Maybe he's not here." As they walked deeper into the room, Victoria became more unnerved. Mascara-filled tears flooded her eyes and ran down her cheeks, leaving black smudges down her face. Her eyes began to burn as the smoke irritated her sinuses.

"Sharon, I can't see. I'm going to stand over there." She pointed to a far wall and dabbed her eyes with the back of her hands, but it didn't help.

"Okay." Sharon walked away before Victoria could say anything further. Squinting, Victoria stumbled toward the far wall. She saw an open window and thought it would give her some relief. She felt someone take her by the arm. She turned to see Bobby standing beside her.

"Did you enjoy the concert?" he screamed into her ear.

Victoria smelled the strong alcohol and tobacco on his breath and stepped back from him.

"Hello." She turned again to another male's voice behind her. She took a quick look at the man but did not immediately recognize him and returned her attention to Bobby, but a young woman was whisking him away. Victoria sighed, disappointed that she didn't get the chance to talk to him.

The other man was still standing beside her. He didn't say anything. He just looked at her. She took a deep breath, but the smoke quickly filled her lungs and she coughed.

"Excuse me." She walked away from him and toward the window. She peered out long enough to let the fresh air fill her lungs. She quickly scanned the room for Sharon, with no luck. The fresh night air rejuvenated her lungs but did nothing for her burning eyes. As she wiped away the tears with her fingertips, a tissue appeared before her face. She looked at it, then at the slightly tanned hand holding it. Her eyes followed along the hairy arm until she reached his face. Their eyes met, and she realized he was Michael Prince. She froze.

"The smoke gets to me sometimes too," he said. His voice was firm, and she immediately picked up on his strong British accent. He urged the tissue toward her.

Victoria finally took it and wiped at her eyes and nose. She managed to capture the tears, but the burning persisted. "Thank you." She was embarrassed that someone had noticed her, and Michael Prince, of all people.

"Maybe this will help." He sat down on a stool beside her and dipped his fingers in a glass of water he held in his hand. He placed a cool wet finger on each burning eye.

Victoria kept her eyes closed.

He then dipped his fingers again and took a piece of ice. Delicately, he placed a small ice cube on each eye, for just a few seconds.

She tried to breathe evenly, but the feeling was too stirring. When she opened her eyes, she found him looking intently at her.

"Thank you." She stared into his face, puzzled as to why he would care about her, of all people. There were plenty of women who would love to share his company. She wasn't one of them. She turned away.

Go away now, she thought. *Go away.* She turned again and saw him still staring at her. She smiled faintly and repositioned herself on her seat, ready to make a quick exit.

"Better?" he asked.

Victoria looked at him briefly. "Yes, thank you." She glanced nervously around the room, hoping her callousness would deter him and he would leave. He didn't. She tried to think of something other than his presence.

Michael asked her something, but she couldn't make it out. "Pardon me?" she asked.

"Did you enjoy the concert this evening?"

Victoria smirked. "You don't want to know."

"I am very interested. Did you enjoy the music?" He inched closer to her.

Before Victoria could answer, a young woman abruptly interrupted their small talk and kissed Michael hard on the lips.

Wow, Victoria thought as she watched the woman throw herself on him. The woman tried to get a date with him for later that night, but Michael dismissed her. She glared at Victoria, pivoted on her heel, and stomped off.

"My apologies," Michael said.

Victoria just shrugged it off. She thought for a minute about his question. She didn't want to hurt his feelings, but she wanted to be truthful about how she felt about the music.

"I'm sorry," she said, shaking her head. "But this just isn't my kind of music. Tonight I just heard noise, that's it."

Michael grinned, appearing to be somewhat amused by her answer. "Noise. You refer to our music as noise. Explain."

"Well, for starters, you can't sing."

"Oh?" His laughter interrupted her.

"Don't get me wrong," Victoria continued. "When you're onstage, you are a wonderful entertainer. You move really well. But you can't sing."

"My music is a different flavor," Michael explained. "Every beat, every sound, means something. Music is a feeling. You are supposed to feel something when you hear it."

Victoria answered, "I did. When I heard your music I felt a headache."

Michael's robust laughter resounded in the room. She was pleased he wasn't offended.

Michael was approached by a young man. Victoria didn't recognize him as one of the musicians, but by the way he laughed and chatted with Michael, she figured they were old friends. As he conversed with Michael, he occasionally directed his attention toward Victoria. She didn't like the way he looked at her. She felt she was being undressed.

"Hello." He stepped away from Michael and stepped in her direction. When he reached her, he pulled her to her feet and grabbed her by the waist in a swift motion. She was caught completely off guard.

"Are you partying with us tonight?" he asked as he tried to pull her lips to meet his.

Victoria immediately leaned back to avoid his lips.

"It ain't that kind of party," she said, leaning back so far that her back was almost parallel with the floor. If he removed his arm, she would certainly tumble to the floor.

Michael pulled the man up by the shoulder, edging him away from Victoria. They stood a few feet away as Michael whispered into the young man's ear. The man turned to Michael, apologized, then left. But it was enough for Victoria. She decided she had had enough of this for one night.

"It was nice meeting you, and good luck on your tour," she said, and turned away. She quickly scanned the room in one last attempt to locate Sharon. Before she could step away, Michael took her arm to prevent her from walking past.

"You can't leave now. We haven't finished our conversation."

Victoria looked at him. *Why is he pursuing this?* she wondered.

"I would really like to continue talking with you," he added.

"I can't," she said. "It's very smoky in here, and I really should go before my eyes start to bother me again."

"Then not here. Someplace else." He took her hand and led her to a door on the opposite side of the room.

Victoria assumed he was escorting her to a quieter room. She saw him motion to one of the bodyguards, who immediately joined them. They were rushed outside the coliseum into a waiting limousine before she realized they had exited through some sort of escape door.

"What the hell is going on?" she yelled as the limousine sped off down the road. "Where are we going?"

Michael answered her nonchalantly. "To my hotel room."

Victoria was stunned. Immediately she sprang from her seat and banged on the glass partition that separated them from the driver.

The bodyguard in the front seat turned and looked at her.

"Stop the car!" she yelled.

The driver looked at the bodyguard, who then looked at Michael. Michael reached up to touch her, and she panicked. She swung at him and landed a solid punch on his face.

"Shit!" he yelled in pain. "What in bloody hell did you do that for?" He covered his nose as blood ran between his fingers and began to blanket his hand.

"I'm not going to your hotel room!" she yelled. "Tell him to stop the car or I'll scream."

"I asked if you wanted to go someplace to talk, and you said yes."

"I did not say yes, and I never said I would go to your hotel room. Listen, you got the wrong person. Take me back now."

They were silent as Michael looked at her. Her chest rose and fell quickly beneath her shirt.

"I just wanted to talk to you without interruptions." He took a towel and some ice from one of the compartments and applied it to his nose. "I haven't had a conversation like this in a long time, and I thought it was refreshing. I meant no disrespect."

She watched him as he tried to stop the bleeding. She couldn't believe she had gotten herself into this, and she had no idea how to get out of it. She was in his car. He could do anything he wanted to her. This could be the end of her life. She would never be a lawyer or see her family again. She felt tears of panic welling in her eyes as she began to shiver.

"Turn the car around," Michael yelled to the driver. "Go back."

Victoria looked at him. Was he for real? Immediately the driver made a U-turn and headed back. She stopped shivering as they drove toward the coliseum.

"My apologies once again. My intentions were not to offend you."

They were silent again as the awkwardness divided them. Victoria saw the disappointment on his face and, oddly, felt sorry for him.

"Is anyone else going to be there?" she asked, remembering the man in the party room. She wondered if Michael had whispered to the man to meet them at the hotel.

Michael answered her, "No, just the two of us. Promise."

"I don't know," Victoria replied. "I don't feel right about this."

"You really shouldn't be worried. You do a good job of defending yourself." Michael examined his nose in the mirror.

"You frightened me," Victoria said, not offering an apology. Her eyes didn't leave him as her fingers began to twist the fabric of her skirt.

"I'm not in the rape business," Michael answered her, looking at her nervous hands. "I take it for granted that every woman I meet wants an invitation to be sitting where you are at this moment."

"You never offered me an invitation." Her face was hard and unemotional as she stared at him.

"Where are my manners?" Michael moved closer to her and took her hand. He placed the blood-spotted towel on the seat beside him.

"Would you care to join me for casual conversation, expensive champagne, and maybe some hot and heavy sex?"

Her expression eased as she looked at the softened smile that crept across his face. She noticed the gentle way he touched her hand.

"No." Victoria laughed and shook her head. The nervous twisting of her fingers stopped. She couldn't help but notice the swelling on his nose. She took the ice-filled towel and applied it.

"Ouch." He flinched.

"Sorry," she said but continued to hold the towel to his nose. "This is way off base for me, but okay, I'll go. But one wrong move and your nose won't be the only thing that'll be black and blue tonight." Michael laughed at her threat and promised to be on his best behavior.

She turned and eyed a white telephone. "May I?" she asked, pointing to the phone.

"Be my guest."

Victoria picked up the phone and dialed Sharon's cell phone number. After only two rings, she picked up.

"Hello?" Sharon yelled into the phone.

"Sharon, it's me."

"Where the hell are you? I've been looking all over this place for you!" Sharon yelled.

Victoria held the phone away from her ear until Sharon stopped screaming. "I'm fine. I left. I have a way home."

"You left?" Sharon yelled.

"Yes, but it's okay," Victoria said, wondering if she should tell Sharon that she was sitting in a limousine with Michael Prince. She decided against it. Sharon would never believe her anyway.

"You met a man, didn't you? Oh, you little tramp!"

"I have to go. I'll see you when I get home," Victoria said, trying to urge Sharon off the phone before she asked too many questions.

"I won't wait up for you." Sharon laughed.

"Bye, Sharon," Victoria said and hung up the phone.

"Everything's okay?" Michael asked after waiting quietly for the call to end.

"Yes. I just didn't want her to worry about me."

They continued to talk as the driver turned around and headed back in the direction of the hotel.

"Can we drive around?" Victoria asked as she glanced out the window.

"Certainly." Michael instructed the driver to continue driving. He circled downtown Cincinnati several times. Victoria served as tour guide as they drove past Cincinnati's crowning glories.

"Can we walk?" she asked. "Are you allowed?"

Michael smiled and told the driver to park. The bodyguard let them out and remained a few feet behind them as they walked along the deserted streets. Downtown Cincinnati was quiet at two o'clock in the morning save for a few cars that passed them.

"What is this place?" Michael asked.

"Proctor and Gamble Towers. I remember when I was a little girl before the Towers were built, but I can't remember what was here before. It seems the Towers were always here. Beautiful building, isn't it?" she asked as she stopped in front of the white stone building. "Downtown was so much different then. On that corner there used to be a White Castle restaurant," she said, pointing down the street a bit. "My family and I used to go in there late at night and order one dollar's worth of White Castles, and we'd get a whole bag of 'em." She laughed at the memory.

"You grew up here?" Michael asked.

"Yes, born and raised. What about you?"

"Oh, I grew up in a small town north of London."

Victoria nodded. "I've never been outside the States, but Cincinnati really is a beautiful city, especially at night along the Riverfront."

It was a mild night, mid-seventies with a slight breeze blowing. She felt safe for some reason. She didn't know if it was Michael or the fact that the bodyguard walked just a few feet behind them. Victoria closed her eyes and threw her head back, letting the breeze kiss her cheek.

Michael just watched her.

"Ah," she said loudly as she breathed in the night air.

She took him up Broadway Street, then they turned down Fourth Street. They walked past the Maisonette Restaurant, which, she explained, was Cincinnati's only five-star restaurant. She had only eaten there twice in her life. She couldn't afford it, she explained. They walked up Race Street to the Aronoff Center, another one of Cincinnati's spectacular edifices. It was a beautiful brown brick building. Victoria explained there were many Broadway plays shown there. She'd seen *Phantom of the Opera* at the Aronoff.

After walking around the art center looking at the many posters and signs that hung around the building, they walked toward the heart of Cincinnati, the Tyler Davidson Fountain Square. Victoria shared that she loved Fountain Square. She would sit on the granite walls and look at the surrounding buildings. Sometimes she would look over at the Westin Hotel and find someone changing clothes in the windows. She never understood that; they had to know that people could see them.

She watched the water flow through the fountain's spouts and drop into the pool beneath. The lights in the fountain glowed softly, creating a peaceful allure. No matter what time of day she visited Fountain Square, Victoria never felt threatened by anything or anyone there.

She sat down along the fountain's edge and ran her finger through the water.

Michael sat down beside her and slowly dipped his fingers in.

"This is a perfect night to be out. Wouldn't it be devilish to take our shoes off and get in?" Victoria asked with an innocent-school-girl look on her face.

"So, what is the wildest and craziest thing you've ever done?" Michael asked, his fingers weaving along the ripples in the water.

"This night." Victoria laughed. Michael had turned out to be good company. He listened when she talked, and he wasn't making any unwanted advances, which surprised her.

"Excuse me, sir. We have company. I think we should be leaving." They turned around and saw a dark blue sedan slowly pulling up along the curb. The windows slowly lowered as the car came to a sudden halt. She watched as Michael's bodyguard quickly took off his jacket and threw it to Michael. Michael quickly put the jacket around her head as he ushered her to the waiting car. The bodyguard held the door open for them to jump in. He closed the door just as she heard a man yelling and banging on the window. She couldn't see what happened.

"Keep this on your head for now," she heard Michael say. "Don't worry, you're safe."

"What's happening?" she asked as the panic returned to her voice. "What's going on?"

"No worry, it's just paparazzi," Michael said. "We're going to the hotel now."

Victoria did not protest.

"What kind of cologne does he wear? This jacket smells great," Victoria joked. She heard a deep hearty laugh. She sensed Michael had not done that in a long time.

10

Within minutes they arrived at the hotel and Victoria could sense that whoever was following them was still in hot pursuit because everything became rushed. The voices around her spoke quickly; the movements were swift. The jacket remained on her head the entire time.

She heard new voices instructing the bodyguard where to go, and they headed in those directions. Michael's hand never left her arm, and he spoke to her the entire time. He told her when to walk, when to step up or down, what they were doing, and where they were.

They were at the Cincinnatian Hotel, and the limousine had taken them to the back where they would go through a private entrance. The hotel guards would take care of the paparazzi from that point.

Inside the hotel, Victoria felt her feet upon the soft cushioned carpet and the strong scent of potpourri mixed with the scent from the jacket. They were escorted to a waiting elevator, and as soon as they stepped in the doors closed and the elevator began to ascend.

"Were you frightened?" Michael asked, removing the jacket from her head.

"No, but look at my hair," she said, checking herself in the mirror lining the inside of the elevator. She tried to reconstruct the hairstyle she'd spent fifty dollars and three hours in the beauty salon to get. Once again Michael laughed.

He opened the door to the penthouse suite, and Victoria stood with her mouth agape when she stepped inside.

"Oh my God," she said. She felt as if she had stepped into an episode of *Lifestyles of the Rich and Famous.*

They walked upon black marble floors. The furniture was pure white upholstery accompanied by marble-and-glass accent tables.

In a far corner sat a white Baldwin grand piano. The window treatments matched the fabric of the furniture. Wonderful abstract paintings lined the walls, a colorful mural covered the high ceiling. Across the entire length of the far wall was an entertainment center that looked like something out of a futuristic movie.

"Wow," she said. She walked toward the glass wall on the opposite side of the room and stared into the night. "How much is a room like this a night?" she asked, turning to Michael.

Michael smiled as he walked toward the bar. "I don't know," he said, reaching for a chilled bottle of champagne. "I don't write the check." The sound of the cork being released from the bottle echoed in the room. Michael watched the flowing champagne run down his hands as he poured two glasses and handed one to Victoria.

"Could an average person like myself obtain this room?"

"I would imagine so."

They smiled at each other and raised their hands in an unspoken toast. Victoria closed her eyes as the sweet liquid bubbled in her mouth and coated her throat. When she opened her eyes Michael was frowning at her.

"What?" she asked, wondering if she had done something wrong.

He placed his glass on the bar and leaned into her. "What in bloody hell is your name?"

It was Victoria's turn to burst into laughter as she realized she had never introduced herself. "Victoria." She extended her hand to him. "Victoria Jordan. And you?" she added with a wicked grin.

Michael laughed again. "Michael Prince." He took her hand in his and lowered his lips to kiss the back of her hand. "So tell me something about Victoria."

She thought for a minute. "There really isn't much to tell except that I'm a college student and I'm studying to be a lawyer."

Michael nodded. "Law. Now, that's an honorable profession."

Victoria settled against her seat as she sipped again from her glass.

"What brought you to the music hall tonight, Ms. Jordan? I don't believe you came to see me."

"I entered an essay contest held by one of our radio stations here in the city to win the tickets for my roommate. She absolutely adores you."

"Really? Perhaps I'll have the pleasure of meeting her one day." Michael smirked. "What was your essay about?"

"The effect music has on people, their actions, their moods, and their lives. There is some music that I listen to that I have to stop what I'm doing and just listen. It grasps me, you know?"

Michael nodded. "And?" he asked.

"And I won, but I couldn't give her the prize. I had to come too."

"Lucky me."

They were silent.

Why was Michael Prince flirting with her? She found it very interesting and intriguing, but she knew not to make it into anything more than that.

She watched him open a drawer behind the bar, and take out a silver tray with a small amount of white powder in a vial on top and place it on top of the bar in front of her.

She stared as he poured the powder out, picked up a razor, and began separating the powder into rows.

She gasped. "Is that . . . ?" she asked, not wanting to say the word aloud.

Michael nodded. "Would you like?" he politely offered.

She reached toward it and smeared it on her fingers. She'd never seen or touched cocaine before. "No, thank you." She looked at the fine powder on her fingers and wondered about its addictive power. "Do you use it often?"

"When the need arises."

"It can control you," she said, looking from her fingers to him.

Michael took her hand into his, gently separating her powder-covered fingers and licked each one. His tongue glided over her long, polished nails while his eyes remained on her.

"It does not control me. I'm too strong for that," he said, sliding her fingers from his mouth and caressing them.

"Are you strong enough to stop?" she asked, shifting in her seat and taking her hand from his.

"If I want to."

"Could you not do it while I'm here?" Victoria asked as she glanced from the powder to him.

Michael nodded.

Victoria turned away from him, picked up her drink, and walked toward the large windows. She was captivated once again by the view of downtown. One of the sliding doors was partially opened, allowing a breeze into the room. She stood underneath the curtain and let the soft fabric tickle her cheek.

She heard music, then turned around to find Michael sitting at the piano. She walked over and sat beside him. His fingers moved effortlessly across the keys with perfect precision.

"You play beautifully."

"Music," Michael said as he tapped on the keys, "is a feeling." He was repeating what he had told her earlier. "Pretty much like what you wrote in your essay. Do you feel a headache coming on now?"

Victoria laughed and shook her head as the music resounded in the room.

"That's one of the songs from the concert tonight. To me it's the same. It means the same. It makes me feel the same. My music is my life, no matter how I play it or sing it."

"How many instruments do you play? I noticed you with a guitar at the concert."

"Just about all of them. Except a harp. I could never master that." Michael shrugged.

"You can just pick up an instrument, any instrument, and begin to play any song?" she asked sarcastically.

"Well, yes, actually, I can."

Victoria rolled her eyes. She was really beginning to think he was full of it now. No one can do that.

"Who's your favorite artist?" Michael asked as his fingers slid across the keyboard.

"I have several."

"Name one."

"Okay." Victoria closed her eyes and thought for a moment. There were so many that came to her mind. "Regina Belle," she said. "No offense."

Michael stopped tapping on the keys.

"Which song?" he asked.

"'Dream in Color.'" Victoria threw her shoulders back, thinking herself clever. Although it was a beautiful song, not many people knew of it. It received no radio play, and the only reason she knew it was because she listened to the CD constantly. Then the words began to roll off his lips, and her mouth dropped. "Oh my God, how do you know Regina Belle?"

"Victoria, I'm an artist. It's good business to know other artists. I study music and I listen. And besides, it's a beautiful song."

"This is unbelievable. You are so talented." Victoria followed his hands across the keys, then looked into his face. "Michael," she continued. "Why not market this voice, this side of you? Why do you dance across the stage in spandex and jeans and scream into a microphone?"

"Because this side of me does not sell records. To you, Michael Prince is just a name, but that name is attached to an image and that image makes a lot of money. Speck's Records owns the name, therefore they own the image and, in a sense, they own me. I can't change any of it." He played harder and faster until he was banging on the keys. "I can't cut my hair, change the way I dress or the people I party with. It's all about image."

"Then why do you do it?" she asked, looking at the redness that appeared on his fingertips.

"Because I like to eat." He turned to look at her, and they laughed as he continued to play.

"I doubt if you're that pressed for food," she said, laughing. "How can you be happy playing music if you can't play it the way you want?" she asked.

"Look at it this way. You tell me you wish to study law. Hypothetically, let's say you go into a practice for which there is no demand. If there is no demand, there are no clients, and if there are no clients, there is no money, therefore you cannot afford to stay in a room like this." Michael winked at her. "The same is true for the music industry. You do what there is a demand for in order to be successful." He stopped talking long enough to deliver exciting notes on the piano.

"But for the record," he continued, "I am happy with the music that I play. Remember, music is my life. I'm just not happy about being owned."

"How can you change that?"

"Create my own label."

"Then why don't you do that?"

Michael turned and looked at her. "It's not quite that simple, my sweet Vicki."

Victoria blushed.

"It takes a lot to be able to do that. A lot from right here I don't have right now." He pointed to her heart. "Wow. I never talked about that with anyone before. Thank you." He leaned forward and kissed her on the lips.

Victoria did not protest as she closed her eyes and accepted it. He kissed her again, harder this time, with his tongue tracing the fullness of her lips. Victoria pulled away and looked down at the piano.

"Don't be embarrassed," he said. "It's the music." The back of his hand stroked the side of her face. "You are a very beautiful woman, Victoria."

His words wrapped around her and pulled her closer to him, but she resisted and kept a comfortable distance.

Michael resumed playing a soft melody for her while they sat and talked on the bench. She was surprised by how easy she found it to talk to him and how comfortable he was to be with. He was not intimidated by her intelligence, which was something she found very rare among the men she met.

"I like you," Victoria said before she realized she'd let it slip out.

Michael's eyebrows raised. "You do?"

"Yes, I do. You are a very interesting person."

"Ah," Michael said and threw his head back. "Now that's a word I haven't heard in a long time." He continued playing while an uncomfortable silence fell between them. "But you like this side of me, right?"

"What do you mean?"

"The Michael Prince you met at the coliseum, you really didn't like very much, did you?"

Victoria shook her head. "No, I didn't."

"But I'm a package deal. You can't dissect me and keep only the parts you like."

Victoria drew back. He was taking this conversation a lot farther than she had intended for it to go. "I was only making a statement. I didn't mean anything by it."

"Sure you did. If you didn't, you would never have said it. Just be careful not to fall in love with me."

Victoria chuckled. "I'm not going to fall in love with you."

"I think you already have." Michael stopped playing and turned to look at her.

She could have thought of a few things she would like to have called him at that moment, but she didn't. She only returned his stare.

"Remember what you asked me at the fountain?" His voice broke the stifling silence again.

Victoria gazed at him, puzzled by his question. "What is that?" She felt his hand on her back as he began to tease the skin beneath her shirt.

They stood and walked across the floor to the large sliding doors and pulled them open. They stepped out onto the cement balcony as he took her hand and led her to a small Jacuzzi.

"Would you still like to do something devilish?" They sat against the edge of the Jacuzzi.

"I don't know what you mean."

"Would you like to give it a try?" Michael asked, dipping his hand into the heated water.

"I don't have a suit."

He smiled. "You don't need one."

"I don't think so."

"You have a beautiful body. You shouldn't be embarrassed by it." He removed his hand from the steaming tub and let the water drip from his fingers and run down her arm.

Victoria shook her head.

"Are you certain about that?" Again he dipped his hand into the water, but this time he smoothed her black eyebrows with his wet fingers. Several drops trickled down her face.

"Close your eyes," he said as he continued to touch her with his wet fingers.

Her eyes closed, and she listened to the sound of his voice and the beat of her heart.

"Imagine yourself submerged in the water as it begins to heat the blood that runs through you."

Victoria took a deep breath, then opened her eyes and watched the bubbles burst softly against the marble walls.

"I can't."

"Why can't you?" he asked.

"Because I've just met you."

"Victoria, we've spent an entire evening together."

She rolled her eyes and folded her arms across her chest.

"What could be wrong about it?" Michael stood and walked toward the glass doors. "I'll go inside while you undress, and I will not come out until you are in the water."

Victoria still shook her head.

"Consider this an educational experience."

She laughed. "There is nothing educational about being naked in a Jacuzzi unless you are studying human anatomy."

Michael laughed as he stood by the door, a warm smile stretched across his face and his arms folded in front of him. His dark brown hair, now clean and dry from an earlier shower after the concert, lay loosely on his shoulders.

"Okay," Victoria said beneath her breath.

Michael winked at her as he turned and walked back into the suite.

Victoria looked around the balcony for a few seconds searching for any indication that she shouldn't follow through with the idea. She stepped out of her leather sandals. There was nothing alarming about being alone on the balcony and no signs to stop her from this adventure. She slipped her shirt over her head and dropped it onto the cement floor. Her fingers moved quickly across the single button on her skirt, allowing it to fall with the shirt. The black thong bikini was the last to come off.

She stepped toward the Jacuzzi and sat down on the edge. She dipped her right foot into the white bubbles but pulled back as the heat ran up her leg. After taking a deep breath she tried again until her entire right foot was in the water. She did the same with the left foot, then stood in the water shivering until her body adjusted to the sudden change in temperature. Slowly, she descended into the water until her shoulders were beneath the bubbles.

"Feels great, doesn't it?" Michael's voice startled her. She looked up and saw him walking toward her, naked.

Oh my God, oh my God, she repeated silently. Her eyes were drawn to his hairy chest, then to his private area, his legs, and back to his private area. She looked away as she sunk deeper in the water.

Michael walked past her to the bar on the opposite side of the balcony.

"So, what do you think?" He handed her a tall glass of champagne as he stepped up to the Jacuzzi.

"It's fine. Thank you." She took the glass, quickly gulped the champagne down, and reached for a refill.

Michael grinned as he poured her another glass. "Are you sure?"

"Yes," she said bringing the glass to her lips and quickly downing it. She reached for another refill.

"Well, okay, but you might want to slow it down just a tad," he said, pouring the bubbling liquid into her glass.

Victoria took a deep breath and watched as he stepped into the water beside her. His eyes closed as the heated water touched his skin. He held his breath until he was submerged to his shoulders. Then he took a quick breath and plunged his head under for a few seconds before coming up for air.

"That felt great," he said, picking up the glass he had sat on the edge of the Jacuzzi and wiping the wet hair from his face. "How are your eyes?" he asked, taking a drink from his glass.

The question puzzled her until she remembered how they had burned earlier. "Oh, they're fine. How's your nose?"

"I think I'll live." He laughed and touched his nose.

Victoria was captured by his smile, and that worried her. Her stomach turned as the water began to heat her inner thighs.

"When are you leaving town?" she asked, trying to think about something other than the sensation between her legs.

"You kicking me out of Cincinnati so soon?" he asked.

"No, it's not that . . . it's just that . . ." She couldn't finish the sentence because she didn't know why she had asked the question. She shrugged.

Michael stood and took her hand and pulled her up toward him until he stood behind her. Gently, he began to massage her shoulders.

When his fingers touched her skin, a shiver traveled up her spine, causing her to tense even more.

"Relax." He spoke softly into her ear as he massaged the tight muscles in her shoulders and arms.

She closed her eyes and tossed her head from side to side. He ran the tip of his index finger down her arm, up her abdomen and her chest. He circled her breasts, then gently touched her nipples. A soft moan escaped her lips. When she opened her eyes, she quickly moved away from him.

"I'm sorry," he apologized. "I didn't mean to make you uncomfortable."

"No, it's my fault. I have to leave." Confused, she looked around for something to cover herself with, but Michael stopped her before she stepped out of the Jacuzzi.

"Is something wrong?" he asked.

Victoria turned and looked at him. He suddenly looked different to her. He was suddenly intriguing and sexy.

"I have to get out of here."

"Why?" he asked.

She tried to think of an explanation other than the truth: that he was scaring the hell out of her.

"I don't understand how I'm feeling right now."

"And how are you feeling?" Michael asked as he reached out and touched the side of her face.

She took a deep breath and stepped away from his touch again. "Confused. I've never done this before," she said softly.

"You've never made love before?"

Victoria shook her head. "No. I've never been with . . ." Her voice trailed off as she searched for the right words.

"You've never been with a man of my color before?" he asked, attempting to read her mind.

"No, I haven't," she answered, looking directly at him. "And I wasn't exactly looking to be either. I've never felt like this before about someone like you." She stopped talking and took a deep breath.

"Someone like me." Michael smiled. "So, what you are saying is that you wouldn't make love with me tonight because of my color, regardless of the way you feel about me?" Michael stepped closer to her and took her hand. He put it to his chest and guided it along his body. He slid her fingers down his bare chest and put her hand on the hardness between his thighs. "If you don't want to make love with me, Victoria, don't let it be because I'm white." Michael pulled back and looked at her. He picked up the goblet from the edge of the Jacuzzi, and their eyes met as he turned the glass up to his mouth.

"I'm not even supposed to be here," she said in the lowest voice she could manage.

Michael took her in his arms and kissed her hard on the lips, pulling her into him until her breasts pressed hard against his chest.

"If you weren't supposed to be here, then you wouldn't be." With a deep breath, he stepped from her again and whispered, "Victoria, I want to make love to you. Do you want to make love with me?"

She dropped her head and looked into the water.

Michael lifted her head to him and looked into her eyes. "Tell me, Vicki. Tell me you want to make love with me."

Still she didn't say anything. Her voice was lost in her throat.

He kissed her softly on the lips, then leaned back as he looked up at the sky. She heard him exhale deeply as he continued to look up.

"Yes."

Michael lowered his eyes to hers.

"Yes, I want to make love with you."

He quickly took her into his arms and kissed her. She closed her eyes tight as his hands explored her body and the moans escaped her lips.

"Open your eyes. Look at me." His voice was so low she barely heard him.

She looked at him again. Her stomach muscles tightened, waiting to feel him deeply inside her. She felt him enter her and gently move inside her as her legs wrapped around his body. She closed her eyes again and threw her head back.

"Look at me," he said again.

She watched as he moved with her and kissed her neck. Her hands explored his chest as she planted small kisses on his shoulder.

He lifted her from the water and laid her upon the towel next to the Jacuzzi. He whispered her name and kissed her repeatedly, moving slowly inside her while her body quivered.

When she opened her eyes, he smiled at her, then softly kissed her eye. His movements never stopped. She smiled back at him and he joined her in the ecstasy.

They walked to a comfortable cushioned chaise on the balcony and lay in each other's arms, not saying much. Victoria's legs wrapped around his as they looked up at the stars. Occasionally she laughed at a joke he made. Before they fell asleep, Victoria thought again about what Michael had said to her earlier. Perhaps she had already fallen in love with him.

11

VICTORIA

Stephanie and I met for Sunday brunch at a local hotel. There were only a few things that I looked forward to these days, and this weekly ritual was one of them. It gave me a chance to get away from the house and enjoy a few minutes to myself without having to chase Reese or argue with Gerald. Stephanie and I always arrived early enough to have a seat at the window so that we could talk without too much worry of others tuning in.

I sat at the table and sipped from a cup of coffee, only half listening to her rant on about her boyfriend. My mind was on that dream I had the night before and the man in it. I remembered everything about the dream, to the finest detail. I felt as if his presence was real and the conversations actually happened. And when I closed my eyes, I inhaled traces of his scent in the air.

"Are you okay?" Stephanie asked. "You're not your usually chatty self."

I hadn't realized that my eyes were shut, and I held my breath in my lungs. When I opened my eyes Stephanie was looking strangely at me. I exhaled and stirred my coffee while she waited for an answer.

"Have you ever been with a white man?" I finally asked.

Stephanie was about to sip from her soda but drew the glass back when she heard the question. "What?"

"Have you ever been with a white man?"

"Why are you asking me this?" Stephanie leaned forward on the table.

"Because I want to know."

"Well, yeah." She quickly sipped the soda.

"You little tramp, you never told me." Now I was the one intrigued. I thought I knew everything about Stephanie. We'd been best friends since high school.

"Victoria, I don't have to tell you everything."

"I want details." I leaned forward over the table waiting to hear the juicy news.

"Well, there really isn't anything to tell. He was a guy I worked with. We had been kind of flirting with each other, and after the Christmas party one year we both probably had a little too much to drink and we went back to my place, and the rest is history."

I screamed. "I cannot believe you kept this a secret from me!" I grilled her for more details. "Well, what happened after that?"

"What do you mean, what happened? We had sex and that was it. I mean, what more do you want?"

"That's it? Did you guys go out after that? Is there a story to be told here?"

"No, there isn't. I guess I did it to experiment. I wouldn't have a relationship with a white man."

I sat back in my seat and frowned at her. "Why not?"

"It's just not something I would want to do. Relationships are hard enough, why add the pressures of society to it? People staring at you, being discriminated against, who needs it?"

I didn't respond as I took another bite of the sandwich in front of me and thought about the dream again.

"Is there a reason for the questions? Something you want to tell me?"

I shook my head. "No, not really." I swallowed the bite I had in my mouth before I continued talking. "I just had the weirdest dream last night."

"About?" Stephanie asked, urging me along.

I shrugged. "About me and a white rock star."

"A white rock star?" Stephanie raised an eyebrow.

"I know it sounds ridiculous, but it was a good dream anyway," I said, laughing.

"What were you watching before you fell asleep?"

"Videos."

"Ah." Stephanie nodded. "Well, that explains it. And how are things with you and that wonderful husband of yours?" she asked, folding her arms across her chest.

"As delightful as ever," I responded, returning the sarcasm.

"Which means he's still an ass," Stephanie said before taking a long draw from her soda. "Sorry. I didn't mean to say that about your husband."

I was quiet. I didn't see a point in defending him when she was right.

"Do you want to go out tomorrow night?" Stephanie asked. "Maybe you'll meet someone and have an affair."

I snickered. Stephanie would jump at the opportunity to fix me up with someone. She had been trying for months to convince me that the only thing I needed was a man who made me feel like a woman and all of my problems would magically disappear.

"When was the last time you had an orgasm?" she asked.

I peered around to see if anyone had heard her. "What does that have to do with anything?"

"Everything if you're married to a man that makes you have one."

"It's not about sex anymore. I have Reese to think about."

"You sound like your mother," Stephanie said, stirring in her seat.

"Well, good. My mother and father had a great marriage."

Stephanie didn't say anything more about my sex life, and the conversation quickly changed. But after we left the hotel, I drove home in silence thinking about everything she had said. It was true, I sounded exactly like my mother, but was that such a bad thing? I couldn't imagine my mother doing anything as selfish as leaving my father because he didn't satisfy her sexually. My mother never even talked about sex. I'd seen my parents kiss many times when I was growing up, and it was always a simple peck on the cheek or a quick kiss on the lips. I'd never seen them locked in a passionate embrace but that didn't mean anything. My father adored my mother. That much I knew without a doubt.

I thought about Gerald and the sex we'd had the night before and I cringed. I couldn't imagine my father ever making my mother feel the way I felt whenever Gerald touched me.

Then I thought of Michael and the way he caressed me, the way he looked at me, the way he included me . . .

I sighed heavily and shifted in my seat.

Even though it was a dream, it was exhilarating to be awakened again. I wondered if Michael would come back in my sleep tonight and make love to me. I pressed a little harder on the gas pedal, eager to get home and for the day to wind down.

MICHAEL

Exhausted, Victoria lay in his bed. He must have carried her inside when she fell asleep in his arms. Her body was relaxed from the evening's activities. She smiled as she rolled over, thinking of holding him in her arms. He was not there. She opened her eyes to confirm the wrinkled sheets beside her were empty. Hastily, she sat up and searched for any sign of him but the room looked undisturbed except for her clothes placed neatly in a chair.

Victoria bolted from the bed and covered herself with the white sheet as she stepped upon the warm carpet. She walked out onto the balcony. The Jacuzzi was turned off and covered as if it had never been used, and the champagne goblets they drank from were also gone. She walked to the phone and dialed the front desk.

"Mr. Prince has checked out," said the clerk on the other end of the line. "Would you like us to call you a cab?"

VICTORIA

Another night of sex with Gerald. I hated men. Gerald for not loving me, and now Michael. I thought about the last dream. What was the reason for that? Was it to tell me that I would never be loved? Why did *he* have to disappoint me too?

Dad, where are you when I need you? If my father were alive, I could have talked with him about the dream and he would have told me what it meant. I hated him too, for dying when I needed him the most.

Gerald left early in the morning. His movement around the bedroom woke me up, but instead of getting out of the bed, I pulled the cover over my head. I was going to be late for work, but I didn't care. When I finally got out of bed, Reese was awake and ready for her breakfast.

I slipped into my bathrobe and walked about the house in a stupor. Everything seemed to move in slow motion. The soreness between my legs reminded me of the sex Gerald and I had the night before, and the weight on my chest made me feel like I had lost my best friend. I poured Reese a bowl of cold cereal for breakfast instead of making the usual pancakes she loved to devour with syrup. I ignored her protest and sat at the kitchen table sipping a strong cup of black coffee. After she realized that I wasn't giving in, she ate the cereal.

With her fed and ready to go, it was my turn to get dressed. Reese lay comfortably across our bed and watched the morning cartoons while I headed to the bath. I left the door open so she wouldn't feel that I'd left her alone.

I started the shower, turning the handle farther left than usual, and watched the steam quickly rise to the ceiling. My robe slid from my shoulders and gathered at my ankles.

I stepped into the bathtub and let the water beat against my chest, hoping the burden would lift and wash down the drain along with the tears that flowed from my eyes.

12

MICHAEL

It had been a month since Victoria's night with Michael, and she still couldn't believe that she had awakened alone in the hotel room.

She awoke many mornings with puffy red eyes and was forced to hide them from the world behind sunglasses. Question after question ran through her head as she tried to understand what had happened. How could she have been so stupid as to think that someone like Michael Prince would be interested in her? How could she have thought that the evening meant something?

Unable to reconcile those questions, Victoria decided to put the experience behind her, but the stabbing pain in her heart did not go away. There were times she found herself in Sharon's room staring at the collage of Michael and Kaleidoscope.

"Why do you have so many pictures of him on your wall?" Victoria asked one morning after walking into Sharon's room to retrieve a book.

"Of who?"

"Him," she said, pointing to Michael. "You shouldn't idolize him. He's just a man."

"Yeah, but a hot, sexy man I wouldn't mind getting it on with."

Victoria rolled her eyes and stormed out of the room, slamming the door behind her.

"What is your problem?" Sharon asked, chasing after her. "Why did you just slam my door?"

Victoria was quiet as she tried to calm herself. She paused. Should she tell Sharon what happened that night? Deciding against it, she said, "It's nothing. Sorry," and walked out of the dorm. She sat in the student lounge and watched the other students as they returned from dates or were on their way out. She walked to the pay phone and called home.

"Hi, Dad." It never failed. Whenever she needed comforting, she could always rely on her father's voice.

"How's Daddy's baby girl?" His usual question.

Victoria hadn't realized how much she loved hearing her father say those words until she went away to college. She was Daddy's baby girl, and he had a hard time letting her go. But then again, she wasn't so sure she wanted him to.

"I'm fine," she lied.

"Are you sure?" he asked.

There was a brief silence.

"Dad, how do you know when you're in love?"

"Hmmm." He paused. "I'm going to tell you like this. Some people would say that it's how you feel when you're with that special person, but I believe that it's how you feel when you're not."

Victoria heard him take a deep breath. She wondered what he was thinking.

"But how do you know when it's right?" She fought yet another round of tears.

"There is no real answer to that question. When it's right, you'll know."

"But what if you're wrong?"

"Better to be wrong than to never know. Would you want to

go through life saying, 'What if I had done this?' or 'What if I had done that?'?"

She thought about that as she wiped a tiny tear that escaped from the corner of her eye. Exploring a relationship with Michael was not an option.

"How's Robert?" he asked.

Victoria suspected her father knew she was not referring to her steady boyfriend, Robert.

"He's fine, Dad."

"I like Robert, Vicki. He's good for you. He comes from a good family, and he's a young man who is going to be very successful in his field."

"I know, Dad. I have to go now. Tell Mom I said hi." Victoria quickly hung up the phone. The last thing she needed was to get into a conversation about Robert. She had had many first experiences with Michael that night, but she had also done something she never thought she was capable of. She had cheated on Robert.

Victoria shrugged off any further thoughts of Michael Prince. Whatever it was that happened between them that night just didn't matter anymore because she was never going to see him again. Michael made sure of that when he left her in that hotel room.

VICTORIA

"Victoria."

I looked up and into Frank's face. He was standing over my desk.

"Are you okay?"

"I'm fine, why?"

"I've been standing here for five minutes, and you haven't heard a word I said."

I picked up the stack of papers on my desk and pretended to straighten them out. "I apologize. I just have a lot on my mind. Do you need anything?"

"That's okay. I'll take care of it."

"Are you sure?"

"Yes." Frank hesitated before he walked away. "Anything I can help you with?"

I smiled. "No. I'm fine. I was just thinking about my father." I knew that was a safe answer.

"Oh, I see," Frank said, nodding. "Consider taking advantage of the employee-assistance program. They have counselors you could talk to."

I shook my head. "I'm fine, really."

Frank nodded and walked away.

I sat at my desk and thought about what had just happened. My father had come back to me. It was a daydream, but he was there. I heard his voice.

My smile widened as I swirled my chair and focused on the computer screen in front of me.

I knew Dad wouldn't let me down.

13

MICHAEL

Friday nights were terrible study times in the dorm. All night you would hear the loud knocks on apartment doors with students coming or going, creating havoc in the halls. Unfortunately for Victoria, the library hours were short on Fridays, so she had no choice but to return to her room to study. Sharon had gone out, so at least she had the place to herself.

The apartment dorm she shared with Sharon was equipped with a small living room, kitchen, dining area, one bath, and two bedrooms. It suited both of them fine and provided more privacy than the less expensive dormitories.

Victoria sat in the living room in a dingy pair of sweatpants, a white T-shirt, and socks.

She was heavily into her sociology textbook when the phone rang. She reached over, not losing her place, and answered it.

It was Janet at the front desk. "Victoria, you have a visitor. Do you want me to send him on up?" A student was usually working the desk and sometimes announced when visitors arrived. She had told Robert earlier that she might excuse herself for an hour if she felt she was far enough along. She had been sitting in the same place for three hours. Perhaps a break wouldn't be a bad thing.

"Yeah, send him up." She replaced the receiver, then put a book-mark between the pages. She stood and stretched.

She heard the light knock on the door, and still stretching, she walked to the door to open it. Even in his disguise Victoria recognized him. Immediately she pushed the door closed, but he had anticipated her reaction because his foot was planted firmly in the doorway.

He yelled out in pain, but Victoria still was no match for him as he pushed on the door, sending her stumbling backward into the apartment.

"Vicki, please, give me a minute. I just want to talk to you." Michael walked into the apartment and immediately closed the door behind him. He took off the sunglasses and the hat and tossed them onto the sofa. The fake mustache and beard remained.

"Get the hell out or I'll call security."

"Please, I just want to talk to you," he said, walking toward her.

"Talk to me?" she shouted at him. "You said that to me once before, then you ended up treating me like a whore!"

He stopped and stood silently for a moment before he spoke.

"I want to talk about what happened that night and why I did what I did."

"I don't want to hear anything you have to say. Get the hell out of my room." Victoria whisked past him only to have him grab at her arm, preventing her from reaching the door. At the touch of his hand she turned and slapped him so hard that it seemed to echo in the small room.

Michael froze.

Victoria raised her hand to strike him again, but he caught it in midair. They stood and stared at each other as his face turned blood red from the slap.

He stared at her with a haunting gaze that made her tremble. She wasn't sure if it was from the sting of her hand or something else. She studied him as he closed his eyes and fought tears. His grip on her hand tightened, and she couldn't free herself.

His next move completely threw her off guard. He pulled her to him and pressed her hard against his chest. She felt his heart pounding against her chest. She'd never felt anyone's heart beat so fast.

"I am so sorry for doing that to you," he said as he pulled back from her.

"Just go." Victoria pushed away from him. She didn't want his apologies.

"Please . . ."

"The nerve of you to come back here after what you did. Do you think you have the right to walk over people and treat them like trash because you're Michael Prince?"

"No, I don't."

"Look, I admit it was pretty stupid of me to let that happen between us, and I've learned my lesson but—"

"Will you shut up and listen to me for a minute?" Michael yelled. Victoria stopped talking. He took a deep breath before he continued. "I'm sorry for what I did."

"Okay, fine," she said. "Now leave."

"I'm not finished," he said, grabbing her arm as she walked past him. "Give me a chance to make it up to you."

"Why?"

"Because it's important to me how you feel. Vicki—"

"You can't call me Vicki. Only the men I love and the ones that don't hurt me are allowed to call me that!" she yelled. She walked across the room and leaned against the wall.

"I do care about you," he said.

"I refuse to believe that."

"Why?"

"Because if you did, you would never have left me like that."

"But it's because I care about you that I left."

She stared at him. The room was deathly silent; the only sound she heard was her heart pounding in her chest.

"Then why did you come back?" she asked softly.

Michael walked to her and touched her forehead with his own.

The energy between them was overpowering, and all she could do was close her eyes and fight the urge to kiss him.

"Because the thought of you not knowing the truth was destroying me." He touched her lips gently with his. "I don't want you to be afraid of me. I didn't come back to hurt you again. You have to believe that."

"The way you left really hurt me," she said and pushed away.

"Vicki." He stopped talking and started over. "Victoria, my life is not simple, and you are so different from anyone I have ever met."

"Different how? Your life consists of beautiful women throwing themselves at you. Why did you feel that I was the one you needed to hurt in order to protect?"

"You are as beautiful as they come, and even more. The things I find intriguing about you can never be captured by a camera."

Victoria couldn't say anything. No one had ever said anything like that to her before.

He reached out to her, and she stared at his hand before placing hers in his. He closed his hand around hers, pulled her to him, and held her tight in his arms.

"I missed you," he whispered, and planted small kisses on her ear and neck.

Victoria moaned.

She heard a soft knock at the door and pushed away from Michael just as the door flung open. She gasped when she saw Robert step through the opened door.

"Robert," she said quickly, perhaps too quickly, as she looked from him to Michael standing just inches away from her.

He didn't say anything at first as he glanced from her to Michael. "What's going on?"

"Nothing. This is Michael. He's my . . . stats tutor. I've been having problems and decided to get some help." That was the worst lie she could have ever come up with, but she was not good at lying. There weren't many things for her to lie about.

Robert gave her a questioning look before walking closer to her. "That's funny, because he looks as if he's about to kiss you."

"I was about to give him a hug. I really appreciate his help."

"Oh, I see," Robert said, not taking his eyes off Michael.

Victoria stepped between the two men to lessen the tension.

"Why didn't you come to me if you needed help?" It was true— if she was having problems with math, she could have gone to Robert. Math was his minor, and he often tutored underclassmen whenever he needed extra money. When they first met, he'd tutored her and helped her bring her calculus grade up from a C+ to an A−.

"I knew you were busy with exams coming up. I just didn't want to bother you again." *Was he really buying this?*

"Victoria, I don't like this," Robert said. "I don't know what's going on with you. I haven't seen you in weeks, and now you have another man in your room. Is there anything you want to tell me?"

Victoria shook her head.

"What about you, what's your story?" He turned to address Michael.

Michael shrugged. "I don't have a story."

"Robert, I'll call you tomorrow," Victoria said, hoping he wouldn't press the issue any further. She wasn't sure Michael would back up her lie.

"Tomorrow?"

Victoria nodded. "Yes."

"What about tonight?"

"I can't. I have to study. I'll call you tomorrow." She walked up to him and kissed him hard on the lips. When she pulled back from him, Robert looked at her and she could feel the tension loosening.

"Okay," he said, and walked to the door with her. "But I still don't like it." He kissed her again, and Victoria didn't dare pull away from him. She hoped her kiss reassured him that nothing was going on between her and Michael.

After he left, she locked the door behind him and rested her forehead against it. She heard Michael walking toward her and felt his presence at her back.

"Are you okay?"

Victoria shook her head. "No. "

He wrapped his arms around her and she rested her head against his chest.

She hated lying, but being in Michael's arms brought her more comfort than she'd ever felt from anyone. Including Robert.

He resumed where he had left off, kissing her neck as his hands explored the skin beneath her clothes. When she turned to face him, their lips touched and they kissed as powerfully as they had the first night they met.

Without separating his lips from hers, he lifted her into his arms and carried her to the sofa, where they made love repeatedly, sliding from the sofa onto the floor.

———— 〰〰〰〰〰 ————

Victoria came out of her bedroom and jumped when she saw Sharon standing in the kitchen. "Sharon." She tightened her robe around her. "How long have you been home?"

"Long enough." Sharon giggled. "My, my, my. Sounds like somebody is having a good time tonight. What have you guys been smoking?" She took a drink from the large glass of water she had poured for herself.

Before Victoria could answer her, Michael stepped from Victoria's room and stood beside her.

Sharon immediately recognized him, and the water she had in her mouth sprayed across the countertop. The popcorn bag in her hand tumbled to the floor. Victoria quickly covered Sharon's mouth.

"Don't scream," Victoria pleaded. But Sharon couldn't scream because she couldn't catch her breath.

"Is she going to be okay?" Michael asked Victoria.

"Yeah, this happens every time she gets excited," Victoria explained, and walked her to the sofa, but after two minutes Sharon was still struggling to catch her breath. It had never lasted this long.

"Are you okay?" Victoria finally asked.

Sharon nodded and took a sip of the water Michael had fetched for her. Then she took several deep breaths. "What the hell is going on?" she yelled, leaping from the sofa, slamming the glass of water on the coffee table. "Damn it, this is Michael Prince! What the hell is Michael Prince doing in our dorm?"

Victoria and Michael looked at each other and smiled.

"I don't believe it. My roommate is sleeping with Michael Prince."

"You must be Sharon. I've heard much about you." Michael extended his hand to hers, but she didn't touch him. She looked at his hand and then into his face.

"You're Michael Prince!" she exclaimed.

"I know."

Suddenly she jumped into his arms and didn't let go.

"Sharon!" Victoria yelled, but Sharon continued to hold him tight.

Michael laughed and tried to pry her off him.

"Why are you laughing? It's not funny," Victoria chastised him. "Sharon, get ahold of yourself." She peeled Sharon's arms from around his neck.

When they finally succeeded in separating Sharon from Michael, Victoria stood between them to make sure she didn't try it again.

"What the hell is going on?" Sharon demanded.

"Sit down and I'll tell you." Victoria began to tell her the incidents of that night at the concert while Sharon sat and listened, dumbfounded.

"I don't believe it. I looked for you all night and couldn't find you only to learn that you spent the night with my best friend," she said, looking at Michael. "And you." She turned and looked at Victoria. "How could you keep something like that from me? You should have told me."

"I'm sorry. I didn't know how to tell you."

"Well, I'm mad at both of you," Sharon said, and folded her arms across her chest.

"Would a kiss make it better?" Michael said, standing over her.

Sharon looked up and her mouth dropped open. Then she nodded.

Michael took her hand, pulled her to her feet, and planted a gentle kiss on her cheek.

Sharon smiled and touched her face. Nodding, she walked into her room and closed the door.

"That was sweet," Victoria said, wrapping her arms around him.

"I can be sweet sometimes." He looked down and kissed her forehead. They returned to her room and dove into the bed and continued talking. She lay in his arms with her head resting comfortably on his bare chest.

"So, tell me, Mr. Prince, do you have a girlfriend?" Victoria asked.

Michael grinned and looked at her. "First of all, you need to know my real name."

Victoria pushed herself up on her elbow and frowned at him.

"My name is Michael Stewart. Prince is my stage name." He kissed her. "Second, no. I do not have a steady girlfriend."

"Oh, I see." Victoria caught the hint in his use of the word *steady*. "And why not?"

"It just hasn't happened. I have associates—"

"Associates." Victoria laughed. "Is that what you guys are calling us these days?"

"Well, how long have you been dating Robert?"

Victoria stopped laughing. "About a year."

"Do you love him?"

"If I did, I wouldn't be with you."

Michael kissed her.

"I have a confession to make," Victoria said, and propped herself on the bed and looked down at him. "This associate is going to miss you when you leave."

Michael fell silent and gently caressed her arm, then stopped and looked wide-eyed at her. "Come with me," he blurted.

"What?"

"Come with me."

"Are you serious?"

"Yes, I'm very serious. I'll call and make the arrangements in the morning."

Victoria stopped him. "Whoa, wait a minute. I can't go with you."

"Why not?"

"Because I can't. I have classes, and my exams are in three weeks. I can't just leave."

"Take them when you get back."

"No," she said curtly.

Michael drew back.

"I know what I want to do with my life, and I'm not going to screw it up so that I can run off to Europe."

"Well, I didn't think it would be such a horrible idea."

"It's not a horrible idea. I just can't do it right now." She had never seen this coming. First he shows up out of nowhere, and now he expects her to just drop everything and run off with him. She couldn't do that no matter how much she wanted to be with him.

"So what happens now?" he asked, looking up at her. "I don't want this to be over."

Victoria looked down into his shining eyes. It was hard for her to believe that he had the capacity to care as much about her as she did about him. "The semester is over in three weeks. I can visit then, if you like."

"I would like that a lot." Michael smiled and pulled her down to him and kissed her.

14

VICTORIA

I sat in the counselor's office with my purse resting on my lap. I had decided to take Frank's advice and look into the employee-assistance program and scheduled a half-hour session. I had to talk to someone. My mother made me feel as if I was whining. My sisters and I were never close enough to discuss personal problems, and they felt the same way my mother did. They thought Gerald was a king of a husband and I'd really lucked out. And although Stephanie meant well, I really didn't believe my problems would go away if I had an affair. The last thing I needed to do was to bring *another* man into my life.

I spent more time lost in my daydreams than ever before, and they were becoming more and more elaborate. My housework was weeks behind, Reese needed help with her reading, and I passed all of the filing on to Cynthia at the office. My life was coming apart, but all I wanted to do was lock myself in my room and slip into a world I had complete control over.

I waited to be called into the counselor's office, but the longer I sat in the room, the more ridiculous the whole thing appeared. I sat in the cushioned chair with a clipboard of forms given to me by the receptionist.

This person is going to think I'm nuts, I thought. My right leg shook nervously as I clutched the straps of my purse, ready to dash for the door.

I'll give it one more minute, I thought, and looked at the second hand tick around my watch.

I'd made up my mind. If the counselor didn't arrive within the next few minutes, I was out of there.

"Victoria Chandler?"

I looked up at the cheerful woman standing over me with a clipboard in her hand.

"Yes," I said, and stood up.

"Hi," she said, extending her hand. "I'm Nancy Harris. My office is this way." I shook her hand, then she led the way down a short white corridor toward an open door. She stepped inside and waited until I was in before closing the door. "That is a lovely dress," she added.

Oh, goodness. This woman is too cheerful, I thought. She looked as if she didn't have a worry in the world.

"Thank you." I took a deep breath, trying to conceal my nervousness.

"Please have a seat." I eyed the empty cushioned chair across from her desk, sat down, and returned my purse to my lap.

Nancy flipped through the forms I'd completed earlier while sitting in the lobby waiting to be called. "Tell me a bit about yourself," she finally said.

I shifted in my seat and dropped my purse to the floor. There wasn't really anything to tell her about me that wasn't already written on the forms she held in front of her. I didn't feel it was an appropriate time to tell her about the daydreaming. "Well, I'm married, and I have a five-year-old daughter."

She nodded. "And how long have you been married?"

Read the paper. "Five years. We were married when our daughter, Reese, was a few months old."

"Reese. That's a beautiful name."

"Thank you. She's named after her great-grandmother."

"Are your parents still alive?"

"My mother is. My father died right after Reese was born."

"Oh, I'm sorry."

"We were very close." My eyes began to water, and I fought to keep the tears from falling.

"How about your relationship with your mother?"

"It's great."

Nancy nodded. "Where do you and your husband live?"

"North Avondale."

"Oh, really?" Nancy said, looking excited. "I grew up in North Avondale, right off Reading Road near Xavier University."

I added, "My husband graduated from Xavier University with a degree in engineering."

"Excellent school." Nancy nodded. "Do you attend any of the basketball games?"

"My husband does, but I don't. I attended Ohio University, but I didn't graduate."

"And how did you meet your husband?"

"We met at a nightclub and he swept me off my feet," I admitted. *But he has long since slammed my feet back on the ground.* I hadn't felt swept away by Gerald in years.

We talked for a half hour about my past and how I met Gerald, and that was it. I had come here to talk about the turmoil in my life, and all she wanted to talk about was a love story.

"Well, let's see." Nancy grabbed a calendar and scanned the dates. "I would like to see you back in one week."

I looked at her dumbfounded. That was it? We hadn't talked about anything. I hadn't even told her why I had come today.

"Can you make an hour appointment next week?"

I shrugged. I wasn't sure I wanted to.

"You're not here today because everything is perfect, and a half hour really isn't enough time for us to talk, but it's a good beginning."

I nodded, even though I wasn't sure if I agreed with her. There was nothing I wanted more than to be able to do things with Gerald. I would be thrilled to accompany him to an Xavier basketball game or take a walk with him, but neither seemed likely to happen.

I thought about the wish I had made after Reese was born that Gerald would marry me so that we would be a real family.

I had gotten my wish, but we had never felt like a real family, with a real marriage at its center.

15

JAMES

Victoria and Monica walked into the house and headed straight into the family room, where they slumped on the sofa. Victoria kicked her heels off and rested her feet on top of the coffee table.

"That was fun," Monica said, and propped her bare feet on the coffee table as well.

"Yes, it was," Victoria agreed.

"Did you enjoy yourself?"

"Yes, I did. Thank you." She reached to give Monica a hug. When she settled in her space again she burst into laughter.

"What's so funny?" Monica asked.

"Larry and John," she answered, lowering her voice to an alto, and Monica started laughing as well. "Can you believe those guys? Larry had a permanent ring around his finger but swore he wasn't married. He probably took the ring off at the door. And John. Oh my God. That man didn't have any teeth."

Monica laughed harder. "He had teeth, Victoria. He just didn't have any at the bottom."

"Same difference."

"But hey. They did buy our drinks," Monica said, coming to their rescue.

"Well, yes, they did. They were good for something." They had gone to a small jazz club to get Victoria out of the house. The crowd was older than the patrons at the Wilderness, and the chances of running into James were slim.

James, she thought. It had been a month since that awful night on the Riverfront. He had called her a few times in the beginning and left messages, but she had never called him back. She couldn't risk it.

"Please tell me you're not thinking about him again."

Victoria didn't say anything. He was out of her life, and it had to be that way even though it didn't stop her from thinking about him.

"You have got to stop this. You ended it, now get over it."

"I'm trying!" Victoria yelled, and pressed her head against the cushion.

"Well, if you're going to continue to torture yourself like this, then I suggest you call him."

"I can't."

"Why not? He's close to eighteen, and he's not a student at our school. You can date him."

"I cannot imagine sleeping with a seventeen-year-old."

"Then don't sleep with him."

She shook her head. It still just didn't seem right to her.

"Face it, Victoria, you're in love with the guy. I don't think you would be doing anything wrong by going out with him. Men do it all the time."

"I can't. I don't trust myself. I love everything about him." She took a deep breath. "What in the hell is wrong with me?" she said, and slapped herself in the forehead.

"Stop that." Monica grabbed her hand and held it. "There is nothing wrong with you." Monica squeezed her hand. "You didn't know, I didn't know. But I think you should call him."

"I'll think about it."

They settled on the sofa for moment in silence while Victoria contemplated calling James. If she did make that decision, it wouldn't be tonight.

"You want something to drink?" Victoria asked, standing up and heading into the kitchen. "I assume you'll be sleeping in the spare room."

"Yeah, I could use another glass of wine. And put some popcorn in the microwave."

"Yes, ma'am," Victoria said, and saluted her. The doorbell rang just as she stepped over Monica. "That better not be Gerald bringing Reese back. I told him to keep her until Sunday." She grumbled and walked to the door. When she stepped into the narrow hallway, she looked toward the door and stopped cold.

"Oh my God," she mumbled.

"What's wrong?" Monica asked, and jumped from the sofa and stood beside her. "Wow. We really talked him up."

Victoria turned and darted back into the living room.

"What are you doing?" Monica asked, chasing after her. "You can't leave him out there."

"Yes I can," she said, pacing.

"Victoria, if you don't let the man in, I will."

"Is he still there?"

Before Monica could peek around the corner, James rang the doorbell again. "Does that answer your question?"

Nodding, Victoria took a deep breath, then stepped into the corridor again and walked toward the front of the house. She slowly turned the handle and opened the door until she had a full view of him.

"Hi," he said, standing with his hands buried deep inside his jeans pockets.

"What are you doing here?" She stepped out onto the porch with him. Her heart pounded against her chest, but she couldn't tell him that standing close to him made her nervous.

"I wanted to talk to you, but you won't return my calls."

"That's because we agreed not to see each other again."

"That was your decision. Not mine."

"James, please don't make this difficult for me." She looked at the ground.

"How do you think I feel, or do my feelings matter?"

Victoria shook her head.

"My feelings don't matter?"

"That's not what I mean. It's just that it would be very difficult for us to have a relationship."

"But not impossible?" he asked.

Victoria didn't answer him.

"Difficult but not impossible, right?" he asked again.

"I suppose."

"I'm willing to try."

Victoria folded her arms at her chest and looked to the ground again. Her mind was racing. There were too many obstacles they'd have to overcome. She would have to alter her entire lifestyle to accommodate him. She wouldn't be able to share a bottle of wine with him or go out to a club with him again. She couldn't even agree to meet him there because if it was ever challenged, she would be accused of abetting his entrance into an adult facility where alcohol was readily available to him. That could cost her her job for improper behavior, and she couldn't have sex with him for the same reasons. He was not eighteen yet. It would not be acceptable.

"You're thinking about it, aren't you?"

"Yes."

"And?"

Victoria shrugged. "I don't know. It'll be a very big sacrifice."

"I think you should give me a chance," he said, and took her in his arms.

She didn't step out of his embrace. She felt wonderful being in his arms. He lifted her face to him until their eyes locked. She knew he was about to kiss her, but she couldn't stop him. James's kisses lifted her high above the ground. She closed her eyes and accepted his kiss.

It was the same kiss they'd shared on the Riverfront. Gentle at first, then he moved deeper into her mouth and touched her tongue with his. When he pulled away and looked at her, she knew without a doubt that she was not going to walk away from him again.

16

Victoria stayed late to grade papers. It had been only a week since she'd reconciled with James, and they'd talked every night since. She couldn't wait to finish grading the papers so that she could rush home and talk with him again. If he didn't have too much homework, maybe she could invite him over. Kissing him was still a thrill, and she looked forward to it every time she saw him.

She didn't look up when she heard her door open because she expected it to be Monica inquiring how much longer she would be. She hated taking work home, especially now, since James was in her life.

"I'm almost done," she said, putting a red X across one of the answers marked on the test.

"Are you Victoria Chandler?"

Startled by the male voice, she looked up. The man had a familiar handsome face, but she couldn't place where she had seen him before.

"Yes," she said, staring at him.

"I'm Jonathan Mitchell. James's father."

Victoria's heart sank, and she stood up, to do the only logical thing she could think of. "Oh," she said, and walked from behind her desk. "Please come in." She motioned for him to take one of the student desks opposite her desk, which he accepted.

"I'm not one to beat around the bush," Jonathan said. "My wife and I are concerned about your relationship with our son. You may very well be a nice person, but we feel that you are simply too old and too experienced for James."

She wasn't prepared for this. She and James hadn't even discussed how he would tell his parents about her or the fact that he had already done so. She fumbled to her chair and sat down.

"Excuse me," she said, taking a deep breath. "I wasn't prepared for this."

"Neither were we when James informed us of his relationship with you."

She had to gather herself quickly. Jonathan Mitchell had not come to her classroom to bargain with her. If she was going to continue seeing James, she had to somehow convince his parents that it was a good idea.

"I understand how you must feel."

"You have no idea how I feel," he interrupted her. "I have a teenage son who's growing up a lot faster than I want him to."

"I really care about James."

"Are you having sex with my son?"

"No," she snapped. "James and I are not involved like that. I promise."

"I am going to have you investigated, and if I find out that you've been involved with anyone else underage, I will make sure you never teach again. Now, that I promise."

Victoria stared at him and took his threat seriously, but it also made her angry. He had no right to make accusations like that without knowing anything about her.

"Mr. Mitchell, I don't like what you're implying."

"But I'm sure you understand where I'm coming from."

"Did James tell you how we met?"

"Yes. He said you met at the mall."

"Did he tell you anything else?"

"Is there more to it?"

"There's a lot more to it. Were you aware that James had a fake identification card?"

Jonathan looked squarely at her. "A what?"

Victoria paused, knowing perfectly well that she was about to confide information about James that she was sure he didn't want his parents to know. "James used a fake identification card to get into the Wilderness."

"The Wilderness?"

"Yes. James and I did meet at the mall, but I saw him prior to that at the Wilderness. I had no idea he was seventeen years old until later, and when he told me, I ended it."

"James did not tell me this."

"I have my suspicions why he left that part out, but you need to understand how all this got started. I did make a decision to continue seeing your son, but it wasn't because he's seventeen. It was because after being separated from him for a month I really realized that I care a great deal about him." She had his attention. The lines on his face softened and the huff she heard coming from his nose calmed.

"Okay, but now that I know about this, I'm not going to allow him to continue going to the Wilderness with you."

"When I found out he was seventeen, I told him I couldn't go to the Wilderness with him anymore."

He raised his eyebrows. "You did?"

"Yes, I did. I can't take that chance of losing my job. I know he's too young to be in the Wilderness, and I can't contribute to that."

"And how did he take it?"

Victoria reached into her desk and took out her purse. She rummaged through her wallet until she found what she was looking for, then handed it to Jonathan. "That's the card he used to get into the Wilderness. He gave it to me because he wanted me to know I could trust him. I just haven't gotten rid of it yet."

Jonathan looked at James's picture on the card, then flipped it over and examined the card. "How did he get this?"

Victoria shrugged. "I don't know, but he's not alone. All of his friends have one."

"I see," the man said, and put the card in his wallet.

"If it's any consolation to you, he doesn't drink. I've never seen him with alcohol."

"Then why does he go there?"

"To dance. He's a great dancer." Victoria smiled. She tried to clear the smile from her face, but she couldn't.

The room became uncomfortably quiet. She wondered what Mr. Mitchell thought of her now, but more important, she wondered how James was going to feel knowing that she'd tattled on him.

"I must say that I was not expecting this."

"Mr. Mitchell, I'm not out to hurt James. I really do care about him."

"I don't doubt that, Ms. Chandler, but that doesn't change the fact that he's still seventeen and you have already experienced many things in your life. His hasn't begun yet."

Victoria felt as if he had reached into her chest and grabbed hold of her heart and was determined to squeeze the life out of her. If he forbade her from seeing James, she couldn't fight it and she knew it. "If you object to me dating James, I have no choice but to respect your decision," she said, staring down at her desk. She picked up a pencil only to place it back down.

"I object to you dating my son, and I don't want you seeing him anymore."

The words stabbed her heart, and she couldn't look up. She placed her hand over her mouth to cover the trembling lips. Her hand shook as she fought to keep the tears from falling, but she couldn't stop them from trickling down the side of her face.

Mr. Mitchell rose to leave without saying anything further. When he was out of sight, she dropped her head to her desk and cried.

17

VICTORIA

I picked Reese up from school, then headed to my mother's. I was in no hurry to go home. When we arrived, Reese darted from the car and fled across the street to play with the neighbor's grandchildren. Reese always enjoyed coming over to my mother's house because there were plenty of children around.

"What's wrong with you?" my mother asked as I sat quietly on the deck. I sipped from a glass of iced tea I had poured when I walked in.

"I'm not in love with my husband anymore. I'm not sure if I ever was." I shrugged. "I don't know what to do." I fought the tears that were beginning to burn in my eyes.

"Well, Victoria, you have Reese to think about now."

I took a deep breath. I was thinking about Reese, that was the reason I was still in the marriage. "I'm just not happy." I slumped into my seat and stared off over the beautiful yard. You could always find my mother weeding, seeding, or pruning. Just about every flower imaginable grew in her gardens. My father had planted the first bulbs many years ago, and my parents' yard quickly became the envy of the neighbors.

"Gerald called me. He asked me to talk to you. Said you've been acting funny."

I turned and looked coldly at my mother. "Gerald called you?"

"Yes, he did. I told him I would talk to you. I don't know what to say about you young girls. In my day . . ."

I wasn't listening anymore. Gerald called my mother. Why? What was he trying to do?

"What did he say?" I asked, interrupting her in midsentence.

"He said you've been acting weird. Daydreaming a lot."

"That's it?" I asked, looking crossly at her. She was known for withholding information.

"Well, he said that things weren't going too well with you guys and that you keep putting demands on him."

"What!" I screamed. "He said I was putting demands on him? How dare he!" I stomped my feet on the wood. "Did he say anything at all about the things he's been doing?"

"Victoria, you know how men are—"

I interrupted her again. "That is not an answer." I was so furious I could no longer sit still in the chair. "Did he happen to mention how he forces me to have sex with him?"

Before I had the chance to say anything further, my mother slapped me. I was stunned. My eyes widened as I looked at the creases of anger around her eyes. "A husband cannot force his wife to have sex with him. You are his wife. He provides for you and your daughter. It is your duty."

I couldn't move. Tears began to roll down my cheeks.

"That is the problem with you young girls, so damn liberated." She sat down, slowly pulling her legs out in front of her. I could see the signs of pain on her face as she massaged the muscles in her legs with her hand. "Gerald works hard for you and Reese. You have a good man. Don't be so concerned about how you feel when you're having sex. Who gives a damn about how good the sex is? You got too much Hollywood in you." She stood again and pointed her finger at me. "Do you know how many women would love to be where you're at? You better realize that. You let go, it won't take long before some hussy snatches him up. Then some other woman will be living in your house, sleeping with your husband. You better think about that and get that Hollywood out of you," she murmured as she returned to her garden. "I'm going to have to get over to your house. Lois tells me your garden is just as pretty as mine." Just like that, she totally changed the subject. I watched her kneel and begin picking at the weeds. Her way of dismissing the conversation.

The tears streamed down my face. I knew that I could never confide in my mother again about anything that happened between me and Gerald. And my sisters were out of the question because they would definitely run back and tell her everything I had said.

As I walked away from my mother's house, I felt more alone than I ever had in my life. I called for Reese as soon as I reached the car, and she jumped into the backseat and quickly fastened her seat belt.

"Mommy, are you crying?"

I shook my head and quickly wiped the tears. "I'm okay, honey." I forced a smile, then turned around and looked at her. "Did you have fun?" No matter how many tears I wiped away, I couldn't hide the redness.

"Mommy, why are you crying?" Reese asked, ignoring my question.

"It's not important, honey," I said, and pulled out of my mother's driveway. As I drove away, I wondered if anyone would ever come to my rescue. If anyone could hear my screams.

My vision was blurred, and I could no longer see. I pulled to the side of the road and shielded my face so that Reese couldn't see the tears pouring from my eyes.

18

JAMES

It was carnival season in Cincinnati, and Reese and Victoria had made plans for the entire day. Victoria packed extra clothes just in case they got on any rides that involved water. Monica couldn't join them this time because she'd made plans with her latest boyfriend, so it was just the two of them. It was the first time since Reese was born that Gerald would not be joining them.

Once they were at the carnival, Reese didn't seem to care that her father wasn't there. She wanted to get on all of the rides and sample the pink and blue cotton candy.

Victoria happily obliged and bought her cotton candy and a caramel apple sprinkled with nuts for herself. As they walked through the crowd toward the Ferris wheel, Victoria felt a hand tap her on the shoulder. When she turned around, she saw James standing inches away from her.

The first couple of days after they were forced to break up, James called her from school until she told him not to anymore. Integrity was everything to her, and she wanted to make sure she didn't do anything to upset James's parents. That was one battle she didn't have the energy to fight.

"James," she said, looking around her for any sign of his parents.

"Hi," he said to her. "Hello, Reese." He bent down and kissed her on the cheek. He made sure he didn't leave her out. Reese giggled.

"How are you?" he asked, straightening back up and looking at Victoria.

"I'm fine. How are you?"

"I'm well."

They stared at each other for what seemed forever. She wanted to kiss him so badly she could almost taste him in her mouth. It had been almost a month since they'd split up again, but this time was a lot harder than the first because it was not her choice.

"Who did you come with?" she asked, making small talk just to keep him standing near her.

"I'm here with my friends. What about you?"

"It's just me and Reese."

"Would you mind if I joined you?" he asked.

She hesitated before she answered him.

"I don't know if that's a good idea."

"It's a carnival," he said. "We're allowed to hang out with friends and have fun at the carnival."

"I miss you," she said, fighting the emotions welling up inside her.

"I miss you too." He reached for her hand, and she touched his. "Come on. I'll walk with you guys," he said, pulling her closer to him and joining in with them.

Victoria could tell Reese had taken an immediate liking to James. She clung to his hand as they walked around the carnival grounds and did not let go. They ran into a few of James's friends, but he did not leave her side the entire time they were there. They took fun pictures together in a photo booth and Victoria knew she would treasure them for the rest of her life. Looking at them almost made her cry. She had never been as happy as she was when she was with James. She wanted more than anything to be with him.

She hated when it was time to say good-bye, but Reese just couldn't keep her eyes open any longer. James lifted her into his arms and carried her all the way to the car, where he laid her down on the backseat, sound asleep.

Instead of walking away, he pulled Victoria into his arms and held her against his chest. They stood quietly in each other's arms as they leaned against her car. His fingers were buried in her hair as he held her.

"I have to leave," Victoria whispered.

"I know," he answered, but he didn't move from his spot. "I can talk to my parents again."

Victoria separated from him and stared into his eyes. "I don't think that would be a good idea."

He nodded, agreeing with her. He had protested their decision loudly at first, to the point that it had gotten to be an ugly scene and his parents accused her of disrupting their family.

He leaned forward and kissed her softly on the lips. Then again, longer. When she finally pulled away, she immediately got into her car and drove off without looking back.

When she reached her house, Reese was still asleep. Victoria picked her up from the backseat and carried her inside. Her limp body was hard to balance as she struggled to unlock the door. She took Reese straight upstairs to bed, deciding it would be best to let her sleep and give her a bath in the morning.

After taking Reese's shoes off and tucking her under the sheet, she turned the light off and headed back downstairs.

She felt exhausted, physically and emotionally. Seeing James was exactly what she needed, but it was hard saying good-bye.

She poured a glass of wine and sat on the living room sofa staring at the photos she'd taken with Reese and James. They'd all made some pretty silly faces.

She heard a soft tap on the door. She placed her wineglass and the pictures on the coffee table, then peered into the corridor toward the front door.

It was Gerald.

She frowned and opened the door. "What are you doing here?" she asked.

"I wanted to see Reese, but I assume she's sleeping now."

"Yes, she's asleep."

"Can I come in? I need to talk with you."

Victoria paused for a minute and looked at him. Gerald was a big man, standing six feet four inches tall and weighing well over two hundred pounds. When they stood together, he towered over her five-five frame. She had always been attracted to tall men, and it was the first thing she noticed about him when she first met him. She had always thought he was handsome.

She decided against arguing with him and stepped aside to let him through.

"What do you want to talk about?" she asked as soon as she sat down.

"I just wanted to talk with you. We haven't talked in a while."

She looked up at him puzzled. Talk? They'd never talked. Not even when they were married. That was one of many reasons why they'd divorced.

Gerald walked to the sofa and eyed the pictures lying on the coffee table. He picked them up and scanned through them. "I see you went to the carnival."

"Yes, we did," she said, sipping from her glass.

"And who's the stud?"

Victoria laughed. "He's a friend."

"A friend, huh?" he said, placing the photos on the table again. "A boyfriend?"

"No." Victoria shook her head. "A friend."

"I remember when we used to go to the carnival together. The three of us."

Victoria looked up at him. He wasn't making any sense. "Have you been drinking?"

"Are you going to offer me a glass of wine?"

"I don't think so. Did you want anything?" she asked, looking up at him. He still hadn't told her the reason for his visit.

"Why are you in such a hurry to get rid of me? Your boyfriend here or something?"

"I just want to be alone," she said placing the glass on the table.

"Tell me more about your boyfriend," he said, sitting on the sofa beside her.

Victoria turned to face him and frowned. There was no way in hell she would confide in him about anything. They didn't have that type of relationship. The marriage didn't end on good terms, and they'd never managed to become friends.

"I don't want to talk about it."

"I think I should know."

Victoria grimaced. "It doesn't concern you," she said.

"If you're going to be bringing another man around my daughter, it concerns me."

Victoria had enough. "This is the reason why you and I could never be friends. I think you should go now." She rose from the sofa only to have Gerald push her down again.

"Have you had sex with him yet?"

That did it. "Get out," she snapped. She tried to rise from the sofa again only to have Gerald hold her down. "What do you want?" she yelled.

"Maybe I want my wife back. You used to like it when I touched you." He pulled her toward him and tried to kiss her.

Victoria pulled away from him. "Will you stop," she said pushing him off of her. "I want you to leave." *Damn him. Damn him for ruining this day for her.*

"No you don't." Within seconds Gerald pinned her to the sofa and snapped the button off her shorts, sending it flying across the room.

"What the hell are you doing?" She put her knee into his chest. Even as she fought him on the sofa, she was sure he would stop. But he didn't. "Stop it!" she yelled, using all of her strength to push him off of her. But she was no match.

He pulled her shorts at the zipper, and all she could hear was the fabric tearing from her body.

What the hell is happening? she thought as she continued to fight him. She didn't think to scream. She just wanted him off her.

"This isn't funny," she said, kicking and pushing on him. Her shorts were no longer on her body. It still hadn't clicked with her what was happening. A part of her thought he was testing her, trying to see how far he could take it before she gave in. But she wasn't going to give in. She wasn't in love with him anymore.

She felt his hand fumbling with her underwear and reaching inside to touch her. She tried to sit up only to have him press down harder on her. Her eyes widened and her breath paused when she felt him enter her. She hadn't realized he had unzipped his pants. This wasn't a game anymore. He was raping her.

"No!" she screamed, and tried to twist her body from underneath him. She tried to scream again, but he dropped his chest over her face to prevent any sound from leaving her mouth. He pinned her arms to her sides to keep her from fighting while he continued to thrust hard inside of her.

She couldn't breathe. He lay on top of her while she squirmed, gasping for air as the weight of his body pressed her head deep into the sofa cushion. She panicked.

She stopped resisting him. She just needed to turn her face far enough to breathe. She shook her neck hard and pushed her chest into him, trying to get him to budge just enough to free her nose. It was taking too long and she felt her body getting weaker, but she kept trying until she managed to twist just far enough to free her nostrils from underneath his chest. She panted, getting the air into her lungs. Gerald was still thrusting inside her.

"You like that, don't you?" she heard him say.

Victoria remembered what it was like living with Gerald. During the short two years of their marriage, she was forced to make love to him whether she wanted to or not. His need for sex almost every night killed her desire for it. There were nights when he thrust inside her so hard she'd wake up the next morning sore, the walls of her vagina raw from his penis pounding inside her when she was too dry to accept him.

Tears began to fill her eyes. She thought those nights were over once they were divorced. She never imagined she would have to go through that again.

"I knew you'd stop fighting it," he said. "You always liked me inside you."

He'd thought she stopped fighting him because she was enjoying it. He had no idea he'd almost killed her. She knew she had to get away from him or he'd never stop. She waited until she felt his grip loosen. She managed to squirm to the edge of the sofa, causing them both to fall to the floor. She kicked the lamp with her foot and sent it shattering to the floor. She picked up a large piece of the broken black ceramic and clutched it tight in her hand until she felt the warmth of her own blood running down her arm. With the little energy she had left, she slashed the piece hard across his face.

In an instant he yelled out and jumped to his feet. He reached up to his face and touched the blood streaming from the gash across his cheek.

With him off her and not thinking of much else, she crawled away from him and hurried toward the door. If she could just get it open, she could scream for help and someone would hear her. But Gerald reached her just as she reached for the handle. He twisted her arm hard and pulled it behind her back, then shoved her face hard into the wooden frame. The impact sent her limp to the floor.

He grabbed a lock of her hair and pulled her back into the living room while she kicked and tried to free her hair from his grip.

She felt a hard sting across her face that sent blood sputtering from her mouth. She felt it again, then again, until she lost count. This time she knew he was going to kill her. He was not going to stop until she was dead. Her body fell feebly to the floor.

Victoria lay on the floor, drifting away. She heard a thump and struggled to open her eyes to see what was happening. Was he getting something to finish her off? She had to do something to stay alive.

Then she heard it again. She opened her eyes wide enough to see James and Gerald fighting.

James. She tried to open her eyes wider to make sure she saw correctly. It *was* James. She saw him land a punch hard across Gerald's jaw, sending him scrambling. He tripped over her body and stumbled backward onto the coffee table. The sound ricocheted through the room. Gerald lay sprawled on the floor with his legs trapped on top of hers.

James ignored Gerald's motionless body and ran toward Victoria and lifted her into his arms.

She tried to open her eyes so she could see him, but all she managed was to barely lift her lids. It was enough for him.

"Thank God," he said, then gently placed her head against the floor again and ran across the room.

She heard him rant into the phone, giving details about her and Gerald, before he returned and sat on the floor with her.

"Victoria," he said, lifting her into his arms. "You have to stay awake, okay?" He brushed her hair from her face.

She heard him, but she was weightless. She felt nothing, no pain or worries. Her body floated like she was in a conscious sleep.

"You can't fall asleep. Talk to me," he said, and shook her until she opened her eyes again. "Did you have fun at the carnival?"

She wanted to smile, but the muscles in her face were paralyzed.

"Open your eyes, Victoria," he said, looking down at her.

This time she managed to narrowly open them and focus on him. He had blood on his face. She wanted to reach up and touch him, but her arms wouldn't move. Her body felt the same way it did after she was given an epidural when Reese was born. It was the worst feeling she had ever had, looking at her legs and mentally telling them to move and they wouldn't. But this time she couldn't move anything.

Her eyes filled with panic.

"It's okay," James whispered. "You're going to be okay." He must have seen the fear in her eyes. "Victoria, where's Reese?" he asked.

Her eyes fluttered in determination to say something. She opened her mouth far enough to utter a sound. "Uhh," was the only thing that came out.

"Upstairs?"

She blinked at him.

He sighed. "Okay. I'll take care of her. Don't worry."

Before she could try to do anything more, she heard sirens coming closer to the house. James reached for a pillow from the sofa and placed it under her head before he darted for the door. She waited on the floor, struggling to keep her eyes open like James said.

Other people were in the room, but they moved about so quickly that they were only a blur to her. She felt an oxygen mask secured around her head, and she began to breathe into it. Her body was lifted onto a gurney and wheeled toward the door. She glanced around the room, trying to catch a glimpse of James. As she neared the door, she saw him standing near the wall, out of the way of the medics who had come to take her to the hospital.

His face was the last thing she saw before everything faded away.

Her eyes blinked several times as she tried to focus on the room and where she was. The bed surely was not her own—it was too narrow. When she managed to open her eyes, she knew immediately that she was in the hospital. She remembered everything that had happened, up to being wheeled from the house. She had no idea how long she'd been here.

Her eyes stopped on James slumped in a chair beside the bed. His eyes were closed, and a Band-Aid was stuck to his face under his eye. She continued to look around the room and saw two other people: a man and a woman she didn't immediately recognize.

When she looked harder, she realized she had seen the man before. It was James's father. *What was he doing there?*

She reached her hand up and touched her face. A thick pad of gauze covered half of it. Her mouth was swelled so large it felt like it could touch her nose. A cut inside her lip was stitched together, and the thread left a stale taste on the tip of her tongue. She tried to lift her head, but a sharp pain from her neck prevented her from even raising it off the pillow. She squealed.

James heard her and jumped from his chair to the bedside. "You're awake," he said, taking her hand.

She had so many questions she didn't know where to begin. How long had she been asleep? Where was Reese? What happened to his hand and face? Was Gerald dead?

"How long have I been here?" she said softly. Her throat was dry, and it hurt when she talked.

"Two days."

"Reese," she said, and tried again to sit up in the bed.

James stopped her. "Reese is fine. She's with Monica."

Victoria relaxed on the bed again. "And Gerald?" She needed to know if he was dead, even though she was sure she would not mourn his death.

"He bumped his head on the table, but it just knocked him out. They've arrested him, and he's not going to hurt you again. I promise." He squeezed her hand and sat on the bed with her.

She saw his father come closer and stand beside James. The woman beside him took his hand and placed her other one on James's shoulder.

James stood and said, "Victoria, this is my mother. And you've met my father."

Victoria looked at the woman, not knowing what to say. This was not the best situation to meet her.

"Hi, Victoria," the woman said, as friendly as she could be, considering the situation. "It's nice to finally meet you. I've heard a lot about you."

"I wish it could have been under better circumstances." Victoria started to cry. She was sure this would erase every hope that they would reconsider their decision. "I never meant for him to get hurt or into any trouble."

"Please, don't worry about that. We're just glad that James was there to help you." She took Victoria's hand and squeezed it. "James called us and told us what happened. Our son has never given us any reason to doubt his judgment, and he says he wants to date you. We're not going to stand in his way."

Victoria looked from the woman to James. Was this for real? James's smile reassured her that it was for real.

She continued, "I've met your daughter and she's a delightful little girl. I look forward to seeing both of you around more." A smile crept across her face.

Victoria nodded.

"And if you could have seen some of the dates James has brought home . . . well, we figure he could have done a lot worse," his mother said and giggled.

"Thank you, Mrs. Mitchell," Victoria said and wiped a tear from her eye.

"Please, call me Katherine."

19

VICTORIA

First I received a card from Nancy, the counselor, asking me to make another appointment. I promptly threw it away. A few days later she called. Feeling that this woman was not going to go away, I agreed to meet with her again with the intention of dismissing the case at the end of the session.

When I arrived for my appointment after work, there were other people sitting in the lobby. I smiled at them as I walked by and wondered what problems had brought them here.

I picked up one of the outdated magazines, but before I had a chance to leaf through it Nancy stepped from her office and called me back.

"How have you been?" she asked, smiling as I walked into the room.

"Fine, thank you." I sat down in an empty seat and looked around at the paintings on the wall.

"So, when we last met we talked about you and your husband," she said, picking up her folder. "I'm glad I got you to open up to me. I could tell you were a little nervous. That usually happens the first time. Now, let's talk about Victoria. Tell me something about Victoria."

I took a deep breath. "I don't know what to say. There really isn't anything about me that's worth mentioning."

"Where do you go when you need to get away? Is there a special place for you?"

I took a deep breath and thought of all the places I escaped to. "Eden Park. I love sitting there."

"Why is that?"

"I sit alone and no one bothers me and even though there are hundreds of people whizzing by, it's still quiet. You know what I mean?"

"Yes, I do."

I smiled. "When I'm sitting on a bench in Eden Park looking across the river I can close my eyes and reach deep inside myself and think. It's the only place I can go and really focus on what's going on inside me."

"Does your family ever go with you?"

"I take Reese, but Gerald doesn't go with us. He used to, but not anymore."

"Why is that?"

"Well, because it's the place I go to escape. If I took Gerald, it would add stress to the only place that I find peace, and then I would have nothing."

———

There was no reason to rush home after I left Nancy's office. Gerald was picking Reese up from school, so that gave me a few minutes to spare. Naturally, after bringing up the subject to Nancy, I found myself driving to Eden Park.

I drove around the circle into the park and immediately began looking for a parking space. As usual, all of the spaces along the entrance drive were taken, so I drove farther into the park, passing the empty play area. On weekends that area would be overflowing with children swinging and sliding. Driving on, I finally found an empty space and pulled in.

I sat on a bench and looked out over the river into Newport or Covington. I could never tell the difference. I propped my feet up on the stone wall, placed my arms on top of the bench, threw my head back, and took a deep breath. I looked at the sun as it began to paint an orange horizon across the sky. Off in the distance I saw a plane as it made its way toward the airport. A few minutes later I saw another plane heading for its destination.

MICHAEL

The weeks dragged by as Victoria waited until the end of the semester to join Michael in the United Kingdom. It would mark her first time traveling beyond the United States.

The end of the semester came after she completed her sociology exam. A driver in a black Cadillac sedan met her at the dorm to take her to the airport. She scooped up the duffel bags she had packed the night before and rushed down the stairs to the waiting car.

She could not conceal the enormous smile spread across her face as she rode in the backseat of the car to the airport. She had spoken to Michael almost every day on the telephone since he left the States. Being en route to meet him was an enormous thrill.

Victoria and Sharon had stayed up most of the previous night concocting a plot to tell Robert or her parents if they were to ask for her while she was out of town. Victoria wasn't ready to confront either of them about Michael because she wasn't sure what her relationship with him was.

She arrived at the airport in plenty of time for her flight to London, and the plane departed the Cincinnati–Northern Kentucky Airport on schedule. She remained awake for the entire ten-hour flight to London. She was too excited to sleep. She thought about Michael and what it would be like seeing him when she stepped off the plane. The whole affair was too incredible to even think about. She experienced such a high being with Michael, one she had never achieved with anyone before in her young life.

It seemed, at first thought, that she and Michael would have nothing to share because they were as different as two people could be. However, their differences didn't stop them from keeping each other up for hours sharing stories. She loved listening to Michael talk about his life on the road and his music.

The Michael Prince that was displayed to the world and the Michael Stewart that she shared her thoughts with were so different. She knew about Michael's reputation, thanks to Sharon, and the contradiction puzzled her.

As she sat in the reclining leather seat, her mind drifted to her first night with Michael. Every bit of common sense she had displayed in the past years would have prevented her from ever going back to that hotel room with him. But the more she thought about it, the more she realized that night was meant to happen.

And the sex.

Victoria shifted in her seat when she thought about it. The kisses, the touches, the way he looked at her—everything he did set her on fire.

The plane landed at Gatwick Airport just south of London.

"Excuse me, ma'am." Victoria stopped the flight attendant on her way out of the airplane. "This is my first time out of the country. What do I do once I'm inside the airport?"

"Do you have anything to declare?"

"No."

"Then it should be fairly simple. Just go to the green channel and show your passport."

"Thank you." Victoria walked toward the airport concourse following passengers who appeared to know where they were going. She managed to arrive at customs, where she had her passport stamped without being asked any questions.

That was easier than expected. She had thought the process would entail a thorough search of her purse and bags and a brisk frisk by some overpowering woman, but none of that happened. From there she wandered to the baggage-claims area, then took out the instructions Michael had given her over the telephone. She walked out of the automatic sliding glass doors onto the sidewalk buzzing with travelers. A damp breeze lifted her hair as she stood close to the entrance. She didn't want to wander far and risk getting lost.

Her eyes checked over the travelers, then stopped when she saw a familiar face. It was the bodyguard she recognized first. He stood inches in front of Michael, concealing him from view of anyone who would recognize him beneath the dark sunglasses and the sports cap.

Her heart began to pound against her chest. A warm smile spread across Michael's face as she walked toward him. When she reached him she didn't have a chance to utter a word as his lips covered hers. When he pulled away from her, he rushed her into the waiting car as the bodyguard closed the door behind them.

"Tracy will get your bags," Michael said, mentioning the guard by name for the first time. Once again Michael didn't wait for her to speak as he pulled her close and covered her lips again. Tracy returned with her bags, and the loud thump of the trunk drew them back from their embrace.

"I am so glad you're here," he said, kissing her again.

Victoria smiled and realized how much she had missed him.

"I'm glad I'm here too."

The hour drive to Michael's home in Islington seemed too short. Victoria talked exhaustively about the final three weeks of the semester and her exams. Michael gave a brief history of Islington, the borough just outside London's financial district that was home to many entertainers and public figures. In his own neighborhood, Highbury Village, he was free to roam the streets without being disturbed.

The limousine pulled up in front of a small Victorian terrace house, and Victoria squinted at it. "You live here?" she asked as they climbed out of the backseat of the limousine.

"Yes, and for the next week so will you." He pursed his lips and kissed her softly on the temple, then led the way along the cement walkway.

"It's not what I expected." They took about five steps to the house as Tracy disengaged the security alarm and opened the door. He walked in ahead of them and turned on the lights.

"What were you expecting?"

"A castle, I suppose."

Michael laughed. "Contrary to my name, I'm no prince." Once inside, they stepped into the first of two sitting rooms in the three-story house.

"Wow," Victoria said as she stood agape, looking at the rooms. The looks of the house from the outside were very deceiving. She glanced around the meticulously decorated room as Michael began the tour. On the first story were the usual kitchen, dining room, and entrance onto a terrace and a small garden located at the back of the house. On the second story were four bedrooms, a bathroom, a shower room, and the other sitting room. The entire third story was one bedroom with an adjoining bathroom and a shower room. A small open balcony overlooked the garden in the back of the house.

They stepped onto the balcony and enjoyed the breeze and the moonlight.

"I would never have known this place was so big just by looking at it from the outside. Why do you have five bedrooms?"

"I have lots of friends," he said, smirking.

"So, which one of these rooms will I sleep in?" Victoria joked.

Michael took her hand and led her back into the house. "In here with me," he said, wrapping his arms around her and kissing her neck. Victoria slipped off her shoes and let her feet sink into the soft carpet.

"Are you tired?" he whispered into her ear as his tongue lingered on her earlobes.

Victoria moaned. "A little. A hot bath would be wonderful."

Michael kissed her again on the neck and led her into the bathroom equipped with a black whirlpool tub.

"That would definitely do." She giggled.

"Everything you need should be in here." Michael kissed her hand before he turned to leave her alone. "Take your time."

Victoria slipped out of her jeans and T-shirt as the tub filled with bubbling hot suds. When she stepped into the bath, she closed her eyes and exhaled. She slid deeper into the water, letting the bubbles soothe the fatigue from her body. Her head rested on a soft white pillow.

When she finished with her bath, she sprayed herself with perfume and slipped into an undershirt and panty set.

She opened the door from the bath to see Michael relaxing in front of the fireplace on a white oversized pillow on the floor. The floor around him was littered with soft red rose petals, and a tray of cheese, fruits, and champagne was beside him. He reached out to her as she joined him on the floor.

"Was your bath satisfactory?" He handed her a tall glass of champagne as she sat between his legs and pressed her back against his chest.

"Very." Victoria sipped from the glass and felt the chill run down her throat. Michael picked up one of the petals close to her and began to caress her body with it. "Where's Tracy?" she asked, wondering whether he might wander in on them.

"He's left."

Victoria nodded as Michael continued to caress her with the petal, his fingers never stopping. They sat in silence for a few moments as she enjoyed the sensation. "Wow." Victoria laughed as the petal and champagne began to tickle her.

"Wow what?" Michael said, laughing.

"This is just . . ." She shrugged.

"I missed you," Michael said, squeezing her leg as it rested on top of his.

She turned to face him. "I missed you too," she replied, and exhaled deeply as she stared at him.

"What is it?"

"I'm overwhelmed," she said. "Nothing like this has ever happened to me before. What I'm feeling for you, I've never felt before. I can't help wondering what I'm doing here." She looked around at the incredible room, then back at him. "I'm in the United Kingdom, sitting in front of an incredibly handsome man, in this unbelievable house, and I'm asking myself, can this be real? Can this man feel for me as I feel for him? What is happening here?"

Michael stared at the questioning expression on her face. She saw the seriousness in his eyes as he pondered her question.

"Vicki, I don't know how to answer that. I know how I feel when I'm with you. I enjoy your companionship tremendously."

"Michael, I feel great with you as well, but we're going to great lengths to be together. You traveled to Cincinnati, Ohio, of all places, to find me, using only the information I gave you on our first and only night together. And now I'm in your home, sitting beside you enjoying champagne, in front of a wonderful romantic fire amid rose petals. This is not your everyday meeting." She wasn't sure where she was going with the conversation, and by Michael's expression, neither was he.

"I must be honest with you, Vicki," he said, placing his glass on a tray. "I haven't thought much about what happens next. I wanted you here with me because I wanted to spend some time with you. I don't think much about long-term relationships, which would explain why I've never had one."

"So, after this week I go back to Cincinnati, you go about your daily routine, and we act as if none of this means anything? Do you call me up when you're in town and we get together and have sex, then you disappear again? Is that what this is?"

"I don't know what type of commitment I can offer you, or any woman for that matter. My life is on the road. That is what I do, and I don't want to change it."

Victoria listened to him with a somber look. She wasn't sure what answer she was hoping for, but she knew that wasn't it. She felt a hurtful jolt in her heart.

"So what you're saying is that I will be just like the hundreds of other women in your life, an associate?"

Michael paused before he answered her. "That's not what I'm implying."

"No, that is what you're implying, and I'm not sure if it's okay with me. I have so much more to offer."

Michael didn't say anything.

She continued to sit on the floor, her arms crossed in front of her and her legs tucked beneath her. She felt ridiculous having such a tantrum. What did she expect from him? She would be lying if she said she didn't suspect this all along, but the reality of it hurt.

"I'm sorry. I didn't mean to react like that. I know about your reputation, but I agreed to come here anyway. I wasn't exactly flying blind." Victoria smiled to lessen the tension that had developed in the room. "I have a life in Cincinnati. My family is there, my school, my friends, my boyfriend—"

"Boyfriend?" Michael stopped her.

"Yes, I do have a boyfriend. I believe you've met him."

"I thought you were going to end that relationship."

Victoria looked startled. "I never said that."

"No, you didn't, but I assumed that you were going to." Michael bit his lip before he continued. "Have you had sex with Robert since I left?"

Victoria looked at him and realized he was very serious. "Does it matter?" she asked.

"You're making this seem as if I don't care, and that isn't true. I care very much. I just don't know what the hell to do about it." The soft carpet drowned the sound of his fist slamming into the floor.

He reached for his glass and refilled it, then stood and walked to the fire.

Victoria kneeled on the carpet and folded her arms across her chest. "I'm confused. I don't understand why you're upset."

Michael looked straight at her. The glow from the fire burned in his eyes. "Victoria, you just told me you've been with another man. How can you not understand why I'm upset?"

"Damn it, Michael, haven't you been with another woman since you've left me?"

"That is a different situation!" he shouted.

"Why, because you're Michael Prince? That is total bullshit!" Victoria walked to him and stood inches from him.

Michael emptied his glass, then placed it on the mantel. "I don't like the idea of you being with another man."

"Well, Michael, if you can tell me not to expect any form of commitment or relationship from you other than casual sex from time to time, then don't expect me to sit at home and wait for something more."

Michael dropped his eyes and stared at the floor. "Is that what you want from me, a relationship?"

Victoria paused. "I don't know." She lowered her eyes and shook her head. "I mean, this thing between you and me was never supposed to happen." She made a sweeping motion between the two of them. "Things like this do not happen to people like me. I was to graduate from law school, marry Robert, live in an affluent suburban neighborhood in Cincinnati, have two or three beautiful black children who would go to private school and live boringly ever after."

"You do realize that we've just taken verbal swings at each other just to make some meaning out of all this."

Victoria nodded.

"A relationship with me would never be simple."

"I know that."

Michael took her into his arms. "First of all, you have to stop saying that this was never meant to happen. If that were true, it wouldn't have." He lifted her face toward him. "Promise?"

Again Victoria nodded.

"Do you still want me?"

She smiled. "Yes."

"It won't be easy, for me or for you. There are some things about me . . . my life . . ." Michael stopped talking and bit his lip.

"Are you trying to change my mind?"

"No, I'm just saying that you're going to have to be patient with me. I've never had a serious relationship, but I want to give us a try." Michael paused and took her hand into his. "Will you be patient with me?"

Victoria thought about his question. She didn't fully understand what he was referring to, but the Michael Stewart she had come to know was wonderful and worth the effort.

"I promise," she said, as Michael wrapped his arms around her. She felt warm and safe in his arms, but heaviness appeared in her chest as her thoughts drifted to words spoken by her father after one of her childish temper tantrums.

He had stood inches from her, looked into her eyes, and said, "Sometimes, Victoria, we get what we wish for."

20

Victoria fell asleep on the floor in Michael's arms. When she awoke early the next morning, Michael had carried her to the bed and wrapped a quilt around her. She searched the room for him, but he wasn't there. She rose from the bed and draped a bathrobe around her. She walked to the large glass doors and swung them open so that the gentle morning breeze filled the room. The sun was emerging on the horizon as she stepped onto the cold stone balcony. She stood looking over the rail onto the immaculate landscape surrounding her, then sat on one of the wrought-iron chairs and took in the warmth of the view.

She heard Michael come into the room and walk out to join her on the balcony, his T-shirt and shorts drenched with sweat. He sat in a chair opposite her and slipped off his running shoes.

"That felt good," he said, then stood and kissed her. "Sleep well?"

"Yes."

"Good. I'm going to take a quick shower. How about us walking to get some breakfast. I know an excellent pub not far from here where we could have a delicious meal."

Victoria frowned, a bit disappointed. "You don't want me to cook?"

"Why would you want to do that? You're on holiday."

Preparing breakfast was the only domestic skill she could use to impress him. She had cooked for Robert after their first night together, and now he was convinced she was a wizard in the kitchen.

"I want to cook."

"You don't have to."

"You don't understand," she said with a sigh. "Do you want to know if I can cook?"

"No, not really."

"I'm trying to impress you."

"Oh." He nodded. "You cook very well?"

"No, not really."

"Well, then, that's settled."

"Want some company in the shower?" she asked, giving up.

Michael grabbed her hand and they walked to the shower. Afterward, they dressed and walked to the pub for breakfast. It was the first time they had been together alone in public. Tracy did not accompany them. As Michael had pointed out, his presence in Islington wasn't remarkable as lots of celebrities lived there. He was just one of the commoners. He explained that if they ventured onto Oxford Street it would be quite a different scene.

After the plentiful breakfast of bacon, sausage, fried eggs, mushrooms, tomatoes, baked beans, and coffee, they returned to Michael's terrace house. They walked along a stone pathway toward the back of the house to a small storage building. He opened the door to reveal his collection of motorcycles: two Harley-Davidson road bikes and a Buell sports bike. Victoria walked around each one, fingering their crafted chrome frames.

"Do you mind?" Michael asked.

"Not at all. I love them."

Michael fetched her the extra leather riding jacket and helmet he had hanging in a nearby closet, and they were off. He was going to give her a personal tour of London.

The tour began with a trip to the London Zoo, which Michael loved, followed by lunch in Regent's Park.

"Is that where you studied music?" Victoria asked, pointing to the Royal Academy of Music, then taking a bite of the chicken-liver paté and toast they picked up along the way.

"Oh, no. The principal of the Royal Academy would never admit me."

"I don't understand."

"My flavor of music would not qualify for the Royal Academy. But my mother attended the Academy and went on to join the London Symphony Orchestra. She was a pianist."

"Does your mother live nearby?"

"No, no, she doesn't." Michael finished his toast and stood. Victoria got the feeling he didn't want to continue the conversation. When lunch was over, they returned to the bike and Michael headed north of the city with the sun beaming behind them. He took an abrupt turn down a very small and isolated brick road, then stopped.

They were parked in front of a small abandoned house. Thick wooden planks covered all the windows. The house looked as if it had been abandoned for a very long time.

"What is this place?" Victoria asked.

Michael seemed distant. A dark shadow had come over his eyes as he stared at the house. "I grew up here," he said, never taking his eyes from the house.

Victoria was quiet as she watched him staring off. He dismounted the bike and gazed at the small home as if he were seeing an apparition. He began to walk toward the house as if in a trance, oblivious to her and everything else around them.

Not wanting to be left alone, Victoria joined him and entwined her fingers with his. "You want to talk about it?" she asked. There was obviously a story behind those wooden planks.

"No." He didn't say anything more as he squeezed her hand with each step toward the house. Victoria didn't dare pull away.

Inches from the house, he stopped. He stared at the front door as if he was expecting it to fling open. Moments passed and he remained fixated on the house. When he snapped out of the trance, he turned and briskly walked back to the motorcycle, leaving Victoria standing alone.

"Let's go," he said.

Victoria ran to catch up with him. When she reached him and hopped on again, he started the bike and rode off. She wanted to talk to him about the house but didn't know how to bring it up. She decided to wait until he mentioned it.

Instead of returning to his home, they rode to Speck's studios in central London. When they arrived, Michael introduced her to studio workers and the other band members of Kaleidoscope. The rhythm guitarist, Bobby, remembered her and gave her a hug. He explained that he wasn't surprised to see her because Michael spoke of her often.

Everyone gave her such a warm welcome. She was surprised that no one seemed to give her race a second thought. Victoria took a particular liking to Michael's personal assistant, Nicole, who was also black. Nicole walked Victoria around the studio while Michael excused himself and disappeared with several other musicians.

Several minutes passed before Michael rejoined them in one of the meeting rooms. He appeared more relaxed than he had been all afternoon. Victoria watched as he walked from person to person, slapping them on the back and laughing. He seemed to know everyone there, and she was thrilled he was cheerful again.

After a short time Michael led her to a recording room. He kissed her hard on the lips.

"I've been wanting to do that all day."

"Then why didn't you?" she asked, snuggling closer to him and falling limp in his arms.

Michael smiled, then kissed her again. "Thank you for being here," he said. "It means a lot to me." The light from the overhead lamp twinkled in his eyes.

"Thank you for wanting me."

They kissed again as their bodies leaned backward onto the mixing console.

"Michael," Victoria managed to say as he planted soft kisses on her lips. "Michael, what are you doing?"

"I want you."

"Here?"

He nodded.

She thought about someone coming in, but Michael wasn't concerned. She easily stepped out of her pants as he pulled her to the carpeted floor, their bodies interlocked as they made love. It did not take her long to climax. With Michael, it never did. She curled her body and rolled on top of him. She looked at his naked body beneath her as she continued to hold him inside her.

They lay on the soft carpet, her body resting on his as they caught their breath. They looked up as they heard the door click. Michael grabbed a shirt thrown beside him and draped it across her back, shielding her body from view.

"So this is where you two stole away to." Bobby stood in the doorway and looked at them lying on the floor. "Hello, Victoria," he taunted. Victoria could hear the giggle in his voice. "It's so nice to see you again. Are you enjoying your stay?"

Victoria didn't answer as she buried her head in Michael's shoulder.

"Close the bloody door!" Michael yelled.

She heard the door closing, but not before Bobby burst into hysterical laughter. She and Michael remained on the floor a few minutes longer and laughed themselves.

"Let's go," Michael said as they stood and dressed. He held her hand when they rejoined the others. Victoria could imagine how they must have looked. She didn't have anything to make her hair neat again, and neither of them had taken the time to tuck their shirts in. They had that glow that said they'd just had sex.

They said their good-byes to everyone and rode back to the house in silence. Victoria's head rested on Michael's back while she admired the scenes that whisked by. Taking a deep breath, she closed her eyes and let him lead the way home.

21

After making love, Michael wrapped his arms around her as they lay in bed and watched television. They stayed up much of the night snacking on fruits, cheese, and wine, laughing at the comics on the BBC.

Later in the morning, they returned to the studio for rehearsals. Victoria stayed out of the way by following Nicole around and discovering more about the work she did for Michael. Nicole also told her the story of how Michael had found Victoria in Cincinnati. After he had returned to England, he asked Nicole to find the radio station in Cincinnati that held the writing contest and get more information about the winner.

She blushed.

Later that night, Kaleidoscope was scheduled to play at a private party for one of the execs of Speck's Records. It was to be an informal affair, but it was important for Victoria to look good, so she and Nicole went shopping on Oxford Street.

Victoria loved hanging out with Nicole and never felt uncomfortable with her but was tempted many times to ask questions about Michael. She never gathered the nerve to ask, and Nicole didn't volunteer any information.

After stopping in several shops but not finding anything to her liking, Victoria finally walked into a popular designer store and decided on a long black silk skirt with an unbelievable split to the thigh. The slightest wrong move would reveal everything under the skirt. It was daring and the type of thing Michael Prince's girlfriend would be expected to wear. Instead of choosing the matching black silk shirt, Victoria picked a short tight-fitting shirt made of red silk. She also decided on red sandals and long dangling gold earrings to match. Nothing came with price tags.

Nicole explained, "It's sort of a reality check. If you have to look at the price tag of anything in this store, you shouldn't be in here."

Victoria flinched.

Nicole told her to pick out a few additional outfits for the road, which she did. She chose a few sweaters, two dresses with all the accessories to match, and an exquisite leather jacket she would never find at home.

Then they headed to the spa to have facials, manicures, and pedicures. Afterward they shared a massage room and talked.

"Do you do this often?" Victoria asked as her masseuse worked magic on her shoulders.

"About once a month. But if something really gets to me, I just come here and have a massage."

"This is my first."

"Oh, you should make it a routine. Spoil yourself from time to time."

Victoria made a mental note that she would take Nicole's advice.

After their outing, Victoria was dropped off at the terrace house. Michael was already at the party, and she would be taken there later. The limousine and the driver would drop Nicole off at the studio, then return for her. Victoria thought this arrangement was odd, but she figured there had to be a reason for it.

Before dressing for the party, she took a quick nap to regain some energy. When she awoke, she began to put on her makeup. She never wore a lot. Her collection consisted of pressed powder, blush, eyeliner, and lipstick. Then she began to dress.

"It's party time," she sang as she examined herself in the mirror and bounced out of the room to the waiting driver on the street below.

The party was held in the solarium ballroom on the top floor of the recording studio. The windows provided a breathtaking panoramic view of London.

Victoria searched for a familiar face as she walked around the room. Every time she took a step, she bumped into someone. For the first time since arriving in London she began to feel inept. When her eyes met one of the other guests, she just smiled and kept walking. She grabbed a glass of champagne from the waiter's tray and downed it as she continued her stroll.

"Where is he?" she mumbled as she stood at the open bar and inspected every face around her. She spotted him as she began her third glass of champagne. Michael and the other members of Kaleidoscope entered the room, and it immediately became alive with robust laughter and louder music. The women flocked to Michael and the other band members. Victoria watched as several trays of cocaine began circulating.

She watched Michael as he mingled with the guests, particularly the women. There were two beautiful women walking with him, a blonde and a brunette, one on each arm. Their outfits revealed more body than she would ever dare to expose. She frowned as the women took turns kissing and caressing him.

Michael's arms were wrapped around them, pulling them closer to him and kissing them hungrily on the lips. Her heart fell into her stomach as she watched him squeeze the blonde's breast.

The band members made their way to the stage with Michael grabbing the microphone and a guitar. The music was loud and raucous as Michael screamed into the microphone. His head moved so fast, Victoria thought his neck would snap. She noticed how quickly he began to perspire. The room was very well air-conditioned, but the sweat poured from his body.

He performed wildly on the stage, with incredible energy. This behavior was so different from what he had shown her earlier. She could have sworn she had never met him.

Kaleidoscope played three songs before calling it quits. Victoria made her way from the bar, slowly walking toward Michael. She stood inches in front of him. When he turned and looked at her, she saw no sign of recognition on his face. His eyes were wide and his facial expression blank. He looked as if he had never seen her before in his life.

"Michael," she said as a tray of cocaine reached her. She looked from the tray back to him.

Then it hit her. Michael was high. She hadn't realized it until now. That explained everything. Without knowing what to do, she turned away and headed for the exit. She pushed strands of hair from her face, but she felt nothing. She was numb.

"Vicki!" Michael called after her.

She heard his footsteps following her down the corridor. When she was out of the room, she looked around. She had no idea where she was going.

"Vicki, stop!" Michael yelled after her again. He finally reached her as she found the elevator door.

"Are you okay?" he asked.

She was visibly shaken, but she didn't want him to know exactly how messed up she really was. "Yes, I'm fine," she said looking down at the carpet. "I just needed to get out of there."

"You're a bloody awful liar."

"I don't know what to say," she said, shaking her head. "You're flying pretty high right now."

Michael closed his eyes as he leaned his head against the wall. "I needed a little help tonight, that's all," he said, rubbing his face.

"I knew that you've used cocaine because I saw it our first night together, but I never thought I would actually see you high."

They were silent.

"I wasn't thinking," Michael said, breaking the silence. "I'm sorry."

"What are you going to do about it?"

Michael looked at her, puzzled. "What do you mean?"

"Are you going to get help?"

Michael shrugged. "It's not a problem, just something I do sometimes."

Victoria stared at him. He didn't honestly believe that, did he? "It's going to become a bigger problem one day."

"I got it under control. It doesn't control me."

Victoria took a deep breath, deciding not to pressure him. She didn't want him to think that she was a controlling nag. "Okay," she relented.

Michael took her into his arms and softly touched her face. "You care about me, don't you?"

"Yes, I do, and I don't want you to get hurt."

He kissed the top of her head. They stood quietly in the hall holding on to each other. Her head rested on his chest as she listened to the thump of his heart and wondered if it was normal.

She thought about everything she and Nicole had done to prepare for the evening. She had put a lot of effort into looking good for him tonight, but he was too high to even notice.

22

VICTORIA

Sitting opposite Gerald in the car when we left the grocery store, I thought about James, the rape, Michael, and his drug problems. I couldn't explain why I would daydream about a rape, but I knew where it came from. Every time Gerald and I had sex, I felt like a victim, but in real life there wasn't anyone who could come and rescue me. And when Gerald fell and hit his head, it was what I wanted to do to him. I wanted to hit him so hard that it would knock some sense into him.

We stopped at an intersection, and I glimpsed three young women walking on the sidewalk beside the car. Nothing about them set them apart from any of the other women we had passed. I noticed that one of the women looked at our car, then turned to the other girls, and they also looked. Then they began to giggle. I slowly turned my head to see that Gerald had a fine smile across his face.

"What the hell are you doing?" I asked.

He turned to look at me, then quickly wiped the smile from his face. "Nothing." He accelerated, passing the young women.

"You're flirting with them while I'm in the car?"

"They looked at me and smiled. I smiled back. It was nothing."

"I'm sitting right here!" I screamed with my teeth clenched and the muscles in my forehead tightening. The thought that he had enough audacity to ogle other women while I sat beside him was repulsive.

"You're making a big deal out of nothing, okay?" he said, trying to end the conversation. "If you wouldn't have gained so much weight, I'm sure somebody would want to look at you too."

My first thought was to smash his head against the window, but a cough reminded me that an innocent five-year-old sat calmly in the backseat. Instead, I turned and glared out the window again with my fist tightly clutched against my face.

MICHAEL

When Victoria returned home to the States, she received a welcome she was not prepared for. Photographers came from everywhere and started snapping her picture. Sharon even rushed to the library one afternoon and pulled her out so that she could watch a segment of a tabloid television show that had photos of her and Michael together and a video of them getting into the limousine at the studio party. Almost every kiss they had shared was captured on film.

She could not recall ever seeing anyone with a camera, and she definitely hadn't seen anyone with a video camera.

"Oh my God!" she screamed. "My father is going to see this!"

The telephone in the apartment rang constantly with calls from reporters requesting exclusive interviews. She recognized some of the names of the magazines but not all of them. Most were tabloids.

She couldn't walk to class without being harassed by reporters or blinded by a camera flash. Several times she and Sharon returned home only to find more reporters and photographers swarming the halls interviewing their friends and asking questions about her. Studying in the library was now a luxury she no longer had. The intrusions became such a problem that the dorm complex had to hire extra security to keep the reporters out.

As a result, her grades dropped and she was now in jeopardy of losing a number of her scholarships. If that happened, she would either lose her apartment with Sharon or she would have to get a job to subsidize the cost. Working a part-time job would take away valuable study time.

She spent most of the time since she'd returned from England locked away in her room with the telephone unplugged. She couldn't talk to Michael because of his travel schedule, which did nothing to calm her anxieties. Everything happened so fast, she didn't have time to prepare for the intrusion. For some reason she hadn't thought about how her life would change because of Michael, and he hadn't bothered to warn her.

The Black Student Council office was the only place she could go and find solace. For some reason, the photographers didn't follow her there. She sat in one of the conference rooms and read from her sociology textbook. She heard the front door when it opened but didn't bother getting up.

"I thought I'd find you here."

Robert walked into the room and sat down hard in a chair opposite her. The look on his face was beyond anger. It was contempt.

"You lied to me," he said, pointing at her.

Victoria dropped the pencil she held in her hand and met his stare.

He started to say something more but held back his words and bit down hard on his lip before he spoke again. "That was really fucked up, what you did," he said, then stood up and started pacing the floor.

She wanted to apologize to him, but she doubted it would make a difference. The scorn in his voice would not go away just by her saying the right word. "I'm sorry," she said, softly. She felt obligated to at least make an attempt.

"You should have said something. You should have told me before you even got on that plane."

"I know. I just wasn't sure if I wanted to lose you." As soon as she said it, she knew that was the wrong answer.

"So, I was a backup just in case things didn't work out between you and your white lover?"

This is going to get ugly, she thought, then shifted in her seat. "Robert, I can't justify what I did. It was wrong and I can't make it right." Knowing that nothing she said was going to make things better, she continued, "Everything happened very quickly, and I didn't know what I wanted to do. I didn't do the right thing by you, and for that I am sorry. I didn't mean to hurt you."

She watched the anger in his face grow deeper. She had never known Robert to be a violent person, and she'd never seen him mad before.

"You and I slept together after I met him in your apartment, and there is no way you're going to tell me you didn't fuck him that night."

Victoria just stared at him.

"The sight of you is disgusting. I'm transferring out of here so that I don't ever see your face again. I cannot believe that you could be so stupid."

She drew back. "Stupid?"

"You're a white man's bitch. That's all you will ever be to me."

"This conversation is over," she said, gathering her books.

"Well, maybe it's a good thing you are with him because I have no intentions of marrying a stupid bitch."

"Go to hell," she mumbled, and left.

───※───

"Are you okay?" Sharon asked as she walked into Victoria's room.

Victoria sat on the bed with her legs pulled up to her chest. She wiped the tears from her eyes and shook her head. "This is becoming a bit more than I bargained for. Robert said some pretty awful things to me."

Sharon sat down on the bed and tried to comfort her. "Victoria, what did you expect? You cheated on him."

"But it's more than that."

"Then what?"

"It's because Michael is white. I cheated on him with a white man, and he will never forgive me for that."

"Does it matter if he forgives you?"

She shook her head. "No, but it makes me wonder what the rest of the world thinks about my relationship with Michael. Robert says the only reason Michael wants me is for sex. Is that what people are going to think?"

"Michael can have any woman he wants, black or white."

"I know that, so why does he want me?"

"Have you asked him?"

"No."

"Do you want to be with him for the right reasons?"

Sharon's question caught her off guard. "What do you mean?"

"Why do you want to be with Michael? You know about his lifestyle and that beautiful women throw themselves at him every day."

"Am I not beautiful enough to be with him?"

"That's not what I'm saying."

"Then what are you saying?"

"Don't try to build your self-esteem by being with Michael."

"There's nothing wrong with my self-esteem!" Victoria yelled.

"Okay," Sharon said, waving her hand. "Let's drop this conversation. If anyone should be upset with you about Michael Prince, it should be me. You stole my man."

They laughed and hugged each other until they were interrupted by the telephone.

"Ugh, I can't believe I forgot to unplug that," Victoria said, hesitating before she answered it. "Hello!" she screamed into the receiver.

"Vicki?" She cringed as she immediately recognized her father's voice.

"Dad!" she said, surprised to hear his voice instead of that of a reporter. She gripped the telephone and squeezed her eyes together waiting for him to yell at her.

"Young lady, we have been trying to get ahold of you for days!" he screamed into the receiver.

"I'm sorry, Dad, but I've been pretty busy."

"I was on my way to that school."

"I'm sorry. I didn't mean to worry you."

"I want you to come home. I want you to come home now."

"Dad, I can't come home right now. There are two weeks left before midterms. I just can't leave right now." Victoria's mind drifted to her lack of accomplishments so far this semester. She had three very important papers due, but thanks to the generosity of her professors who knew the pressure she'd been under, she received extensions on two of them.

It took her ten minutes to explain to her father why she couldn't come home. The schoolwork was a valid excuse, but the truth was she just didn't have the energy to go into combat with her father. She promised to go home as soon as the semester was over. She thought it was wise not to mention that she had made plans to join Michael in England as well.

Dealing with the reporters and Robert was one thing, but dealing with her dad was going to be something entirely different. He was too boisterous, too powerful, and too intimidating to be taken lightly.

After hanging up the telephone, Victoria rested on the bed and stared up at the ceiling to collect her thoughts. She thought about Michael and wished he was there to help her get through all this.

She reached across the bed, grabbed her criminology book from the nightstand, and began to read.

23

Summer vacation was going to be different this year, Victoria realized as she finalized her plans to spend two months touring Europe with Michael. The media frenzy around their relationship had eased, but the details of the union were still a hot topic.

After she finished the last exam, she drove home as promised. The drive was just a little more than an hour, but today it seemed much longer. Normally, Victoria looked forward to her mother's wonderful home-cooked Southern meals, but not this time. As she drove along the busy highway, she rehearsed what she was going to say and how she was going to defend herself.

"Everything happened so quickly," she repeated aloud. "I just didn't get the chance to tell you guys before the reporters showed up." She shook her head and tried again.

"I just didn't know that I was going to get involved with him. It all happened so quickly." Again she shook her head.

"I'm screwed."

When Victoria pulled into her parents' driveway she immediately spotted her sister's car. She always looked forward to seeing her family and sharing stories. Unfortunately, this visit would be different. She knew everyone wanted details of her relationship with "that man." But most important, they would want to know why she hadn't told them.

When she got out of the car, she was bombarded with hugs from her niece, nephew, and her two sisters. No one mentioned Michael. They went inside and dinner was served. The subject still did not come up as they stuffed themselves with turkey, dressing, collard greens, macaroni and cheese, and sweet potato pie.

Victoria put a forkful of dressing in her mouth only to glance up and notice Elaine staring at her. The eye contact with Elaine convinced her that her father had forbidden them to talk about Michael at the dinner table.

After dinner she joined Lois and Elaine on the front porch for casual chitchat as they often did.

"Girl, you're going to have to tell us something, quick before Dad comes out," Elaine said, peering into the house. She had moved closer to Victoria and lowered her voice. "What's going on with you and this white man?"

"We're dating," Victoria answered simply.

"Dating my ass, you're going to have to do better than that. You flew to Europe to be with him and didn't tell us shit. Dad is furious."

"What is he saying?"

"Victoria, he saw the pictures. What do you think he's saying?"

Victoria sat back in the chair and sighed deeply. How was she going to handle this? She was wrong not to tell them about her trip, but she had her reasons.

"Personally, I can't believe you're sleeping with a white man," Elaine continued, still peering inside the house. "Damn, Victoria, what was wrong with Robert?"

"Nothing was wrong with Robert. My relationship with Michael has nothing to do with Robert."

"He is gorgeous for a white man, but how is he . . . you know?"

Victoria looked at her oldest sister. That was it. That was what she wanted to know. She wanted to know how Michael was in bed. Victoria grinned. "I have no complaints."

"I've heard," Lois spoke for the first time during the conversation, "they're only good for money."

"Oh, Lois, shut up," Victoria and Elaine said simultaneously at the ridiculous remark.

"Does he treat you right?" Elaine asked.

"Oh, yeah. When we walk down the street, he holds my hand. When we lie in bed together, he wraps his arms around me and holds me. He doesn't have sex with me just because I'm lying naked beside him. He'll massage me until I fall asleep. When I talk, he listens, and when I'm at the other end of the room, I can turn in his direction and see him looking at me, smiling." Victoria exhaled.

Her sisters were staring at her.

"What's going on out here?" Her father's voice broke the silence as he stepped onto the porch. He looked at all of them until his eyes rested on Victoria.

"Nothing, we were just talking," Victoria answered.

"Victoria, come take a walk with me," her father summoned.

"Will Mom be joining us?" she asked, hoping. Her father was always on his best behavior when her mother was around, and Victoria was sure that if her mother joined them, he would be less curt with her.

"No, she will not be joining us."

Damn, they must have already discussed that.

It was time. He was going to let her have it, and it wasn't going to be pretty. Victoria nodded and walked behind him down the flight of stairs toward the back of the house. She knew exactly where he was taking her—to his territory and domain. The deck.

Years ago, her father built the deck, and he made sure everyone knew it. "Built it with my own bare hands," he would say. Whenever he wanted peace and quiet from the rest of the world, he retreated to the deck.

They walked slowly up the steps leading to the sitting area. She heard every creak the wood made; it seemed to be talking to her. Warning her, perhaps.

He sat in his usual seat and looked out on the yard. His calm demeanor surprised her. She had thought he would be ranting and raving, but he did none of that. He looked at his flower garden, each seed he had carefully planted. Every spring and summer morning, she would find him on the deck having his coffee and reading the newspaper. Victoria often thought of her parents and the way they did things. She could never imagine herself having everything in her life so well put together.

"How's school?" he quietly asked while taking off his eyeglasses and cleaning the lenses with a lint-free cloth he kept in his shirt pocket.

Victoria sank in her chair, unable to relax. She looked around the gardens as he did, trying to remain calm. "Fine. My grades dropped a bit this semester, but I should be able to bring them back up next semester."

Her father only nodded as he put his glasses back on his round face. "Would that have anything to do with your involvement with a certain man we've been reading so much about? And why did I have to learn about my daughter's involvement with this man from strangers?"

Victoria took a deep breath. It hadn't taken him long. The battle had begun.

"I thought I knew you, Victoria. I thought I knew all my daughters. But I was wrong. I don't know you at all."

Victoria wanted to sink deeper into her chair and hide within the cloth that covered the pillows, but she knew she couldn't do that. She sat up straight and prepared herself.

"I never thought . . . I never thought you would cross over," her father said. "I never thought you would do that. I thought you were smarter than that."

"Dad—" Victoria began, but he cut her off.

"Don't you know what they used to do to black women? They used to come at night and rape them. And you, my daughter, are sleeping with one voluntarily."

Oh, that hurt. She felt a stab in her heart when he said that. She took a deep breath and closed her eyes tight to ease the burning. She had never known that her father felt so deeply about this. They never talked about it growing up because no one in her family had ever brought home anyone who was not black.

"Victoria, you're dating a white man. As if that isn't bad enough, you pick the worst one you could find. A rock-and-roll, drugged-out punk. My God, you went to college and got stupid."

Victoria gasped. *Stupid?* This was the second time she had been called stupid. She was being hit hard, and no one was giving her time to catch her breath. Her father had never called her a name before. She had always been Daddy's little girl, never anything other than that. The tears started to roll down her cheek.

"Robert is a fine, young, educated *black* man," he said, continuing his assault.

"My relationship with Michael has absolutely nothing to do with Robert," she said softly. "I didn't plan for this to happen, it just happened." She wiped tears from her face.

"I don't understand," her father said. "I just do not understand how you allowed this to happen."

Victoria very proudly proceeded to tell her father an abbreviated version of how she met Michael and of how he found her again. Her father just sat in his chair and shook his head.

"You slept with a man hours after meeting him."

Victoria stared at her father. She did not mention sleeping with Michael that night, but she knew her father was not dumb.

"Dad, we have established a commitment—"

"A commitment," he interrupted her. "What type of promises has he made?"

Victoria fell silent. Everything that she and Michael had discussed had been intimate, and she wasn't going to go into details with her father.

"Victoria, you can't possibly think this man is going to be honest with you. Use your brain. You're not that naïve. He's going to sleep with you and marry a white woman."

"We've just started dating, and neither one of us has ever mentioned marriage. If we do, there is no reason why he wouldn't consider marrying me."

"When you're intimate with someone, marriage is always in the back of your mind whether you discuss it or not, and I'm telling you it won't happen."

"Why not? Do you think I'm not good enough?"

"You're a beautiful black queen. Of course you're good enough, but that is not the point."

"Then what is?"

"Is he good enough to marry you?"

Victoria paused. She had never considered whether Michael was good enough for her. She was too busy wondering if she was good enough for him.

"I know you will be a terrific wife and you will love him and do whatever it takes to make your marriage work. But will he love you the way he is supposed to to make you happy?"

"I don't know what you're talking about. Michael is successful—"

"Michael's success has nothing to do with you and his ability to be a good husband. Is he going to be seen in public with you, or is he going to hide you away? Does he want a family? Will he be truthful and faithful to you? You need to be able to answer those questions before you get involved with him."

Victoria was stumped. Hadn't her father heard anything she'd said? Michael went through the trouble of traveling to the United States to find her. Of course he would be able to make a commitment to her.

"If Michael had only limited interest in me, he would have just left and never come back."

"Not true. A man will tell you everything you want to hear to get back into your bed. And he'll say it perfectly. Don't go by what he says or what he used to do. Pay attention to what you see."

Victoria looked at her father dumbfounded. They had never talked like that before. These were things that should be coming from her mother, but her mother had never said anything like that to her before either.

Her father continued. "Pay attention to his lifestyle because that is what you will be marrying. From what I see on television, Michael is known to be in the company of beautiful women and a lot of drugs." His voice trailed off. "Are you on drugs?"

"No, I'm not on drugs." She stood and walked toward the railing. She didn't know if she should be angry, complimented, or offended by everything he'd said. He had called her stupid, a beautiful queen, and now a possible drug addict all in the same conversation.

"We all get wrapped up in fantasies sometimes. I'm sure this is very exciting for you. You're traveling to exotic places and you're meeting famous people. Don't lose focus on reality."

"And what exactly is that?" she asked, turning to face him.

"Just open your eyes and see him for who he is."

"How can you tell me to do that when you haven't?"

"I beg your pardon," he said, retreating to his chair.

"You say that he's not capable of making a commitment to me just because of his career and because he's white. You haven't taken the time to get to know him."

"And have you?"

"He asked me to join him this summer, and I'm going to. I leave in two days." Victoria folded her arms in front of her and faced her father, but he wasn't having that. He stood up and towered over her.

"I didn't raise you to be a fool. If you want to be a fool, then you go ahead and be a fool." He stood only inches away as he looked down upon her. "Until you come to your senses, I have nothing further to say to you." He brushed past her and walked toward the front of the house.

Victoria stood agape staring after him. She had never known her father to be a hypocrite. How could he tell her to open her eyes and see the real person when he refused to get past his color? She lost respect for her father, and that was something she'd never thought would happen.

<hr />

For the two days of her visit, Victoria found it extremely difficult to be in the same room with her father. She would look at him and feel a tingle in her nose followed by burning in her eyes as she kept the tears from falling. She wanted so badly to make him understand what was happening between her and Michael. They were falling in love, and it was beautiful.

"Are you still going to do this? Are you still going to London?" Her father stood in her bedroom doorway and watched her packing a few things she needed for her trip. The weather was fair in the U.K., and Michael had instructed her to pack light. She was scheduled to take the early-afternoon flight, and her sisters volunteered to drive her to the airport.

"Yes, I am. Michael is expecting me."

Without saying anything, he turned and walked away.

Victoria stared at the empty doorway where he had stood. Her nose started to tingle again, but she refused to shed a tear.

Lois and Elaine escorted her to the airport as promised. Victoria was quiet most of the way even though she appreciated their company and the fact that they had not shunned her as well.

"You have to follow your heart, Victoria," Elaine said. "If your heart is with Michael, then that's where you should be. You're not Daddy's little girl anymore, and you can't live your life the way he wants you to. Do what's right for you." Victoria wondered what had happened in Elaine's life to give her such wisdom.

She smiled and squeezed her big sister's hand. She was glad somebody understood.

24

Victoria arrived in England ten hours later. After leaving the plane and going through customs, she looked around the busy airport expecting to see Michael standing nearby, waiting for her. The nerves in her stomach were jumping as she giddily stood looking from side to side, but she did not see him. As she continued to look about the busy area she did see a familiar face, but it wasn't Michael's.

"Hello, Ms. Jordan." Tracy reached out to take her small duffel bag.

"Hi, Tracy. Is Michael waiting in the car?" she asked, removing the bag strap from her shoulder.

"No, he could not get away from the studio. He instructed me to return you there." Without further words, he escorted her to the parked limousine and opened the door for her to get in.

Disappointed, Victoria slid into the backseat and settled against the soft leather seat, preparing for the drive into London.

"How long have you worked for Michael?" Victoria spoke as Tracy wove in and out of the airport traffic. Almost every time Michael appeared in public, Tracy was there. She wondered if he had family of his own.

"Three years," he replied briskly.

"You're not from here?" Victoria asked, quickly picking up on the fact that he did not have the same English accent as the others.

"No, I'm from L.A. I met up with Michael while he was on tour there about three and a half years ago. He offered me a job as his personal bodyguard, so here I am."

Victoria nodded as she listened to him and was grateful she didn't have to struggle to find words for a conversation.

"Ms. Jordan, I hope you don't mind me saying this, but you don't look the type," Tracy said after a brief silence.

Victoria frowned. "Excuse me?"

"The type I am accustomed to seeing with Michael. You don't look the type."

"And what type is that?" she asked, giggling.

"I think you know the type I'm talking about." Tracy was not smiling. "Be careful."

Now she was baffled. Was this some sort of warning? Should she be fearful of being here?

"What do you mean by that?" she asked as she leaned forward in her seat.

"There's a lot that goes on with these guys. Sex, drugs, it's all here." His voice was stern and protective.

"And Michael?"

"He's Michael Prince. What more do you need to know?" He didn't say anything further as he broke away from the traffic heading into London.

Victoria settled against the leather seat again and glanced out the window. Her father's words and Tracy's warnings echoed in her ears.

What was she supposed to do with that information? she wondered.

○○○○○○○○

They continued their drive into London in complete silence. When she walked into the studio, everyone immediately recognized her and informed her where she would find Michael. She forced a smile as she made her way through the halls. She needed Michael now more than she ever had. She needed his reassurance to calm her worried mind.

She heard the music the second she stepped off the elevator. Slowly she walked down the long carpeted corridor toward the door where the music was coming from. She wanted to find Michael and get out of there. She was in no mood to party.

Taking a deep breath before she opened the door, she swung it open and closed her eyes as the smoke rushed into her face. Her nostrils quickly filled with the mixture of tobacco and marijuana scents as she walked in.

The dimly lit room was filled with people. She conversed briefly when someone stopped her and welcomed her back. She hugged her, not remembering her name, and continued walking about in search of Michael. The first person she recognized was Bobby, and she rushed to him.

"Hey Victoria, welcome back," he said loudly and threw himself into her arms. When he kissed her hard on the cheek, she smelled the alcohol and marijuana on his breath. "How have you been?"

"Fine, thank you," she said, trying not to breathe in. "Have you seen Michael?"

"He's over there," Bobby said, pointing.

She saw him sitting away from the crowd but in the company of many women. He held a rolled marijuana cigarette and took a long drag from it. Victoria watched as he passed the joint to the women around him.

With her eyes watching his every move, she walked toward him as if she were watching a scene being played out in a movie. She stood in front of him, unable to move or speak to get his attention.

"Hey." He rose from the sofa, removing his arm from around the shoulder of the woman sitting beside him, and walked to her. He pulled her into him and kissed her hard on the lips. The taste of marijuana and the scotch he had been drinking was on his tongue.

Grimacing from the taste, she quickly stepped back from him.

"How was your flight?" he yelled over the music.

"Fine." She couldn't find words to say more as her agitation with the party grew. "Can we get out of here?" As she waited for an answer, she felt a presence close behind her. When she turned, a woman walked briskly past her and stood close to Michael. The woman passed him a joint she held in her hand as she very casually slipped her other hand around his waist. Then she turned and blew a soft cloud of smoke into his face.

Victoria watched in bewilderment at the exchange. Immediately, she knew this woman was not just a groupie.

"Sonya, this is Victoria," Michael said, backing away from the woman.

"Oh." The woman turned and looked at Victoria, then took her arm away from him. "Hi." Sonya extended her hand toward Victoria, who looked at the outstretched hand and then at the woman. She was beautiful. She was tall, slender, and slid comfortably into Michael's arms.

"You son of a bitch." Victoria was looking at Michael, ignoring the extended hand. "Is she the reason you couldn't meet me at the airport?" Without waiting for an answer, she turned and headed for the door.

This trip was a huge mistake, she thought, shaking her head.

"Vicki, wait," she heard him call after her as she walked briskly toward the door, dodging the many people blocking her path.

"Vicki, please." Michael took her arm as she reached the door. "I need to explain," Michael pleaded.

She turned with fury to meet his eyes. She wanted to yell, she wanted to run, she wanted to kick, she wanted to scream, but all she could do was look at him.

He stammered, "I can explain."

"What the hell could you possibly explain? You're sleeping with another woman. What is there to explain?" Her voice was loud and emphatic. Those standing nearby clearly heard the exchange. Sonya heard her too, because she saw the woman drop her head and move toward the back door.

"Your girlfriend is leaving. Perhaps you should go catch her." Victoria pulled away from him and stormed out the door. With

Michael close behind, she walked quickly down the hall, where she spotted Tracy standing by the elevator.

"Victoria . . ." Michael took her by the arm again, only to have it yanked again from his grasp.

"Don't touch me," she said sharply. She turned away from him and spoke to Tracy. "Could you please take me to a hotel?"

"Bring the car around and drive us back to the house," Michael ordered.

Tracy dropped his eyes and went to get the car.

"I'll get a taxi," she said angrily as she began to walk away. Michael quickly grabbed her arm before she had the opportunity.

"No you won't." He held her arm tightly, ushering her away from everyone.

Seconds later, Tracy pulled up and Michael rushed her inside the car. They sat quietly in the backseat as the limousine sped down the road. Victoria huddled close to the door, putting as much distance as she could between her and Michael. Tears began to fall rapidly from her eyes, but she quickly wiped them away.

"Vicki, I'm sorry." Michael slid across the leather seat and sat closer to her. "I'm sorry." He picked up her hand from her lap and squeezed it.

"Sorry isn't going to get it this time, Michael." She continued to dab at the tears.

Michael took a deep breath and leaned back in the seat, his hand tight on top of hers.

"I don't understand why you asked me to come here," she asked after a long silence.

"I wanted you here."

"Why? You can have any woman you want, why me? Why bother?"

Michael sat up straight and faced her. He brought his hand to her face and caressed it with the tips of his fingers. He traced the side of her face as he put his hand on the back of her neck and touched her forehead with his own.

"I need you." His voice cracked.

Victoria separated herself from him and leaned against the window. She turned her head and faced the window, only to see his reflection in the glass. She watched as Michael squeezed his eyes shut and threw his head against the seat.

"There are things I can't talk about," he said as he began to tousle his hair.

"What things?"

He was silent for a long time before he answered. "The house . . ."

"What house?"

Michael continued to tousle his hair. "Sometimes I just want to forget," he said as he closed his eyes tight.

Victoria turned to see the creases across the corners of his eyes. "What are you trying to say to me?"

Michael grabbed his chest and pressed hard against the leather seat. He began to pant as if he was fighting to breathe.

"Oh my God!" she screamed. Her first thought was that he was having a heart attack. She grabbed him and laid him flat on the seat.

"Michael!" she screamed. She was about to turn and bang on the partition that separated them from Tracy when Michael grabbed her hand and pulled her down to him.

"I'm okay," he said, still gasping for air. He continued to hold her down as his breathing slowed to normal.

Victoria's head rested on his chest as he began to whisper into her ear. "Vicki, the way you feel right now and the things that are happening right now are the reasons I ran from you after our first night together. You scared the bloody hell out of me. I fell in love with you."

Victoria rose to meet his eyes but he pulled her back down as he continued to whisper in her ear. "I didn't want to hurt you, but I knew I would."

She squeezed her eyes shut, trying to keep the tears from falling. When she lifted herself up and looked down at him, the tears fell.

"I love you," he whispered to her.

Victoria pulled herself from his chest and sat across from him.

Michael rose from the seat and kneeled down in front of her. He held her face in his hands as he stared into her eyes.

She dropped her eyes, unable to look at him. "I don't know—"

"I can do better," Michael interrupted her. "I can do better. I promise." He planted small kisses all over her face as he wiped the tears with his thumb. "Please stay with me. Will you stay?"

Victoria raised her eyes and met his. Her face was still in the palm of his hands as she nodded. Michael took a deep breath as if he had been holding it for a long time or as if it were the first breath of his life.

25

Victoria rested in bed, her naked body snuggled against Michael's, his arms wrapped around her. She could feel his breath against her ear as she stared into the darkness thinking about the night's events. She thought about the disappointment of not seeing him at the airport and the hurt afterward.

"I want to tell you I love you, but for some reason it doesn't seem to be enough," Michael said.

Victoria didn't say anything as she toyed with the hair on his arm and continued to stare into the darkness until he fell asleep.

Morning arrived, and they enjoyed a casual breakfast at the pub near Michael's home. They sat alone on the back terrace, surrounded by beautiful flowers and ponds, while other patrons ate inside. Victoria spoke maybe five words. She had been hurt before, but never like this.

In the past, if someone simply said something the wrong way or if she didn't agree with an idea, she walked away. It was never hard to leave someone your heart was not with in the first place.

"You're quiet. What's on your mind?" Michael asked, placing his fork on the small table.

Victoria shook her head as she picked at her plate of grilled kippers. Although it was a very common dish in the U.K., the idea of eating fish for breakfast did not appeal to her, even though she had promised to give it a try.

"Would you like to order something else?" Michael asked.

Victoria shook her head no and put a forkful of the kippers in her mouth.

"Talk to me, Vicki." Michael leaned against the back of his chair.

Victoria put the fork down and covered her face. She tried to hide the tears that were beginning to fall, but she couldn't. They streamed between her fingers, and her sobs replaced the sounds of nature around her. When there were no more tears and her sobs could no longer be heard, she looked up at him and wiped her eyes with the back of her hand.

Michael picked up the cloth napkin from the table and handed it to her. Still, he didn't say anything.

"I'm sorry," she said, wiping her eyes with the napkin.

"I understand."

They were silent as she dried her eyes.

"Do you feel better?"

Victoria nodded.

"Are you ready to leave?"

She nodded.

They rose from the table and walked from the pub along the streets of Camden Passage, undisturbed. The conversation picked up as she managed to smile while they browsed the antique shops. The air in the U.K., Victoria noticed, was usually damp, with clouds overhead. It sprinkled a lot, not heavy downpours, but it was usually wet. Michael was an avid collector of art and artifacts, and he picked out several pieces that would look great in her apartment and in her room.

They spent much of the day walking, stopping only for drinks and a light lunch of chicken-liver paté and wine. The late-afternoon walk came to an end, and it was time to return to Michael's place to prepare for another concert. Nothing was mentioned of her morning tears or the events of the previous night.

They arrived early at Wembley Arena, where the concert was to be held. While Michael made his usual preparations, Victoria got the opportunity to assist Nicole with paperwork and to sit in on talks with the facilitator to make sure all legalities were met. She was getting firsthand experience of the business aspects of the music industry.

Kaleidoscope shared the stage that night with several musical groups. During Kaleidoscope's performance, Victoria remained backstage but had a full view of the stage. Her eyes did not leave Michael as he paraded around. She admired his energy and understood why he was so popular with the women. Everything about him was sexy. The way he walked, the way he moved his lips, his screams, his whispers, the way he held the microphone, everything.

The band began to play the song Michael sang to her their first night together. Of course, this was the original rock version, but he dedicated the song to her, then turned and pointed to her as she stood backstage. To hear him speak her name in front of thousands of screaming women took her breath away.

As the concert went on, Nicole grabbed Victoria's arm and took her inside one of the dressing rooms. There she had laid out five gowns. A makeup artist and hairstylist stood by.

"What's going on?" Victoria asked as Nicole began to size her up with the gowns.

"There's a party after the concert. Sonya will be there." Nicole held a gold dress to her and nodded. "Wear this one." It was an extremely elegant gold-laced, double-layered silk gown. From the waist to the floor, the bottom layer was a transparent silk, a slightly lighter shade of gold than the top layer. When she stood in the light, the contours of her body would easily be seen. The top of the backless gown was the same silk lace of the layer underneath the skirt. When she took the gown in her hand, it seemed to weigh no more than an ounce.

"You're kidding, right?" Victoria asked as she held the gown against her body.

"No. Put these on." Nicole handed her two pads to lift her breasts. As Victoria eyed the gown, she could see that her breasts would be exposed and only the nipples would be covered by a slightly thicker lace. "Trust me," Nicole said before Victoria had a chance to protest.

Victoria shrugged, then slipped out of the jeans and shirt she had on. "Nicole," Victoria said as she sat down for the hairstylist to get started, "who's Sonya?"

"She's a model. A very well paid model."

"Who is she to Michael?" Victoria asked.

Nicole said nothing as she helped with the transformation. Victoria understood the silence. When everyone had finished with her, Victoria looked at herself in the mirror and felt like a princess on her way to meet her prince. She smiled at the beautiful woman staring back at her.

"Thanks, Nicole. I really appreciate this."

"It's my job," Nicole said. They both knew that this was far from being in her job description.

∞∞∞∞∞∞

The concert lasted several hours, but the time flew by. Afterward, it was off to the parties held in hotels around London. Victoria arrived at the first party with Michael, Bobby, and two other members of the band. She smiled as they were photographed but tried desperately to avoid photographers.

All night she was introduced to studio execs and people she would never remember. In fact, Michael made it a point to whisper to her after an introduction if she needed to remember that person. This made her laugh.

"Your laughter is comforting," Michael said.

Victoria turned toward him, and he kissed her softly on the lips. As she walked around the atrium with Michael, she couldn't help but notice when Sonya arrived. Her escort for the evening was a very popular musician from one of the other bands that had performed at the concert. Sonya's presence was like a magnet. She had such beauty and grace that as soon as she stepped into the room everyone turned to look at her.

"You're very beautiful tonight," Michael said to Victoria as they stood off in a corner.

Victoria grinned. "Thank you."

"Where did you get that dress?"

"A woman never reveals all of her secrets." She laughed.

"Let's get out of here," Michael announced as he loosened his tie. "We've spent two hours with these old chums." Michael gathered Bobby and his date, Chloe, and they left the party. Following close behind were Tracy and a few other bodyguards. When they reached the limousine, Michael popped a bottle of champagne. The four of them sat in the limo laughing and joking. Victoria learned that Chloe was also a model and a regular at Kaleidoscope concerts.

They drove from the downtown hotel to one in the West End. This party was much quieter and more secluded. Only invited reporters lingered taking pictures. After Victoria and Michael arrived, they were escorted to a suite and given the key. They were obviously staying the night. She noticed a change of clothing for both of them had been placed in the bedroom.

They changed into jeans. Michael explained that this was not the kind of party they had just left. This party would be attended mostly by friends. As they dressed, Michael opened up another bottle of champagne.

When they walked down the hall to the private suite, the other members of Kaleidoscope were already there, as were several other musicians from the concert.

"Go mingle," Victoria said, nudging his arm.

Michael turned and looked at her.

"You don't have to baby-sit me. Go talk with your friends. I'll be fine." She walked away from him and turned around to see him smiling at her.

She picked up a glass of champagne at the bar. Chloe whisked by, grabbed her by the arm, and led her to a circle of women. One of them was a model Victoria recognized. Another was a student at London University majoring in fashion design, another was a photographer, and the other was an aspiring actress. All of them were in some way involved in the entertainment industry and were more than eager to fill Victoria in on the dirt.

Their talk became laughter, and several men joined in on the conversation. Another round of champagne followed. As Victoria finished her glass, she began to feel funny. She knew how her body responded after drinking too much, but this felt strange. As she tried to excuse herself, someone took her arm and she felt a breath close to her ear and a hand slipping underneath her shirt.

"I've been watching you." She heard the voice in her ear, but she couldn't do anything. She felt herself walking or being walked away from the noise and everyone else. Her mind was so vacuous she couldn't think if she should resist. Before it went blank she saw the most beautiful shades of red, green, and yellow flash before her eyes and she smiled, thinking how bright the colors had been.

Victoria awoke in bed, naked, a thick comforter covering her body. She turned on her back and stared up at the ceiling. She blinked rapidly, trying to focus on the room and to remember how she'd gotten there.

She tried to sit up in the bed, only to be greeted by a sudden dizzy spell that forced her to lie flat. When the room stopped spinning, she tried again until she was sitting upright. Her eyes focused, and she saw Michael standing on the balcony looking out over the city. The sun did little for the gloom that was cast on his unshaven face.

She was surprised to see that he was wearing the same thing he wore the night before. He held a large coffee mug in his hand and slowly sipped from it.

"Hey," she said, despite her tongue sticking to the roof of her mouth.

Michael jumped and quickly walked into the room and sat down beside her. She looked into his face and immediately saw his red, swollen eyes.

"Hey, how you feel?" he asked, lifting her hair from her face.

"I don't know." She took a deep breath. "What happened? Did I have too much to drink?"

Michael picked up a glass of orange juice that was on the table beside her and put it to her lips. She sipped slowly, and the cold juice began to excite her taste buds. When she'd had enough, Michael placed the glass on the table and took her hand again.

"Last night at the party . . . do you remember the party?" he asked as his fingers caressed her hand.

She thought for a few seconds. Yes, she remembered being at the party, but she didn't remember leaving. How did she get back to the room?

"Yes, I remember the party. It's kind of hazy but I remember. I don't recall leaving."

"Well, at the party . . ." Michael stopped talking and licked his bottom lip. "You were drugged."

Victoria gasped. "What?"

"You were drugged with what is known in the U.S. as a roofie. Do you know what that is?"

Victoria shook her head.

"It's the date-rape pill," Michael said, then paused.

Victoria's mouth dropped open as her heart fell into her stomach.

"You had quite a bit of champagne, and when he gave you the pill I think you just passed out. That's why you don't remember leaving the party. Amnesia is a side effect of the drug."

"But I just had the champagne and I didn't taste anything different. I would have been able to taste something in my drink."

"No, no, not roofie. It has no color, no taste. There was no way for you to know it was in there."

Victoria trembled as she clutched the sheet. "Was I—"

"No, nothing happened," Michael said, stroking her face to reassure her. "I saw him as he tried to walk you out, and I ran over to you. I carried you back here and put you to bed."

Victoria let the breath out of her lungs. "Are you sure? You're not lying to me about this, are you?" Her hands were still trembling as she gripped the sheets tighter.

"I promise, Vicki. Nothing happened. I got to you. I wouldn't lie to you about that." He took her hands and squeezed them.

"Oh, God," she said as she buried her face in his shoulder.

"I have been apologizing ever since you arrived." Michael pulled away from her and walked to the balcony. "I wanted this to work, you know. After fumbling things up when you first arrived, I promised myself I would do better, and now this." Michael turned to face her. "Maybe you should think about returning to the States."

Victoria stared at him as her mind went numb.

"What if I hadn't gotten to you in time . . ." Michael turned away from her again and grabbed the edge of the glass door leading to the balcony.

"Michael," she called to him, but he didn't answer her. "Michael," she repeated as she reached out to him.

He turned around and looked at her outstretched arms. He took three steps and fell into her arms.

"I don't blame you for what happened at the party. That wasn't your fault. I just have to be more careful." Michael lay in her arms, and she rocked him until he fell asleep.

〰〰〰〰〰

They slept the remainder of the morning in each other's arms. When Michael awakened later that afternoon, they shared a much desired bubble bath. They returned to bed, where they sat up nibbling on fruit, biscuits, and crisps while watching television. Later, they invited Bobby and Chloe to their suite. Michael picked up the guitar and performed a solo that was absolutely astonishing. Victoria sat on the edge of her chair with her head resting in the palm of her hand and her eyes glued to him. When he finished playing, she walked over to him and kissed him so deeply that they excused themselves and rushed into the bedroom, leaving their guests spellbound on the sofa.

〰〰〰〰〰

For two months she toured the U.K. and Scotland with Michael and Kaleidoscope. On the morning she was to leave, she awoke and found a very beautiful diamond-and-emerald ring on her ring finger. She sat up and searched the room for Michael. She got out of bed, put on a housecoat, and walked down to the second story. She found him in the sitting room sitting at the piano. She raised her finger and pointed to the ring.

Michael smiled. "Do you like it?"

"It's beautiful," she said, touching the ring.

"We're going to be apart for a long time. I wanted you to know that you will go with me wherever I go." He held up his hand to reveal a matching ring on his finger.

Victoria brought her hands to her mouth as tears began to fill her eyes. She walked over to him and squeezed him hard against her breasts.

"I love you so much," Victoria whispered in his ear.

"I know," Michael said. "I love you too."

26

VICTORIA

"You want to come over to my house tonight?" Stephanie asked as we talked on the phone.

"Why, what's up?"

"I'm having company."

I paused long enough to take in the hidden message. "Who's going to be there?"

"Edward, and his brother."

Ah, now the truth is told. Stephanie was trying to fix me up with Edward's brother. "Steph, I don't think so."

"He's cute, Victoria, and he has a good job."

"I don't know," I said, shaking my head. Being with another man was the last thing on my mind.

"Just come on. I told him about you, and he's excited to meet you."

"Does he know I'm married?"

"Yes, he's married too, so you guys can keep it discreet. Just come over and meet him." Stephanie hung up before I had a chance to protest any further. After thinking about it, I got up from the sofa and told Gerald I'd be back.

When I reached Stephanie's house, I saw the mystery man's car parked in the driveway. I slid my fingers along the paint, trying to pick up some kind of vibe from it. I shook my head, telling myself I shouldn't be there.

"Come on in." Stephanie met me at the door and quickly escorted me downstairs. "Victoria, this is Kevin. Kevin, this is my friend Victoria." Then without waiting for us to shake hands, Stephanie left the room.

"Hello," Kevin said as he eyed me up and down. "Stephanie failed to mention how beautiful you are."

Oh, God. I lowered my head so he wouldn't see me as I rolled my eyes. I knew that all he wanted from me was someone to have sex with.

"Thank you. I can't stay long. I have to get back home." I walked over to the sofa and sat down. Kevin nodded and followed me.

"Understand. So tell me, what do you like to do?" he asked as his hand found its way to my leg.

"Meaning?"

"Do you like going to movies, dancing?"

"Yes, I do." I took his hand in mine and held on to it to keep it from exploring up my skirt.

"The next time you want to hang out, you can just page me." He wrote down his number on a piece of paper and handed it to me. "Don't lose that."

I nodded, taking that to mean, "Don't let your husband find that."

"You're a nice-looking woman."

"Thank you. Maybe we could take a walk sometime and talk," I said, shifting the conversation.

"Yeah, that would be nice. We should do that." He put his hand on my leg again and slid a finger slightly up my skirt. "Why do you wear such baggy clothes? You have a nice ass. You should show it off."

At that point I knew that Kevin was not listening to me. He couldn't care less about getting to know me or what was on my mind. If I told him about my dreams and desires, he wouldn't listen. I had one of *those* at home. I didn't need another one. "I have to go now," I said, getting up from the sofa. "It was nice meeting you, Kevin."

"Be sure to call me. You and I should really hook up."

I looked at his eyes, and they were not on my face. He was peering around to stare at my behind. He even went so far as to crook his neck and made a noise inside his throat that I assume was supposed to be a compliment. It was not. The thought of turning around to walk out of the room didn't appeal to me, but then I found pleasure in knowing that his stare would be the closest he would ever come to touching me again.

I hurried out of the room and gave him a full view of my behind as I left. I wished I had the nerve to smack it and toss a finger up at him. I reached the front room where Stephanie and Edward were sitting watching television, laughing and sharing a joint.

"You leaving so soon?" Stephanie jumped from the sofa and hurried toward me. "How did it go?" she whispered in my ear.

I took her arm and pulled her to the door as I walked out. "Next time you want to introduce me to someone, let it be someone who wants a little more than just a piece of ass." I waved at her and walked to my car, where I burned the number in the ashtray, then headed home.

27

JAMES

There was a unique bond between Victoria and James. Victoria boasted about how easy it was to talk to him because there were no sexual stresses in their relationship. She enjoyed entertaining him and his friends in her home. For one thing, it kept them off the streets and out of trouble. There was no alcohol for them to get into at her home or cigarettes they could smoke.

One thing Victoria did miss was going out dancing with James. She loved to dance, but they could no longer go to the club. They did enjoy going to movies or on picnics, or just staying home, renting movies, and talking.

When she felt the need to be around people her own age, she and Monica would go to one of the local clubs to dance while James hung out with his friends doing his own thing. Not once did she question him about his activities, nor did he question her. It was the most trusting relationship she had ever had in her life.

For the most part Victoria was able to get along with James's friends, but she couldn't conceal her resentment of his ex-girlfriend Tai. Monica teased her about being jealous of Tai and James's friendship, which was not true. She wasn't jealous of it, she just didn't like it. She was particularly ticked off by the way Tai made references to James in a sexual way. She had to stop Tai a few times when she did this, by reminding her that James was *her* boyfriend and she didn't appreciate it. Victoria also didn't like the way Tai very aggressively tried to befriend her. This obvious put-on made her very weary.

The conversation came up again as they lay across the bed watching a movie. After ten minutes of unsuccessfully trying to persuade James to be leery of Tai's motives, Victoria decided to drop it and to concentrate on the movie.

She lay on her stomach, her elbows resting on the soft comforter while her head rested in the palm of her hand. Her legs, bent at the knees, were crossed in the air.

"Are you comfortable?" he asked, lying beside her.

"Yes." Contrary to how it may have looked, she found the position very comfortable. As she watched the movie, she felt James's feet entwine with hers. She smiled and continued to watch. Soon her feet began to sway. She looked over at James, and he only smiled.

"What are you doing?" she asked.

"Nothing," he said as her legs again swayed to the other side.

Victoria laughed as he continued to push her legs. When he stood up, Victoria thought the play was over but it wasn't. He grabbed her legs and began to tickle her feet. She burst out laughing and flipped over on her back trying to break free from him, but he was too strong.

"No!" She laughed as she tried to kick from his grip. James released her feet but worked his way up her side, straddling her. They laughed heartily until she felt his mouth on hers. She pulled on his bottom lip with hers as he pulled back from her only to go back to her and kiss her again, deeper.

She wrapped her arms around him and pulled him down on top of her. He lifted her shirt and cupped her breasts, squeezing her nipples. She moaned as he slipped the white cotton shirt over her head and took one of her breasts into his mouth. Her fingers ran feverishly in his hair as he sucked on her swollen nipples. She felt his hand fumbling with the zipper on her shorts, and she reached down to help him.

She never knew what it was, but something grabbed at her as her fingers entwined with his. When she opened her eyes she stared at the ceiling and remembered.

"Oh my God." She pushed him off her and sat up quickly on the bed.

"What is it?"

She took quick breaths, trying to get a grip on what she was doing. She wiped her face as she tried to calm down. "We can't do this." She scrambled to the other end of the bed and grabbed her housecoat.

"What?"

"Oh, I am so sorry." She hid her face in her hands.

"Please, don't do this."

"I have to."

"Vicki, who's going to know?" he said, sliding off the bed and walking toward her. Before he could touch her, she backed away.

"I can't believe you're doing this." He stopped walking toward her and sat down on the bed.

"I'm sorry."

"Do you want to be with me?"

"Yes, I do."

"Then why are you doing this? I'm not a virgin."

"James, please don't do this to me."

"We've been dating for months. Everyone knows about our relationship, so you're not going to lose your job. Your ex-husband is on trial for what he did to you, so you're certainly not going to lose your daughter. I want to know why you're running away from me."

Victoria took a deep breath before she looked at him again. She remembered the promise she made to his parents.

"James, I made a promise that I would not force you to grow up too fast."

"You know that I'm not a virgin, right?"

"Yes. Tai makes me very aware of it." She cringed at the thought.

"So, I won't be doing anything with you that I haven't done already."

"But that doesn't justify it."

"I don't understand what you're getting at."

"Yes, I want you, but it's just not time."

"Are you ashamed of me?"

"That's ridiculous. Of course not."

"We have a solid relationship, yet you won't make love with me. I don't understand that."

"We don't have to use sex to strengthen our relationship."

James stared at her. His desire to be with her would not let him understand what she was saying. "Forget it." He picked up his car keys and stormed out.

28

VICTORIA

I sat in the soft cushioned seat flipping through the pages of *Ebony* magazine waiting for Desiree to finish setting up her booth and call me back. When it came to getting my hair done, I always made the first appointment of the day because I didn't want to wait for hours for my turn in the chair.

"I'm ready for you, honey," Desiree finally said, swiveling the chair toward me.

When I sat down, she raised the chair and fingered through my hair. I was long overdue for a retouch on my perm.

"Your hair sure has grown. What are you getting done today?" She lifted several strands, looking at the condition of my scalp.

"The usual."

Desiree stopped fingering through my hair and looked at me through her mirror.

"Now, Victoria, you've been coming to me for almost a year now, so I feel I can be honest with you."

I looked at her reflection in the mirror, curious where she was going with this conversation.

"Short hair makes you look old. You'll look much younger with longer hair." She reached into her drawer and pulled out a lock of human-hair extension and held it to my head. "See what I mean?" She turned the chair so that I could see my reflection in the mirror. "Do you want me to add some extension?" she asked, beginning to manipulate my hair while looking at my reflection in the mirror.

"No," I said sharply. "I don't want to be bothered with long hair."

Desiree frowned when I turned her down. "But—"

"No," I said, cutting her off. "I don't want it."

She relented. "Okay, it's your hair." She threw the extension back in the drawer, grabbed the scissors, and resumed her conversation with the beautician in the space beside her.

She talked about the surprise birthday party her husband had thrown for her on a riverboat. He had invited all of her relatives and friends, and no one said a word about it. He had planned everything from the catering to the music; all she had to do was show up. She then showed off a diamond tennis bracelet that he had given her. She stopped working on my hair and walked around the boutique showing it off.

"You like it?" she asked, stopping at me.

"It's lovely. How long have you been married?"

"Two years," she said proudly.

"Two years. And he does all that?"

"This is the time when he should. In ten years he's going to be sick of me." She laughed.

"I've been married for five years, and my husband has never done anything like that for me."

"Then leave his ass and find you a man who makes you feel special." She put the scissors to my hair again and began clipping.

"It's not that simple," I said rolling my eyes. "I have a daughter."

"Then your daughter needs to see how a man is supposed to treat a woman, otherwise she's going to marry someone just like her father because that's all she's seen. How is she going to know that it's supposed to be different if she's never seen any different?"

I didn't say anything. It couldn't be as simple as that. I had a responsibility to make sure my daughter was provided for and had the best life possible. I couldn't give her a home in the suburbs or pay her tuition to one of the best schools in the city. She loved her father. What type of mother would I be, taking her away from her father?

Desiree turned my back toward her again. "Now. Let me finish cutting your hair."

JAMES

Victoria had taken a shower and gotten into bed. She had dozed off a few minutes before the phone rang.

"Hello," she said sleepily into the phone.

"Were you asleep?" It was James.

"It's okay," she said, sitting up in the bed. "I wasn't expecting to hear from you tonight."

"I want to apologize. I was wrong for leaving the way I did."

"No, it's my fault," she said. "I'm the adult, and I should never have allowed things to go that far."

"Vicki, if I am going to continue to be your boyfriend, please don't treat me like a child."

Victoria grimaced. She hadn't realized she was doing that. "Do I do that a lot?"

"No, you don't. But it comes out from time to time."

"I'm sorry. I don't mean to."

"I know," he said. "There's another thing I need to talk to you about."

She didn't say anything but waited for him to continue.

"Prom is coming up."

Again she grimaced. She hadn't thought about that. Attending James's senior prom would present a very awkward situation. She was casually acquainted with a lot of the faculty at James's high school because she would bump into them from time to time at the jazz club she and Monica went to. Some of the men even asked her out, but she turned them down. She told the truth, that she was involved with someone, but she never said with whom.

"When is it?" she asked. She wanted to know how much time she had to think of a good reason to tell him why she couldn't go.

"Next week."

"Next week!" She shot up in bed and gripped the phone tighter.

"Don't get so excited," he said. "I'm not going."

"Why not?"

"Because I know you wouldn't want to party with a bunch of high school kids, and I understand that."

She exhaled. "Would you really do that for me?"

"It's the truth, isn't it?"

Now she felt horrible. James had every right to attend his prom, and her apprehension was not a good enough reason for him not to go.

"James, I want you to go," she said, biting her lip. God, she hoped she wouldn't regret saying that.

"I'm not going to the prom alone. It's no big deal."

But Victoria couldn't drop it. "I'm serious, James. I want you to go."

James was about to add something, but she interrupted him.

"I want you to ask someone to the prom."

"Yeah, right. You want me to take another woman out?"

"Yes, I do. I trust you, I love you, and I want you to go. It's important."

"Why?"

"Because this is your life and I can't hold you back. I went to my prom, and you have a right to go to yours." She exhaled.

"You sure about that?"

"I'm very sure. Just be home by ten o'clock."

<hr />

As prom day drew closer, Victoria wasn't so sure she had made the right decision. She became more and more apprehensive, but she said nothing. Was she throwing him into the arms of another woman? Things had been tense since that night when she refused to have sex with him, and now this.

She tried to rationalize everything, but she found herself crying at times. She had never met anyone who made her as happy as James did. They were at different points in their lives, and she knew the time would come when she would have to let him go.

Finally, prom night arrived, marking the end of the longest week of Victoria's life. She had hardly seen James that week because he was busy preparing for the prom. She wanted to give him his space, but she also wanted to know details of his evening.

Victoria knew James wasn't going to have any problem finding a date, but he didn't mention whom he had asked. She wondered if he was taking Tai. She cringed at that thought.

Victoria had the day planned—actually, it was Monica who had made the plans because Victoria was too depressed. She and Monica had gone out that morning to the mall to have facials and to get their hair and nails done. Afterward she wasn't ready to go home, but Monica had to leave because she had a date. They had left Reese with Monica's sister, who offered to keep her for the night. At first Victoria resisted, not wanting to be alone, but Reese was having so much fun playing with Monica's niece that she didn't have the heart to take her away.

When Victoria returned home, the house was empty and quiet and she couldn't call James. She sat and stared at the television even though she wasn't watching it. When the doorbell rang, she welcomed the intrusion.

She looked through the glass in the door and saw James standing on the porch, smiling at her. Slowly she opened the door. "What are you doing here?"

He looked so handsome that it took her breath away. His small beard was neatly trimmed. His hair was cut low, just the way she liked it. His skin was smooth, clear, and glowing. He was wearing a splendid black tuxedo with an emerald cummerbund, bow tie, and handkerchief. And when he smiled at her, she froze.

"Oh my," she said as she stepped back from him.

James smiled. "Are you going to invite me in or what?"

She shook herself, then stepped aside to let him in. When he walked in the doorway she noticed a large, beautifully wrapped silver package in his hand.

"What's going on?" she asked as she closed the door behind her and looked at the package.

"I'm on my way to the prom."

"Where's your date?"

James smiled again and handed her the package. After frowning at him, Victoria took the package and opened it.

She could only stare at the beautiful silk emerald gown. Even in the box it was the most gorgeous thing she had ever seen in her life. She placed the box on the sofa and lifted the gown from between the tissue paper and hugged it to her body.

Confused, she looked at him. "I don't understand."

"You and I have a date for the prom. Our prom. Just the two of us. I know you insisted that I go, but Vicki, I couldn't imagine being anywhere without you. If I am going to have the time of my life, it has to be with you by my side, not anyone else."

Victoria's mouth dropped open. "Are you serious?"

James nodded. "Go get dressed."

The largest smile of her life crept across her face as she ran upstairs to her room. She threw off her old jeans and T-shirt and slipped carefully into the delicate silk gown. When she had finished dressing she examined herself in the mirror. She took her hair and pinned it up off her shoulders. She searched through her jewelry box and found a pair of gold-and-emerald earrings.

Taking a deep breath, she turned and walked to the stairs to meet James. He stood at the bottom landing waiting for her and held his hand out. When she reached him, he pulled out a beautiful diamond necklace.

"My mom wants this back," he said as he clasped the necklace.

Victoria laughed.

With the help of his parents, James had reserved a small hall in the city. His mother decorated it for the evening using all of her creative talents to make the room perfect for a prom. Silk plants lined the walls, and the dinner table was lavishly set with elegant black china and an emerald linen tablecloth. A beautiful arrangement of wildflowers sat atop their table in a sparkling crystal vase with candles burning beside it. Their names were inscribed in gold on the crystal goblets placed on the table.

She also learned that James had recruited Monica's help. It was Monica's job to get Victoria prepped without knowing she was getting prepared for the prom and to baby-sit.

Dinner was served by the catering service Katherine had hired. Their servers were dressed in black tuxedos. A photographer had arrived for just a short while to take pictures at Katherine's request. Soon after they had finished dinner the catering service left.

The first dance of the evening was to their prom theme song, "New Beginning" by Tracy Chapman. The prerecorded music was playing on an elaborate stereo system. They danced until the glow of the sun appeared in the window. Then they walked to the waiting limousine and drove to Eden Park to watch the sunset.

When James escorted Victoria to her front door, they were quiet, as they had been for the last few hours. When he turned to kiss her good night, she held on to him as long as she could.

"I don't want you to leave," she said softly as he held her.

"It's not time," he said. He kissed her softly on the cheek, then walked back to the waiting limousine. He blew a kiss as the car sped off down the road.

30

The party began promptly at nine o'clock, and the house filled with teenagers from James's high school and his friends from the neighborhood. Some students from the high school where Victoria taught were also present. She felt a bit out of place socializing with some of her students, but being with James and looking forward to the following night more than compensated for any uneasiness she felt. Tai was at the party too, of course, and although Victoria despised the girl, her presence didn't bother her.

"The party is great," Victoria said to Katherine as they prepared more food in the kitchen. For most of the night the adults tried to stay out of the way.

"Yes, it is," Katherine replied.

Victoria flinched at the bland tone in Katherine's voice. "Katherine, I don't know if it's me, but is something wrong?" Victoria asked. "Did I do anything to offend you?"

"No, why do you ask?"

"Because you've been very curt with me all night."

Katherine looked at her and shook her head. "You're right. I'm sorry." She touched Victoria's hand and squeezed it.

"Anything on your mind?" Victoria asked.

Katherine took a deep breath and placed the platter back on the table. "Yes, there is. We need to talk." She took Victoria by the arm and led her into the empty family room and closed the door behind them. "James won a scholarship to George Washington University."

"That's wonderful!" Victoria said, putting her hand to her chest.

"He's not taking it," Katherine said.

"What do you mean, he's not taking it?"

"He's turning it down because he doesn't want to leave you."

"He's not taking it because of me?" Victoria frowned. "Are you sure?"

"Yes, he told Jonathan and me this afternoon."

"Katherine, I swear I didn't know anything about this."

"I believe you, but I don't know what to do. On one hand, you were the best thing to have happened to him. He started focusing on his grades and joined the youth-in-government club. But now he's reached a point where he has to go forward—"

"And I'm holding him back," Victoria said, finishing her statement.

"I didn't say that."

"You didn't have to."

Katherine hugged her before walking out and rejoining the party.

Victoria stayed in the room and sat in the large leather chair. What was she going to do? Should she tell James to go to Washington, or should she let him choose a school in Cincinnati? She wouldn't have to worry about losing him if he stayed in Cincinnati. He could get his undergraduate degree at Ohio University, then go on to Ohio University Law School and everything would be okay. They could be happy together. She would spend the rest of her life making sure he wouldn't regret giving up the scholarship for her.

She couldn't lose him. She just couldn't lose him.

"Vicki."

She jumped, startled out of her thoughts.

"Are you okay?" James asked.

"Yes, I'm fine." She forced a smile and held out her hand for him to join her.

"Why are you sitting in here alone?"

"I had to sneak away for a minute and think."

"About what?" he asked, pulling her from her seat toward him.

"Making you happy."

"I like that," James said as he kissed her. He held her in his arms as they continued to kiss.

It was good to be away from the crowd and in his arms. She kissed him hard and didn't want to let go. They slid further onto the sofa until she was lying on top of him and his hand caressed the skin underneath her shirt.

"Excuse me, you two." Jonathan had walked into the room and looked at them lying on the sofa. "You do have guests out here."

James and Victoria looked at each other, embarrassed, but laughed. They rose from the sofa and rejoined the party.

James arrived at her house early Saturday evening to help her prepare the meal. It was difficult for them to finish cooking because they kept stopping and kissing. After sampling the food, they followed with a five-minute passionate kiss.

Miraculously, they finished cooking the meal without burning it, then sat down at the table to eat. They nibbled their food and stared at each other. Victoria was determined to get through this. She had planned this day for a long time, and she wanted it to be perfect. She didn't want to just rush into bed with him. She wanted to cook for him, she wanted to wait on him, and she wanted him to know how much she loved him.

As they sat quietly at the table, James removed a small black box from his pocket and placed it open on the table.

Without him having to say anything, she knew what it was and her heart dropped from her chest into her stomach. She looked at it and then at James. She watched as he picked up the box and removed the small, simple diamond solitaire from its velvet holder. He took her left hand, bent down in front of her, and slipped the ring on her finger.

"Will you marry me?"

Her mouth would not open. She wanted to say yes more than anything in the world. She had won his heart. He was going to stay in Cincinnati, and they could be together forever.

She mumbled, "I don't know what to say."

"Say yes." He was still holding her hand while her heart pounded inside her chest. It was too much. She couldn't take the pounding any longer. She drew back from him, stood up, and stumbled to the other side of the room, almost doubling over.

James walked up behind her. "Are you okay?" he asked, reaching out and taking her into his arms.

"Yes," she said as she turned away from his touch.

"What is it?"

Victoria stood, using the back of the sofa for support as she tried to look at him. When she finally did she nearly broke into tears. "Why didn't you tell me about the scholarship?" she finally asked.

James shrugged. "It's not important. I'm not taking it."

"Why not?"

"Because I'm not," he said. He walked to her and took her in his arms. "Now, how about concentrating on something more important, like our future together."

"This is important. I need to know why you didn't tell me about the scholarship."

James stepped back and stared at her. "Don't do this again."

"Do what?"

"Run away from me."

"I'm not running away from you, but I need to know," she pleaded.

"What do you want me to say, Vicki? You know why I'm not taking it."

Her heart felt like it had stopped as she burst into tears. "Oh God," she said, dropping her head and praying for strength.

"Don't do this, Vicki. Don't do this to me again."

She continued to cry. "I can't." She walked over to him and placed the ring in his hand. "I can't."

James fell back against the wall.

"I am so sorry."

"You kept saying, 'It's not time, it's not time.' You never had any intentions of being with me, did you?"

"That is simply not true. I want to be with you."

"No, Victoria, it's not time. And guess what?" He turned and stared at her. "It will never be." He turned away from her and walked out of the house, slamming the door behind him.

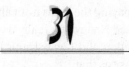

VICTORIA

"Have you ever given any thought to going back to school?" Nancy asked as I sat in her office one afternoon.

"Many times, but I've never pursued it seriously."

"Why not?"

"Because I never knew what I wanted to do with my life. I attended classes but never did exceptionally well."

"Maybe because you weren't taking the classes that suited you."

I shrugged.

"What were some of the things you've considered?"

"Well, anything that's technology-based makes good money."

"Are you a technical person?"

"No, but I'm told that if I want to make enough money to live off, I need to be in technology."

"Making a lot of money is nice, but will it make you happy?"

"Probably not."

"So what do you want to be when *you* grow up?" Nancy asked.

I took a deep breath and thought about some career ideas I had entertained once upon a time.

"There are two areas I've given serious consideration to: teaching and law."

"Oh, really," Nancy said, straightening up. "You have some good schools right here in Cincinnati to choose from if you pursue either one of those."

I waved her off. "It doesn't matter. I can't afford to go back to school, and I don't have the time. Gerald has made it perfectly clear that fully supporting me was not his responsibility. I have financial obligations, and I don't make a lot of money. Gerald, on the other hand, makes very good money, which eliminates my chances of getting financial aid."

"What about student loans?"

"They have to be repaid, and I don't have the extra cash."

"You don't begin paying the loans until after you finish school."

I had to give it to her; Nancy was really trying to jog my hopes of continuing my education. But I was skeptical; it all sounded good, but it was never as easy as that.

"I take it you've given up on that option."

"I've given up a long time ago, along with many other things."

"Things like what?"

"Things like happily ever after," I said.

"You don't believe in happily ever after?"

"No, I don't."

"But there can be happiness."

"Well, just call me stupid, because I haven't found it."

"That doesn't make you stupid."

"Well, it must be, because Gerald calls me stupid every day for everything I do. My mother thinks I'm foolish for not thinking I have a wonderful life. And Stephanie thinks I'm daft for at least not having an affair. I can't seem to do anything right in anyone's eyes."

"Victoria, you're not stupid," Nancy repeated.

"My life is a mess, and all I want to do is to lock myself in my room and daydream about how my life could be or would be, and I have no idea how to make it any better." Tears started to stream from my eyes. Nancy handed me a tissue, and I sat there and cried.

Nancy waited until my sobs grew quiet and I wiped my nose before she spoke again. "How often do you daydream?" she asked, handing me another tissue.

"Every chance I get. That's how I escape. They're not sappy stories, and I don't know why they come to me the way they do. And I can't talk to anyone about them because everyone would think I'm crazy if I told them some of the things I think about."

"Well," Nancy said, sitting back in her seat and crossing her legs. "Tell me about them."

MICHAEL

Commencement day approached at Ohio University, and Victoria and Sharon were among this year's graduating class. Sharon had already accepted a position in the physical-therapy department of a hospital in Boston. She was returning to her hometown to be with her family.

Victoria hadn't committed herself to any school. She wasn't sure if she wanted to stay close to her family or to relocate. Among her choices were Harvard, Yale, UCLA, Princeton, and Ohio University Law School. Any of those would have been good, but she wasn't sure which direction to take because she hadn't discussed it with Michael.

It was uncertain whether Michael would make it to the ceremony. She understood his hectic traveling schedule, but she had worked so hard for this moment and she wanted to share it with him. Even if he couldn't attend, she would most definitely be joining him for the summer touring.

For the Jordan family, graduation day was the social event of their lives. Not only was Victoria graduating from college, she was going on to become a lawyer. That made her parents and sisters proud, and they boasted of her accomplishments to everyone in the neighborhood.

"What are you doing?" Sharon asked as Victoria pulled back the curtains and scanned the auditorium, standing on her toes.

"I'm looking for Michael."

"Victoria, I don't think he's going to make it. Come on." Sharon pulled her from the curtain and back to her place in line.

The commencement exercises began, and the students were led out into the auditorium. The ceremony lasted two hours, and when it was over, the new graduates, degrees in hand, rushed to meet family and friends on the back lawn for the reception.

Victoria ran to her parents. "I did it!" she screamed, and leaped into her father's arms, then her mother's. She searched the grounds for her sisters and saw Michael and Bobby standing with them. She screamed.

"You made it!" She jumped into his arms, almost sending them both to the ground. "Did you get here in time for the whole thing?"

"Yes, we saw the entire ceremony," Michael said, and hugged her tight.

She turned and gave Bobby a hug. "This is incredible. You guys made it." She took Michael by the hand and led him to her father.

"Dad, this is Michael." Full of smiles, she introduced the two most important men in her life to each other. "Isn't he wonderful?" she said, and kissed Michael.

33

The party given in her honor later that night was held in her parents' backyard. Sharon and her family also stayed for the festivities, and it was indeed a soulful affair. Her cousin provided the music, while all other family members ate collard and mustard greens, baked beans, potato salad, macaroni and cheese, barbecue ribs from her father's famous secret recipe, fried chicken, peach cobbler, and sweet potato pie. Michael marveled at how delicious everything was.

Everyone spent the evening eating, laughing, and dancing. She and Michael danced heartily on the lawn to all of their favorite tunes, fast and slow. She challenged her younger relatives to dance contests, which she easily lost. She just couldn't keep up with them. Michael even tried, and when he tripped over his own feet everyone laughed. Victoria even noticed a chuckle from her father, who remained stern-faced most of the day.

The delight of the evening came when her cousin played her favorite Regina Belle tune. She immediately turned to Michael.

"Did you—"

Michael smiled. "I might have."

Victoria walked into his arms, where she stayed for the remainder of the night. Before long it was dark, the only light coming from the poles situated around the lawn. The music continued on the CD player, though her cousin, the evening DJ, had left a long time ago with almost everyone else. Those who remained had gone inside, and she and Michael were still dancing on the lawn.

"Victoria! Michael!" Victoria turned to see her mother walking toward them. "I prepared the guest room for Michael and his friend, and of course, Victoria, you have your room. We're going to bed now. Good night." She kissed both of them on the cheek.

Victoria smiled at Michael, who also smiled. "Thanks, Mom," Victoria said as she kissed her mother on the cheek. "We'll be in shortly."

Her mother turned and walked back into the house.

"Separate rooms, huh?" Michael laughed. "You want to go get a hotel?"

Victoria laughed. "No, that would be obvious and rude." She pinched him. "My parents are old-fashioned. They don't allow couples to sleep together in their home unless they're married."

Michael said, "Oh, is that right?"

They continued to dance as Victoria felt his hand pulling her closer to him.

"What about getting married?" he asked after a brief silence. "If we were getting married, would they allow us to sleep in the same room?"

"I don't know. I never asked." She held him as she listened to the music in the background and the sound of his heart in her ears.

"Well, I think we should find out," Michael said.

She stopped dancing and looked at him. "What are you talking about?"

Michael didn't answer her. He lifted her arm, spun her around and into another dance. She shrugged it off and continued to dance. Michael spun her around again, but when she faced him this time, he stopped and looked directly at her.

"Will you marry me?"

She froze.

Think, Victoria, think. What is he asking you? Her mouth fell open. Was he asking her a question regarding their sleeping arrangements? Was he asking her if she *would* marry him *if* he asked, or *would* she marry him because he *was* asking?

"What are you asking me?" she asked nervously. Was she getting worked up for no reason at all?

Then Michael knelt down in front of her and looked up at her.

"Oh my God," she whispered, watching his knee touch the ground.

"Victoria Jordan, will you marry me?"

She backed away from him and put her hand to her mouth to keep from screaming. "Oh my God," she repeated.

Michael smiled and reached for her hand again. "You're having a hard time with this, aren't you?"

She nodded. "Are you asking me to marry you?"

"I'm trying to, but you're backing away from me saying, 'Oh my God.' Can you help me understand if this is a good thing or a bad thing?"

"Yes." She smiled and touched his face.

"Yes?" he asked.

"Yes." She nodded.

"Yes what? Yes you will marry me, or yes you're going to help me understand?"

"Yes, I will marry you."

"Oh," Michael said, then a huge smile crept across his face. "I'm glad we've established that."

Victoria laughed. "You look so cute down there," she said giddily.

"I look vulnerable down here," he said, and took the large diamond solitaire from his pocket and slipped it on her finger.

Victoria looked at the ring on her finger and smiled. "Oh—"

"Don't say it," he interrupted. "Just say you like it."

"I love it."

"Good," he said, and stood up to kiss her. "Are you ready to go inside?"

Victoria swallowed hard and nodded. She put her hand into his and they went inside. He walked her to her room, and they stood outside her door and kissed passionately until her back thumped against the door.

They saw the light come on in her parents' room and chuckled softly. Seconds later they saw her father emerge from his bedroom with his housecoat draped around him. Michael kissed her softly on the cheek, then stepped back.

"I'll see you in the morning." He let go of her hand and made his way to the guest room, saying good night to her father as he passed the kitchen.

Victoria chuckled as she heard the exchange.

She walked into her room and closed the door behind her. When she fell on the bed she screamed into the pillow. She and Michael were going to get married! Married. She was going to be Mrs. Michael Stewart.

She turned over on her back and stared up at the ceiling, squeezing the pillow to her chest. *Married,* she repeated. *She was marrying Michael.*

Slowly, she pulled herself from the bed and began to undress. She had just slipped into her favorite Mickey sleep shirt when she heard the first tap on the window. Thinking she was imagining it, she ignored it until she heard it again. Cautiously, she walked to the window and drew back the curtain to see Michael standing on the other side.

"What are you doing out there?" Hurriedly she opened the window.

"Shhh." He put his finger to his mouth to quiet her as he jumped and climbed in the window. Victoria reached for his arm to help him, being extra careful not to make any noise. When he was in, they stopped and listened for the sound of feet coming down the hall. After seconds had passed, he pulled her into his arms and kissed her hard on the lips.

"You really didn't think I was going to let my future wife spend this night alone, did you?" he asked. Then he kissed her again.

Victoria melted in his arms as they fell upon the soft carpeted floor and made love.

<hr />

They slept that night in each other's arms and woke up long before anyone else, so he could exit her room the same way he had entered it. Victoria took the opportunity to shower and dress before others were up, wanting to do the same. By the time she had finished dressing, the house was full of voices. She joined her mother and sisters in the kitchen to help prepare breakfast.

It was Elaine who first noticed the ring. Just as Victoria told them that Michael had proposed to her, her father walked in, followed by Michael and Bobby. The room immediately became festive again. When the excitement had finally subsided, everyone sat down for a huge breakfast of sausage, bacon, eggs, grits, home fries, and toast. It was enough food to feed a small army.

Everyone offered opinions as to what they should do for their wedding. Elaine thought she should marry next summer, since it took at least a year to plan a huge wedding like the one they should have. Lois thought of a big winter wedding. The more everyone talked about the wedding they should have, the more Victoria withdrew.

"I was hoping for a nice, quiet, intimate affair," Michael said, taking her hand.

Victoria smiled and realized that he'd noticed that she didn't like any of her family's ideas. "So was I," she said.

"How about here, one week from today?" Michael asked as he stared into her eyes.

"Perfect." She kissed him.

"Are you crazy?" her mother protested. "Do you know how much planning goes into this?"

"Keep it simple, Mom. We want it simple." She kissed him again.

"That's easy enough for you to say. You're the one getting married, not the one who has to plan it."

Victoria dropped her head on Michael's shoulder. "We've created a monster." She laughed.

"There are so many people to invite. Elaine, go get a pencil and a piece of paper," her mother ordered, and Elaine immediately left the table in search of the items.

"What about your family, Michael?" Mr. Jordan asked. "Will they be attending?"

Michael drew back from Victoria and stared at the table. "No, no, they won't be."

Mr. Jordan asked, "Why not?"

"I have no family. They died."

"Everyone in your family is dead?" her father asked.

"I'm the only one," Michael said, looking sternly at her father.

"Michael, you never told me that," Victoria said, interrupting their stares.

"I don't like to talk about it. It happened a long time ago." He looked at Bobby, then shifted in his seat.

"How did they die?" her father persisted. He wasn't letting the issue rest so easily. "Things like this should be discussed before you get married."

"Dad, please. He doesn't want to talk about it." The subject was dropped.

—∞∞∞∞∞∞—

After breakfast, Victoria telephoned Sharon at their hotel. She was thankful she caught her and her family before they left for Boston. She asked Sharon to be her maid of honor.

Sharon screamed. "You're marrying Michael?"

"Yes!" They screamed together.

"Of course I'll be your maid of honor. Oh my God!" Sharon screamed again.

Victoria laughed. "I know what you mean. I kept saying that too."

That week she, her mother, Sharon, and her sisters frantically prepared for the wedding. Victoria happened upon an absolutely beautiful white silk dress. It was off the rack, nothing designer, but it was the most beautiful dress she'd ever seen. Michael asked her repeatedly if she needed money, and repeatedly she turned him down. This was one thing she wanted to do on her own.

For the remainder of the week, Bobby stayed in a hotel under Victoria's father's name while Michael continued to stay at the Jordans' home in the guest room, although he snuck into Victoria's room at night. The day before the wedding Michael joined Bobby at the hotel.

That night he and Bobby shared drinks and hors d'oeuvres with a few of Victoria's cousins and her father at the hotel as they threw him a small, downgraded version of a bachelor party. The girls gave Victoria a small bridal shower. She received many wonderful gifts, including edible and sexy lingerie.

When the wedding day finally came, Victoria couldn't believe how nervous she was and broke into tears. Her mother warned her she had better stop crying before she ended up with a headache and red puffy eyes on her wedding night.

"It's not like you'll be doing anything new anyway," her mother mocked.

"Mom," Victoria said, not believing what her mother had said.

"Oh, Victoria, please. We know Michael sneaks into your room at night. How stupid do you think we are?"

Victoria's mouth dropped open as her mother laughed.

"Mom," Victoria said when the laughter stopped. "How do I be a good wife?"

"Just be true to each other. Don't take each other for granted."

"Oh, Mom, that's old advice."

"But it's good advice. The way you feel right now is wonderful. Hang on to it because it doesn't last. There are going to be days when he makes you so mad you want to just slap him," her mother said, chuckling. "And there will be days when you take him into your arms and cradle him like he's a baby from your womb. You got to take the good with the bad and just hang on."

"What if I fail? What if I do everything wrong?" Victoria fought to control the panic welling inside her.

Her mother took her hand and squeezed it. "You and Michael are going into this with a lot of strikes against you already."

Victoria dropped her eyes, but her mother lifted her face back up and looked at her. "I've seen the way Michael looks at you. He loves you and he's willing to try. That's the most important part right there. It's not going to be easy. Be patient with him. I think he will make you happy."

Victoria smiled and kissed her mother.

"But of course, if it gets too bad, run like hell and bring your ass back home."

Victoria laughed.

When everyone was finally dressed, they stood around and looked at one another. They were all so beautiful. Sharon had selected a mint green off-the-shoulder dress. Her sisters, serving as hostesses, had decided on silk cream shirts and mint green pants. Her mother looked like royalty in a mint green gown she already owned.

Victoria waited patiently for her nephew to announce Michael's arrival. A few minutes later, he came running into the house screaming that they were there. The nerves jumped around in Victoria's stomach, and she couldn't stand still. Everyone left her alone and made their way outside as the music began to play. Her father met her at her bedroom door and stole an extra minute to hug her.

"You're so beautiful," he said, hugging her tight.

Victoria smiled and held on tight to him. "And I'm still Daddy's baby," she said, and kissed the tear that escaped his eye.

"I know I was very hard on him earlier. I just want you to be happy."

Victoria nodded. "I know."

"Are you ready?" he asked as he entwined his arm with hers.

Victoria took a deep breath and nodded, then let her father lead her down the white runner to meet Michael.

VICTORIA

I could not recall Gerald ever asking me to marry him. I thought about it many times but never could come up with an actual proposal. His exact words were, "We should just go ahead and get married."

There were times when I tried to enact scenes from my day-dreams, but Gerald was never cooperative. So I gave up. But there was one thing I really wanted to do.

"Let's go to a spa," I said to Stephanie.

We were sitting at our usual seat in the park watching Reese play. This time Stephanie had brought one of her nieces so Reese could have a playmate.

"To work out?" Stephanie asked.

"No. A full-service spa to get a massage and a facial and get our hair done."

Stephanie's face lit up. "That does sound like fun. When?"

I faked a cough. "You know"—I coughed again—"I feel a cold coming on."

Stephanie laughed. "That's strange." Then she coughed. "So do I."

When we returned to Stephanie's house, we browsed the Internet until we found a spa that suited us, and we made an appointment for the next day.

I was exhilarated. I had something to look forward to, and that made all the difference in the world. I couldn't wipe the smile off my face.

The next day I met Stephanie at the spa to begin our pampering. By four o'clock we had sat in a sauna and had a body wrap and full-body massages with the sound of the ocean in the background. Our hands and feet were manicured and pedicured, our hair was washed, conditioned, and styled. Before we left for home, we stopped and ate a tuna-salad sandwich.

I had never felt so relaxed in my life. My body felt as if it were floating on a cloud when I arrived home. Gerald had picked Reese up from school, and as usual, they were sitting on the sofa watching television. I walked over to Reese and gave her a big hug and a kiss and began to tickle her.

"You're in a good mood tonight," Gerald said.

"Yes, I am. I had a good day."

"What brought all this about?"

I shrugged. "I had a good day," I said simply. I didn't want to go into details with him because I knew he wouldn't understand.

Gerald turned his nose up at me and continued watching TV.

"It was a beautiful day today, wasn't it?" I walked to the large picture window and leaned against the wall. The sun was still shining as bright as ever. We couldn't have picked a more perfect day for our spa adventure.

"Have you been smoking those funny cigarettes?" Gerald interrupted my thought.

I laughed but ignored his question.

"You have, haven't you?"

I decided to go ahead and tell him about my day. The way I felt, not even Gerald could ruin it. "I went to a spa today. I took the day off work, and Stephanie and I went to a spa. It was wonderful." The grin on my face stretched from one ear to the next.

Gerald frowned. "You wasted money on a spa?"

"It wasn't a waste of money at all. I have some money saved."

"How much?"

"Why?"

"How much?"

"None of your business."

"I want to know how you get to save money to go to the spa and all of my damn money goes into this damn house!" he shouted.

I turned and looked at Reese as she sat on the sofa looking at her father. "Hey, honey, why don't you run outside and play on your swing," I said.

"Okay." Reese jumped up from the sofa and ran out the back door to play in her backyard clubhouse.

"You really need to watch what you say in front of her."

"You didn't answer my question."

"I pay my bills, Gerald."

"Well, since you have all this extra money to throw away at the spa, I have some bills you can pay." He got up from the sofa, went into the kitchen, retrieved some envelopes from the bill drawer, and threw them at me. "Why don't you pay these so that I can go to a spa?"

I took a deep breath, trying to keep the smile on my face. There was no way Gerald was as hard-pressed for money as he claimed to be. He made four times the amount of money I made. He bought a new car every four years, and now he was driving a new BMW. He had a closet full of clothes, and the mortgage on our home was about 5 percent of his monthly income, which he took advantage of by making extra payments. He also paid Reese's tuition. Gerald was good with his money even though he kept his actual portfolio a secret from me.

I was responsible for my personal debts including all of the utilities, food, and clothes for Reese and myself. I managed to pay myself one hundred dollars a month, which I did faithfully, putting it into a savings account. Contributing to a savings account was a necessary expense. My mother had taught me that.

"Always pay you first," she had said.

But Gerald was still ranting. "You can start paying half of the mortgage."

"What?" I yelled. "I can't do that."

"Why not?"

"I can't afford it."

"Well then, get a second job so that you can start paying it."

"And what about Reese? Who will take care of her?"

"If you can go to a spa, you can help me pay this damn mortgage," he said, ignoring my question.

I didn't think that he could ruin my day, but I was wrong. "Fuck you!" I yelled, and stormed out of the room and ran upstairs.

Evil. He was just damn evil. He couldn't have cared less about the money I spent at the spa because he spent at least that much in video games. What pissed him off was that he saw me happy and he was bent on destroying the smile on my face.

I felt tension building and a headache creeping into my temples. I walked to the bathroom, took the bottle of Excedrin from the medicine cabinet, and swallowed two capsules. When I returned to the bedroom Gerald walked in and my headache exploded.

I fumbled to the side of the bed and pulled the blanket over my head.

MICHAEL

The morning after the wedding, Victoria, Michael, Bobby, and Nicole left Cincinnati for London on a private jet. Michael had remembered to call Nicole and had her flown into Cincinnati. After the wedding, Nicole issued a press statement and shared some of the photos.

Immediately following the wedding, the skeptics began to predict how long the marriage would last. Many of them gave it less than a year.

After a brief two-day stay at Michael's home, they boarded the private jet again, bound for an exclusive resort on a remote section of an island near Jamaica. While there, they took a yacht to Jamaica and toured the island because Victoria had never been there. Their honeymoon lasted three weeks.

At night Victoria would often roll over to feel Michael sleeping beside her. When she opened her eyes to watch him sleep she smiled. She was actually in love with her husband.

After the second month of their marriage, much of the hype had dissipated and it was possible for them to resume their early-morning walks. They also ate out a lot because Victoria had never acquired her mother's touch in the kitchen. Most of her meals were thrown in the garbage can. Victoria loved the walking and the eating out because they were able to talk with no interruptions from the television or the telephone. It was decided during one of their walks that she was going to attend law school at UCLA.

The following month they traveled to Los Angeles to make all the necessary arrangements for Victoria to begin school in the fall and to find a place for them to live. Before leaving London, Michael had arranged to meet with a Realtor in Los Angeles. The biggest debate between Victoria and Michael was whether to rent or buy.

They decided to lease a condo in Malibu. Victoria loved the master suite, which was designed so that they could enjoy the beauty of the sunrise in bed or in the small solarium attached to the room. The walls were feather-painted in a light gray with a hint of burgundy. A gray marble fireplace accented the far wall. The window treatments and bed ensemble were a lighter shade of burgundy. On beautiful sunny days the room was so comfortable it was hard to get out of bed. The solarium became one of Victoria's favorite spots, a place to study or to relax with a glass of wine.

Each of them had a fully equipped private office. Hers was not far from their bedroom, while Michael's was in the front with an attached deck. Victoria declined this office because she knew she would spend more time daydreaming than working.

Victoria stayed at the condo alone most of the time while Michael made frequent trips to and from London and other places around the globe, separating them for the first time since they were married.

Victoria absolutely loved the beach, the crystal blue water, and the sunsets. She loved taking strolls along the shore and burying her bare feet in the hot sand. There were no better sights than the sun setting over the calm blue Pacific Ocean and the sun rising behind the mountains.

Autumn marked the beginning of law school for her, and it was as she had expected, hellish. Her mornings and nights were no longer spent walking along the beach. They were spent reading. She would end the day by sitting on the balcony with her head buried, studying contracts and preparing briefs. A criminal-law textbook replaced the morning paper. When Michael returned she was barely able to talk to him because she was simply too busy. It was nothing for her reading assignments to top two hundred pages in a given night.

When Michael was in town she would pull herself from her studies long enough to enjoy a few drinks with him until they were both drunk. Also, when there was time, he would give her piano lessons, which usually ended up with the two of them making love on the floor. On one particular occasion, after they had had way too much to drink, Michael took out a portable recorder and they taped what became their song, "Dream in Color."

When the song was finished, they laughed and fell to the floor.

"You were awful," Michael said as they burst into another round of laughter.

"You don't have to worry about me quitting my day job," she said, laughing.

───── ◊◊◊◊◊◊◊◊ ─────

During her second semester the students were advised to join a study group and she signed up. At the end of the week she met her three new study partners in one of the library's meeting rooms. First there was Diedra, who was a lot like Victoria. Fresh from her undergraduate studies at Stanford, she was attending law school on scholarship. Then there was Paul, an older white man who had been an accountant for several years before deciding to give law school a try. And finally there was Bruce, an African-American man who'd been a police officer with the LAPD for two years before deciding to take on law in a different way. Bruce was the genius of the bunch and an excellent speaker. He was invited to run for president of the student council of the law school, which he did, and he won. He obviously had a knack for the law, and he let it be known that his intentions were to work in the Los Angeles County Prosecutor's Office.

The study group met once a week in the library. A special rapport developed between Victoria and Bruce, and he became her first real friend since she moved to California. They began meeting for study time in the library, and she even had him over at the condo a few times. They would sit in the kitchen and study until the wee hours. It didn't take long for the paparazzi to pick up on the late-night guest at the Princes' home. She immediately had to do some explaining to Michael. When the incident blew over, she decided that the late-night study sessions alone with Bruce were probably not a good idea.

It wasn't difficult for the press to blow the friendship out of proportion. Not only was Bruce extremely intelligent, but she would have to be blind not to have noticed that he was very attractive. Victoria didn't deny that fact to herself or anyone, but she was happily married, and despite the gossip, she and Bruce remained good friends and study partners.

There were times during their study sessions when she would stop and call Michael or she would simply talk about him to Bruce. Bruce would always look at her and smile.

"I'm boring you, aren't I?" she would ask as she once again drifted into a conversation about Michael.

"No, not at all," Bruce said. "I like watching you smile."

Victoria dropped her head. "I'm sorry. I don't mean to talk about him so much. I'll stop."

Michael did manage to return home a few times during the semester, which always made her happy, and when the year ended she flew to London to be with him.

Almost immediately upon arriving in the U.K., Victoria knew Michael was back on drugs. She saw it in his eyes and by the way he acted. He tried to hide it, but she could tell he was trying too hard to be normal.

When it was time for her to return to the States, Michael begged her to stay with him longer. She couldn't, and they had their first argument. She didn't understand his behavior at all because he knew classes were scheduled to begin the following week and he knew she had to prepare for them, but he continued to pursue the matter. She tried desperately to get him to compromise and join her in California for just a few days. But he wouldn't. She hated leaving him like that, and the moment she walked into the condo she called him.

Three months went by before he was finally able to come to the States. As usual, she was thrilled to see him, but she could tell the friction was still there. He was quiet and withdrawn most of the visit. After two short weeks, Michael announced he was leaving the next morning.

Victoria flipped, and they had another argument. When he left the next morning she was not there to say good-bye, and she regretted it the whole day. When she figured he would be home, she phoned him to apologize. The phone rang a few times before it was finally answered. It was late in London, so she knew she was probably waking him up.

"Hello?" It was a woman's voice. Startled, Victoria said nothing.

"Hello?" the woman said again.

"Excuse me, I must have the wrong number." Immediately Victoria hung up the phone and dialed the number again.

"Hello?" It was Michael.

"Hi, it's me. Are you alone?"

"Yeah, I'm alone."

Victoria sighed. "I just wanted you to know that I'm sorry about what happened and that I love you," she said, cupping the receiver. Her head rested on a large pillow as she looked up at the ceiling. "I miss you so much," she said softly.

"I miss you too," he said.

They talked until she heard his voice begin to trail off. She knew he was tired, so she let him hang up and get some sleep. After replacing the receiver, Victoria lay across the bed and stared up at the ceiling until she drifted off to sleep.

35

Michael was able to return to the States a total of four times that year. On their second wedding anniversary he called from Australia. He promised to try to make it home, but when she got the call, she knew he would not make it.

She called Sharon and begged her to come to L.A. for an extended weekend in the spring, and Sharon did. The entire visit Victoria cried on Sharon's shoulders. A few months later Michael's picture started appearing on the cover of the tabloids again, but this time they were of him and his old flame Sonya. More and more stories of Michael and Sonya surfaced until it became impossible for Victoria to dismiss them as pure coincidence.

That summer Kaleidoscope had a two-month hiatus and Victoria planned for her and Michael to do a lot of talking and making up. She prepared to join him in London because things were better for them there. She couldn't begin to understand why. When she started making travel plans, Michael surprised her and called her from the Los Angeles airport to tell her he was on his way. Excited to see him, she paced around the condo tidying up, took a quick shower, and sprayed herself with Michael's favorite scent.

The second he walked in, she jumped into his arms and kissed him so hard they fell on the floor.

Michael laughed. "I take it you're a bit horny."

"Oh, yeah." She had his clothes off in a few seconds flat.

They made love repeatedly that afternoon, stopping only to move from the living room floor to the bedroom. When Victoria fell asleep, it was still pretty early in the evening. When she awoke a few hours later, she walked into the front room and found Michael sitting on the soft carpet smoking a joint. He leaned against the sofa with his arm thrown over it. His hair had grown longer and was stuck between his back and the sofa.

The music of David Sanborn played softly in the background. Victoria stood in the doorway with her arms folded across her chest and watched him inhale deeply on the rolled cigarette and let it out through his nose. She looked into his face, and although he was unshaven, she found him extremely sexy.

"Hey," she said to get his attention. When he turned toward her she smiled. "You look relaxed." She walked over and sat down on the sofa beside him. "Want some company?"

Michael was quiet as he took another draw from the joint, then stubbed it out in the ashtray.

"You didn't have to do that." Victoria picked it up from the ashtray, grabbed the lighter, and flicked it on the joint.

"What are you doing?" he asked.

"What does it look like I'm doing?" She took a draw and held it in her mouth before letting it out through her nose. "I'm enjoying a smoke with my husband." Before she had a chance to put it to her mouth again, Michael snatched it from her.

"You don't smoke." He stubbed it out in the ashtray again.

"Michael, I've smoked a joint before."

"Your father will kill me if he knew you were smoking. He would swear I had something to do with it."

"My father would still like to believe that I'm a virgin." She chuckled, then snuggled closer to him. "I've been thinking." She kissed him softly on the cheek. "I don't have to start school this fall. I could take the semester off and spend a little time with you. We could take a minivacation."

"What are you talking about, Victoria?"

"I'm talking about us. We haven't been spending a hell of a lot of time together, and that bothers me. I miss you."

"Great, now your father will accuse me of forcing you to drop out of school."

"Michael, will you stop talking about my father? I'm trying to save my marriage here. I don't like the way things are turning out."

"Well, maybe you should never have married me!" he yelled as he got up from the floor. Victoria dropped his arm and leaned against the sofa.

"What the hell is that supposed to mean?" Victoria screamed.

Michael walked out of the room and Victoria followed him to their bedroom only to find him slipping a sweatshirt over his head.

"Where are you going?"

"Out," he said, then rushed past her. She heard the door slam behind him.

She was bewildered. What did she do wrong? Why was he so upset? She had thought he would be thrilled about the idea of them spending more time together. She walked into the solarium, sat down on the cushioned chair, and stared outside.

What is happening to my marriage, she wondered. Michael was isolating her and she couldn't reach him. Something was going on with him, but she had no idea what.

Michael didn't come home that night. Victoria fell asleep in the solarium, and when she awoke, she took a long shower, then put on a sweater and a pair of soft cotton drawstring pants. She grabbed the newspaper and walked out onto the wooden deck with a cup of hot cappuccino and tried to read the morning paper, hoping that he would come back, but he did not.

She didn't do much that afternoon because she still waited for Michael to return home. She took a slow walk on the beach and wished that he was with her. It was such a beautiful day. The sun was shining as bright as she had ever seen it, and boats and jet skis dotted the ocean as pleasure seekers took advantage of the day.

When she returned to the condo she checked the answering machine for any calls, but there weren't any. She called the L.A. studio and found that Michael had stopped by earlier in the day but had left with a group of people some hours before. She asked whom he had left with, hoping that it would be someone she'd be able to contact. Among the group were Bobby, Richard, the drummer, Sonya Campbell, and a few other ladies.

Sonya Campbell, Victoria thought. Michael and Sonya *were* involved again. That would explain his behavior, his disappearance, and the woman's voice she heard when she called his house a few months ago. She never forgot that because she was sure she had dialed the correct number.

To keep from overreacting, she walked to the beach and let the waves wash over her. She didn't even bother to change clothes as the surf rose high above her head and smashed down over her body. The stronger waves pulled her feet from underneath her and carried her deeper into the ocean. She'd stand and walk closer to the shore and do it again and again until she was worn out.

Dripping wet, she staggered into the condo, pulling her sweater and pants off at the door. She headed straight for the shower and washed the salt water from her body and her hair. When she was all cleaned up, she put on a silk lounger, grabbed a wool afghan, and went back out onto the deck.

There was still no sign of Michael as she sipped from another cup of cappuccino and stared up at the quarter moon.

36

She lay across the bed with the afghan over her. She hadn't meant to fall asleep in that position, she had only wanted to lie down for a second and feel the blanket against her body. She heard the shower in the bathroom and knew that Michael had finally decided to come back home.

When she turned over, she saw his clothes thrown sloppily on the floor and smelled their foul odor. She picked them up with her fingertips, took them into the kitchen, put them into a bag and tied it up. When she returned to the room, the shower had stopped and she went into the bathroom with him.

He stood in front of the mirror with a razor in his hand. The five o'clock shadow that made him so adoringly sexy had grown into a sloppy beard. His wet hair fell flat on his shoulders, and a fluffy white towel was tied around his waist.

Victoria watched as the razor cut every trace of hair on his face until it was once again smooth and immaculate. He poured some aftershave lotion into the palm of his hand and blotted it on his face. When he was done, Victoria walked up to him and grabbed both of his arms and looked at their undersides.

"What are you doing?" he asked.

She didn't reply.

"I'm not a junkie, if that's what you're looking for." He pushed away from her and walked into the bedroom.

"I know you're back on drugs and you've shut me out of your life. I need to know what's going on with you."

"There is nothing going on, Victoria. Just the usual stuff."

"You can't say that to me when you've been gone for a day and come back home unshaven with stinky clothes."

"I've just been out."

"For an entire day?" Victoria took a deep breath. Michael was not going to cooperate. "Okay, let's try this a different way. What's going on between you and Sonya?" Victoria cursed herself. One thing she'd learned during her studies was to never ask questions when the answer can destroy your case. She really didn't want to know what was going on between Michael and Sonya because the evidence was right in front of her face. Michael ignored her, and that made her angrier. He walked to the bed to lie down.

"You didn't answer me."

"I know I didn't answer you because I don't think you want to hear the answer."

Victoria's mouth dropped open. "You asshole!" she yelled, then snatched a pillow from the bed, threw it at him, and stormed out.

She found herself driving. She didn't know where she was going. She just had to be far from Michael and the mess her marriage had become. She drove to the only place where she was able to find some solace, the school library. There were times when she had gone to the school simply to sit in the library and read one of its many newspapers or magazines.

When she walked into the huge library she was not alone. Many students taking summer classes were busy studying. Quietly, Victoria sat in one of the soft plush chairs in the lounge area and selected a newspaper. She read the words on the page, but her mind didn't retain anything. She found herself rereading entire paragraphs because she hadn't remembered what she had just read.

"Hey, you, wake up."

She looked up and saw a friendly, familiar face staring back at her. Instantly she smiled. "Hi, Bruce. What are you doing here?" She placed the newspaper on her lap as he sat in a chair opposite her.

"I'm taking my last class. I graduate at the end of the summer."

Surprised, she looked at him. She had known that he carried a heavy load during the regular semesters and took several classes during the summer months, but she had had no idea he had accelerated so much.

"Wow, that's wonderful," Victoria said, reaching over and hugging him.

"I take the bar in December, so it's still crunch time," he said, smiling. Bruce was always so carefree. She enjoyed his high spirits and terrible jokes.

"Are you okay?"

Victoria tried to smile, but the tears began to flow and she broke into a quiet sob.

Bruce took her by the hand and led her out of the library. They got into his car and he drove as she cried in the passenger seat. She filled him in on what was happening in her marriage and told him she felt powerless to do anything about it.

"There's nothing I can do but sit back and watch my marriage fall apart." She continued to cry heavily until all of the tears had fallen. "I'm sorry, I didn't mean to bring this down on you like this."

"Victoria, we're friends. You don't need to apologize. I just wish I could do something to help. You could always come and stay with me for a while, if you need to get away."

Victoria smiled. "Thanks, Bruce, but I don't think that would be such a good idea."

They drove around town awhile, stopped to get something to eat, then drove back to school. Bruce walked her to the lounge, where he stayed with her.

"You don't have to stay with me," she said, feeling guilty for keeping him. "I'll be fine."

"It's no bother. I was on my way home anyway."

She noticed a sudden surprised look on Bruce's face. When she turned around, she saw Michael walking in their direction.

She was shocked. Michael had never come to the school before, and he wasn't dressed in any of his usual disguises.

"Well, this is a pretty interesting sight," Michael said as soon as he reached the table. "My wife enjoying a cup of coffee with her lover."

"What?" Victoria stared up into his face. "We were talking."

"Yeah, I can see that," he said, looking at the coffee in front of them. "What the hell do you need to talk to him about at this hour?"

"You have a lot of nerve!" she yelled. "You have no right to accuse me of anything."

"Do you want to sleep around, Victoria?"

"Wait a minute," Bruce said, stepping between Victoria and Michael. "I think this is getting out of hand."

"This is none of your business," Michael said, pointing at him.

"If you come in here with alcohol on your breath, standing in front of her and pointing at her like you're about to hit her, I'm making it my business."

"Hit her? I would never hit her."

"That's not the way it looks, man, so I advise you to go sober up."

"Who the hell do you think you are! This is my wife. This is a matter between me and my wife!" Michael yelled, brushing his chest against Bruce.

"You're drunk!" Bruce yelled back.

"Stop it!" Victoria rushed between the two men and pushed them apart. It would have been only a matter of seconds before someone threw the first punch. "Bruce, I have to go. Thanks for everything." She excused herself and picked up her purse from the floor.

"You do not have to go anywhere with him. He's drunk."

"Bruce, I'll be fine," Victoria said, and headed toward the exit holding her head down as she passed inquiring eyes. Michael walked quickly behind her.

"How dare you?" She turned to him the moment they stepped outside the lounge.

Michael walked past her toward his car.

"Oh no you don't." She grabbed his arm before he could walk away from her and turned him around to face her. "Why did you do that?"

"I came here to apologize, and you're sitting with Bruce. How quickly can I be replaced?"

"There is nothing going on between Bruce and me, contrary to you and Sonya."

Michael threw his hands up in the air. "So you say."

"You're nothing but an alcoholic and a drug addict. You need help!" she screamed, then immediately put her hand over her mouth.

"Is that how you feel about me?"

She sighed. "I love you, but I think you should get some help."

"Maybe you just shouldn't be married to me anymore." Michael backed away from her, got into his car, and sped off.

She drove home frantic. She should never have called him those things no matter how mad she was at him. He needed to feel that she would be there for him. Her calling him names was only going to push him further away. And now he was mad at her, and that didn't help either. She needed to get home and apologize and try to make him understand that she was not deserting him.

When she reached the condo, she saw his Porsche parked sloppily in the carport. She rushed from her car and ran inside. She quickly searched for him on the deck, but he wasn't there.

"Michael!" she called out, but she heard no answer. She walked into the bedroom and found him there, packing. "What are you doing?" she asked, walking into the room and standing beside him.

"I'm going back to London, alone."

Her heart sank. Michael was leaving her. "Oh no, you can't do that," she said, and began removing the clothes that he had already placed in the suitcase.

Michael grabbed her by the arm and forced her down on the bed.

She looked up at him.

"I'm leaving," he said through gritted teeth. "You don't need to be married to an alcoholic and a drug addict."

"I shouldn't have said that to you, and I'm sorry," she said, crying. "But we can work this out. You can get help."

"You're still saying it. I would only need help if I had a problem. I've told you before, I do not have a problem."

"Michael, you have a problem."

"Don't you think I would know if I was an alcoholic?" he yelled. "My father was a bloody alcoholic, and I am not my father!"

Victoria stared into his face and squinted. "Your father?"

Michael backed away from her and stormed out of the room. The last sound she heard from him was his tires screeching across the pavement as he sped down the drive.

37

VICTORIA

I was seeing Nancy twice a week now, and I actually looked forward to talking with her without hearing criticism and, in most cases, personal opinions. Talking with anyone else was out of the question. My mother was stuck in the sixties. My sisters were struggling with their own lives and were not in any position to help me. Nancy became a welcome relief.

"What about other women?" Nancy asked during a lunchtime half-hour session.

I raised my eyes to Nancy, trying to understand what she was asking me.

"Do you suspect he's having an affair?"

I took a deep breath and pressed my back against the padded fabric. "All the signs are there. I don't know who she is, and I don't want to know."

"And how does that make you feel?"

"Mad . . . cheated . . . but not surprised."

Nancy was quiet.

"The way he looks at other women . . ." The image of his face came to mind. His smile was warm, friendly, inviting. "He hasn't looked at me like that in years."

"What would it take for him to look at you like that again?"

I could tell Nancy was struggling to understand why there was so much contempt in my marriage. It was something I struggled with every day myself.

"I don't think he ever will. He blames me for ruining his life."

"And how did you do that?"

"I got pregnant."

"And that ruined his life?"

"He thinks so. After I got pregnant he lost interest in our relationship and me. If I plan a romantic evening, he doesn't show up. If I wear sexy lingerie to bed, he won't touch me. It seems the only time he wants to have sex is when he's sure I don't want to. And I never want to anymore."

"It seems he's trying to get back at you."

"Seems that way. He wanted me to have an abortion. He didn't want to get married."

"Maybe he wanted to marry someone else."

That sent a jolt through my heart. "I don't know."

"You ever ask him?"

"No."

"Why not?"

"Because I was just as good as anyone else, and I wanted us to be a family."

"But you suspected that he may have wanted to marry someone else?"

I said nothing.

"Victoria, is that why you got pregnant?"

"No." I turned and looked sternly at her. "I got pregnant because that was what we wanted. Both of us."

Nancy didn't say anything. Instead she concluded the meeting and handed me a card with my next appointment on it.

I took the card and shoved it into my purse, then stormed out of her office.

JAMES

It had been four and a half years since that awful night of Victoria and James's breakup. James went away to George Washington University, and Victoria had not seen him or heard from him since. He had simply disappeared from her life like he said he would.

But she thought of him constantly, especially now that he would be graduating soon. She wanted to know how he was doing and what his plans were. Was he staying in Washington, or was he coming home? Victoria gathered the nerve to drop in on Katherine and Jonathan one afternoon. It had been a year since she last saw them because it was too hard to visit and not be a part of their lives.

Oddly, during one of Victoria's better days, Katherine had telephoned and asked her if she was free for lunch. Despite the short notice, Victoria accepted. It was difficult not talking to James, but it was even worse not knowing anything about him, and this was her opportunity to find out everything.

When she arrived, Katherine was already at the table waiting for her. Something about her looked strange. Katherine was a stylish woman. Victoria had never seen her leave the house unless her makeup was perfect and every strand of hair in place. Today she wore jeans and a long polyester shirt, like she had just stepped out of the garden. She looked deep in thought as she sat sipping from a coffee mug waiting for Victoria to arrive. Katherine's thoughts seemed to be far away from the café as she sat with a long, worried look on her face that immediately alarmed Victoria.

"Hi," Victoria said, and Katherine quickly turned toward her.

"Oh, hi, Victoria. I'm so glad you could make it." Katherine stood and gave her a long hug. "How's Reese?"

"She's great."

"Why didn't you bring her? I miss her."

"She's at Monica's. I didn't know how this afternoon was going to go, and I don't want to cry in front of her again. She has seen me cry too much lately."

Katherine gave her a pitying look, and Victoria was immediately sorry she had said that. The last thing she wanted was to be pitied.

"How's Jonathan?"

"He's great. Working hard as usual. I'm trying to convince him to retire, but I think they're just going to have to kick him out before he does that."

Victoria chuckled. "He loves his job."

"Too much," Katherine added.

"And how's James?"

Katherine put the cup to her mouth and took a slow sip. "He's doing well. His graduation is in three weeks. He's graduating magna cum laude," she bragged.

"I never had any doubt," Victoria said, smiling.

"He had us worried after you and he broke up. For a while there we thought we'd lost him. He started drinking and lying around the house and said he wasn't going to college."

"I didn't know that."

"Well, there are a few things you don't know."

Victoria cringed. What exactly did she mean by that?

"Well, he's going to be staying in Washington. He got a scholarship for law school."

"That's wonderful."

"Yes, it is. He's doing very well." The smile on her face was short-lived, and she looked down at the table. Victoria got the feeling that Katherine was purposely leaving something out. "How are you, Victoria? Are you dating?"

That was an out-of-the-blue question. "No, I'm not."

"Are you waiting for James?"

"I don't know. I just haven't found anyone yet."

Katherine nodded.

"Katherine, is everything okay?"

"Yes, everything is fine. Please forgive me, but I have to cut our lunch short. I have to get back home. Jonathan and I had an emergency, but I didn't want to cancel."

"Is everything okay?" Victoria asked. "Anything I can do to help?"

"No, no. Everything will be fine." Katherine rose to leave, and Victoria stood with her. Before Katherine walked away from the table she came and stood in front of Victoria and hugged her. "I want you to know that no matter what happens, you and Reese will always be welcome in my family." Katherine squeezed her and then turned to leave.

"Katherine—"

"I have to go, honey. Kiss Reese for me, please," she said, then hurried out the door.

<hr/>

With time to spare before she had to pick up Reese, Victoria decided to walk around the mall. She stopped outside the jeweler and searched the display for a small gold ring she could get Reese for her birthday.

She was startled when she heard her named called. She turned around searching the crowd, but she didn't recognize anyone. When she returned her attention to the rings, she heard it again. This time she turned and searched every face that came her way. Then she saw her. It had been a long time, but Victoria immediately recognized Tai.

"Victoria, hi!" Tai rushed into her arms and hugged her like they were long-lost friends.

Victoria tapped her on the back gently and quickly pulled away from her. "Tai," she said. "How are you?"

"I'm great. Getting bigger." She giggled.

Victoria agreed. She looked at the young woman's face and body. She had picked up a little weight since the last time she had seen her, at James's birthday party.

"How are you doing?" Tai broke into the conversation. "And how's your daughter?"

"We're doing well, thank you."

"How old is Reese now?" She was still going, smiling the entire time.

"She'll be ten soon."

Tai gasped. "Oh my! It doesn't take long, does it?"

"No, it doesn't. It was nice seeing you." Victoria began to walk away.

"It was great seeing you too. I'm going to have to tell James I ran into you when I get back to his house."

Victoria stopped. "James is in town?"

"Yes, he's at his parents' house."

"I just had lunch with Katherine, and she didn't say anything about it." Victoria frowned. *That is just so unlike Katherine.* Why would she not tell her James was in town?

"I suppose she told you about the baby?"

Victoria squinted. "What baby?"

Tai paused. "James and I are having a baby. Katherine didn't tell you?"

Victoria stood frozen. That was it. That explained why Katherine was behaving so weirdly. She must have invited her to lunch to tell her about Tai and James's baby but decided against it. Victoria wished she had.

"Congratulations," she finally managed to say. "I didn't know."

"Isn't that wonderful?" Tai giggled.

Victoria was speechless as she looked at Tai. Then she went from shocked to mad.

Wonderful? Victoria thought. *Wonderful for whom? You bitch, you bitch, you bitch.*

"Isn't it funny how things turn out?" Tai was the only one talking. "We should go someplace and talk about old times."

"No, I don't think so," Victoria finally said.

Tai looked at her dumbfounded.

"I don't like you, Tai, and you've never liked me, so it's not necessary to pretend."

"Well, you don't have to be nasty about it. I thought that maybe we could put the past behind us, considering—"

"Considering that you've managed to manipulate yourself into James's life? Is that supposed to make me like you?"

"You're still such a bitch," Tai said.

"Whatever, Tai. You have a good life." Victoria took a step away from her.

"People get nasty in their old age," Tai said, snickering. "No wonder James doesn't want to have anything to do with you."

Victoria stopped and turned around to face Tai again. "And if he had any sense, he would get rid of you, too."

"Well, you see, that's where you're wrong. He can never get rid of me now."

"Is that what you think? You think that you having his child is going to make him love you?"

"He does love me."

"No, he doesn't. Do you want to know what he once told me about you? You were something to do. You were something to do then, and you're still just something to do."

"It doesn't matter what you say. I'm the one having his baby."

Victoria shook her head and quickly walked away before she slapped her.

38

VICTORIA

I sat on the bench at Eden Park, watching Reese as she played. She was a beautiful little girl. Her pigtails flopped up and down as she ran to take her place in line for the slide. Reese loved wearing pigtails even though she hated getting her hair combed. She was such a tender-headed little thing.

I watched her as she laughed all the way down the slide. Her laughter made me laugh until my heart ached.

Reese was not a mistake. I wished things between Gerald and me were better, but I could never look at Reese and see her as a mistake. She wasn't a problem child at all, actually, and because she was so well behaved, she made my life a little easier. Perhaps Gerald had wanted a son. Maybe if Reese had been a boy, things would have been different.

I heard Reese laugh with some of the other kids, and I smiled at her. I turned around and stared across the river at Kentucky.

MICHAEL

Four weeks had gone by since Michael left, and Victoria still had not heard from him. She'd barely left the house in that time, for fear of missing his call. School started without her because she never made it to class, forcing her into an unofficial withdrawal.

She struggled every morning to get out of bed. When she did, she took long hot showers and put on her housecoat. Many days she went without eating. She simply didn't have the appetite or the strength to cook anything. When she did try to cook, the sight and smell of the food made her sick. Her stomach became so upset by food she stopped trying to eat.

It wasn't until she awoke one morning so weak she couldn't get out of the bed that she realized something was wrong with her. She pulled out the telephone book from the drawer next to the bed. She scanned through it for telephone numbers of anyone who could come and help her. There were only a few names on the list: Bruce—she was sure he wouldn't want to see her; Diedra—they had never become friends; her family back in Cincinnati; Sharon in Boston; Bobby's L.A. apartment.

Bobby? She remembered hearing his voice on the answering machine a few days ago. She wondered if he was still in town. She dialed his number.

"Hello?" she heard him say.

"Bobby, it's me, Victoria."

"Hi, Victoria. How are you?"

"I don't know. I don't feel too good."

There was silence. "I'll be right there." He hung up.

She heard the click as she lay on the bed with the receiver still in her hand.

Soon afterward she heard the constant chimes of the doorbell, but she couldn't move from the bed. When she focused again, she saw Bobby on the balcony outside their bedroom. He was banging on the glass.

Victoria forced herself from the bed and stumbled to the floor. She heard Bobby yelling for her to get up and try again. She did. She stood and made her way to the glass door and opened it. When she did, she collapsed in his arms.

When Victoria woke up, she found Bobby sitting beside her, smiling. She looked at the IV attached to her arm, then glanced around the small white room.

"Well, hello, sleeping beauty," Bobby said as he stood and reached for a glass of water. He put the glass to her mouth and let her drink.

"Thank you," she said, and let the water wet her dry lips. "What happened?"

Bobby smiled at her as he reached for the house phone. She heard him tell the nurse that she was awake. "How do you feel?" he asked, moving the falling strands of hair from her face.

"Tired." She struggled to make the words come out. "How long have I been asleep?"

"Since yesterday morning." He brought the glass to her mouth again, and she readily accepted it.

The doctor came in. Bobby moved to the window and out of the doctor's way as he quickly examined her.

"How do you feel, young lady?" he asked, and squeezed her hand.

"Tired, but fine. What happened?"

"You haven't been eating and you were dehydrated. We've been feeding you with this since you've been in here." He pointed to the

IV in her arm. "Victoria, I need to tell you something that I don't think you know." He put her chart down and looked at her hard.

Victoria quickly looked at Bobby for clues of what he was about to say, but Bobby only smiled.

"Is something wrong with me?"

"You're pregnant."

"What?" she said after a short silence.

"You're about four weeks pregnant. We did an ultrasound and the baby is fine, and we want it to stay that way. You need to start eating, okay?" He rubbed her arm and smiled at her.

Victoria looked from the doctor to Bobby. She had heard him say she was pregnant, but she didn't believe it.

"I can't be pregnant. I'm on the pill."

"Well, you're pregnant, and if you're still taking birth control pills, stop."

Victoria's mouth dropped open. "Are you sure?"

The doctor nodded. "When you get out of here, make an appointment with an obstetrician. They can take it from there, okay?"

Victoria nodded.

"Good. Now I'll leave you two alone." He looked at Bobby and walked out of the room.

Victoria stared straight ahead. She couldn't believe it.

"Oh, Bobby." She covered her mouth with her hand and was quiet for a few minutes, trying to come to grips with everything. "Has anyone called Michael? Does he know?"

Bobby shook his head.

"I have to tell him." She sat up in the bed excitedly. "I have to find him. I'm going to London when I get out of here, and I will find him."

"Victoria, I don't think that's a good idea."

"Bobby, this baby is what we need. Once Michael finds out about the baby, he'll come back." Victoria was convinced she was right.

Bobby took her hand and squeezed it.

───※─────

Victoria and Bobby boarded the private jet to London. Bobby insisted on joining her for the trip so she wouldn't be traveling alone.

She immediately understood why Bobby and Michael remained such good friends.

"How long have you known Michael?" she asked, making conversation. They had a ten-hour flight ahead of them.

"Since we were sixteen."

"Really? What was he like?"

She didn't see the smile she had expected. Instead Bobby leaned back against the leather seat and frowned.

"There were problems."

Victoria leaned forward. "He mentioned his father being an alcoholic. What happened?"

Bobby turned to face her. "Michael told you that?"

"Yes, he did, the night he left. I thought Michael's family was dead."

"They are," he said, then picked up a magazine and began flipping through it.

"You're not going to tell me, are you? Why are you so loyal to him?"

"I've known him a long time," Bobby replied. "He's like my brother. We've been through a lot over the years. I've seen him hit bottom and get back up." He shook his head. "I don't know where he's at right now."

"So you would agree that something is going on with him?" Victoria asked.

Bobby nodded. "Something, but I don't know what."

When they reached Gatwick Airport, a car was waiting to take them to the house. They tried several times to reach Michael on the car phone but could never get through. Victoria sat quietly as they drove through the streets of London. She didn't know what to expect once she got there, but a part of her was afraid.

They parked on the street outside the house. All the lights were turned off, and Victoria wondered if Michael was even there. They walked to the front door and Bobby reached for the buzzer, but she stopped him.

"I have a key." She reached into her purse for the key, then slipped it into the lock. When it clicked, she pushed the door open and they walked inside. The ashtrays were full of cigarette stubs; goblets and shot glasses littered the table.

"I'm going to check upstairs," Victoria announced and walked up to the third-story bedroom. The door was partially opened, and she heard Michael's breathing in the darkness. She smiled.

Slowly she pushed the door open and stepped into the room. She fumbled in the darkness for the lamp when she heard an unfamiliar sound.

Michael was not alone. She found the lamp and turned it on. In the bright room, she saw Michael lying in bed. The person beside him was Sonya. Her naked body was covered partway by a thin white sheet.

The bright light startled the sleeping pair, and Michael jumped up. After blinking several times, he saw her standing in the doorway looking from him to his lover.

"Shit." Michael darted from the bed and grabbed a pair of jeans from a nearby chair.

Victoria watched as Sonya sat up in bed and pulled the sheet over her body.

"Come on." He tried to take Victoria's arm and lead her out of the room, but she wouldn't move. She jerked her arm from his grasp. She looked around the bedroom; it looked as if they were living together. Perfume and toiletries that did not belong to Victoria were laid neatly across the brass vanity.

Once again she felt his hand on her arm. She didn't jerk her arm away this time. She just slowly moved it from his grasp.

"Please don't touch me," she said softly as she shook her head. She was too numb to say much of anything else.

"Let's go downstairs."

"You left me for Sonya?" She turned to face him. "Is that what this is?"

"Vicki—"

"Answer me, damn it!" she yelled. "Did you leave me for Sonya?" That's when she felt the pain for the first time. It started in her back, and she straightened up to relieve it.

She heard Bobby running up the steps. When he stepped into the room he saw Sonya and turned his head.

"Come on, Vicki, let's get you out of here," Bobby said, taking her by the arm.

"What the hell are you doing here?" Michael demanded.

"I came with Victoria looking for you. I see we found you."

"What the hell are you doing hanging around my wife?"

"Your wife? You don't give a damn about your wife."

"Don't tell me who I don't give a damn about."

Victoria screamed.

Everyone turned to look at her as she doubled over on the floor. The front of her dress was covered in blood.

"Shit." Bobby ran to her.

"What the hell . . ." Michael froze.

"Call 999. We need to get her to the hospital."

"What in bloody hell is going on?" Michael yelled.

Bobby turned to face Michael and whispered, "She's pregnant."

VICTORIA

I heard the scream and immediately jumped up from the bench and searched the playground for Reese, but I didn't see her.

"Reese!" I screamed out. Panic ran through me as I turned and looked all around. I still didn't see her.

"Reese!" I screamed again, then I found her sitting on the ground near the pond. I ran across the winding drive to get her.

"What happened?" I asked, and dropped to my knees beside her.

"I fell." She stretched her leg out and showed me her skinned knee.

"Why did you leave the play area? You were not supposed to leave the play area." I was gripping her so hard that my fingers were buried in her arm and Reese cried out in pain. When I realized what I was doing, I let go of her arm and pulled her to my chest.

"What would I do if something happened to you?" I said, and hugged her as tight as I could.

39

MICHAEL

After she was released from the hospital, Victoria flew to Cincinnati. Her parents met her at the airport.

With her mother holding her right hand and her father the left, they walked from the concourse to the parking garage.

"You're home now," her mother said to her as she slid into the backseat of their car. When her mother closed the door, Victoria looked up and saw the tears in her eyes. That made her own eyes water as well.

It wasn't long before her parents' home became a paparazzi heaven. The telephone rang nonstop, and reporters harassed the neighbors for stories. They wanted to know about the baby. They wanted to know about the breakup. They wanted to know if the father of the baby was someone other than Michael and whether that had led to the breakup. There were all sorts of stories conjured up as to why Victoria and Michael split. The only truth that was printed was that Michael was now with Sonya.

Seeing pictures of Michael and Sonya together was extremely painful. Victoria stopped going to the grocery store with her mother because she just couldn't stand to look at them any longer. During her second week at her parents' house, Sharon flew in to visit her. Victoria was so happy to see her that she broke down in tears the moment they hugged.

Much to her surprise, during her stay at her parents', Nicole called her from London and Bobby came to visit twice. The people she considered friends—Sharon, Nicole, and Bobby—were making sure she got through this.

Also to her surprise, her father proved to be the most supportive. Victoria had prepared herself to be scorned and ridiculed for marrying Michael, but he did none of that. She could tell he was trying very hard to lift her spirits because they started doing some of the things they used to enjoy together. They went for long drives, took walks through the woods, and sat out on the deck and talked.

"Dad," Victoria said, putting her coffee cup down and turning toward her father. "I'm sorry if I brought you any grief."

Her father patted her hand. "You could never bring me grief."

"I guess you want to say, 'I told you so.'" Victoria hid the pain with a chuckle. "That's what I get for being hardheaded, huh?"

He took her hand and squeezed it but said nothing.

Victoria continued. "I don't know what happened," she said, and shook her head as she thought back to the days that were filled with laughter. "I don't know if I did anything wrong, and if I did, he wouldn't tell me."

Her father leaned toward her. "Victoria, I'm going to ask you a question, and I want you to be honest with yourself." He turned her around to face him. "Did you know that Michael had a drug problem before you married him?"

"I knew he did drugs occasionally, but I assumed—"

"You assumed what, that it would just go away?"

"No, I assumed that he would stop taking them when he saw that it was affecting our marriage, that he would do whatever necessary to preserve it."

"There is a whole process involved with drug addiction that requires more than Michael just waking up one day and saying he's not going to do drugs anymore because he married you. He has a disease. It has nothing to do with you or anything you did wrong in the marriage. I'm not even sure if Michael realizes that it's a disease. And because he can't stop, it makes him feel powerless and hopeless and he gets himself buried deeper by getting involved with women and more drugs. I have no doubt that Michael loves you because I saw it in his eyes when I walked you down the aisle. But that means nothing if he doesn't get help."

"But I should have been able to do something. I am his wife. I should be able to help him."

"He has got to help himself first." Her father took her head into his hands and wiped the tears that streamed down her face. "All the love in the world is not going to help Michael if he doesn't get help for his disease."

Victoria shook her head, not accepting that she was powerless to do something, anything. Strong women were supposed to be able to stand by their husbands and support their families in crisis. Her family was falling apart, and she couldn't do anything about it.

"I wanted my marriage to be like yours. I wanted it to be perfect."

"Your mother's and my marriage wasn't always this way. We had some rough times too."

Victoria shrugged. "An occasional argument? Everyone does that."

"Victoria, your mother kicked me out at one point."

She stepped back and frowned. "I don't remember that." She shook her head.

"You were very young. I had a drinking problem and I needed to get my life together. Your mother kicked me out until I did. Why do you think I take so much pride in the house and this deck? It's because I lost it all and I had to hit bottom to realize what I had lost. When I did, I fought like hell to get it back, and I ain't letting it go again."

"But this is different . . ."

"Listen to me," her father said, shaking her. "This is *not* different. You have got to let it go, otherwise you're going to end up just like him."

Victoria bit her lip. "I feel like I failed him." Her heart was heavy, and she couldn't bring herself to look directly into her father's eyes anymore. "I knew Michael was slipping away, and when I found out that I was pregnant, I saw a chance to hold on to him just a little while longer. I just wanted him to see that we were a family and that I loved him." Victoria squeezed her eyes shut. "I feel like I failed at everything." She leaned into her father's chest and cried.

"You cannot save Michael or your marriage by giving up everything you've worked for just to be by his side and hope that one day he'll come around."

"But I wanted to just hold on a little longer . . ."

"Michael must make peace with himself first before anyone can help him."

"And what if after he makes peace, he discovers that he was never in love with me? I'll lose him."

Her father lifted her face up to meet his eyes. "And if that happens, you must remember that you can't lose something that never belonged to you."

———— ◊◊◊◊◊◊◊◊ ————

After a month in Cincinnati, Victoria decided to take her father's advice and attended an Al-Anon meeting. She found it intriguing enough to go back. Many of the men and women in the group had experiences similar to hers. It was astonishing to realize that their thoughts mirrored her own; many of them too learned the hard way that they couldn't save their loved ones from self-destruction.

Throughout that month, she never heard from Michael.

By the end of the third month, she returned to California. Bobby extended the invitation for her to stay at his apartment because she couldn't bring herself to go back to the condo. He was in London and had the keys immediately sent to her.

Once settled into the apartment, she returned to the law school to talk with the dean of admissions about completing her final year. She had barely finished her second year before her world turned upside down. The dean allowed her to reenroll after she explained to him what had happened. He seemed genuinely pleased that she decided to continue her studies.

Bobby phoned her often to make sure she was doing okay. She was, and she thanked him profusely for his help.

A few days before she started classes, the postal carrier knocked on the apartment door. Reading the return address on the certified envelope, Victoria immediately knew what it was. Michael had filed for divorce.

Victoria sat on the sofa and cried before she found the courage to open the envelope. She called Sharon first and read it with her on the other end of the phone. She paused when she read the amount of the monetary settlement.

"That's a lot of money, Victoria," Sharon said, breaking the silence. "How much money is Michael worth?"

"I have no idea. We never got into a discussion about money. He has people who take care of everything."

"You've never gone over his financial records?"

"Why on earth would I do that? I'm not worth anything. I had about two hundred dollars in the bank when I married him, and he never asked me how much money I had. "

And besides, Victoria thought. *Michael was always generous to me during our marriage.* She had unlimited use of his credit cards and he bought her a Lexus sport utility vehicle as a wedding present, which she still owned. There were many luxuries Victoria would miss not being Mrs. Michael Stewart, such as sitting in the audience at events such as the Grammys and the American Music Awards. Kaleidoscope never won anything but they were selected to perform at the MTV Music Awards. There Victoria actually got the chance to shake hands with Regina Belle. It was one of the most exciting moments of her life.

"You're a college student," Sharon was saying. "You're not supposed to have any money. Well, how does it feel to be independently wealthy?"

Victoria wiped the tears from her eyes. "I would rather have my husband back."

Sharon sighed. "I know."

They were silent for a few moments.

"Are you going to get a lawyer?" Sharon asked.

"It would probably be wise, but it's not necessary. I think I'm going to have someone read it just to make sure I didn't miss anything, but he's not trying to screw me."

"I'm so sorry, Victoria."

"So am I."

The initial meeting with Michael's attorney was short and to the point. He first advised her that it was her right to seek separate representation, which she waived. He then went over the divorce settlement in depth with her. He told her that Michael wanted an amicable divorce, which explained why he offered a very generous settlement. He then asked Victoria if she accepted or rejected the offer.

She accepted.

Since it was an uncontested divorce, the process went quickly. Four months later Victoria received the preliminary divorce agreement in the mail, and she read over it again. Everything was exactly as she had signed, with nothing out of the ordinary. She did not have to be present for the final hearing, but she went, hoping that Michael would do the same. But he didn't.

During the short hearing the divorce was granted on the grounds of irreconcilable differences. Mr. Anderson represented both parties, and there were no objections from either side. Victoria sat alone at a table on the other side of Mr. Anderson, hearing only portions of the proceeding. Her eyes glanced most of the time at the empty seat beside Michael's lawyer.

She had not seen or spoken to Michael since she left him in London. When the judge asked her whether she would like to return to her maiden name, she agreed. He also explained to her the details regarding the gag order, which prohibited any discussions with the media of any details of the divorce and the settlement.

"I understand," she replied. And as quickly as it had begun, the marriage was over.

When she left the courtroom that day, she was once again Victoria Jordan. The significance of that was marked by the absence of photographers as she descended the stairs of the courthouse. Her life over the past four years had been ducking and hiding from reporters whenever she was in public. Without Michael by her side, Hollywood wasn't interested in Victoria Jordan.

———— ◊◊◊◊◊◊◊◊ ————

The transition back into normal life was not a difficult one. When Victoria finally finished school, she purchased a two-bedroom condo not far from the UCLA campus. It was nowhere close to what she had become accustomed to in Malibu. In fact, many of the hotel rooms she and Michael had stayed in were much better. She didn't have an ocean view, but she looked forward to decorating the place and bringing it to life. Most of her rooms had fresh paint but with no borders, and her bedroom furniture was a mattress and a box spring.

One of her first visitors was Bobby, who flew to the States regularly.

"Very nice. Modest," Bobby said when he walked in and took a look around, but she heard the sarcasm in his voice.

"Oh, shut up." She punched him in the arm and went into the kitchen to prepare a small lunch. When she was done, she handed him a turkey sandwich and chips on a paper plate.

Bobby looked at the plate, then at her.

"I know that you're accustomed to being served from the most expensive china, but I haven't gone shopping yet." She forced the plate into his hand.

Bobby laughed and took the plate. "It's okay. Gives me a reality check."

"I've been working pretty hard, but I'm hoping to be able to devote more time to decorating."

Bobby laughed. "How does it feel being Counselor Victoria Jordan?"

Victoria smiled. "Wonderful. My parents flew out for graduation. It wasn't the party I had after I got my undergraduate degree, but it was nice. We went out for dinner afterward, and they stayed for the whole weekend. I got to show them California, and I took them to Disneyland."

They talked and ate and tried to catch up on the happenings of mutual friends on both sides of the Atlantic. Soon it was evening, and Victoria turned on the television. They hadn't discussed whether Bobby would stay the night, but as the hour grew late, Victoria felt comfortable having him. They were close enough friends that his prolonged presence was never a problem.

They sat comfortably on the sofa. Bobby had slipped off his shoes, and Victoria changed into an oversized sleep shirt. She fetched a blanket from the bedroom and pulled it over both of them as she sat opposite him with her feet in his lap. They talked and periodically glanced at the television.

Their conversation was interrupted as they heard blaring from the TV reporter's mouth the words, *"The recently divorced rocker Michael Prince and his live-in girlfriend, model Sonya Campbell, have purchased a one-point-two million dollar home in the affluent Hampstead Heath. The house was previously owned by actor Everett Lewis. Many London observers are citing Mr. Prince's rekindled affair with longtime girlfriend Sonya Campbell as the cause of the collapse of his marriage to UCLA law student Victoria Jordan."*

Victoria's mouth dropped. "I really didn't need to see that," she said, and went into the kitchen to get a bottle of wine and two glasses.

"Well, I can tell you that things are not as they appear," Bobby said.

"What do you mean?" Victoria waited until Bobby pulled the cork from the bottle, then held her glass toward him for him to fill it.

"I wish there was a way you could talk to him."

"Why?"

"What you see on television is not the way it is. He's not very happy, and he's slipping farther and farther away."

"He just bought a million-dollar house with his girlfriend. It looks like he's doing okay to me."

"Like I said, it's not as it looks. He hasn't been in the studio, and we've been canceling sold-out concerts because he won't show up. We've had to put the tour on hold because of him. There's a lot of money being lost, and if he doesn't straighten up, he's going to be without a label and slapped with an enormous lawsuit."

Victoria almost spilled her drink. "Can they do that? He started the band."

"But he's under a contract, and he has breached it. Michael Prince can be replaced."

Victoria paused as she took a sip of her wine. "What's wrong with him, Bobby?"

Bobby placed his glass on the table beside him. "I don't know, but he's going to kill himself if he doesn't stop."

Victoria put the glass down on the table and pulled her knees up to her chest. "What can I do? He won't talk to me." Victoria began to rock, unsettled by the news. Her eyes couldn't hide the hurt and the concern. But she was powerless to help him.

Bobby reached for her and held her. "I apologize. I shouldn't have brought you into this."

"It's not that I don't care," Victoria said. "I do care, I just can't do anything if he won't even talk to me."

Bobby laid her head on his chest to comfort her, and she didn't bother moving from his embrace. It was comforting to be in someone's arms, to be held again. She hadn't realized how much she had missed it until that moment. She closed her eyes and settled her head closer to his heart as she wrapped her arms around his body. She exhaled.

She felt his hand at her back, caressing the skin underneath her shirt. His fingers slowly moved to the nape of her neck and twisted the strands of her hair. With her eyes still closed, he tilted her head to meet his lips as he lowered his face to her.

The first kiss was gentle. She felt just the softness of his lips. Then he kissed her again, deeper; the moment his tongue touched hers, they pulled apart.

"I am so sorry," he said, and backed away from her. He pulled his long brown hair from his face and looked away from her.

Victoria stared at him, speechless until she took several quick breaths to calm the racing nerves and feelings that were going on inside her. "Bobby," she began, but Bobby interrupted her.

"We both know this can't happen, right?"

Victoria nodded.

Bobby exhaled loudly, then leaned against the sofa with his head resting on the pillow. He took several deep breaths before lifting his head to look at her again. "I do have a confession to make," he said, chuckling softly. "Do you remember the day we met?"

"How can I ever forget?"

"Do you remember when I saw you backstage?"

Victoria nodded again.

"I was going to ask you out. When I met you at dinner, there was something about you I really liked."

Startled, Victoria drew back.

"But I got pulled away, and when I came looking for you, you were gone. Imagine my surprise when Michael told me who he spent the night with that night."

"Oh, Bobby, I had no idea."

"Of course not. There was no reason for you to," he said, and took her hand. "Things turned out the way they were supposed to. You ended up with Michael because that was the way it was supposed to be."

"Even now?"

"Even now."

Victoria smiled.

"I should be leaving," Bobby announced, and stood up. He took Victoria by the hand and led her to the door with him. "Take care of yourself," he said, and kissed her softly on the forehead.

Victoria sighed heavily, understanding that Bobby was saying good-bye. They had crossed a line that they could never erase, and their love for Michael was strong enough for them both to know that if the drugs didn't kill him, the knowledge of her and Bobby spending a night together would send him to his grave.

40

Victoria would never forget that phone call as long as she lived. It came after one of the worst days at the office. Her desk was piled high with papers and reports that she was unable to touch all day. When she left for home that evening, she was frustrated with all of it.

She drove slowly and kept herself focused by blasting the radio and letting the cool ocean air hit her face from all angles. The moment she stepped in the door she started taking off her clothes and made a path to the bathroom. She turned on the bath water and made it as hot as she could stand it, then poured an entire cupful of bubble bath under the stream filling the tub.

Slowly she stepped into the softened water and slid into the bubbles until her neck rested on her white bath pillow. She closed her eyes and let the bubbles ease away the tension of the day.

When she stepped from the water an hour later, her toes and fingers were wrinkled. She splashed on some cocoa-butter oil, then slipped into a silk nightshirt. The second her head hit the pillow she was asleep.

She sat straight up in bed when she heard the noise. She waited. Then she heard it again. It was the telephone. She reached over and picked it up.

At first she didn't recognize the voice, then she heard the heavy accent. "Who is this?"

"Victoria, it's me, Nicole."

Finally Victoria put a face with the voice. "Nicole." She reached over and turned the clock toward her. It was two-thirty in the morning.

"I may be out of line, but . . ." Nicole stopped talking for a moment. "Michael was in an accident last night, and it doesn't look too good."

Victoria pushed the blankets from her body. "What happened?" she practically screamed into the receiver.

"He hit a tree. He was trapped inside the car, and it took them an hour to cut him out of it and get him to the hospital. He's in a coma. I just thought you should know before you read about it in the papers."

Victoria heard Nicole sobbing.

"Where is he?"

After getting the information from Nicole, Victoria called the airlines and was told to come to the airport and try to get a flight on standby. If not, the next available flight wouldn't be until the next evening. Hurriedly, she threw a few items into a duffel bag, grabbed her passport, and dashed to the airport. It was the first time in her life she was glad not to see a police officer.

It cost Victoria twenty-five hundred dollars to reach London that day. At Gatwick Airport she went through customs as usual and dashed to the taxis.

At the hospital, Nicole met her at the service entrance far from where all of the media attention was being focused. Nicole, with the help of a nurse, slipped Victoria into a nurse's uniform so she wouldn't be recognized and took her to Michael's room.

There he was, lying in bed covered with bloody bandages, IVs, and electrodes. Cardiac and neurological monitors attached to the electrodes gave off a constant hum and series of beeps. Victoria looked up at the blood-pressure monitor and saw the numbers go up and down. She had no idea if they were good or bad. Every few seconds the electrocardiograph machine printed waves across a long strip of lined paper that folded into a neat pile when it hit the floor.

Victoria walked to him and took his skeletal hand into hers. She could clearly see the blue veins. Drugs and alcohol were literally eating him alive. His once tanned vibrant skin was now pale and rigid.

She touched his face, bent down, and softly kissed his lips.

She couldn't say anything at first. She just stared at him and the miracles of modern medicine that were keeping him alive.

"Oh, Michael." She stroked the side of his face. "If only I could help you." She wiped the tears from her eyes and held his hand carefully so as not to disturb the IV. "I am so sorry for the things that went wrong with us. I loved you."

She kept talking to him. She talked about the good times and things they had done together. "You know what? I brought something with me. I hope you don't mind, but I thought you might like it." She searched her bag for the cassette player. She took out the cassette that was already in it and replaced it with another one. When she pushed Play, the sound of laughter and music reverberated in the room.

"Do you remember this?" She laughed. It was the recording of the one time she had made a complete fool of herself trying to imitate Regina Belle. As she listened to the missed beats and the awkward singing, she laughed. When she looked at Michael and saw no change in his expression, she cried.

"Please don't die. Give me a chance to say I love you again."

The door closed behind her. "How dare you!"

Victoria jumped and turned around to the angry face of Sonya.

"How the hell did you get in here!" Sonya screamed.

"I—"

Sonya looked at the nurse's uniform Victoria had on and turned toward the door. "I'm getting security."

"No, please don't." Victoria dashed toward the door and stopped her before she had the chance to reach it. "I just needed to see him."

"You have absolutely no right to be here!" Sonya yelled.

"I know, but I needed to see him."

"He divorced you. He doesn't need to see *you*."

"I only wanted what was best for him."

"Then don't be here when he wakes up." Sonya brushed past her and took the seat beside Michael's bed.

Victoria took another look at Michael before she left, then stood outside in the corridor and peered into his room through the small glass window on the door. She watched Sonya pick up his hand and hold it.

"That should be me," she whispered softly, and touched the glass. She slipped out of the hospital and boarded the next flight back to California.

41

VICTORIA

"Are you finished, honey?" I asked Reese when she put her fork down.

She nodded.

"Could you go to your room so I can talk to your father?"

This got Gerald's attention. "Talk to me about what?"

"I'll tell you in a minute."

"She doesn't have to leave. Go ahead and talk."

Reese looked at me with questioning eyes.

"I don't want to have this conversation in front of her."

"Why not? She's a member of this family, and anything you have to say can be said in front of her."

"No, it cannot. Go to your room, honey."

Reese ran from the table before Gerald could make her sit down again.

He tossed his fork onto the table and pressed his back against his chair. "What's going on?"

"I've been seeing a counselor for the past few months. I go after work and sometimes at lunch."

"A counselor? You mean like a psychiatrist or something?"

"She's not a psychiatrist."

"I see." He nodded. "And why are you doing this?"

"Because I needed someone to talk to about things."

"What things?"

"Things with our marriage and my life."

"And how much is this costing us?"

"Nothing. The job pays for it."

"Oh." He put a forkful of green beans in his mouth and began to chew.

"She thinks it would be a good idea if you would come to a session with me." I tossed some green beans around with my fork, not picking any of them up.

"Why?"

"To talk about our marriage."

"What's wrong with our marriage?"

I snickered. "What's *right* about it?"

"What, you're not happy?"

My mouth dropped open. Was he serious? "You're joking, right?"

Gerald put his fork down and leaned back in his chair. "Is your counselor telling you I'm not a good father and I'm not a good husband?"

"No, but we just need to talk to someone."

"I'm not going to talk to some head doctor. You can forget it." He threw his napkin on the table.

"Why does everything have to turn into an argument with you?

I just asked you to come to the counselor's office with me so that we can talk."

"We don't need a counselor. If you got something to say to me, say it now."

"Why do you resent me so much? All I ever tried to do was be a good wife to you! Why won't you let me do that?"

Gerald was quiet at first. "We're just very different and we want different things."

"That has nothing to do with you going out of your way to hurt me. We've been married for five years, and you are mean and spiteful to me. Why?"

"Victoria, I wasn't in love with you when we got married."

I took a deep breath and held back the tears. "Then who were you in love with?"

He almost said a name but thought twice about it and stopped. "It doesn't matter anymore."

"It does matter because if things don't change, you're going to wake up and find yourself alone."

"I'll never be alone."

"And why is that? Do you already have someone waiting for you?"

"I just know that I will never be alone."

"Will you go with me to the counselor's office?"

"No."

"Thank you. That's all I need to know," I said, and walked upstairs to our bedroom to lie down.

42

"He wouldn't come," I said. "He's not interested."

"What does this mean for you?" Nancy asked.

I shook my head. "I don't know."

"How do you feel about your marriage at this point in time?"

"I'm at the end of my rope. I've tried everything that I think is humanly possible to save this marriage, but I'm up against a man who doesn't want to save it."

Nancy leaned forward in her seat and took my hand. "Be prepared to accept that you may have to go on without it."

JAMES

Victoria was in the kitchen baking cookies that Saturday afternoon for Reese's school's bake sale. She had just put a batch in the oven when she heard the doorbell ring and ran to get it.

The moment she saw him standing outside her door it seemed the world stood still. She saw him through the glass before she even opened the door and stood in the corridor for a few seconds taking in the sight of him. It had been three years since she ran into Tai at the mall. She hadn't seen James since he graduated from high school.

Tai had had a boy, which Victoria knew because she saw the pictures at the Mitchells' house. She had only visited twice after the baby was born and couldn't go back. It was too painful to see a picture of James's likeness sitting on the mantel.

She finally walked to the door and opened it, but found it difficult to speak. "Hi," she managed to say.

"If this is not a good time, I can come back," James said, looking at the dishrag in her hand and the apron around her waist.

"Don't be silly. Come in." She stepped aside to let him enter.

James looked around. "Everything is exactly the way I remember it," he said, nodding.

"Well, I haven't done any redecorating."

"You didn't have a need to. You always kept everything looking great."

Victoria smiled at the compliment. "I tried." She walked farther into the house until they were in the living room. "Please, have a seat." She pointed to the sofa, and when she did the ring on her finger shimmered in the sunshine.

James took her hand and looked at the ring. "You're engaged?"

She drew back her hand and bit her lip. "Yes, I am."

They sat down on the sofa, Victoria opposite him.

"When is the wedding?" he asked.

"Later this year. It's going to be a small affair." Victoria stopped talking and sniffed the air. "Oh, no!" She rushed into the kitchen, where the scent of burnt cookies was even stronger. Hurriedly she slipped on the oven mitt and grabbed the cookie sheet, but it tilted from her hand. When she reached for it with her other hand, she burned herself and pulled her hand back, and the cookie sheet fell to the floor.

"Ouch!"

"Are you okay?" James walked into the kitchen and helped her pick up the cookies from the floor. "Do you feel a sense of déjà vu?" James asked as he bit into one of the salvageable cookies.

Victoria smiled and thought about that day at the mall when she dropped her packages and James knelt down to help her.

After they had picked up the cookies they returned to the living room and sat on the sofa.

"How's PJ?" Victoria asked, sitting cross-legged on the sofa.

"He's great. His grandparents are out spoiling him again." James grinned.

"You sound very proud of him."

"Oh, I am. He's great. Smarter than I was at his age."

"I'm happy for you." Victoria squeezed his hand.

James took her hand and looked at the ring again. "Do you love him?" he asked.

Slowly, Victoria pulled her hand away.

"I'm sorry," he apologized. "That was out of line."

"No, it's okay. It's just that no one ever bothered to ask me that before." Victoria thought about Richard. She met him a few months after learning of Tai's pregnancy. He had been a good friend, someone she could talk to. "He's a good man," she said after a long pause. "He's very stable, considerate, and he's great with Reese."

"And?" James asked, looking at her.

"I'm sure I do. It's just different."

"How so?"

"With Richard everything is comfortable and predictable."

"Wow, that sounds . . ." James paused. "Boring."

Victoria laughed. "Well, he's older, you know."

James nodded. "I guess I was too young for you."

"At one time, yes, you were. But you taught me how to laugh again." Victoria paused and took a deep breath. "We had a good time."

"Yes, we did."

They looked at each other silently. Victoria broke the spell and turned her eyes down at the sofa. "For a long time I didn't have anyone in my life because no one could measure up to you. I was lonely and I wanted to be with someone. It took me a while to accept that you had moved on with your life. It was hard. Enough about me, what about you? Have you and Tai tied the knot and planned more babies?"

"Oh, no. I can't see that happening."

"Really? But I thought—"

"What happened between Tai and me probably never should have happened, but I have a son now and I'm going to be there for him. I don't have to marry a woman I don't love in order to be a father to my son. He's with me all the time. I support him financially, and I'm active in his life. Tai knows where I stand with her."

"Are you sure? I remember mentioning to you about Tai's motives many years ago, and you denied it."

"I didn't see it because I didn't want to. Or maybe a part of me wanted to hang on to her just in case you and I didn't work out. One of my youthful mistakes." James snickered.

"Wow, you've grown up."

"Victoria, I have to tell you something." He took her by the hand

and looked at her finger. "When I arrived at the university, I had no intentions of staying. I wanted to be with you, and I came close many times to walking out. But I fell in love with the place and I fell in love with learning. Then I wanted to stay and graduate. I stayed away because as much as I loved it, I still would have given it up for you."

"James, I wanted you to become whatever you desired. That was why I did what I did. It wasn't because I didn't love you."

"I know. I've always known that. And I've always hoped that I could come back and make things right for us." He took a deep breath and looked at her finger again. "Am I too late?"

Victoria was stunned. What was he asking her?

James looked into her eyes and held her hand in his. "I want us to do this again. Start over and get to know each other as adults. There is nothing holding us back now. Unless . . ." He dropped her right hand and held only the hand where she wore Richard's engagement ring. "Unless you marry Richard."

"But what about Washington?"

"I'm going back to Washington. My future is there right now."

"Where do I fit in?"

James paused. "Long-distance relationships are a bitch, but I guess we could attempt it for a little while."

"And then . . ."

"Hopefully, you'll fall in love with Washington too."

James stood and pulled her up with him. She was standing next to the man she always knew James would become. He was strong, handsome, confident, assured. When she looked up into his face, he closed his eyes and kissed her softly on the lips.

"Think about it, okay? I'll wait." He kissed her again, then headed for the door.

"James!" Victoria called out, stopping him before he reached the door. "I guess I have to give Richard his ring back."

James turned around and looked at her.

She continued. "I don't have to think about it. The answer is yes."

He walked to her, then took her into his arms and kissed her. A spark traveled through her and ignited her entire body. James was the only man who could make her feel that way with just a kiss. She felt it the first time he had ever kissed her, and now she felt it again. She was thankful that some things didn't change.

"It's time," he whispered, and he lifted her into his arms and carried her upstairs into her bedroom.

After eight years, Victoria and James finally made love.

44

MICHAEL

"Yes?" Victoria asked as she pressed the intercom button that connected her office phone to the receptionist's desk in the lobby.

"There's a young woman out here to see you," Georgette said.

"Who is it?" Victoria asked, still pecking on the keyboard.

"She says she's an old friend."

Victoria stopped typing. *An old friend? Sharon?*

"Send her in." She jumped up from her chair and ran to the door to greet Sharon. When she saw Nicole, her mouth dropped open.

"Nicole!" Victoria screamed. "Nicole!" She ran into her arms and hugged her. "What are you doing here? I thought you were someone else."

"Well, I'm on holiday and I just wanted to stop by and see you before I go back," Nicole said.

Victoria screamed again and hugged her. "This is wonderful. Come in." She stepped aside to let Nicole into her office at the prestigious law firm. "Sit down."

Nicole sat in a leather chair and crossed her legs.

"How long will you be in town?"

Nicole shrugged. "I haven't really decided. I'm on a shopping spree."

They laughed.

"I know how that is," Victoria said, leaning on the edge of her desk with her hands folded in front of her. "I can't believe you're here. This is wonderful. Where are you staying?"

"Beverly Hills, of course." Nicole laughed.

"Of course," Victoria repeated, laughing along with her. "Well, come stay with me. It's not in Beverly Hills, but it's a nice house."

Nicole nodded. "I would love to."

"Wonderful. We have so much catching up to do. Are you hungry?"

"Famished."

Grinning, Victoria called her secretary and told her she'd be taking the rest of the afternoon off.

Their first stop was the small café nearby where they ate almond pasta salad and grilled chicken for lunch while Victoria filled Nicole in on her relationship with Bruce, her job, and the things she had been doing over the past few years.

Then it was time to shop, and Victoria loved to watch Nicole shop. She always got a kick out of the way Nicole fussed about things and tried to match fabrics. Nicole was very particular about what she wore.

After their brief shopping spree, they drove to the house that Victoria shared with Bruce in an affluent suburb of Los Angeles. Once inside, Victoria gave Nicole a quick tour of the room where she would be sleeping. The moment Nicole saw the swimming pool in the back of the house, she insisted that they go for a swim.

"This is a great place, Victoria," Nicole said as they sat poolside after swimming.

"Thank you, but I can't take the credit. It was like this when I moved in."

"Oh?"

"This is Bruce's house. I bought a condo after Michael and I divorced, and I lived there for about a year. Then I ran into Bruce and we started dating. He asked me to move in and I did."

"Wow, such a love story. You and Bruce have known each other for years."

"Yes, we have, but I wouldn't call it a love story. Two lonely people sharing their time together is more like it." Victoria tried to force a smile, but all she could manage was a tight grin.

They continued talking about the house until they both shivered as the temperature began to drop. They went into the house to shower and change and met in the family room, where Victoria had started a fire. They sat on the floor in front of the fireplace and talked.

Victoria decided to order Chinese. While they waited for the food to arrive, they opened a bottle of wine Victoria had gotten from the cellar and placed in the refrigerator. They were on their second bottle when Bruce finally arrived. Victoria stood to introduce them.

"Honey, this is my wonderful friend from London, Nicole. Nicole, this is Bruce."

"Hello, Nicole. Pleased to meet you," Bruce said, extending his hand toward Nicole.

"My goodness, you have such a strong voice. I would hate to be opposite you in a courtroom," Nicole said, shaking his hand.

"And he seldom loses," Victoria added.

"I think you ladies are feeling pretty good." Bruce picked up the bottle of wine and peeked inside.

"We were just talking about old times. We have some good memories."

Nicole threw her arms around Victoria, and they hugged and laughed again.

"I'm going to leave you ladies alone so that you can continue reminiscing."

"Do you want to join us for a drink?" Victoria asked before he walked out of the room.

"No, you go ahead and have fun. I have to get up early in the morning and head back to the office. Good night, ladies." Bruce left them alone while he went into another room.

"Did I make him uncomfortable?" Nicole asked when Bruce was out of earshot.

Victoria shook her head. "No, he's always like that. He doesn't socialize much. He works a lot."

"Well, with both of you guys being lawyers, why don't you go into practice together?"

"Well, for starters, I'm in corporate law and Bruce is in criminal law. And he'd never leave the prosecutor's office. It was his dream to work there, and I think the man would work for free if they asked him."

Nicole laughed. "Guess what I brought with me," she said suddenly and jumped up. She didn't wait for Victoria to guess and ran into the guest room and came back with a large gold book.

"What's that?" Victoria asked.

"Pictures," she announced, opening to the first page.

"Oh, I don't know," Victoria said, putting her hands over the pictures.

"It'll be fun," Nicole said, and turned the page. The first picture was of Victoria and her first day in London.

"Oh, no, look at that hairdo!" Victoria laughed and pulled her hand back.

They smiled and giggled at the photos, until they reached the wedding pictures. The laughter immediately stopped.

"You were a beautiful bride."

Victoria smiled as she scanned the photos. "Thank you. I'm glad Michael thought enough to call you. I had completely forgotten."

"You were too busy planning your wedding." Nicole turned the page. "Do you ever think about Michael?"

"All the time. There were times in the beginning when the phone rang and I answered it, wishing it was him. But it never was."

Nicole grinned wickedly. "Why don't you call him? You can use my cell phone."

"I would never do that."

"Why not?"

"What would I say to him? I haven't talked to him in years, and besides, he's with Sonya."

"They broke up long ago."

"I haven't heard anything about that."

"Well, if you've noticed, you haven't heard *anything* about Michael lately because he has kept things very low-key. He wants it that way now. Do you want me to call him for you?" Nicole asked. She was about to stand, but Victoria pulled her down.

"No," Victoria refused, shaking her head wildly.

"Why not?"

"Because he divorced me and hasn't contacted me in years."

"But things are different now. He's clean and he's recording again and he's doing very well. You would be very proud of him."

Victoria shook her head. "But he still hasn't contacted me. I've gone on with my life now. I have a life with Bruce."

"Are you in love with Bruce?" Nicole asked.

"He's a good person."

"And . . ."

"And what?"

"That's it? He's a good person? Is that how you describe the man you would spend the rest of your life with?"

"What more do you want?"

"What about passion and desire?"

Victoria looked at Nicole and shook her head. "You're dreaming."

"No I'm not. Isn't that what you had with Michael?"

"Yes, I did, but it didn't work out, so I had to wake up from my dream," Victoria said, closing the photo album.

※※※※※※

Victoria lay in bed that night staring up at the ceiling. After hours had passed, she finally got up and walked to the large closet. She took a wool afghan from the shelf, wrapped it around her body, and walked out onto the adjoining deck and sat.

Talking about Michael rekindled feelings in her that she had forced herself not to experience in a long time. She missed being in love. She missed feeling loved. She remained on the balcony until the morning sky turned a burnt orange as the sun crept onto the horizon. Then she fell asleep.

When she awoke, she was still sitting outside. She walked inside the house to find that Bruce had already left for work. She took a quick shower, changed into a pair of jeans and a T-shirt, and joined Nicole in the kitchen. Nicole had already made coffee and had a basket of fresh muffins delivered from the bakery down the street.

"You didn't have to do that," Victoria said, walking into the kitchen.

"Well, I probably won't do it again either. It cost me a small fortune to get them to deliver."

"This is not London." Victoria laughed and picked up a blueberry muffin and sat down. "So what's on your agenda for today, more shopping?" She took a bite of the muffin and followed it with a sip of coffee.

"Actually, I'm leaving this morning."

Victoria stopped as she was about to take another bite. "It's not because of last night, is it? I'm sorry . . ."

"No, it's not that. I really do have to get back. I'm having a birthday party, and I want you to come."

Victoria's eyes grew wide. "What?"

"I want you to come to my party."

"In London?"

"Yes, please say you'll come."

"Nicole, I don't know. I haven't been to London since . . . you know."

"I know, but things will be different this time. Please say you'll come."

"Oh, I don't know. I would love to, but . . ." Victoria paused for a moment. The idea of going back to London was both exciting and frightening. The thought of possibly seeing Michael again scared her. "I have to talk to Bruce about it first, okay?"

"Okay, that's fair," Nicole said. "Call me the moment you make a decision. And Victoria, I really want you to come."

After finishing breakfast, Victoria watched Nicole gather her things and get into a waiting cab.

Now she had the entire day to herself. She could go to work, but she wasn't in the mood. She slipped on a comfortable pair of sandals and drove to Malibu. She walked up and down the beautiful beach until she happened upon the condo that she and Michael once shared. She didn't know if he still had rights to the property, but it was just as beautiful now as it was then. She wanted so much to go inside.

She started walking toward it but stopped when she saw a young couple leaving. She turned and walked in the opposite direction.

45

VICTORIA

It's my birthday, I thought. *I wonder if he'll remember.*

Will he give me flowers? A card? I hope he sends flowers to the office. Cynthia's husband always sent her flowers at the office on her birthday.

No flowers came. *Maybe they're at home,* I told myself.

At home there was no sign of Gerald. *He could be out buying a present or a cake.*

Hours passed, and no Gerald. Would he surprise me with a party like Desiree's husband?

By the end of the day, he still hadn't come home to wish me happy birthday.

46

MICHAEL

Victoria noticed the flowers on her desk Monday morning but didn't think much of them. She worked as usual and only occasionally glanced at the beautiful arrangement. Every Monday after that another assortment arrived.

"Things must be going pretty well," Georgette said one morning, bringing Victoria a fresh cup of coffee. She stopped and smelled the roses.

"What must be going pretty well?" Victoria asked, tapping away on her computer, not even bothering to look up.

"With whoever is sending you flowers every week."

Victoria looked up at her. "What are you talking about?"

"The flowers, Victoria. Who's sending you the flowers?"

Victoria looked at the bouquet on her desk, then back at Georgette. "I thought the firm was supplying them."

"You've got to be kidding! You don't know who's been sending them?" Georgette started fumbling through the arrangement for a card.

"No, I haven't given them a second thought. I've been so damn busy. What if Bruce has been sending them and I haven't even thanked him!" She put her hand to her mouth.

"Well, I think you better do a lot of making up tonight, and real good," Georgette joked as she smelled the flowers again and left the office.

Victoria sat at her desk and looked at the flowers again. Maybe Bruce had been giving some thought to their relationship. Since she moved in with him, she had learned so much about him that she hadn't known before. Bruce talked about the law all the time. His knowledge of the law, which she had admired so much in college, was now boring. He had no other interests.

There were no evening walks to watch the sunset or early-morning strolls under the sunrise. Bruce always got home late from work and left before she got up. There was no more walking barefoot in the sand. Bruce hated the beach, which was really strange for someone who was born and raised by the ocean. There were no more rides through the streets, stopping alongside the road to enjoy lunch or coffee at a small café or restaurant. Bruce hated sitting in the grass and eating outside.

Victoria sighed again as she picked one of the beautiful roses from the vase and brought it to her nose. Slowly she smelled the sweet aroma of the petals as she closed her eyes.

Bruce, she thought. Maybe she could have done more for the relationship. Maybe they could buy another house and it would be their house and not Bruce's. Maybe they could talk about getting married and having children.

She shrugged at that thought. That was going just a little too far. She took a whiff of the flowers again and picked up the telephone. Surprisingly, he was in his office.

"Hi, honey," she said into the receiver, a little more cheerful than she had been in a long time.

"Hello. This is a pleasant surprise. How's your day going?" Bruce asked. He had such a virile voice. She always loved to listen to him, especially when they talked on the phone.

"Great, thank you. Do you have any plans for tonight?"

"No, not at all." She heard him rustling through papers.

"Good. Could you be home in time for dinner?"

"Sure. Seven-thirty sound good?"

Victoria glanced at the clock on her wall. "Seven-thirty sounds wonderful."

"Good. I'll see you then." She listened to the sound of his receiver click before she replaced her own. She smelled the flowers once again. "He's so sweet."

〰〰〰〰〰〰

Victoria left the office early that night. When she arrived home, she began to prepare a simple vegetarian meal. Neither of them were strict vegetarians, but they enjoyed the variation. Before Bruce arrived she started a fire in the fireplace, changed into a silk camisole set, and put on some soft music.

When Bruce arrived he changed clothes and they sat in the living room and ate, discussing their cases. Bruce usually gave her some pointers since he was much more experienced at the investigating end of things. Whenever she hit a dead end, he could always find another angle.

They were lying on the floor in front of the fireplace. Victoria kept her eyes closed and listened to him as she toyed with the hair on his arm.

"Let's not talk about law tonight, okay?" she said, shifting around to face him. "First of all, I want to say the flowers are beautiful. Thank you." She kissed him.

"What flowers?"

"The flowers you've been sending me."

"I wish I could say I have, but I haven't been sending you flowers. Someone's been sending you flowers?"

"Yes, for almost a month now. I thought it was you." She returned her attention to the fire.

"No, it's not me. You want me to have someone check it out for you?"

"No, no, that won't be necessary." She resumed toying with the hair on his arm.

"No card?"

"No, Georgette and I looked for one today."

"It's probably an old client."

"I suppose, but why?" She rested her head against his chest and looked into the fire again. She felt his hand fondling her breast. "How about another drink?" She moved away from his advances and walked to the bar to pour a glass of scotch.

Scotch. She hadn't had scotch since . . .

She drank it in one swallow.

"What's wrong?" Bruce asked.

"Nothing." She poured another and swallowed.

"I don't think you're telling me the truth."

"Well, would you like to cross-examine me?" she asked with a hint of sarcasm that Bruce didn't miss. "I'm sorry. That was completely unnecessary."

He took the scotch glass out of her hand and led her to the sofa. "Talk to me. What's on your mind?"

She didn't hesitate telling him what was wrong. When it came to dealing with Bruce, there was no way she could bullshit him. "I'm disappointed that it wasn't you sending the flowers."

"I see. Is that all?"

Victoria thought for a minute. "No."

"I'm listening." He folded his arms and leaned against the sofa.

"Is there anything else you want to do besides being a lawyer?"

Bruce shook his head. "No."

Victoria sighed. "I didn't think so."

"Victoria, you knew me in law school and how driven I was about my law career."

"But that was then. This is now. We've graduated and it's time to live."

"I'm living. I'm happy with my life."

"But what about having a family and traveling and having a real relationship?"

"You don't think we have a real relationship?"

"No!" she yelled and fell on the sofa. "No, I don't!" Victoria hid her face. Bruce was the last person in the world she wanted to hurt. "I like traveling and I like socializing and I like doing things that don't require a law book." She took a deep breath. "We have a beautiful deck with a breathtaking view of the sunset, but we've never sat out there together to watch it."

"Victoria, I'm not Michael."

Victoria looked up at him, her eyes moist with tears. "Am I trying to make you into Michael?"

Bruce nodded. "I think you were hoping that we could evolve into doing the things that you enjoyed doing with Michael, but that's not me. I am the same person you knew in school. I didn't change."

"I know, but I was hoping for something a little more." Victoria hid her head in her hands again.

Bruce sat down beside her and held her. She rested her head on his shoulder.

"Bruce, I'm sorry."

"Don't be." He rubbed her back and let her cry a few quiet tears.

"Nicole is having a birthday party in London, and she's invited me." Victoria wiped the tears from her eyes.

Bruce touched her face and kissed her forehead. "Then I think you should go."

47

Victoria flew from L.A. to London and took a taxi from the airport to Nicole's apartment in Clerkenwell. Nicole had arranged for a messenger to meet Victoria at her apartment with the key and the number to her cellular phone because she was unable to be there. Victoria dialed her as soon as she got settled.

"Nicole."

"Victoria, wonderful, you made it," Nicole said, horns blaring in the background. "Are you finding everything okay?"

"Yes, I am," Victoria said.

"Bloody London traffic. I'll be there as soon as I can. I have to run now before some jackass hits me. Bye."

Victoria laughed and hung up the phone. She walked around the quaint apartment and found her way to the second-story shower room. She took a quick shower and changed into a pair of jeans and a T-shirt.

When she emerged, she felt refreshed. She took a deep breath and smiled. There was something about being in London that was very familiar to her. She walked down to the first story and stepped out onto a small terrace in the back. She sat down on a fabric chaise and took a nap.

When she opened her eyes again, she stared up at the sky listening to the quiet of nature around her. Then she heard the buzzer. Realizing she had heard the sound before in her sleep, she jumped off the chaise and rushed to the door.

Without expecting to see anyone but Nicole, she threw open the door and was staring into Michael's face.

She froze.

"Nicole told me you were here," he said.

Victoria stared at him, unable to move.

"Is this a bad time?"

"No," she finally said. "No, come in." She stepped aside and let him enter.

"Thank you."

She didn't know what to do or say. She stuffed her hands in her pockets and looked around the room.

"A bit awkward, huh?" Michael said.

Victoria smiled. *That's better,* she thought. "I'm just a little shocked. I knew I would probably see you. I just wasn't expecting it to be so soon."

"You want me to leave?"

"No," she said taking him by the arm. "No, not at all. I'm glad to see you." She led him into the sitting room, and they sat down. He looked good and he looked well.

"I love what you've done with your hair," she pointed out.

"I cut it," Michael said, running his hand through his dark brown hair.

"Yeah, I can tell. It looks good."

"Thank you."

Victoria yawned. "I'm sorry," she said, covering her mouth.

"Did I wake you?" he asked.

"I dozed off earlier on the terrace. It's okay." Victoria smiled again and shook her head. "This is a bit awkward." She laughed. "I've been thinking about you and how you were doing."

"Really?" he asked.

"Yeah. It's been a long time."

Michael smiled.

He has such a wonderful smile, Victoria thought. So warm, so reassuring. "I'm starving. Would you like something to eat?" she asked as she rushed to the kitchen.

"Are you going to cook?" he asked, following her.

"Yes. What would you like?"

"Are you trying to impress me again?"

Victoria laughed. "I can't believe you remember that."

"Did you learn to cook?"

"No, not really." She laughed.

"Well, let's go then." He took her by the hand and led her to the door.

She slipped on her shoes and they rushed out. Parked in front of the apartment was Michael's Harley-Davidson Roadster. Victoria sighed. She always loved that bike.

"Is it okay?"

"It's great. I just hadn't realized how much I've missed it."

He helped her with her helmet. He sat on the bike, then held her hand and helped her on. "Hold on," he said as he revved up the engine and sped off. She wrapped her arms around him as she slid closer to his body.

"That sounds so smooth," she yelled into his ears against the wind. She felt his smile on her cheek.

They rode to a small restaurant and enjoyed a lunch of fresh bread and baked chicken. It didn't take long for the awkwardness to wane, and soon they were talking and laughing freely.

The lunchtime ride turned into a full-day adventure. They cruised through the streets, and when they hit the less populated countryside, Michael purred down the road at top speed, hearing her mixed screams and laughter as they hit sixty-five, then seventy miles per hour at her goading.

"Go faster! Go faster!" she yelled as he reached seventy-five miles per hour.

"That's as fast as I'm going with you, young lady. Get over it." Then he slowed down.

They stopped along an open field of beautiful soft green grass and took off their shoes and walked. At a knoll overlooking the countryside, they sat down. Michael did most of the talking, stopping long enough to notice that Victoria didn't immediately open her eyes after she blinked.

"You must be tired." He stretched his jacket out on the ground, then motioned for her to join him. "We'll rest here for a moment." He lay flat and let her use his chest for a pillow.

Within minutes she was fast asleep.

"Vicki." The sound of her name broke into her dream. "Vicki." She lifted her head and glanced around the countryside. The sun was fading.

"How long have I been asleep?" she asked, stretching.

"About an hour."

"Why didn't you wake me sooner?"

"No way."

"Did you get some sleep?" she asked.

"No, your trademark snore kept me up," he said, grinning.

"I don't snore," she said, but wondered if she did.

Michael laughed as he helped her up off the grass. She brushed the grass off her backside, and they walked back to the bike.

They rode for a while but not in the direction of Nicole's apartment. Victoria remembered seeing some of the sights before. She pulled away from Michael as she glanced around the neighborhood. Why did it look so familiar?

Michael slowed down and parked the bike on a hill. Victoria suddenly remembered where she was. It was that little house again. The one he had brought her to many years ago. But this time the house wasn't boarded up. It was beautiful. The grass was green, and flowers were planted neatly around it. Small children played in the street nearby.

"I remember that house," Victoria said, looking over the hill. "This is the house where you grew up."

"Yes," he said, standing beside her and looking at it. "There's a story I need to tell you about it."

Victoria turned and looked at him, waiting to hear the truth about his past and his family.

"My parents were musicians," he began. "Both of them were. Pops was very skilled on the violin, my mum on the piano. They were in different troupes, and they met at a party, fell in love, and were married. Mum quit when she became pregnant with my sister and me."

His sister? Victoria never knew Michael had a sister. She opened her mouth to ask about her, but he stopped her.

"Please, let me finish," he said, holding up a finger. "My sister and I learned music before we could talk." He smiled. "As we grew older Pops stayed out more, taking in women and alcohol. He was a drunk. Every night he would stumble into the house with the stench of the neighborhood pub. Most of his money and time were spent in that little pub right there." Michael pointed to a boarded-up building less than two blocks away.

"Eventually Pops was dismissed from his company. It was bound to happen." He paused. "Mum went back to work and was very good, very successful. She got lots of work. Pops loathed her success, and the fighting started. They fought all the time. I watched my mum age twenty years in a matter of months. She was once a beautiful, angelic gentlewoman, and I watched her deteriorate into an angry and hostile person. The music that kept us together as a family was no more. She gave it all up for him. She was a very unhappy woman. She never said it, but we saw it in her eyes. She used to smile and laugh, but that stopped."

Michael paused.

"About that time Bobby and I started the band. It was a far cry from the discipline of the Royal Academy, and Pops had it in his mind that that was where I was going. He wanted me to go into the classics, be like him, when being like him was the last thing I wanted to do.

"One night, he stumbled into the house again after one of his alcohol binges, and he and Mum started fighting. The screams were so loud they woke up my sister and me. When I went into the sitting room, I saw him leaning into my mother, hitting her and hitting her. I yelled for him to stop, but he wouldn't. He just kept hitting her."

Michael couldn't stand up any longer. He sat down and continued to look at the house. "Blood was everywhere." He quickly got agitated, stood up again and started pacing. His hands flailed about, gesturing as if he were back inside the house and she could see the exact image he did.

"Inside the letter drawer my father kept his gun."

Victoria raised her hand to her mouth. She knew what he was going to say.

"I told him to stop, Victoria. All I wanted him to do was stop hitting her. He was killing her."

"Oh, Michael." She stood and walked over to him and wrapped her arms around him.

He pulled away from her and looked down at the house again. "He died a few days later, in the hospital. I killed him, and I wasn't sorry that I did." Tears rolled down his face. "Such a terrible way to feel about your own father," he said, and wiped the tears away.

"Mum . . ." He walked to the embankment again and looked at the house. "Mum died a few days later. Then it was just me and my Jessica." There was a smile on his face when he spoke of his sister.

"I tried to take care of Jessica, but the trauma was too much for her. At one point she really tried to get herself together, but she couldn't stay that way and was in and out of mental hospitals for years. There were moments when it appeared she would be well enough to come home, but then she would relapse."

He paused and took a deep breath before he continued. "I was eighteen at the time, and Bobby and I were doing gigs around London, nothing big. The phone rang and I rushed to the hospital."

Victoria listened intently. It was history repeating itself. The drinking, the problems at home, and the trip to the hospital were all very familiar.

"Jessica overdosed on sleeping pills. She was sixteen years old and stunning. She had her whole life ahead of her, and she ended it." Michael stopped talking and held his head down.

"Why didn't you tell me?"

"I never told anyone. Bobby and maybe some of the people from around here know the truth, but no one ever spoke of that day again." He paused for a moment and looked out at the house. "I sold the house as part of my healing process. Beautiful, isn't it?"

"You should have told me."

"My life fell apart before my eyes, and I felt powerless to stop it. All I had to look forward to was the next high. It's so easy for me to say that I would never have put a finger on you, but I don't know. I was becoming my father, and I didn't want to become him in that way."

"You could have given me a chance to help you," she said.

"You couldn't have helped me. No one could have."

"I wouldn't have been able to solve your problem, but at least I could have been there to help you through it. That was my job."

Victoria didn't say anything as she looked out over the hill at the little house. She folded her arms in front of her. She wasn't sure how she was supposed to feel, but she was angry that he hadn't told her sooner. Maybe things would have turned out differently if he had.

"Are you okay?" he asked, walking up behind her. He took her into his arms, and she leaned her head on his chest. They both looked at the house.

"No. I'm angry."

"I was pretty messed up back then, Vicki. I didn't know what was good for me and what wasn't. I didn't even know I was messed up. I thought I had everything under control." He stood beside her and took her hand.

"It's too late now to know what kind of wife I could have been."

"I hope you've been enjoying the flowers," Michael said, changing the subject.

Victoria turned to look at him. "It was you?"

Michael nodded. "I had to do something to let you know I was thinking about you. If that upsets you, I'm sorry. I just had to do something."

Victoria stared at him. She didn't get him. By not confiding in her and trusting her, he destroyed their marriage, and then he goes and does something like that.

"I don't know how to take you."

"What do you mean?"

"Since our first night together you have given me so many reasons to never speak to you again, but for some reason I can't stay mad at you. I should have known it was you sending the flowers."

"There was no way for you to know that," Michael said, lifting her chin up to him. "I'm sorry about everything." Michael touched her, so tenderly, and lifted her face to meet his eyes. "I'm especially sorry I made you regret marrying me."

"I've never said I regret marrying you. There were times when I didn't like you very much. But I never regretted marrying you."

Michael exhaled. "It's getting late. I think I should get you back to Nicole's."

"I don't want to go back just yet. If that's okay."

"Where would you like to go?"

She thought. "Do you have a place nearby?"

"I still have the house in Islington."

"I thought you and Sonya purchased a home together."

"We did, but I kept mine. She now has the house in Hampstead Heath."

"Okay. Let's go to your place."

"Are you sure?"

She thought back to the history they had together in the house in Islington, and she was sure he had thought of it too. "Yes, I'm sure." She took his hand as he led her back to the bike. She held on tight as they rode through the familiar streets. When they reached his house, she paused outside the entrance and looked at it. There were a lot of memories behind those doors. She remembered what had happened the last time she'd been here, and it saddened her.

"Are you okay?"

"I'm fine. Will you please stop asking me that?"

Michael led the way to the house and let them in.

"New furniture," she said, looking around the room. "I like it." She touched the sofa, and it was so soft it seemed to just close around her finger.

"Thank you. Can I get you anything?"

"No, I'm fine." She sat on the sofa and looked at him. "I just want to take my shoes off and relax." She slipped her sandals off and looked up at him. She held out her hand to him.

Michael took her extended hand and joined her on the sofa. He began to massage her feet. They looked at each other and smiled.

"What did I do right to deserve you?" he asked.

Victoria shook her head. "You don't have me yet."

48

Victoria awoke the next morning to the smell of fresh coffee. When she turned over on the sofa and opened her eyes, she saw a tray full of breakfast muffins, bagels, and fresh fruits. She sat up to see Michael returning from upstairs. He was wearing a long white terrycloth robe with a towel in his hand to dry his hair.

"Morning," he said. He draped the towel around his neck and walked to the table to pour a mug of coffee.

Still fully dressed, Victoria sat up on the sofa, wiping the sleep from her eyes as he sat down beside her and smiled.

"Sleep well?" He handed her a mug.

"Yes, thank you," Victoria said, accepting the coffee. She took a quick sip, then placed it on the table. She needed to stretch, so she stood and leaned forward and back to rid herself of the morning stiffness.

"Stiff?"

"A little," she said and reached for a muffin.

"I didn't know what you wanted, so I took the liberty of getting everything," Michael said.

"From where?" she asked as she bit into a blueberry muffin.

"I have friends," he said, smiling.

"This is good." She took another bite and watched the smile creep across his face.

"Victoria, I need to ask you a question," he said. His serious expression made her heart beat a little faster.

"What is it?" She held the remainder of the muffin in her hand before putting it in her mouth and waited for him to continue.

"Would you go to Nicole's party with me?"

She exhaled in relief. "Yes. I would love to. But you do realize that if we show up at the party together, it will cause quite a stir."

"Yes, I am very much aware of it, and I don't care. I would like you to be my date."

While there were many questions swirling around her head, she said again, "I would love to." She reached for a fresh strawberry and took a bite.

Michael returned Victoria to Nicole's apartment and told her he would come for her around eight o'clock that evening.

She rang Nicole's buzzer and heard her footsteps running to the door. When Nicole opened the door, she grabbed Victoria and pulled her inside.

"I want details."

Victoria laughed. "Well, good morning to you too."

"Yeah, yeah, yeah," Nicole said, urging her on.

"We spent the night talking, and it was wonderful." Victoria walked into the apartment and sat down in the sitting room.

"What do you mean, talking?"

"Talking, you know, sharing conversation, ideas, and thoughts." Victoria smiled wickedly. "He asked me to be his date for your party."

Nicole screamed. "Did you say yes?" She sat down next to Victoria.

"Of course I said yes, as if that's a surprise to you." Victoria stood and walked to the window and looked out. She was trying so hard to compose herself, but the truth was she was exhilarated.

"What do you mean by that?" Nicole asked.

"Oh, don't try to play Miss Innocent with me. I'm not stupid. Let's start with your sudden arrival in L.A. and now this party. This has been one elaborate scheme concocted by you, with Michael's help no doubt, to somehow get me back to London."

"Well," Nicole said, standing and walking briskly past her. "It's my birthday." She walked out of the room, then peered back inside. "And you don't even have to buy me a present."

Nicole stayed around the apartment for just a short time before she headed into town to complete the preparations for the party, telling Victoria that she would meet her there.

For the rest of the day Victoria stayed alone in the apartment getting ready. Unlike the previous parties she had attended when she was younger, this time she did not have to rely on what Nicole could pull out of her magic hat.

She decided on a short cream-colored knit dress. It showed every curve of her slender body, which she kept in very good shape by working out three days a week. It was more of an effort for her at thirty than it ever was at twenty-one.

A few minutes past eight, she walked into the sitting room and checked her makeup one last time in the mirror. Everything was in place. Her hair was neatly pulled up into a French roll. Her gold earrings and necklace were in delicate balance with her dress. Her designer perfume touched every delicate pulse of her body.

She nodded at the woman in the mirror.

She was walking to the door to check outside when the buzzer rang. She was so nervous that the sudden intrusion made her jump. She took a deep breath, then opened the door.

Michael stood before her with a simple white rose in his hand. He was so handsome, his face clean-shaven, his dark brown mane combed back and slicked down. He wore a pair of nicely tailored brown slacks and a cream silk button-down shirt.

"You look great," he said as he stood in the doorway.

Victoria modeled the dress, then turned around and took the rose from him, inhaling its sweet fragrance.

"Thank you. And you likewise." She stepped aside and let him in. He kissed her lightly on the cheek, and her body shivered at the touch of his lips.

"Would you like a drink?" she asked, walking to the bottle of champagne she had put on ice an hour before. She reached for the chilled glasses and set them on the table next to the champagne.

"No, thanks. I've been dry for more than two years. But please, don't let that stop you." He took the bottle from her and twisted the cork.

Her stomach dropped. She had forgotten about his alcoholism. "Michael, I'm sorry. We don't have to have this." She took the bottle from him and placed it in the ice.

"Victoria, it's okay. If you want a drink, I want you to have a drink."

"Michael—"

"End of conversation." Michael picked up the bottle and poured a drink for her. Before she sipped it, he picked up the other glass and walked into the kitchen.

"Nicole usually keeps club soda for me," he said. When he returned, he held a bottle of club soda in his hand and poured it in his glass.

"To our renaissance," he said, and clicked her glass with his.

<hr />

She finished two glasses of champagne before they hurried from the house and into the waiting limousine. When they arrived at the restaurant where the party was being held, it was just as Victoria had predicted. The cameras immediately started flashing.

It was a happening place, and they blended in very well with old friends. Victoria received hugs, kisses, and well wishes from just about everyone. When she scanned the room for a particular face, she found him standing among a group looking at her. He raised his glass and toasted her. He seemed too busy to interrupt now, but she definitely wanted to speak to him before she left.

The party was everything Victoria remembered parties from the Michael years to be. Very festive and very loud. But she was having the time of her life mingling with old friends and making new ones.

"How long are you staying?" she was asked repeatedly.

"I don't know. A week or so." She really didn't know. She needed to get back to the office and reclaim the caseload she'd dumped on one of her colleagues.

"Are you enjoying yourself?" Michael had walked up behind her and put his hand around her waist.

"Yes. I'm glad I came." She turned to face him and stared into his eyes.

"Do you think anyone would notice if we sneak out of here?" he asked.

"Yes."

They laughed.

"Meet me by the door in five minutes," he said, then dropped her hand and walked away.

Victoria spotted Nicole on the other side of the room and walked over to whisper in her ear.

Nicole blushed. "Don't rush home."

Victoria made her way toward the door. She saw Michael approaching from the other side and waved to him. As she did, she felt someone take her by the hand and twirl her around. It was Bobby.

"Do I at least get a hug before you guys sneak off?" he asked.

Victoria walked into his arms and hugged him tight. "Hi! How are you?"

"Pretty good," he said as Michael walked up. "I see you guys have been doing some much needed talking."

Michael slipped an arm around Victoria's waist and pulled her to him. "What are you saying to my woman?" he said jokingly.

Your woman, Victoria thought. *That's interesting.*

"I was telling her how beautiful she looks tonight." Bobby kissed her on the cheek.

"Thank you."

"We're about to get out of here," Michael said to Bobby, turning Victoria away from the conversation. "Call me later. There's something I want to talk to you about."

"I'll do that. It's nice seeing you again, Victoria, and I hope it will be a regular occurrence."

Victoria walked back to Bobby and hugged him again. "Thank you. For everything." She kissed him on the cheek and turned to join Michael.

They sat in the limousine quietly as she leaned against him and stared out the window into the night.

"I have a surprise for you," Michael said as they rode through town. He picked up the car phone and paged the driver to give him the new instructions. A few minutes later they pulled into the parking lot of a small white building not far from the restaurant. The words RENAISSANCE RECORDS were engraved on a brass plate in front of the building. Victoria touched it as they walked in.

Inside, he pointed to the collage of pictures on the wall. Some of them she remembered. Then he walked her to the recording studio where all the magic took place.

"How did all this come about?"

"Well, after the accident I tried to sign with a record label, but no one wanted me. I can't say I pretty much blame them. I was quite a snot."

Victoria laughed.

"Then I was driving through town and noticed the sign and it hit me. I was truly given a second chance at life, a rebirth, you could say. It was time for me to do what I've always wanted to do."

"It's a big step," Victoria said, walking around the studio.

"Yes, it is, but it's working. We are doing very well. I stole Nicole from Speck's. It cost me quite dearly too, I might add."

Victoria laughed. "And she's worth every pound, I'm sure."

Michael nodded. "Yes, she is. She has made this possible," he said, pointing to Victoria and himself.

"Do you think we would have done it on our own?"

Michael shook his head. "Not a chance. We're both too proud." He walked into her arms and kissed her. Victoria closed her eyes as his lips lingered on hers. The kiss was as if she had kissed the wind.

Michael stepped back and held up one finger. "One second," he said.

He walked to the far wall and changed the lighting. Victoria looked up as blue, red, and green lights illuminated the room. Then he walked to the sound system and fumbled with the sliding knobs. Victoria watched him, not quite understanding what he was doing until she heard the music. It was their song.

Victoria laughed and ran into his arms.

"Hi, Dad," Victoria said, smiling into the receiver.

"Victoria? It's five o'clock in the morning. What's wrong?"

"Nothing's wrong, Dad. Nothing is wrong at all. I just needed to call you. I'm . . . I'm in London." There was a brief silence before her father responded. She knew that would be all she needed to say.

"I just have one thing to say, Victoria."

Victoria braced herself and closed her eyes.

"I just want you to be happy," he said.

She opened her eyes and smiled. "I am happy. I am very happy."

"That's all I ever wanted."

"I love you, Dad."

"When are you coming home?" he asked.

Before she answered, she turned and looked at Michael sleeping in the bed. "I am home."

VICTORIA

Happily ever after. I thought about that infamous phrase: happily ever after.

Life with Gerald continued as it always had. James and Michael had come into my life and had managed to live within me for months without Gerald or anyone ever knowing how lost I really was.

I drove to my mother's house for lunch. I needed to confide in somebody. I needed someone to know what was happening to me. I needed my mother.

It was a beautiful sunny day, so I didn't bother going into the house. I knew where my mother would be. I walked toward the backyard and found her, just as I predicted, on her knees, pulling the dreaded weeds from her beloved perennial garden.

"Mom!" I called out. The sound of my voice startled her some-what, but she smiled as soon as she realized it was me.

"What you doing here, girl? Didn't you have to work today?"

"I'm on my lunch break." I walked onto the deck and poured myself a glass of sun tea she had prepared. "I need to talk to you," I said, and sat down on the cushioned chair.

I watched my mother lift herself from the ground, a little more slowly than she had the year before. She had picked up a little weight over the years. Perhaps too much for her legs to support.

"Need help?"

"No, I'm okay," she said, and stood and took a deep breath, then dusted the dirt from her gardening clothes.

"I think you need to lose some weight."

"Oh, be quiet. I'm old and I enjoy eating." She walked toward the deck. "What brings you here, anyway?"

I poured her a glass of tea and handed it to her before I began to trouble her with my burdens. "I miss seeing you and Dad working in the garden together. I wish Gerald and I could find something to do together. You and Dad had the best marriage." I shook my head. "Do you miss him?"

"Sometimes," she said, and sipped from the glass. "But we didn't start working in the garden until after he stopped hanging out all night."

I frowned. "Dad never hung out all night."

"Ump."

"What is that supposed to mean? I remember you and Dad waking up early in the morning and working in the garden. When we all moved out you guys started taking weekend trips and going to movies."

"Victoria, you were the baby. Of course that's what you remember because you didn't see the hellish days."

I frowned.

My mother waved it off like she always did. "It doesn't matter anyway. Things were different back then."

"No," I said, stopping her from changing the conversation. "I want to know. What were things like?"

She leaned back in her chair and took a sip of her tea. "The reason your father and I started working in the garden is because he couldn't hang out all night anymore. He got older and he used himself up."

"Used himself up? What is that supposed to mean?"

"He couldn't perform anymore, Victoria. You got to remember this was before they came out with that Viagra. So, the garden, the house, and you girls became his obsession."

"What!" I screamed, practically jumping from my chair.

"Girl, I should have left your father years ago, but life without sex suited me just fine."

"How long was it since you guys had sex?"

"Years. I stopped counting how many."

I looked at my mother, dubious that she had lived this life with my father. I had thought their nights were filled with as much passion as they put into everything they did together. "But how did Dad make you feel when you were together?"

"You mean sexually?" she asked.

I nodded.

"In the beginning it was wonderful, but after we started having children things changed. Your father changed." Her face went blank. "Enough about that. How's my grandbaby, and when are you and Gerald going to give me another one?" She smiled broadly. "Don't tell your sisters, but Reese is my favorite. She ain't as mannish as them hoodlums your sister got." She shook her head and sipped again from her glass. "Something wrong with them kids."

"Mom, how come you've never told me this before?" I asked, ignoring her remarks about my niece and nephew.

"Tell you what?"

"About Dad. About how things were?"

"Because it wasn't important for you to know. What went on between me and your father stayed between me and your father. Your sisters remember."

"That's probably why they're both single and not looking," I murmured.

"Gerald's a good man. He does what he's supposed to do."

"He does what he's supposed to do for Reese. He doesn't do shit for me."

My mother looked stone-faced at me. It was the first time I had ever sworn in front of her. "What's wrong with you?"

I remembered the conversation I'd had with Desiree. She was so right. I had to do something to save my daughter.

"I have to go back to work." I stood up.

"Victoria!" she yelled out to get my attention. "Don't do anything foolish. Gerald is a fine man. He's just young. He'll come around. I could have left your father many times, but it wasn't about me anymore. It was about you girls. Don't mess that child up and take her away from her father."

"And when she grows up, she'll have the luck of being just like her mother and marrying someone just like her father." Not bothering to hear her response, I walked to my car and drove back to work.

※※※※※※

I walked to the room we called a cafeteria, but it was really just a small room with a couple of vending machines, a coffee machine that made the worst coffee in the world, and two small round tables. No one ate lunch there, and its only purpose was to serve as a smoking lounge when it was too cold to go outside. My boss, Frank, was a smoker, so no one was going to complain about violations of the no-smoking policy inside the building.

I stood in front of the snack machine trying to decide between the Oreos and the Famous Amos cookies.

"Hello, Victoria." I turned to the sound of my name and found a gentleman standing beside me braving the coffee machine. His face didn't look familiar.

"Hello," I said, then turned my attention back to the cookies. Famous Amos won.

"How are you today?" he asked.

"Fine, thank you." I paused. "How do you know my name?"

He laughed. "You've seen me before. Many times actually. But I do have to admit that in the two dozen times I've been in here this is the most you've ever spoken to me."

I glared at him. He hadn't answered my question.

"Lawrence Taylor, with Taylor Freight." He held his hand out for a shake.

I raised my eyebrow in recognition. "Oh, yes. You're one of the drivers." I shook his hand.

"Owner. I'm the owner of Taylor Freight. One of my guys is off sick, so I'm taking his route. You guys are one of my top clients. Don't want to miss a drop. You know what I mean?"

I nodded. "I don't remember seeing you before."

He laughed again. "That's because you never looked at me. Every time I stop in to talk to Frank, you're always sitting at your desk typing with your mind a million miles away."

I nodded again. That sounded like me, all right. "I'm sorry."

"Ah, don't worry about it," he said.

I took a moment to look at Lawrence. He was an older man, perhaps in his forties. I could tell that by the sprinkle of gray hair. Salt and pepper. And his mustache was the same way. His face was smooth deep brown, a beautiful complexion. He looked like a man who took care of himself.

"So, how many cities do you guys deliver to?" Lawrence wasn't walking away, so I continued talking.

"All over. We do pretty good business, and it keeps me busy. On the weekends I just pull out my bike—"

"Bike?" I interrupted him. He must have noticed my excitement because he smiled.

"Yeah, my bike. You ride?"

"No, I don't ride, but I love them. Do you have a road bike or one of those sport bikes?"

"I have a road bike, honey. I'm too old to be bending over like that. Would you like a ride?"

"I would love a ride," I answered without hesitation.

"Well, what are you doing after work? I can swing by and take you for a spin."

I frowned. "I can't. I have to pick up my daughter from school." *Damn, that would have been nice,* I thought.

"What about around six o'clock?" Lawrence countered, rescuing the possibility.

"Six-thirty?"

"Six-thirty will be fine."

"Great," I said.

"Where?"

I thought quickly but came up with the most logical location. "Eden Park. I'll meet you at six-thirty at Eden Park."

Lawrence nodded. "Sounds like a date. You sure it won't be a problem?" He pointed his baby finger at my left hand.

Oh, damn, my wedding ring. "It won't be a problem. We have a date."

I walked back to my desk beaming. For the first time in a long time I was glad I'd come to work that day.

———— 〰〰〰〰〰 ————

I showed up at Eden Park at six-fifteen. I'm never on time for anything, but I was determined not to be late for this. I wore my best jeans and a button-down blue-jean shirt. I even tucked the shirt in, which was something I never did, since I didn't like the curves of my behind. When I got out of my car, I walked across the drive to the benches and sat down. I looked out over the water, constantly glancing back toward the entrance hoping to spot Lawrence.

Why are you getting your hopes up, Victoria? He's not coming. That thought repeated in my mind every ten seconds when I looked at the entrance. I looked at my watch. Six-thirty. *He's not coming.*

Six thirty-five. I rubbed my legs. *Give him time, give him time,* I thought. Then I heard the roar of a motorcycle engine behind me. I turned and followed the cycle until it rounded the drive and rode off the other side.

He's not coming.

I leaned against the seat fighting tears. I had wanted this so much. Talking with Lawrence at the office and making this date had given me something to look forward to. I hadn't had that in a long time.

Again I heard the sound of a motorcycle behind me, but I didn't dare look back. I didn't want to be disappointed again.

It stopped. "Hey, beautiful. Sorry I'm late." It was Lawrence. He was sitting on a black Honda road bike, his legs spread out in front to balance it. The heel of his black boots dug into the pavement for support. He took off his helmet and held it in his hand. "You ready to ride?"

I nodded excitedly and jumped from my seat. When I reached the bike, he put the helmet on me and helped me on.

"Don't let your legs touch that," he said, pointing to the chrome by my calves. "It gets pretty hot, and it'll burn you. Don't want you messing up your legs. Hold on." He started the smooth engine again, and as soon as we began to move, I grabbed on to him and held him tight.

We rode around for hours, through Mt. Adams, Clifton Heights, and into Covington and Newport, Kentucky. We even rode to the airport to watch the planes take off.

"I wonder where they're going?" I asked as I sat on the back of his bike holding him at the waist.

"Sometimes anywhere but here is nice," he said.

"Do you travel a lot?"

"Every chance I get. I'm on the road all the time, and I give myself a vacation at least every four to five months."

"Must be nice," I said, and leaned my head against his back.

"You hungry?" He turned his head slightly toward me. It was getting late, and I hadn't even thought about food, or going home.

"Yes," I said.

He started the engine again and drove into the airport garage, where he parked the bike and we walked in.

"I spend a lot of time here. I know of a nice quiet restaurant where we can eat. We don't want to have any surprises," he said, and winked at me. I got the feeling Lawrence had done this before.

I walked beside him, glancing at his physique out of the corner of my eye. It didn't strike me until that moment how tall he was—over six feet, perhaps six-three. He took long, comfortable strides.

As we walked alongside the busy travelers, Lawrence took my hand. My heart skipped. His hand was strong yet comforting. Rugged but not scratchy. He seemed to be a leader but was not overbearing. I let him hold my hand and didn't want him to let go.

When we reached the restaurant, I looked around. He was right— it was very private, dark with only a few lights hanging from the ceiling. Only the passengers with long layovers would come inside here instead of opting for a quick bite at one of the fast-food restaurants.

We sat down in a booth away from most of the other patrons. A waitress came over to give us water and menus. Lawrence opted for a grilled-chicken Caesar salad, and I wanted the same but added a bowl of French onion soup.

"Comfortable?" he asked once we placed our orders.

"Very. I'm having a nice time."

"Good," he said, then took a sip of his water. "So, how long have you been married?" His question caught me off guard, and I didn't know how to answer him. Was I supposed to lie?

"Five years, almost six." I took a drink of my water. "Are you married?"

"Nah, I'm divorced. Was married twenty years."

"Twenty years. That's a long time to invest in a relationship. Why end it?"

"It was never much of a marriage. I stayed until my son graduated high school and went off to college. That was long enough for me."

"You have a kid in college? How old are you?"

"Forty-three. How old are you?"

"I'm twenty-five. No, wait. I'm twenty-six now."

"Twenty-six. My goodness, you're just a baby."

I laughed. "A baby?"

"My oldest, Jacqueline, is twenty-one, in her third year at Howard. My youngest, Dexter, is in his second year at Morehouse."

"Wow, that's pretty impressive," I said, nodding.

"It wasn't easy. I worried about Dex for a long time. All he ever wanted to do was to grow up and be the next Michael Jordan. It took a lot of banging his head against the wall before he realized that maybe that wasn't it."

I laughed. "You sound like you're a good father."

"I do my best, and I made a lot of mistakes. I was on the road a lot and missed a lot of practices, but I made his games, every single one of them." He took a sip of his water. "How old is your daughter?"

"She's six now and about ready to graduate kindergarten." I laughed.

"You have a beautiful smile, Victoria. You should do it more often."

"If I had something to smile about, I probably would." I picked up my glass and took another sip.

"And why would a beautiful woman like yourself not have anything to smile about?"

I frowned at him.

"What? You don't think you're a beautiful woman?"

I shrugged.

"Look in the mirror, young lady."

"I do look in the mirror, but I don't see what you see."

"That's because it's not how you feel, and you should. You're a beautiful woman."

The food arrived, and luckily the subject changed. The last thing I wanted to do was to turn this meeting into a pity party.

"How long have you been in the trucking business?" I put a forkful of salad into my mouth and looked across the table at Lawrence. He put his fork down and wiped his mouth.

"I got my commercial driver's license right out of high school and went on the road. I made a lot of money for a lot of people until it dawned on me that I could be doing that for myself. So I bought a couple of trucks and hired a driver and we got started. It really wasn't difficult because most of the contacts I already had. I was in business about a year when the company I used to drive for folded and I acquired most of their business. I've been blessed."

"So where did your ex-wife come in?"

Lawrence smiled. "I met her while I was on the road. We dated for about a year, but we really didn't see each other much in that time. I thought I was in love, and I'm sure she did, too. Then my daughter was born. It didn't take long for me to realize that it was a mistake, and I contemplated leaving, but then she got pregnant with my son and that ended that thought. Hell, she would have had a house full of babies if I hadn't put an end to it."

"But what made her so terrible that you couldn't fall in love with her?" I asked. Hearing Lawrence talk about his marriage reminded me so much of what was happening in mine.

"It's hard to fall in love with an unmotivated woman."

I stopped eating and looked at him. "What do you mean?"

"She didn't want to do anything. I couldn't get her to help with the business or start her own thing. She knew the money was coming in and that was good enough for her. She got to drive big fancy cars, live in a big house, and go shopping every other day with the girls, and she was happy. That was all she wanted."

"But she stayed home and raised the kids, and they turned out pretty well," I said. Why was I defending this woman?

"Yes, she did, but that was not her focus."

"Don't you think it was cruel to divorce someone after twenty years of marriage?"

"It would have been worse if I had stayed. There was nothing between us. I did as much as I could with the kids when I was home, but she and I rarely had much to talk about. It wasn't an unpleasant relationship, just not a loving one."

"Did you cheat on her?" I picked up a piece of grilled chicken and put it in my mouth. My eyes did not leave Lawrence.

"Of course," he said without hesitation. "Any time you're having sex with your husband only twice a month and he's not complaining, you better believe he's getting it someplace else."

I didn't say anything more as I chewed.

"Does that make you think less of me?" he asked.

I shook my head. "I think you're very honest."

Lawrence leaned forward, reached across the table, and took my hand. "Why aren't you happy?"

I guess it didn't take a genius to figure out that I was not happily married.

"My story will have you yawn." I looked down at his hand around mine. He began to caress my hand, and I grew tense at his touch. It felt good to have the attention, but I couldn't escape the feeling that this was the last thing I needed in my life. "So what does your wife do now?"

"She got a nice settlement. She is the mother of my children, and how can I say I love them but hate her? They are a part of her. And I didn't hate her. She was who she was, and it just wasn't for me. She bought herself a nice condo so that she wouldn't have to do yard work because that would mean she would actually have to touch dirt."

I laughed.

He continued. "And she works part-time to supplement her income because she still likes to shop."

I doubted Gerald would take care of me so well if we were to divorce. On more than one occasion he'd made it perfectly clear that my happiness was not his concern. I was sure that once Reese was no longer a financial responsibility, Gerald would readily serve me with divorce papers and the twenty years I gave him would be gone.

"Was it hard for her to start over again after the divorce?" I was intrigued by his tale and wanted to know more. I was hoping he wouldn't be offended by my asking.

"No, it wasn't, actually. It was easy for her. Like I said, she was taken care of. The kids were off in college, so she didn't have to worry about taking care of them. She dates and continues doing the things she enjoys. She just doesn't have to worry about whether or not I'm coming home anymore."

"Wouldn't it have been easier for her to leave when she was younger?"

"Maybe, but then it would have been harder for her to maintain the standard of living she was accustomed to and raise two kids."

"Why didn't you leave?"

He shifted in his seat. "One thing about men: when there are children involved, we don't leave. The women usually make that choice. If she would have packed up and left, I wouldn't have stopped her. I would have taken care of the kids and made sure they were comfortable, but I would not have left on my own." He leaned forward on the table. "You have to remember, she wasn't an unhappy woman. She was living pretty good, so it was easier for her to stay."

"Didn't you worry that she was going to leave you and take half of your business and the house and leave you in the cold?"

"She did get half the business when we got divorced, and she sold it back to me. She went her way and I went mine. The business made back what I paid her within a year. You can't put a price tag on freedom."

"Will you ever remarry?"

"I don't rule it out," Lawrence said, squeezing my hand. "I probably shouldn't have told you all that. But obviously something is on your mind." He squeezed my hand again. "And I hope I get the chance to see you again."

I dropped my eyes to the table. "Lawrence, I would like to see you again too, but . . ." I took a deep breath before I continued. "I wouldn't be with you for the right reason."

"And what do you mean by that?"

I shifted in my seat. "My marriage is a mess, as you may have guessed." I sighed. "It would be so easy for me to get involved with you. You're handsome, articulate, fun . . . you would be my rescuer. But I don't want to be rescued. That'll take me from one dependent relationship into another dependent relationship, and I don't want that. I have some unfinished business I need to take care of and some things I need to fix before I can get involved with anyone."

Lawrence grew a huge grin on his face. "Young lady, that was a damn good answer," he said. "When you fix what you need to fix, you let me know."

I smiled. "I will."

And it started the moment I returned to work the next day. Being with Lawrence was the trigger I needed to do what I knew in my heart needed to be done.

I had knocked softly on Frank's office door and waited until I heard him answer before entering.

"What's up?" he asked the moment I walked in.

"Frank, I know this is very irresponsible of me, but . . ." I paused and looked at the top of his head as he scribbled notes on his legal pad. "I won't be back tomorrow." I exhaled.

Frank stopped writing and immediately looked up. "You what?"

"I won't be back tomorrow," I repeated.

He finally dropped his pencil. "Is something wrong?"

I shrugged. "Yes and no. I have to do this, Frank. If I don't do this now, I may never get the nerve to do it again." I looked directly at him and spoke firmly even though it had taken me hours to work up the nerve to walk into his office.

"You're not in any kind of trouble, are you?" He stood up and walked to close the office door.

"No, no, nothing like that. It's just that I need to move on with my life. Professionally and personally."

"Where are you going to go?"

I took a deep breath. "I hear California is very beautiful this time of year."

Frank nodded. "Yes, yes, it is. And you know what? I have a brother who's a manager at a telephone company in Los Angeles. I don't know if they're hiring, but it won't hurt to give it a shot."

I gasped. "Are you serious?"

"Yes, I am." He walked to his desk, grabbed a piece of paper, and scribbled a name and telephone number on it. "Give him a call when you get there, and I'll let him know you're coming."

I stood with my mouth open. I've heard that when you're on the right path, things find a way of working out and when you think there is no resolution, one is found for you. This was my clue that I was on the right path.

"I'm glad you're not angry with me for leaving on such short notice."

After a long silence, Frank finally spoke. "Victoria, when you first came to work for me you were just a kid in college looking for some extra money, which was all right with me. You were so full of life and energy, and you had a smile that stretched from one end of your face to the other. It was beautiful and intoxicating. I didn't mind greeting you every day. I never expected you to stay as long as you did. After you got married and your life changed, I saw you change. I haven't seen you smile like that in years."

I hung my head, shocked that Frank had noticed so much about me.

"That's why I started the Employee Assistance Program." Frank took my hand. "Get your smile back."

———— ◊◊◊◊◊◊◊◊ ————

My face must have looked glum as I drove home that evening, but my mind was clear. I knew what I had to do and I felt good about it, but my emotions were a mix of relief, sadness, and disappointment. I wanted so much for my marriage to succeed. I wanted Gerald to love me, I wanted to be a good wife and a good mother. It seemed I failed at all of that.

For the first time I took notice of the scenes around me.

There was a coffee shop at the corner of Main Street. I could have gone there for coffee in the morning instead of drinking that nasty crap from the machine at work.

A house on Parker Drive was painted a beautiful sky blue.

When did they put that fun land in the park? I could have brought Reese to this park instead of that old run-down one near our house.

"Ouch," I said as my tire rolled over a deep pothole.

When I got to Reese's school, I ran inside and swept her into my arms.

"Are you okay, Mommy?" she asked as my eyes filled with tears.

"I'm fine, honey. I'm just happy to see you. It's been a good day for me." Privately I prayed that she would forgive me for what I was about to do, and that one day she would understand.

At home that evening, all was quiet and normal. Gerald left sometime during the evening and returned a few hours later while I read Reese one of her favorite stories. He peered into her bedroom as I tucked her in for the night.

"Night, Dad," Reese mumbled tiredly. I kissed her cheek before turning off the small lamp on her night table. I walked a few feet down the hall into our bedroom, then quickly climbed into bed and pulled the covers over my legs.

I picked up my book from the night table and opened it to my marked page. But my mind turned instead to the sound of the shower in the other room. A few minutes later Gerald came into the bedroom, a dark green bath towel hanging loosely around his waist. I turned my eyes away from him when he dropped the towel and reached into his underwear drawer. I crossed my stretched legs underneath the covers as he climbed into the bed. When I looked at him again his back was toward me, and the next sound I heard was the faint sound of sleep.

I stared at him. No words of good night came from him. No inquiries about my day. Nothing. I closed my book, turned off the light, and went to sleep.

———

Morning arrived, and I followed my usual routine. I took a quick hot shower, prepared breakfast, and got Reese off to school. I climbed into my car and drove to the nearby U-Haul, where I rented a small trailer and a bundle of boxes.

I started in my bedroom, grabbing clothes still attached to hangers and shoving them into boxes. I opened each drawer, scooped up the contents, and threw them into the boxes. I did the same with every pair of shoes that lay on the floor. Every article of clothing I owned was crammed into six large U-Haul boxes. Then I went to Reese's room, filling four large boxes with her clothes and another two boxes with her dolls and toys. I walked into the family room and confiscated one of three televisions we owned and the small stereo system. From the kitchen I took a complete set of dishes, pots and pans, and eating utensils. Box by box, I loaded everything into the trailer.

It took three hours to pack six years of my life into fourteen boxes. As I turned to leave, I glanced once again at the family portrait that hung on the wall. In that instant I understood what Frank had meant and what was missing from the portrait. It was the smile.

In all of the photos taken before our marriage there was a smile on my face that didn't appear forced or painted. It showed all of my teeth, as if I was filming my own toothpaste commercial. In the family portrait that smile was gone, replaced by a "cheese" for the camera.

I placed the photo on the table and, on top of it, the keys to the house.

My first stop was to the bank to close my savings account. Eight years of saving one hundred dollars a month plus interest had given me close to ten thousand dollars. It wasn't enough to live off of, but it was enough for a fresh start somewhere else. Then I headed to the school to pick up Reese.

I had a difficult time explaining to the principal that Reese would not be back. She gave me a questioning look as I signed all of the papers withdrawing her.

"Where will she be going to school?" the principal asked as she looked outside at the trailer attached to my car.

"I'm not sure, but when I get her enrolled I'll send for her records."

She paused. "Mrs. Chandler, this is rather sudden."

"Yes, it is." I nodded as I signed my name on the final line and handed her the clipboard. "It was a sudden decision." From the nervous expression on her face, I was sure she was worried that I was kidnapping my daughter.

"Reese loves your school. I'll bring her back to say hello to everyone as soon as we get settled in our new home." That seemed to relieve her a bit.

"Please do that. Reese was such a joy to have."

As I walked out of the school, grasping Reese's hand tightly, I silently hoped that Mrs. Smith wouldn't call Gerald or the police.

"Where are we going, Mommy?" Reese asked as she climbed into the backseat and snapped the seat belt around her. She reached for a bag of Doritos from the many bags of snacks I'd brought.

"We're going to a place called California." I handed her a peanut-butter-and-jelly sandwich that I'd made at the house and a can of cola from the cooler.

"Is Daddy coming too?"

"No, Daddy is not coming." I quickly glanced over the map before pulling out.

"Why are we going to California?"

"Because it will be our new home."

"But I like where we live now. I don't want to live in California."

"You say that now, but you will love it."

"I don't know anyone in California. What about my friends?"

"You'll make new friends."

"I don't want new friends."

"Reese, please. Everything will be all right." I took a deep breath as I contemplated turning the car around and going back. I looked at Reese in the rearview mirror. She wasn't eating as she stared out the car window.

"Reese."

"Yes, Mom?"

"I love you."

———— ✺✺✺✺✺✺ ————

Three days of driving followed. Reese made the trip very unbearable with her constant refrain, "Are we there yet?"

Late in the afternoon on the third day, we pulled into a hotel in Redondo Beach, California. After checking in, I took Reese by the hand and we crossed the street to the beach. We ran straight to the water and buried our feet in the waves. It was the first time either of us had ever seen the ocean. Reese watched the waves smash into the sand at her feet.

"Mommy!" she exclaimed as she pointed to the higher waves.

I laughed as I walked knee-deep into the water.

"You're getting wet," she said.

"Come on!" I called out to her and held my arms open for her to join me.

Carefully, placing one foot in front of the other, she walked deeper into the water until she reached me.

"It's cold." She shivered.

I laughed as the waves smashed into our backs. We were home.

We walked around the beach, staying out of the path of bike riders and skaters, and ate pizza and ice cream as we watched an intense game of coed volleyball.

As the night grew closer, we walked back to the hotel and took our much-needed baths. Reese fell asleep the second her head touched the pillow. I watched her as she slept soundly. Any uncertainty I had about making the trip disappeared each time I heard her laugh. I walked out onto the balcony and watched as the orange clouds covered the sky over the Pacific Ocean and listened to the waves smashing against the beach as nighttime fell over Southern California.

⬿⬿⬿⬿⬿⬿⬿

Reese woke me up early the next morning begging to go back to the beach. I agreed that we could but first I had to make some phone calls. I picked up the telephone book and searched for an attorney who specialized in divorces. After finding one and calling to make an appointment with him for the next day, I called Gerald.

"Where the hell are you?" he yelled.

"Reese and I are in California."

"California!"

I held the phone from my ear as he screamed into the receiver.

"You kidnapped my daughter and took her clear across the damn country?"

"I did not kidnap her. We just left."

"You're going to bring my daughter back to Ohio, or I will have your ass locked up so fast you won't know what hit you."

Stay calm, Victoria. Stay calm. "Gerald, I don't want to make this ugly."

"You're so damn stupid."

Stay calm, Victoria. Stay calm. "Whatever." I took several deep breaths before I could speak again. The nerves in my stomach were jumping all over the place. Could he have me locked up for kidnapping? I had no intentions of going back to Ohio, but that was definitely something I needed to discuss with an attorney.

"I'm going to look for a place to live tomorrow, and I have an appointment with a lawyer."

"What gives you the right to take my daughter three thousand miles across the country?"

"Oh, Gerald, please," I said, fed up with his theatrics. "You hardly noticed her when she was three feet from you."

"That is a damn lie."

"You and I both know that this marriage is not working. I want a divorce."

Gerald was quiet.

"We can discuss joint custody, but for now I will seek temporary custody. I am not coming back to Ohio unless I am forced to by a court of law. If you want to fight me on this, I suggest you get a lawyer." My heart was pounding so hard I was sure he could hear it over the telephone. I was standing up to him. Never in the history of our marriage had I stood up to him and called his bluff.

"I put you in a home, I paid the bills, and this is your gratitude? You take my daughter clear across the damn country, and I have no say in the matter?"

"We were three people who lived in the same house together, nothing more. We were never a family."

"My responsibility was to support my daughter, and I did that."

"But what about me? What were your responsibilities to me?"

"You were the one that wanted to get married. You were the one threatening to take me to court for child support and all that crap. I did the right thing."

"That is not marriage, Gerald. That is an arrangement. An arrangement that would have been over the moment Reese was no longer a responsibility."

Again Gerald was quiet.

"Would you like to speak with Reese?" I asked.

"Yes, please."

I called Reese to the phone. She was standing on the balcony looking at the beach, eager to run into the water again.

"Daddy, hi," she said as soon as she heard his voice. I listened to her tell him about the long drive and rave about her first day on the beach.

"She sounds excited," Gerald said as soon as Reese returned the phone to me.

"She is. As soon as we find a place to stay she'll make new friends and I think she'll like it here."

"I'm not happy about the fact that you chose to take Reese to California. I will talk with my lawyer."

The next sound I heard was the hum of the dial tone.

50

We rented a house in Carson, California, a little town about a half hour outside of Los Angeles. The cost of living in California was tremendously higher than in Cincinnati, and it was more than a shock. I was paying two hundred dollars a month more for a smaller house.

Gerald's threats to sue me for custody of Reese ceased after three months. My attorney had filed a motion for temporary custody with the divorce papers, and the order was granted without any confrontation from Gerald or his attorney. With that worry behind me, we settled into our new life.

Reese easily made friends at her new school and was ecstatic to learn that she would be placed in a beginner's Spanish class. Every day she rushed home from school with a new vocabulary word and would get much practice from the neighborhood kids, who were quite fluent. I quickly became an alternate chauffeur, along with other parents, for frequent weekend trips to the beach. After a few times, the other mothers and I decided that we needed to get in on the fun too, and we all journeyed to the beach together in what became a weekly ritual.

The first time I played volleyball in the sand, my legs would not move. Every time the ball came to me and I ran toward it, I sank deeper into the sand.

"Mom, hit the ball!" Reese yelled.

"I'm trying," I said, laughing as I staggered toward the ball. After throwing the ball under the net to the opposing team I prepared myself for the next play. Once again the ball was hit to me, and once again I sank into the sand.

"I really do know how to play this game," I declared, laughing as I fell into the sand. The truth was I hadn't played since high school, but I was quite good back then and I knew I could still play. I just had to adjust to the sand. After a few weeks of sinking and making a complete fool of myself, I began to improve and my legs became strong enough that I could move around and keep up with the others. When we weren't playing volleyball, we were skating on our Rollerblades or swimming.

Frank was true to his word. He called his brother, and when I called him after Reese and I settled in, he was expecting to hear from me and offered me a job on the spot. The pay was a lot better than I had ever hoped, and one of the employee benefits was a tuition-reimbursement program after six months of full-time employment. After biting my nails about it for two months, I gathered the courage to apply for admission to UCLA. When the letter came in the mail, I waited until Reese was in bed before I walked to the backyard patio. I didn't want her to hear me crying if I was not accepted. Skimming over the introduction, I saw the words "We are pleased to inform you . . ." I leaped from the chair and stomped the ground. The letter included dates and times for me to come in to take the entrance exams, which I did. The exam results revealed strengths in mathematics and English, which meant I could skip all entry-level courses. To my surprise, all of my previous college credits were transferred and applied toward my degree, and my work experience in bookkeeping was used as credit for introductory accounting. That brought the total credit hours still needed for a bachelor's degree in education to fifty-two, plus one year of student teaching.

"So I'm not as stupid as you thought," I said aloud, remembering Gerald's famous line. My moment of reflection was interrupted by the telephone.

"Hello," I said after diving over the sofa to pick it up.

"Hi, Victoria, this is Frank."

"Frank, hi. How are you?" I had called Frank when I moved into the house to let him know where I was and to thank him for helping me find the job.

"I'm well, thank you. And how are things going for you?"

"Wonderful. I got accepted to UCLA," I blurted.

"That is wonderful. The reason why I called is that Lawrence wanted to know if it was okay for me to give him your telephone number."

Lawrence. I hadn't forgotten about Lawrence. I left too quickly to say good-bye to him, and I assumed he would just forget about that crazy woman who asked him a million questions.

"That would be great. I'd like that a lot."

Shortly after our one-year anniversary of moving to California, Reese and I traveled to Cincinnati. Stephanie had flown from Cincinnati to visit us once, but neither my mother nor either of my sisters had made the journey. My mother managed to speak with me for ten minutes at a time but only if I phoned her. Elaine and Lois remained cordial, but it seemed we no longer had anything in common.

Gerald picked us up at the airport when we arrived in Cincinnati, and he was not alone. He had a woman with him, and she was pregnant. Very pregnant. When I took my eyes away from her protruding belly, I looked at her face and sensed a familiarity, but I couldn't remember where I might have met her before.

"Daddy!" Reese yelled, leaping into his arms.

Gerald hugged her hard and planted a big kiss on her cheek.

"I miss you," he said.

"I miss you too," Reese said, and gave him a big smooch on the lips.

"Hello," he said, turning to look at me.

"Hi."

"You look nice."

I slapped my hand to my chest. "You giving me a compliment?"

Gerald looked at his girlfriend and then again at me. My guess was that he'd told her many stories about our marriage and probably none of them were true.

"Thank you," I said finally.

"You lost weight," Gerald continued.

"Rollerblades and volleyball will do that."

"You on Rollerblades? I can't see it."

"Well, Gerald, there is a whole side of me that you never got the chance to see." With that he stopped. There was no point in making a fool out of himself in front of his girlfriend.

"This is my fiancée, Kelly," he said finally.

Kelly. I suddenly remembered why the woman looked familiar. It was the same woman who came to his apartment the day I found out I was pregnant.

"Yes, I remember," I said, and reached to shake her hand. I only held her hand a brief second. "I guess this time it's congratulations to you. When is the baby due?"

"Any day now," she said softly, and immediately looked to Gerald.

"Oh, I see," I said, turning my attention to Gerald. "I've been gone a year, and it only took you three months to become involved with someone else, get engaged, and start another family? I'm going to take a lucky guess that this was in the works long before I ever left." I looked from Gerald to Kelly, and both of them stared at me with dumbfounded looks on their faces. "You know what? It doesn't matter anymore," I said, reaching for my bags.

"I'll get those," Gerald volunteered.

"I have them," I said, and he backed off.

We headed out of the airport with Reese holding her father's hand. When we finally reached the car, Kelly sat up front, with Gerald, while Reese and I sat together in the backseat. Reese did all of the talking as she excitedly filled her father in on all the details of life in California.

"I'm staying with my mother," I announced from the backseat. "You can drop me off there."

"We're going to get something to eat. Would you like to join us?"

When I looked in the front seat, I noticed that Gerald was holding Kelly's hand while he drove. In the years that he had been with me, he had never held my hand while he drove. Perhaps it was safe to say that Gerald wasn't a bad guy after all. One thing was for certain: he didn't love me. Perhaps things would be better for him and Kelly.

"No, thank you," I said quickly. It was awkward enough sitting in the same car with Gerald's new family. "I'll see you guys on Sunday."

He nodded.

When I arrived at my mother's, I got out of the car and began walking toward the house.

"Victoria! Hold up!" Gerald called after me.

I turned and saw him getting out of the car, and he caught up with me as I stepped onto the porch.

"Listen." He paused, seeming to search for words. "I know things weren't right between us." He bit his lower lip. "I wasn't ready for marriage when you and I got married, but I did want to do the right thing by Reese and I thought I was doing the right thing by you too, but . . ." He stopped talking and bit his lip again.

"I know, Gerald. You just didn't love me."

He didn't say anything, but the look on his face confirmed it.

"I hope things are better for you and Kelly." I began to walk away, but he held me back.

"They will be, and we want Reese to be a part of our lives. I'm not going to just forget about her. I want her to visit as often as she can."

"Okay." I turned to leave again, but Gerald took my hand and pulled me into an embrace. I couldn't respond. I held my arms at my sides, unable to put them around him. I didn't have any feelings for him anymore. I didn't love him, I didn't miss him.

"I'm sorry, Victoria."

"You made my life hell for six years. I really don't want your apology. I hope you and Kelly have a good life." I turned away. I used my key to open the front door and was surprised that my mother hadn't had it changed to spite me. Inside the house everything was the same, but I hadn't really expected anything different. My mother hadn't changed anything for more than twenty years, and as always it was immaculate. Not a speck of dust could be found anywhere, and nothing was out of place.

As I walked toward the back of the house where I knew I would find my mother, I stopped and perused the collage of snapshots that hung on the wall. One in particular held my attention. It was an old black-and-white photo of my mother when she was a young woman, before she became pregnant with Elaine. Quite a striking beauty she was. Slim, shapely figure, a radiant smile, and beautiful black hair that the wind seemed to lift from her shoulders. She wore a simple tan polyester dress with a three-inch-wide belt that had those dime-sized holes for the belt latch. Definitely not a dress that I would be caught dead in today, but I'm sure that it was quite stylish at the time. The belt revealed the curves my father must have fallen in love with.

All the other snapshots were taken after the children were born, and there were only a few photos with my mother present. None of them showed that same wide-faced grin.

I peeked through the open window and saw my mother fidgeting in her garden as usual. Perhaps because of the considerable weight she'd gained over the years, swollen ankles had become a constant complaint for her. She was forced to walk more slowly, and there were days when she had to stay in bed altogether because her ankles swelled up so much.

She wore her hair up. I'd grown accustomed to seeing her hair in a tight little bun on the top of her head. The black hair in the picture had been replaced by a dull gray mesh. Her daily attire consisted of cotton pants and T-shirts she wore while working in the garden. When she strolled about the house, she wore her gray flannel pullover robe. I hardly ever saw her in anything other than her robe, except of course on holidays when the entire family would come over to visit. Only then would she slip on one of her Sunday dresses. They all fell well below her knees, and I could not recall ever seeing her legs.

"Hi, Mom," I said, walking up to her and kissing her on the cheek.

"When did you get in?" She accepted my simple peck and went about her routine of pulling the weeds from the colorful assortments of daffodils and tulips.

"About a half hour ago. Gerald dropped me off, and Reese is spending the day with him and his fiancée."

My mother shook her head. "I told you."

"You told me what?"

"I told you if you let him go, some other woman was going to get him. I told you. Now you lost him."

"He was never mine to lose. He's happy now. I'm happy now."

Mom shook her head but decided to drop the subject. "I see you're letting your hair grow," she said. "I don't know why you kept cutting it off." She took her gloves off and manipulated my mane, which now hung loosely on my shoulders. "It looks nice."

"Come, let's talk." I took my mom's hand and led her to the deck. We sat down opposite each other while I looked out over the yard. I took a deep breath and closed my eyes as the sun warmed my face.

"I know you don't approve of what I did."

"I think what you did was downright foolish. You had a good husband. He was taking care of you and Reese. You let him go, and for what?"

I began, "After the conversation you and I had before I left, I hoped that you would understand why I did it."

"What is there to understand?"

"I married a man exactly like Dad."

"Gerald is nothing like your father."

"No, that is where you're wrong. I set out to marry a man like my father and succeeded in doing just that. He was like Dad in every way, and I became you. Gerald was never going to look at me the way I desired him because, just like Dad with you, in his eyes, he settled for me."

"Your father loved me!" Mom yelled.

"But would he have loved you if you had never gotten pregnant?"

My mother sat quietly in her chair, her eyes squinting as she looked at me. She wanted to say something to defend herself, to defend my father, but she appeared at a loss for words.

So I continued. "You know, at first I thought it was all about Gerald, our marriage, and how horrible he treated me. But it wasn't just that. I had a part in it too. I never knew exactly who I was and what I wanted from my life before I jumped into a life with Gerald. I thought I could just become a part of his life and that would somehow make me whole, but it didn't work like that."

"This is nonsense. You gave up that right when you had Reese. Children need to be raised by both of their parents. That is what's wrong with this world now."

"I'm not going to argue with you about that because if there was a way I could have kept my family together, I would have. But the price was too high."

"What is that supposed to mean?"

"Why should I give him my youth only to have him leave me when Reese was no longer a responsibility?"

"By then he would have turned around."

"No, they have Viagra now," I said, snickering, and my mother didn't take well to the comment.

"This is all your selfishness!" she shouted. "Your responsibility was to your daughter, and you took her across the country, away from her family and her friends. What type of an example are you setting for her by running away? You should be teaching her to stay and fight. Fight for her marriage."

"I'm teaching her that she does not have to settle."

My mother shook her head. "Things were different in my day. We were stronger."

"That's because in your day, you weren't given much of a choice. We have choices now, and I have a pretty good life. I rent a nice home. I have a decent job until I finish school. Reese is getting a good education. I haven't lost anything."

"You haven't lost anything. But Reese has lost her father."

I gave up. I was not going to be able to convince her that I'd done the right thing. "Let's talk about you," I suddenly said. I stood up and dashed into the house to fetch the picture off the wall. "Introduce me to the young woman in this picture," I said, pointing to the photo.

My mother looked at it and drew back.

"Look at that smile," I continued. "There's a smile on her face that I've never seen before."

My mom took the frame from my hand and began to trace the image with her finger. "Lordy, I haven't looked at this picture in years."

"Sure you do, you dust it every day."

"I see it, but I haven't looked at it."

"When was it taken?"

"We were on our way to a party. There was always a party going on. This was taken a few months before I got pregnant with Elaine. Your father and I loved to dance." She smiled as she continued to trace the photo. "And we was quite good at it too." She laughed. "You girls got the dancing from me." She placed the photo on the table and leaned back in her chair.

I sat down again and looked at her as her eyes saw images of many years ago.

"I haven't thought about that in years," she said. "It was the early sixties, and I was a different person back then." Some memory must have registered in her mind because she began to smile again. I'd never seen a smile so wide on her face before. "My friend Mary and her husband, William, would come over and get me, and we would go to somebody's house. Every weekend somebody had a party. We were never bored.

"William introduced me to your father, and let me tell you, he looked good." She laughed again, then took a deep breath. "They were heavily involved with the civil rights movement back then. They distributed literature up North about what was happening in the South. We were always on the road traveling someplace. They were invited to work in Georgia for one of the first black-owned newspapers down there. William and Mary went, and they ended up settling there and having children. William became some big shot down there, and he wrote several books and went on to teach at one of the universities. We lost contact with them after a while."

She paused.

"Your father and I stayed here because I got pregnant with Elaine and he had a good job at the auto plant . . ." Her voice trailed off as she looked at the shadows of her past. "During those times, working at one of the auto plants was one of the best jobs a black man could get, and he would have been foolish to quit. Especially considering he had a family."

She paused again.

"But that was when everything started to change. Your father changed. He wasn't the same man he was when we married. We didn't travel, and he didn't do much work for the movement either. Said he was too busy for that now, taking care of his family. I always thought he wanted to go to Georgia but felt he had to stay here because of Elaine and me. He never said that though." Mom grew quiet as the smile and laughter were replaced with a frown and tears. "So I made up for it by being the best wife I could. When your father was active in the movement, I was active in the movement. When he stopped, I stopped. When he was happy, I was happy, and when he was not happy . . ." She paused again.

"He wasn't a bad man, no he wasn't. He took care of his business, and I did what I thought a good wife was supposed to do. I took care of my family, and I didn't complain. We weren't as free to talk about sex as you girls are now. That was a private matter between a man and his wife, and you better not tell nobody that your husband forced himself on you. Well, even the minister . . ." She choked back tears as she touched her face.

"Mom, did something happen with the minister?" I knelt down in front of her and took her hand.

She nodded. "He slapped me. It was my fault. I shouldn't have disrespected my husband like that." She wiped the tears with the back of her hand. "I never said anything about it after that and just accepted that that was the way things were. So you see, when your father couldn't get it up anymore, I wasn't going to complain. I hated sex. I hated everything about it. It always made me feel dirty."

She paused again, then looked at me. "Is that what was happening to you?"

I nodded as tears steadily rolled down both of our cheeks and the hint of understanding finally filled her eyes.

"Do you hate me?" she asked me.

"Oh, no," I said, and squeezed her hand. "You were the perfect wife and the perfect mother. I wanted to be just like you."

My mother gave a hollow laugh as she choked back the sobs in her throat. "And you almost became me."

I stood and wrapped my arms around her as she cried on my shoulder.

Were Gerald and Victoria ever in love?

When Victoria met Gerald, she saw a successful and desirable man, the qualities that she thought would make a good husband. This led her to ignore many of the early warning signs that his heart was not in the same place as hers. Although she didn't purposely try to get pregnant, she didn't go out of her way to prevent it. She knew having his child would make him a permanent part of her life, and she thought that they would work at building the solid family that she envisioned they could create together. But Gerald never had any intentions of the marriage succeeding. His focus was on their daughter and his commitment as a father but never his commitment to Victoria.

Why do you think Victoria fantasizes about James, a man so much younger than she is?

James's age is important because it took Victoria back to the time when she made some crucial decisions in her life. When Victoria met Gerald, she had not yet truly discovered herself or listened to her heart about what she wanted to do with her life.

Victoria and Michael are worlds apart—she is an African-American woman and he is a British rock star. What were you trying to say with this relationship?

This was actually one of my favorite parts to write because sometimes the person who is meant for us may be the total opposite of what we've envisioned for ourselves. I believe so many women and men miss their opportunity for true love, or even being loved at all, because they have closed their minds to certain people they see as not being the right "type."

Victoria didn't have a policy against dating white men; the situation had just never presented itself. Once it did, she had to reach deep inside to understand whether or not she would be cutting Michael off because he was the wrong person for her or because he was the wrong color. I truly believe that when it comes to love, race should not be an issue.

Michael is a rock star with a drug problem. Victoria knows this but marries him anyway. Why?

Their relationship is about acceptance and the old cliché "What you see is what you get." When Victoria married Gerald, she saw that he was reluctant and aloof, but she thought he would grow to accept her, love her, and thus, change. But he didn't. When Victoria married Michael, it was a similar situation. It was wrong for her to marry someone and expect him to change. You should marry someone for who he or she is and not for what you want that person to become.

Are Victoria's daydreams healthy?

Victoria's daydreams were a welcome escape from reality. If she had continued, they could have become unhealthy because they were beginning to affect her "real" life. She had to make a decision about whether to continue her life as it was and escape in the daydreams or change her life so that she no longer needed the escape.

Are you working on another novel?

Yes. My next novel will be entitled *As We Lay* and is about a successful architect and her affair with a married man, who turns out to be the love of her life. There are a few more twists and turns, but you'll have to stay tuned.

The questions and discussion topics that follow are intended to enhance your group's reading of Darlene Johnson's *Dream in Color*. We hope they will provide new insights and ways of looking at this engaging new novel.

QUESTIONS FOR DISCUSSION

1. Victoria knows that she and Gerald are no longer in love. Based on Gerald's actions toward Victoria, do you think that there was ever a time when they were in love? Do you think Gerald feels that Victoria "trapped" him by getting pregnant? Did she? Did Victoria and Gerald make the right decision to get married when Victoria found out that she was pregnant? Would you marry a man you didn't love if you found out that you were pregnant with his child?

2. When Victoria dreams up James, she envisions him as being much younger than she is. James is barely seventeen when Victoria meets him. Why do you think Victoria fantasizes about a man so much younger than she is? Does Victoria do something morally

wrong by dating James when she's a teacher in his school district? Are there certain people whose attraction to each other transcends age?

3. Victoria sleeps with Michael a few hours after she meets him. The next morning, when she wakes up and he's not there, she feels ashamed of her decision. Should she have maintained her original conviction that she would not have a one-night stand with Michael? Would it have been better for Victoria to have had one incredible night with Michael or never to have gotten involved with him? Given the chance, would you consider sleeping with a celebrity? With whom and under what circumstances?

4. When James's parents find out that he's dating an older woman, they are appalled. But eventually they begin to accept the relationship. Do you think that James's parents make the right decision? Why do you think they change their minds about the relationship after they meet Victoria? Should parents be able to determine whom their seventeen-year-old child dates? Is the child obligated to heed his parents' wishes?

5. Victoria tells herself that Reese would be devastated if she and Gerald ever split up. Do you think this is true? Should two parents feel obligated to stay together for the sake of their child? Does Reese seem to notice that her parents don't get along very well? How long do you think you can hide a failing marriage from a child?

6. Before Michael, Victoria had never dated a white man. Then, suddenly, she finds herself falling in love with one. Are there any times when their relationship seems strained because Michael is white and Victoria is black? Would you consider being in an interracial relationship? Why or why not?

7. Victoria knows, almost from the very beginning, that Michael does drugs. When she asks him not to, he agrees to abstain in her presence. Is it right for Victoria to expect Michael to change his lifestyle for her? Are drugs just an inevitable part of a rock star's life? After they're married and Victoria finds out that Michael continues to do drugs, why does she tolerate it and stay with him? Would you stay in a relationship with someone who did drugs regularly? Do you think it's possible to convince someone to stop doing drugs, as Victoria tries to convince Michael?

8. Victoria dreams up James and Michael as a way to cope with her failing marriage. Are these daydreams a healthy way for Victoria to escape her marital unhappiness? Does she get too wrapped up in her daydreams? Is it all right to fantasize about other men once you're married? Have you daydreamed about other men? Would you ever let your spouse know about your daydreams?

9. Victoria finally realizes that she will never be happy if she stays with Gerald. So she takes her daughter, Reese, and heads off to California. Do you think that Victoria will be able to make a fresh start? Is she wrong to take off without telling Gerald about her plans? Do you think that Victoria leaves James and Michael behind for good when she heads to California? How do you think Reese will take such a sudden change in life?

10. One of the most difficult parts of Victoria's relationship with Michael is that they're constantly followed by paparazzi. Is it possible for an international celebrity to maintain any kind of private life? Does the public have a right to know about the intimate details of celebrities' lives? Is public scrutiny something that celebrities must learn to accept? Why do you think people are interested in celebrities' personal lives? Do you follow the lives of any celebrities?

11. Even though Gerald doesn't love Victoria, he's proud that he makes enough money to support himself, Victoria, and Reese. Should Victoria be more appreciative of the fact that her husband pays for them to have a nice house in the suburbs? Would Victoria have left Gerald sooner if she had a good job and felt financially independent? Once you're married, does it matter who makes more money? Is it all right for one partner to support the other, or should everything be split fifty-fifty?

ABOUT THE AUTHOR

Darlene Johnson resides in Indianapolis, Indiana, with her two sons. She is currently working on her second novel, *As We Lay*. She would love to know what you think of *Dream in Color*, and you can e-mail her at brandywinepub@aol.com.